world:
met.

JAMES
FORRESTER

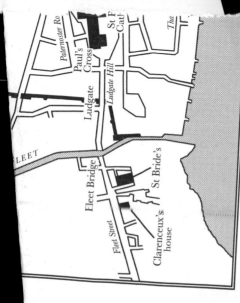

headline
review

First published in 2010 by HEADLINE REVIEW
An imprint of HEADLINE PUBLISHING GROUP

1

Cataloguing in Publication Data is available from the British Library

ISBN 978 0 7553 5601 0 (Hardback)
ISBN 978 0 7553 5602 7 (Trade paperback)

Typeset in Sabon by Ellipsis Books Limited, Glasgow

Printed in Great Britain by
Clays Ltd, St Ives plc

HEADLINE PUBLISHING GROUP
An Hachette UK Company
338 Euston Road
London NW1 3BH

www.headline.co.uk
www.hachette.co.uk

If a man's faith is his enemy
There is no refuge anywhere.

Prologue

❧

Tuesday, 7 December 1563

It was a cold day for a killing. The Scotsman, Robert Urquhart, rubbed his hands and breathed on them as he waited in Threadneedle Street, in London. Watching the door to Merchant Taylors' Hall, he clutched each finger in turn, trying to keep them supple, his grip strong. He cursed the grey December skies. Only when two men appeared at the top of the steps, walking very slowly and deep in conversation, did he forget the chill in his bones. His victim, William Draper, was the one on the left – the jewelled gold collar gave him away.

He studied Draper. Narrow face, grey hair and beard, about sixty. Not tall but well dressed, in an expensive green velvet doublet with lace ruff and cuffs. Eyes like a fox. He looked selfish, judgemental – even a little bitter. You could see how he had made his money: with an ambition as cold and biting as this weather, and with as little remorse.

Urquhart watched Draper pull his cloak close and wait, standing on the bottom step, above the frozen mud. The man continued talking to his less well dressed companion. The carts and pedestrian traffic of the street passed in front of them, the snorting of the horses and the drivers' breath billowing in the cold morning air.

It could not be done here, Urquhart could see that. Not without risking his own arrest. That would be as bad as failure. Worse – for he knew her ladyship's identity. They would torture that information out of him. Arrest would simply require her lady-ship to send another man, to kill him as well as Draper.

He walked to the end of the street and looked back casually. A servant led a chestnut palfrey round the corner from the yard and held it steady, offering the reins to Draper who mounted from the bottom step with surprising agility. Draper offered some final words to his companion from the saddle, then gestured goodbye with a wave of his hand and moved off.

Westwards. He was going home.

Urquhart started forward, walking briskly. He felt for the knife in his belt, the dagger in his shirt sleeve, and the rounded butt of the long-barrelled German wheel lock pistol inside the left breast of his doublet. He hoped he would not have to use it. The noise would bring all London running.

He followed his victim to his house in Basinghall Street. Four storeys high and three bays wide, with armorial glass in the windows. He waited outside for some minutes then drew a deep breath and slowly exhaled, taking a moment to reflect on his mission.

He climbed the few steps to the door and knocked hard. A bald man in knee-length breeches answered.

'God speed you. An urgent message for the master.'

The bald man noted the Scottish accent. 'Another time, sir, you would be right heartily welcome. Alas, today my master has given instructions that he is not to be disturbed.'

'He will see me. Tell him I come with a message from her lady-ship. It is she who bids me seek his help.'

'Regretfully, sir, I cannot disobey an order—'

'You are very dutiful, and that is to be commended, but I urge you, look to your Catholic conscience, and quickly. Her lady-ship's business is a matter of life and death. Tell Mr Draper I have travelled far to see him in his capacity as *Sir Dagonet*. He will understand.'

The bald man paused, weighing up his visitor's appearance and demeanour. He looked at his shoes, dirty with the mud of the street. But the visitor seemed so confident; Mr Draper might well be angry if he turned away an urgent communication brought by a Scotsman. 'Wait here, if you please,' he said, stepping backwards into the shadows.

After several minutes he reappeared. 'Mr Draper will see you. This way.'

Urquhart followed the servant along a dark passageway, through a high hall, and past a pair of large wooden benches piled with bright silk cushions. He noticed a gilt-framed portrait of the master of the house, and another of a stern-looking man in an old-fashioned breastplate and helmet – Draper's father, perhaps. There was a big tapestry of a town under siege at one end of the hall. Above the fireplace were two brightly painted plaster figures of black women in red skirts, their exotic paganism allowing the plasterer to bare their breasts shamelessly. Here was a white-washed stone staircase. At the top, a picture of the Virgin. Finally they came to a wide wooden door.

'What is your name, sir?' asked the bald man over his shoulder.

'Thomas Fraser,' Urquhart replied.

The servant knocked, lifted the latch and pushed the door open. Urquhart crossed himself. He loosened his sleeve, felt the hilt of the dagger, and entered boldly.

The room was long, oak-panelled and warm, and had an elaborate plaster ceiling. Two fireplaces in the far wall were alight, the blazing logs held in place by polished silver-headed firedogs.

The servant turned to his right and bowed. 'Mr Draper, this is the Scotch esquire who has come on behalf of her ladyship. His name is Thomas Fraser.'

Draper was sitting behind a table at one end of the room, looking down at a piece of paper. Urquhart saw the same narrow face and grey beard he had seen outside the hall. He stepped forward and bowed respectfully. He heard the door shut behind him, and the latch fall.

'You come from her ladyship?' the merchant said softly, looking up. There were tears in his eyes.

Suddenly Urquhart felt nervous, like a boy about to steal silver coins from his master's purse. *Why the tears? Was Draper expecting him?* But there was just one thing to do and the sooner it was done the better.

'Sir,' he said, taking another two steps closer, so he was barely six feet from the table. 'I come with an instruction from her ladyship.' He reached for his dagger.

Suddenly a deep north country voice called out from behind him: 'Hold fast! Move no further!'

Urquhart turned. Behind the door as it had opened had been a huge bearded man dressed in a black doublet and cloak. His hair too was black and curled. In his early thirties, he had obviously seen action on more than one occasion. A livid red mark stretched from above his right eyebrow to his right ear. On his left hip he wore a silver-handled side-sword, and he was holding a pistol.

For one throb of his pulse, Urquhart was motionless. But in that moment he understood what had happened. Her ladyship had been betrayed. He did not know by whom, or how, but it left him in no doubt what he had to do. The instant he saw the scarred man move his pistol hand, he pulled the dagger from his sleeve and hurled it at the man's chest. The next instant he rushed towards him, one hand reaching out to grab the pistol and the other fumbling for the knife at his own belt.

When the gun went off, Urquhart was moving forward. And then, suddenly, he was on his side, the report echoing in his ears.

Only then did he feel the pain. It was as if his scream of agony was a sound formed within the severed nerves of his left thigh. There was a mess of blood and torn flesh. He could see splintered bone. As the sliced nerves and the sight of the shreds of bloody meat combined into a realisation of one single hideous truth, he gasped and raised his head, dizzy with the shock. The rip his dagger had made in the black cloak and shirt revealed a glint of a breastplate. The man was drawing his side-word.

'You are too late,' the north country voice declared. 'Our

messenger from Scotland came in the night. Mr Walsingham knows.'

Urquhart screamed again as the pain surged. He thumped the floor, unable to master the feeling. But it was not the wound that mattered – it was the failure. That was worse than the physical hurt. It did not matter that he was a dead man. What mattered was that his victim was still alive.

Eyes blurred with tears of shame, he thrust his hand inside his doublet for his own pistol. The scarred man was too close. But he forced his trembling hands to respond, and drew back the wheel of the lock. Gasping, he twisted round, aimed at Draper's head, and pulled the trigger.

The noise of the gun was the last thing he heard. An instant later the blade of the side-sword flashed through his throat and lodged in the back of his neck, in the bone. And then he was suffocating and tumbling in a frothing sea of his own blood.

It was not an easy death to behold.

1

Friday, 10 December 1563

Clarenceux sat at the table board in his candlelit study, listening to the rain. It drummed on the roof and splattered in the puddles in the street two storeys below. He pulled his robe close around him against the December chill, nuzzling his bearded chin in the fur collar, smelling the wood smoke that had infused the fur over the years spent in the same chair, in the same robe. Thunder rumbled across the sky. The rain seemed to increase in intensity, as if in answer to the thunder's command. He was alone but for his papers and this little halo of golden light.

Ever since the birth of their second child, seventeen months ago, he had spent the evenings working on his heraldic manuscripts, his visitations. His wife, Awdrey, had retired early as usual, to do her embroidery by the light of the candle in the alcove above their bed. He liked to think of her there, needle in hand, in her candlelight, while he worked here at the other end of the house, in his own light. It was as if their evenings were joined by the two golden flames. Even though they were doing different things in different places, they were together.

He reached forward and lifted an old gold cup – once the property of a royal duke, to judge from the enamelled coat of arms it bore – and sipped some wine. He opened the manuscript book before him, and read the first page. The title read: *A Visitation of ye counties of Essex and Suffolke, commenc'd July ye 20th 1561, by me,*

William Harley, Clarenceux King of Armes. That had been two and a half years ago, one of his regular expeditions to catalogue all the gentlemen in those two counties who were entitled to bear coats of arms. Such expeditions were among the most enjoyable aspects of his work as a herald. When war threatened, and he had to ride through enemy territory to confront a king or a general, his responsibilities were far more onerous. And dangerous. But that trip through Essex and Suffolk had been a good occasion; he had met many amiable gentlemen and very few pretentious ones. He smiled at the memory of setting out that day, with his companions all dressed in his heraldic livery. Even Thomas, his old manservant, had joined them, persuaded for the first time to don the brightly coloured clothes of a herald's entourage. He had frowned constantly, and grumbled regularly, but he too had been proud.

Clarenceux was about to turn the page when he heard a knocking sound, down below. Three clear strikes on his front door, echoing through the silent house.

Few people called after curfew. Queen Elizabeth might have abolished the law by which Protestants, religious dissidents and dangerous free-thinkers were burnt at the stake, but everyone was aware that the searches continued. Only now they searched for Catholics. A week ago a Catholic priest had been found sheltering in a house in London. The royal guard had put him in the pillory on Cornhill. In full view of the crowd, they had nailed his ears to the wood. When the blood ran down, they smeared the word *papa* – pope – on his forehead, and laughed as they drank wine and spat it on him. After three hours they sliced off his ears and dragged him, screaming, to the Tower. No one had seen him since.

The echoing thud of metal on oak rang out again.

Clarenceux sat still. His house had never been searched before, let alone in the middle of the night. He himself had never been questioned. He had always believed a man of his rank to be above accusations of religious treason. He had led diplomatic embassies to Germany, Spain, Holland and Denmark. He had declared war on France, personally, in Rheims, on behalf of Queen Mary . . .

The knocking came again, hard, insistent.

But he was a Catholic.

He covered his face with his hands, and whispered a prayer into his palms. He did not have much time. Where was everybody? The boy servants would be sleeping in the back attic. Awdrey would be lying in bed with the baby in her cot. Annie, his daughter, would be in her room. The maidservant, Emily, and Nurse Brown would be asleep in the front attic. Thomas normally slept in the hall on the first floor, but he would think twice about answering the door at this late hour.

Again came the knocking, sounding through the house.

Clarenceux went to the door and lifted the latch. He felt a slight draught on his face. There was darkness beyond, and silence.

In his mind he saw torches by night. He saw himself manacled, being led to the Tower. He imagined the cut of the iron on his wrists, the sound of the chains. The fact he had not done anything treasonable would not save him. It was the use of accusations, the spectacle of men being arrested, that mattered. *He* would matter, a gentleman paraded through the city in his heraldic livery, his ears nailed to the pillory – an example to the people.

Two more heavy strikes on the door.

He looked back into the candlelit room, across at the coat of arms painted on the panelling above the fireplace. They were his family arms, granted to his father, whose portrait also hung in the room. His father's sword was on one side of the fireplace, his own on the other. Like his father, who had served the old king, he was a gentleman. He had rights. But this might be the last time he would see this room. This might be the point at which he lost those rights, and all his status and property.

And so would his family.

He strode to the fireplace and took his sword from its hook on the wall. He picked up the candlestick from the table and left the chamber. The stairs creaked under his weight as he stepped down, feeling his way with his heels against the wooden steps, left hand holding the sheathed sword.

He entered the hall and raised the candle. The light was reflected in a small round mirror on the opposite wall. Further along, to his left, he could see the pile of blankets on Thomas's mattress in front of the fireplace. The fire was now just faintly glowing embers.

'Thomas?' Clarenceux called.

He heard his own deep voice fall away into the silence. He searched the shadows with the candle glow. 'Thomas, are you down here?'

The door in the wall opposite was open. Beyond were the stairs leading down to the main entrance.

'Mr Clarenceux,' came an urgent whisper from below. 'Sir, what would you have me do?'

Clarenceux went to the door. Thomas was at the bottom of the stairs, looking up at him. His shock of white hair, deep-set eyes and heavily lined face gave him a gaunt look at the best of times. Worry made him look even older.

'Open it. If it is the queen's men, they will only return. If our visitors are our friends, they need our help.'

Thomas nodded, and turned to the front door.

Clarenceux lifted his candle to the cresset lamp in the wall to his left. He lit it. The wick began to burn brightly. He heard Thomas shoot open the three bolts on the heavy oak door. The fist of his mind clenched, listening for men's footsteps, for the clink of armour, the knock of a drawn sword against a breast-plate, the men shoving his servant aside . . .

There was a pause.

'It's Henry Machyn. Mr Clarenceux, it's Henry Machyn!'

Clarenceux felt relief shine through him. He smiled. Machyn was harmless, an old man, well into his sixties, with a deep love for the Catholic saints and rituals. He looked down the stairs, and saw Thomas taking Machyn's sopping wet cloak.

The man must be mad to come out on a night like this.

He shook his head and walked briskly back into the hall to light some candles, so he could properly receive his visitor. But as he did so, the darkness of the hall reminded him: it was very late. It was pouring outside. Machyn had called despite the alarm he would undoubtedly cause. Most of all, Machyn's house was at a considerable distance, within the city walls, in the parish of Holy Trinity the Less. What on earth was he doing here, after curfew, in St Bride's, outside the city?

Clarenceux stopped. He turned and looked back at the doorway, lit up by the cresset lamp burning in the staircase wall.

This was not right.

He heard the slow footsteps and the stick of the old man on the stairs, and Thomas sliding the bolts home on the front door.

He walked over to a large elm table that stood by the shuttered windows. He placed his sword on it carefully, and picked up two more candlesticks. One candle was askew. He righted it thoughtfully, and lit both. For a moment he caught a glimpse of his reflection in the round mirror to his left. Brown eyes; short dark hair with a few streaks of grey; short beard trimmed neatly. A kind, enquiring face. He was tall and fit, despite his forty-five years. Riding, walking and sheer intellectual energy had kept him physically as well as mentally strong.

The man who now shuffled into the candlelit room was of an altogether different appearance. Henry Machyn was short, and moved slowly with the aid of his stick, a white-haired hollow of a man. He was drenched from his collar to his shoes. His old-fashioned jerkin dripped on to the rushes, as did the leather-wrapped parcel he carried beneath his right arm. He was fat-faced; his clothes hung from his shoulders as if they had been piled over him. But it was his expression that shocked Clarenceux. He usually had an amiable, avuncular countenance: one belonging to a man who would cheerfully regale drinkers in a tavern with a tall story. But that face, surrounded by a circle of receding white hair, now looked simply bewildered. Two milky blue eyes looked out at Clarenceux: imploring, yet without hope, as if

Machyn had just watched the hanging of a dear friend and was now wishing for death himself.

'Goodman Machyn, what in the name of heaven brings you here at this time?' Clarenceux gestured to his servant, who had followed Machyn up the stairs. 'Thomas, fetch some towels.' He looked again at the deathly face of his friend. 'You know it is perilous to be alone in the streets at night.'

'I need your help, Mr Clarenceux,' Machyn said in a hoarse voice. 'I trusted the wrong man. Everything is gone. It is over for me. The end. And my dearest Rebecca ...' his voice began to crumble; his whole face broke into sobs '... my wife, my son, my friends, everyone ...'

It was as if Machyn's very character had been caught in a trap and sliced in two, and each half was dying separately, in lonely sorrow, unable to reassure the other.

'Goodman Machyn, my friend, what do you mean? Who would want to harm you?

But Machyn did not answer. He was crying openly, his cheeks and beard glistening wet in the candlelight.

Clarenceux stepped forward and put a hand on his shoulder. 'Come now, sit down.'

Machyn shook his head. It took a few seconds for him to regain his composure. 'No, I do not need to sit. I need to talk, to tell you something.' He took a deep breath. 'I know you think you do not know me very well, Mr Clarenceux. But I believe I know you. I have met you many times over the years, and I have always paid attention to your deeds, and your achievements, your integrity. And that is why, now, at the end, I know I can trust you.'

'The end? What do you mean, Henry? The end of what?'

Machyn hesitated, clutching the object under his arm. 'Will you do me the honour of looking after this book for me? It is my chronicle.' He lifted the parcel to draw attention to it.

Clarenceux removed his hand from Machyn's shoulder and took the package. He carefully peeled off the wet leather covering, and let it fall to the floor. The volume itself was mostly dry. He turned it over: it had a fine, thick vellum binding, stamped in the centre on both sides with the design of a whale surrounded by a circle of waves.

'It has been my work for thirteen years,' said Machyn, wiping his face. 'Every event I have witnessed with my own eyes, every funeral for which I provided the black cloth and trappings, every sermon at St Paul's Cross, every execution at Tyburn, every burning of a reformer or a heretic at Smithfield, every procession I have seen through the city ... everything, everything.'

'It sounds like a monumental achievement,' said Clarenceux. 'Bound in vellum, too.'

'Like the volumes in your own library.'

Clarenceux nodded, and smiled briefly. 'Some of them.' His collection of books was probably the most extensive that Machyn had ever seen, but even he had few bindings as fine as this. 'Of course I will ...' he began. Then he stopped himself.

He paused. The room was silent. He could hear the rain outside. He felt uneasy again, as he had when he had heard the knocking.

'Why do you want to give it to me?'

'Because you are the most noble man of my acquaintance. You value old chronicles, and this one is so very precious. It will still be valuable after I am dead. In fact, far more so. I need you to look after it.'

Clarenceux looked away, towards the candles on the table. *So very precious.* Those may have been the words of the man standing in front of him, but they had not been composed in this room. Most of all, it was the word *need* that caused him to think. Machyn *needed* to tell him something. He, Clarenceux, was Machyn's last resort.

'But you have other friends, Henry, and you have a son.'

Machyn shook his head. 'John is not interested in our history or the perilous state of our faith. He is impetuous, and still has the hunger of youth. He wants to see the world. Maybe one day he will not return from one of his voyages. I want this book to last for centuries. Like the chronicles you use when checking your visitations. I always intended that it would come to you in the end. I have bequeathed it to you in my will.'

'You have made a will?' Clarenceux was surprised. Most men waited until they were dying before setting their affairs finally in order.

Machyn raised his right hand. It was shaking. He made the sign of the cross over his face and chest. 'I only ask one thing of you, Mr Clarenceux. Promise me, please, if anything does happen to me, you will go to Lancelot Heath, the painter-stainer . . .'

'Henry . . .'

'No, no. Please,' said Machyn, shaking his head. 'Please listen, for this is most important. If anything happens to me, you must go to see Lancelot Heath, in the parish of St James Garlickhithe. Tell him your name is King Clariance of Northumberland. And tell him I have given you a date. But do not tell him what it is. He will understand.'

'What date?'

'June the twentieth 1557. Exactly like that. June the twentieth.'

Clarenceux looked at Machyn, standing dripping before him. The man was clearly asking him to do much more than look after a chronicle. He could see his lip trembling.

He glanced away. He looked at the light of the candles burning on the table and thought for a moment about Awdrey upstairs, in the glow of her candlelight.

'Henry,' he said gently, turning back to face the old man. 'What meaning has this date? Why need I remember it?'

Thomas returned with the towels. He passed one to Machyn, who wiped his face slowly and dried his shaking hands.

Clarenceux continued. 'Look, my friend, we have known each other for fifteen years at least, maybe twenty. But you have never before come to my house in the middle of the night, without a lantern, breaking curfew. How did you get past the city gates? The city watch? You have never asked me for a favour before, except to borrow a book occasionally. But now you come here in the middle of the night, and ask me to look after this, your own chronicle, and you start talking about its importance after you are dead? And you tell me you have made a will. You are either losing your mind or you are not being honest with me.'

Machyn opened his mouth to speak but uttered no sound. He wiped his eyes and face.

Clarenceux walked over to the elm table. He put the book down carefully and straightened it. He spoke in a low voice, without turning round.

'You know how dangerous it is to possess seditious and heretical writings. You know there are spies. The laws of this kingdom apply to me as well as you.'

'Not in the same way, Mr Clarenceux. No, not in this case. As for the gates ... there is an old elm near Cripplegate. There is a door just behind it that opens on to the tenement of a black-smith called Lowe. He left the door unlocked for me, against the mayor's instructions, as a favour.'

Clarenceux turned and put his hands together, palms against each other. He thought for a moment. Then he let his hands fall to his sides.

'I do not know what to say. Will you not tell me the meaning of this ... delivery?'

'If you ever need to know, you will find out.'

'*If* I need to know? If I *need*?' Clarenceux was aware of his suddenly raised voice. He breathed deeply, trying to regain his calm. 'Henry, I believe I have the *right* to know what you have brought into my house.'

The old man nodded. 'You have every right.'

Clarenceux glanced at Thomas. 'Would it help if we were alone?'

'You have every right to know,' repeated Machyn, 'but that does not mean it is right to tell you.' He held Clarenceux's gaze for a long time. 'No, I trust Thomas, whom I know to be a good man who has spent many years in your service.' He paused. 'But let me ask you this. Why are you a Catholic?'

Clarenceux concentrated. 'Because . . . because it is what I believe to be the whole truth. The way God wants us to pray, the honest understanding of the Almighty – not a matter of faith at one's own will, or partial obedience to God.'

Machyn said nothing.

Clarenceux continued, feeling a little uneasy. 'It is possible to be both a true believer and loyal to her majesty.'

'If you believe that then you deceive yourself,' said Machyn. His white-haired and white-bearded face had a sudden intensity, near to anger. 'When I knocked on your door you must have wondered whether the guard had come for you. It took you a long time to answer.' He paused, searching Clarenceux's expression. 'One can only remain faithful to the queen *and* God if the queen herself is faithful to God. Our present queen is not. You know that. At some point you will have to decide whom to obey: the Creator or His creation. Tell me, are you prepared to live your whole life in fear of that moment?'

Clarenceux looked back at the book on the table. A golden glow touched its pale binding. He walked over to it and put his hand on the cover, feeling the embossed and polished skin.

'In Malory's book, in the Tale of Sir Urry – isn't that where King Clariance appears?'

'Yes. Yes, it is.'

Clarenceux turned. 'Will you assure me, Henry, that I am not putting my family at risk by having this book in my house? Just tell me so, and I will promise you that all will be well.'

Machyn's hand fidgeted with the head of his stick. 'I cannot.'

'Then, have you considered what you will do if I refuse?'

'I believe you will accept, William. You are a good man.' He looked as if he was one of the saints commanding Clarenceux to answer. 'You know God's will. It is in your heart.'

In that instant, those sad eyes *were* the eyes of a saint.

Clarenceux considered. All the world he knew, all the sounds he could hear and all the things he could see were in accord. He did not know what to do but he believed one thing. That it was God's will that he should help this man, his fellow believer.

'This is a test of faith.'

'It is for me, Mr Clarenceux. It has been for a long time. Twice as many years as I have recorded in that book.'

Clarenceux ran his hand over his beard. The fear of having his house searched remained. As did his sense of injustice, and his loyalty to his friends and God. His God. The gentle power that directed him when he was in doubt. The all-seeing watchman without whom he would have no protection from his enemies.

'Very well,' he said quietly. 'I will do what you want, as a favour. But you too must do me a favour. You must explain the real meaning of all this. I need to be prepared.'

'Thank you, Mr Clarenceux.' Machyn smiled for the first time since he had arrived. He stepped forward and reached out with his right hand. He took Clarenceux's and shook it, and continued to hold it. 'Whom else do I know who would understand the significance of King Clariance? If you were to see a quotation from the book of Job, you would recognise it, I have no doubt. You are a man I can trust to fight for justice, for what is true and right. If you need to know the secret hidden in this book, you will find it out.' As he said these last words, Machyn let go of Clarenceux's hand. He crossed himself again.

'The book of Job?'

But Machyn was animated. 'It doesn't matter. You are much younger than me. You will outlive these persecutions. One day you will know what I have learnt, and when that day comes, you will be able to decide what to do ... better than me.' He glanced at the sword on the table. 'You will see justice and truth prevail. Believe me, I want to tell you everything. But there isn't time. If you see Lancelot Heath, and if he gathers the Knights of the Round Table, the way to understand that book will become clear to you. To you, Mr Clarenceux. No one else.'

'Henry, stop. This is confusion, not explanation,' Clarenceux protested. 'The Knights of the Round Table? Who are they?'

Machyn put his hand to his forehead. 'I am sorry. I cannot think clearly. I am a foolish old man. I tried to prepare myself on the way here, so I would know what to say, but ... it has all disappeared.' He let his hand drop to his side. He frowned, clutching his stick tightly. Then his expression became solemn again.

'Listen. I will say this. The fate of two queens depends upon that book.' He nodded, reflecting on what he had just said. 'And now I must go,' he added, turning round and walking towards the door.

'Two queens? You must tell me more, Henry.'

But Machyn kept moving. 'It is very late.'

Clarenceux glanced at Thomas. The servant picked up a candle and followed Machyn.

'Tell me more,' Clarenceux repeated. 'If you want me to look after that book, you must tell me what dangers it holds. I must think about my family.'

Machyn stopped. 'Mr Clarenceux, that book is only dangerous if you know it is dangerous. If nothing happens to me, then you will never know what it holds. Nor will anyone else.' He smiled weakly. 'It is just a chronicle, Mr Clarenceux, the ramblings of an old man in his twilight years, nothing more.' He turned.

'Wait,' Clarenceux said, watching him. 'Stay here tonight, Henry. It is dreadful out there.'

Machyn was at the top of the stairs, silhouetted by the light of the cresset lamp. 'No. Thank you for your kindness, Mr Clarenceux. I fear I would tell you too much. Besides, darkness and foul weather are my protectors. There is a sergeant-at-arms called Richard Crackenthorpe who has men out looking for me. The worse the weather, the easier it is for me to pass along the alleyways unnoticed.' He started to descend.

Clarenceux walked forward. 'Looking for you? Why?'

'You can guess,' Machyn replied. He continued down the stairs with Thomas following. 'The same reason why I had to see you.'

He reached the bottom. Clarenceux remained at the top, by

the lamp. He watched Thomas set down his candle and lift the large wet cloak on to Machyn's shoulders. The candle shone on the side of Machyn's face as he turned to address Clarenceux.

'Go with God, Mr Clarenceux.'

Thomas unbolted and opened the door. Machyn put his hand on the frame to steady himself, and then stepped out into the rain and darkness.

2

Henry Machyn found himself once more in Fleet Street, in the dark. He shuffled across to the houses on the far side, to get out of the rain. He felt tired. The cold bit into his face and hands and he leant heavily on his stick. When he reached the overhanging jetty of a house, he paused. He was safe for the moment.

Lightning flashed across the angled roofs of the houses fronting the street. A moment or two passed, then the thunder came. There was no let-up to this downpour.

I should have accepted Mr Clarenceux's invitation to stay.

He blinked, water dripping from his eyebrows. *No. I did the right thing. It is too dangerous now.*

He stood still, with one hand against a wall and the other on his stick. All his plans ended with Clarenceux and the chronicle. Where to go now? He could not go back home. He needed to find somewhere he could rest, somewhere dry. He could sleep anywhere, he was so tired.

But a glimmer of satisfaction warmed him. He had done it. The book was in the hands of the most intelligent, conscientious and dignified person he knew. A man who could defend himself and had powerful friends. Straining his old eyes, he saw the line of the roof of the herald's house. And up there, on the first floor, there was a chink of yellow light between the shutters; the candle on the elm table. His book was lying beside that candle. Mr

Clarenceux would soon read it. Before long he would read the end – and then he would know.

Despite Richard Crackenthorpe's threats, the book was secure. No royal sergeant-at-arms would dare search the house of a herald, surely. Whatever happened to him now, his part in this act was done. The burden he had borne for the last twenty-six years had been lifted from his shoulders.

3

⁂

Clarenceux stood in the hall, leaning over Machyn's book, which lay open on the table. *The Cronacle of Henrie Machine, marchaunt-ttayler & parrish clerke of Holy Trinitie yᵉ Lesse* was scrawled in a very uneven hand across the top of the page. Beneath it was the first line of the first entry, in an equally unsteady script: *The xiij day of juni 1550 did Ser Arthur Darse knyghte John Hethe paynter & Hare Machyn marchaunt mete . . .* A line or so later he read, *& aftre to Paull's crosse wher we harde a godly sermon by yᵉ gode bysshope of Dorham.*

Clarenceux stared at the first paragraph. It was not just the writing which was appallingly bad; the spelling was awful. He had never seen such a badly written manuscript. Machyn had meant that he and his friends, Sir Arthur Darcy and John Heath, had 'heard a goodly sermon by the good bishop of Durham'.

He turned the page. The next entries were much the same. On the right-hand side was an entry about the earl of Southampton's funeral in August of the same year. Machyn had provided the ceremonial velvet and the black cloth to drape the church, as well as the banners used in the funeral procession. No doubt it had been one of his commissions as an undertaker. That was how the two of them had met: Clarenceux had been the herald at a funeral for which Machyn had provided black cloth and heraldic escutcheons.

He reminded himself of the hard-working ethic of his friend. Machyn was entirely self-taught, and intensely aware of his lack of formal education. That made him humble, self-knowing and perceptive of frustrated desires in others. He was a good man in every way. Clarenceux had no right to criticise his writing. Many men of Machyn's standing could not read or write at all.

He cast his mind back over what he knew of Henry Machyn and his brother Christopher. They had come to London as boys, from Leicestershire, early in the reign of King Henry the Eighth. They had both completed apprenticeships and become members of the Company of Merchant Taylors. Both had been moderately successful. Christopher had owned six or seven shops when he died. Henry's ambitions had been more spiritual and historical. It was wholly fitting that the prized possession of this self-educated tradesman should be not a line of tenements but a finely bound chronicle filled with his own humble lettering.

'Sir,' said Thomas, standing in the middle of the hall, not far from his bed, 'may I ask, will you be staying up? Would you like me to stack the fire?'

Clarenceux looked over his shoulder and glanced first at Thomas, then at the fireplace. Then he remembered the date that Machyn had given him: 20 June 1557.

'Wait,' he murmured, going back to the book. He turned the pages and started looking at the entries.

The xix day of June . . . The x day . . . The xiii day . . . Even the dates were in the wrong order. For a moment he thought that Machyn had made a mistake. But he soon realised that the entries had simply been jumbled up. They had been copied into this book from preliminary notes. There were almost no crossings out.

Then he saw it, towards the bottom of the page. He read the entry silently at first, tracing the scrawl.

The xx day of Junj dyd pryche my lord abbott of westmynster at Powlls crosse & mad a godly sermon of dyves & Lazarus & ye crossear holdyng the stayffe at ys prechyng & ther wrer gret audyense boyth the mayre & juges & althermen & mony worshipfull.

He lifted the book, holding it in the light of the candle, and turned to his servant. 'What do you make of this, Thomas? This is what Henry has written under the date that he told me to remember. It reads: "The twentieth day of June did preach my lord abbot of Westminster at St Paul's Cross, and made a goodly sermon of Dives and Lazarus, and the crosier held the staff at his preaching; and there was a great audience, both the mayor and judges and aldermen and many worshipful." There it ends. All I can think of is that he meant "worshipful men". I was there that day.'

'Respectfully, sir, even if you were there, I do not understand why that is so extraordinary.'

'Nor do I, Thomas. Nor do I.' Clarenceux glanced again at his servant. He looked tired. 'No, Thomas, I will not need a fire. Go back to bed. I am sorry you were disturbed.'

Thomas nodded his thanks. But he did not move.

'Yes?'

'Sir, it was a relief to me . . . that it was Goodman Machyn.'

'I know. I feared the same.'

There was a deep silence. The thought of being paraded in chains to the Tower once more passed across Clarenceux's mind.

'Good night, Thomas.'

'Good night, Mr Clarenceux.'

Clarenceux snuffed out one candle, left one on the table for Thomas, and took the last with him up the stairs to his study. He shut the door behind him and put the book on his table board. He pulled his furred robe back around him, put a felt cap on his head, and sat down. Once more he opened the book and began to read.

4

enry Machyn's arms ached; so too did his legs. With an awkward, painful twist of his wrist between the planks of the fence, he touched the latch, turned it and unfastened it. He pushed the gate, which creaked open. Picking up his stick, he heaved himself forward into the yard, chilled to the bone. He stepped into a puddle but did not care at all, since his feet were already too soaked for it to make any difference. He did not even bother to lock the yard gate behind him. All that mattered to him was that he was heading to a place to rest his head in the dry. If it was the last thing he ever did, he wanted to lie down in the warm.

He stepped forward, stumbling, reaching out with one hand, feeling for the stable door. It was further than he remembered. At last it was there, wet wood beneath his fingers. Water ran down his face as he moved along, feeling for the handle. He found it. But the door was shut fast. *No! Please, no – let it open. Let me find some rest here.* His fingers caught on the edge of the frame, and ran, slowly, up the edge. They felt a wooden swivel latch, and undid it.

The sound of rain on the roof, and the sweet smell of hay and horse dung. Machyn heard the horses stir, and his own short breaths. Feeling dizzy, he moved towards the ladder leading up into the hayloft. The horses moved uneasily in the blackness. Machyn felt the rung of a ladder and tucked his stick under his arm. He began to climb. He told himself that at the top of this ladder was a place where he could at last lay his head down, and sleep on the hay, as he had done as a boy in the stable adjoining his father's mill. Another step, a steadying of his foot, and another heave of his tired body on one leg. The dizziness increased. He needed to hold himself still. But a minute or two more, that was all it would take. He put his forehead against the ladder. A minute or two. And then he would be safe and dry.

Whatever was to happen to him tomorrow, he would at least spend this night in peace. Crackenthorpe would never think of looking for him here, in Mr Clarenceux's stable loft.

5

It was past midnight but Clarenceux could not close Machyn's chronicle. Every so often he noted his name Harley or his title Clarenshux; for the earlier years there were many references to Norrey, Norroy or Norray, when he had been Norroy King of Arms. He saw an entry dealing with a feast held by the Worshipful Company of Skinners, of which he was a warden. He turned back a few pages and noted the funeral of Lady Darcy: *& ther was ij haroldes of armes, Mr Clarenshux and Mr Somersett in ther ryche cottes.*

He flicked backwards and forwards. *Norrey. Clarenshux . . .* His titles echoed in his mind as he read them over and over again. Among the previous year's entries was one that mentioned the proclamation that the English and Scottish queens would meet. Elizabeth and her Catholic cousin, Mary, Queen of Scots. The proclamation had been made in both English and French, and, Machyn had noted, *with a trumpett blohyng and a harolde of armes Mr Clarenshux in a ryche cotte with a serjant of armes.*

Clarenshux again. He began to feel uneasy. This was almost a chronicle about him. True, there were many other entries that did not name him, or have anything to do with him; but the world of Henry Machyn, as contained in this book, revolved around him. Machyn had almost been spying on him. Events in Machyn's own life were hardly ever mentioned. But there were many references to Clarenceux's personal life. Here was one

26

describing the baptism of his second daughter. Another referring to his marriage. Another referring to his promotion from Norroy to Clarenceux. Another about his visitation of Suffolk.

Clarenceux looked around his study. He looked at the book presses: one stood against the side wall, the other at the far end of the chamber. He looked at the fireplace and the painted carved wood above. His coat of arms. He looked at the chest, and the books on it, and the piles of books on the floor. A loose piece of paper had fallen out of one. A few vellum indentures were piled beside it. He looked at his table board, scattered with vellum deeds and books. Three candlesticks, two of which were without candles, stood there. Four quills, two of which needed sharpening. A knife. A metal pen. Ink. Red wax for his seal. Everything was normal, untidy, and connected to him.

He turned back to Machyn's chronicle.

This was not like a chronicle. This was more as if someone else – Henry Machyn – had been writing the diary of another man's life, *his* life. Why on earth would anyone write someone else's diary for them? He pulled his robe closer against the cold. Machyn had spent the last thirteen years writing a chronicle about him, and had never previously breathed a word about it. Why? What did that entry for 20 June 1557 mean?

. . . dyves & Lazarusw . . .

He crossed the room, and reached for a New Testament that lay on the top of the book press against the far wall. Taking it back to his table board, he turned to Luke, chapter sixteen, and started to read, in Latin, the story of the rich man and the poor man, Lazarus. The rich man gave nothing to Lazarus, and so ended up in hell, while the poor man was taken into heaven to be with Abraham.

Was Machyn referring to himself as the poor man and him, Clarenceux, as the rich one? He read on. The rich man begged Abraham to send Lazarus to his brothers, to tell them to give generously to the poor. Abraham replied that the living brothers had the writings of Moses and the prophets. If they would not listen to those ancient texts, they would not listen even if a man were to rise from the dead.

Clarenceux rubbed his eyes, unable to make sense of the story. Why did it apply to him? He had no brothers. Did Machyn think that he, Clarenceux, had not been generous enough to the poor? Surely not. As for the reference to ancient texts – did it mean that men in the future should pay attention to chronicles? Like Machyn's own? Was that all there was to this?

Thunder rolled across the sky. Still the rain continued.

He put the Bible back on the shelf and turned again to Machyn's book. If this was really about preserving the past, why had he been given the book now? Surely Machyn had more to write? *I asked Machyn the wrong question. I should not have asked 'why me?' but 'why now?'*

He turned to the last page. The bottom half was blank. His eye settled on the last passage. It read: *The xj day of Desember I haue Machyn wrytre of this cronacle dyed beyng kylled by ye order of Ric^d Crackenthorpe queenes serjant att armes. Esperance.*

Clarenceux felt as if he had been punched. Machyn killed? By this Crackenthorpe? *That date is tomorrow. What did Machyn say? 'If anything happens to me'? It isn't a case of 'if'. He believes he is going to die. He believes it so sincerely that he's written it in his chronicle.*

Clarenceux shook his head, his thoughts whirling. *Machyn cannot mean to kill himself. Not unless he has some mad idea of doing so and blaming his enemy, through this book. But what does he mean by Esperance? What does hope have to do with his own murder? He mentioned the name of Crackenthorpe on the stairs as he left. He must have known that I would make the connection. But if he had something to say, why did he not tell me? He was more concerned about the book itself, and making sure that I took charge of it.*

Machyn was concealed in a great cloak of darkness, thunder and falling water. Clarenceux had no hope of finding him before morning. He might as well go to bed. But how could he? He would not be able to sleep, knowing what he knew. Besides, if Machyn's prediction was right, there were only hours to spare.

He pushed open the shutter to his study and looked down. He felt the cold air on his face and heard the rain on the tiles and in the street. It was pitch black. He could not even see the outline of the roofs on the other side of the road. He pulled the shutter to. But as he did so he caught sight of a book on the table board, the one he had opened just before Machyn had knocked. *A Visitation of yᵉ counties of Essex and Suffolke* ...

For heaven's sake, Machyn's life is at stake. And I am worried about getting wet.

He threw off his robe, lifted the candlestick, and went downstairs. 'No, don't get up, Thomas,' he commanded, as he marched along the length of the hall. He pulled back the carpet draped over a chest, lifted the lid, and pulled out his leather boots and travelling cope. 'I'm going out to search for Machyn,' he explained, seeing Thomas raise himself on to one elbow in the shadows. He unbuckled his shoes, tossed them across into the corner of the hall. 'Is there a lantern by the back door?'

'By the door to the kitchen, sir, as always. But Mr Clarenceux, can you not hear the weather?'

Clarenceux started to pull on his boots. 'I know it is bad, Thomas, but I fear for his life. Tell my wife where I am, if she asks for me. I'll be back by dawn.'

6

Clarenceux and Thomas were not the only men awake that night. Across London, in dark bedchambers, dozens of people were stirring uneasily at the sound of thunder and heavy rain. Some men were lying beside their wives, imagining the mud on the roads in the morning, or worrying about money, or disease, or business, or God, or death. Women were awake, listening to their husbands' snoring, or their children crying, or the breathing of babies in cradles beside them, hoping that they would survive the cold nights of winter. And a few lay thinking of the searches for heretical texts, and the brutal beatings and trials of those who were found practising the old faith. Had God deserted them? Was this what their queen wanted for them: to be terrorised into this new Protestant faith? Everyone was in darkness, feeling their way around bedchambers, cradles, fears, doubts, injustices.

Among those who were not sleeping were two richly dressed men in a large, high-ceilinged room of a grand new house on the Strand. One of them was in his early forties. His clothes were formal: a deep red velvet robe with gold buttons and shoulder studs, and an elaborate chain of office upon his shoulders. He wore a small ruff round his neck, which was almost concealed by the folds of the hood of the robe. His long reddish-brown beard was full, and his moustache equally so. His eyes were tired – there were folds of skin beneath them – but they were not unkind. His middle fingers were laden with rings. He was standing, concentrating on a paper document, which he now set down on a fine linen-covered table. Leaning forward, he marked the paper with a quill pen. *Cecil*. He put the pen back on its holder and reached for a cup of wine.

'More traitors, Sir William?' asked his companion, who had been waiting for some while.

'More than ever, Francis. This business is like killing beetles. You see one, and you pick up a stone nearby to crush it, and in so doing you find a dozen more of the damned things crawling around beneath that stone.' Cecil lifted another paper, glanced at it, and then shifted his gaze to the other man. 'Talking of crushing, this informer of yours, is he going to live?'

Francis Walsingham was a small, neat man of thirty-one. His black beard and moustache were trimmed short. His hair had begun to recede on the sides, forming a widow's peak; this he tried to cover up with a black cap that fitted tightly to his head. He was dressed entirely in black – doublet, hose and robe – apart from his white ruff and a single gold ring. Although small, he had the look of an ambitious man, not a compassionate one. He did not smile often, and when he did, it did not signal pleasure so much as the achievement of a personal goal.

'So Draper is *my* informer now, is he, Sir William?' Walsingham walked towards the fireplace. He opened his robe to feel the heat and stood looking into the flames. 'He will live. Probably. I do not greatly care. How much he knows is what interests me.'

'You have no more information about his attacker?'

'No. It was stupid of Crackenthorpe to kill him. The pistol was German, very expensive, but anyone of rank could have bought it. The knives were from various makers in London and the north. They tell us nothing.'

'So, what are you going to do?'

'I have not decided. If we let him go, will he act as bait? Or will he warn Machyn and the others?'

Cecil set down his paper. 'I do not believe we have a choice.

If he will not tell us about the chronicle, it is likely that he knows little or nothing about it. I'm sure you have tried your usual methods. We must be more imaginative, more creative.'

Walsingham walked towards his patron and lifted a goblet from the table. 'That would be dangerous.'

'Our situation was far more dangerous before the message came from Scotland. Only we did not know it.'

Walsingham nodded. 'I did think of burning Machyn's house, on the assumption that we would destroy everything inside, including the chronicle.'

'Fires are dangerous in London.'

Walsingham's eyes narrowed. 'What concerned me was that we would be unable to verify the chronicle was there. We would always be worried that he had given it to one of the other so-called Knights of the Round Table. How many of them are there? Draper said four but that seems too few. So, we do not know. But I do know you could not look her majesty in the eye and tell her that you simply *think* that the chronicle has been destroyed. Lord Dudley would pour scorn on you – and in front of her. You would be forced from her presence.'

Cecil did not react. Walsingham was often direct like this with him, to the point of rudeness. He was the same with others too, even the queen herself. It was an unfortunate side effect of his intense focus, his determination to achieve results. It was best ignored.

'I am not going to fail her, Francis,' Cecil replied calmly, looking at the next item on the pile of papers. 'You might be too young to remember her brother's settlement of the throne but, believe me, it still rankles with her majesty.'

Walsingham noted the comment about his age. 'I might be younger than you, Sir William, but I know. You signed the document by which King Edward disinherited both his sisters ...'

Cecil looked up sharply. 'So did Dudley's father, the duke of Northumberland.'

'But when King Edward was dead, and Mary seized power, and executed Jane Grey, you blamed Northumberland entirely.

You stood by and let him be executed as well. And now his son is her favourite. In jumping between these stepping stones, you have only narrowly avoided being swept away by the torrent.'

Cecil retained his composure. 'I sometimes suspect that you forget to whom you are speaking. I was only a witness of that disinheritance, not the protagonist.'

Walsingham set his cup down carefully on the table. He looked Cecil straight in the eye. 'I never forget to whom I am speaking, especially not when it's you, Sir William. I am grateful for your patronage every hour of the day. I am grateful for my place in Parliament. But you would not continue to value me if I forgot your weaknesses. You should pay more attention to them your-self. And every lie you utter is a weakness, for every lie is a hostage to the truth. I *know* you were more than a witness. You confessed as much to the late queen. I heard so from those who were there.'

Cecil hesitated, then made himself smile. 'True, Francis. How true. I too would have been executed if it had not been for the late queen, God rest her soul. And her sister, our blessed Elizabeth, God grant her long life.' He paused, allowing Walsingham to try to guess what he might say next. 'It is somewhat ironic that I should be so profoundly grateful to a Catholic queen as well as a Protestant one. Do you not agree?'

Walsingham said nothing. It was not ironic, it was a mark of Cecil's genius. And he, Walsingham, knew it more than anyone. Anyone, that is, except Elizabeth herself.

He wandered back towards the fireplace. 'The reason I came this evening is not to delight you with my manners. I am aware that certain talents, such as flattery, are quite beyond my abili-ties. Nor can I debate the finer points of religious tolerance and treason with you. I am more interested in finding these Knights of the Round Table. Like you, I do not think that Draper knows more than he has already told us. He is a coward, like most selfish men. He would not have given us the name of Henry Machyn or told us about the chronicle if he was trying to conceal the plot. So, I propose that we let him go – to be bait on the end of our fishing line – and that we watch him. But when we get Machyn, or any of his accomplices, how far do we go to get the truth?'

'If you are asking whether your men may apply torture ...'

'It is a delicate subject, I fully understand. Some of Draper's friends are wealthy.'

'You also appreciate that her majesty does not approve of painful techniques.' Cecil picked up his cup of wine and took a sip. He set the cup back down again, turning it between his fingers on the table. 'However, she does not approve of rebellion either.'

'So, if the enmity of these men is sufficient to warrant it?'

'Then God will thank you for doing what you have to do.'

Walsingham nodded. He turned to leave. Cecil's voice made him pause.

'Do not forget, Francis, that as long as Elizabeth is queen, God is not just all-forgiving. He is Protestant too.'

7

Clarenceux walked cautiously through the darkness of his stable yard, holding the unlit lantern in his left hand and reaching out with his right for the wall. Rain dripped down the side of his face. He felt stone and moved to his left until he touched the wooden gate. It was unfastened. *The stable lad must have failed to close it properly.*

A shutter banged somewhere; otherwise he could hear nothing except the incessant rain. He moved slowly along the dark of Fleet Street, running his hand along the front of his neighbour's house. He wished it were not quite so dark – just a clearer sight of a roofline would have helped.

He wondered which way he should take. How was he to get past the city gates? They would be closed, and the city walls were impossibly high. He knew that certain houses abutted the walls but he had no idea where he might climb up. He had no option but to find the door by which Machyn himself had come, by the Cripplegate elm. Machyn must have gone back that way, returning to his house. To his wife, Rebecca, and son John.

Clarenceux could just make out the shadowy shape of St Bride's Church, and the line of the city wall along the far bank of the Fleet, leading down to the Thames. He could hear the water of the river gushing under the bridge ahead. Knowing the road well, he walked a little faster, with his arms out in front of him in case he should trip over some unseen obstacle in his path.

Here was the bridge. The river below was in full spate. He could smell the refuse that littered the banks and see the shadow of the city walls. Some nights when the weather had been better he had stood at this spot and looked down to the Thames, seeing the moon in the water. Not tonight.

On the city side of the Fleet the wall made a sharp turn, and moved away from the river up the hill to Ludgate. Abutting the wall were two lines of houses, one behind the other. He walked on, wiping the water from his face, until he came to the looming blackness of Ludgate itself. The gate was shut fast, but Clarenceux was reassured: he was cold and wet but he knew where he was. He turned and followed the line of houses built along the wall to the north, along the line of the Old Bailey.

He came to a corner. The tall shadow on his right was Newgate. Muffled shouts came from within a building nearby; a fight must have broken out in the prison. He sighed, despondent. At this rate it would take him all night to reach Machyn's house.

Ahead was the gate of the old priory of St Bartholomew the Great. Once it had been a beautiful church. He cursed the old king – as he always did when he came here – for Henry the Eighth had ordered the destruction of the nave and all the abbey buildings. Twenty years had now passed; what was left was a paltry wreck. That was the thing that enraged him about Protestants. They might speak from conviction, and they might seek God's will just as fervently as those of the old religion – but then they recklessly destroyed things of divine beauty. That could not be done with God's blessing. They spoke for themselves, not with God in their hearts.

He wiped his face and leant against a wall. Ahead there was an intense dark shadow – St Giles's Church: it would not be much further to the elm. He could see the outline of the city's north wall and Cripplegate ahead. He made his way towards it until he felt the cold stone of the gate tower beneath his hand. He stepped carefully forward, slipping in the mud, and pressing himself against the wall. He sensed the elm, which grew from the side of the bank, and then felt its bark. He moved between it and the wall. Here was the door, still unlocked. It creaked open, and he went through.

He was now in a dark sheltered yard, somewhere just inside the north wall of the city, as blind as he had been when he first stepped out of his house. He reached up and felt the wet shingles of a low roof. *It must be a stable of some sort, or the blacksmith's forge. What's the smith's name? Lowe. Not that he is likely to appear now, not in this weather.*

Clarenceux's knee struck stone. He bent down and felt a large water-filled cistern. *Water for the forge.* He moved around it: not far away was another door. He found the latch and opened it tentatively. He closed the door behind him and started to walk down the right-hand side of the street.

Holding the unlit lantern in his left hand, he ran his right over the walls and shop fronts, doors and stone pillars. He bumped into barrels, mounting blocks, carts, cases and piles of wood. His ankle clipped a crate lying in the darkness in the street. At one point he slipped and fell in the mud, landing on his hands and knees in the wet slime, fumbling around in the dark for his lantern and hat.

Why am I doing this? Machyn's problems are his own.

No. He needs my help. And despite his age, he managed this journey in the dark. So I can too.

A dog started barking nearby. Trembling, he reached out, and felt the stone of a pillar. It was the church gate of St Mary Aldermanbury.

O blessed saviour Jesus, help me.

He leant against the church wall, gasping. He felt pain in his hand, and realised he was grinding his palm into the stone of the church wall. What was happening to him? Fear. To go on would be to leave the comfort of the church and enter a deeper, malevolent darkness: a darkness in which he would be as fully visible to the Devil as if it were daylight, and all the iniquities of the city at night would be invisible to him.

8

⧜

Lying in the darkness, Rebecca Machyn wiped the tears from her face. She turned in the narrow bed. *What have we done to deserve this?*

She remembered Henry's words, and his kisses. And his tears. And the emptiness of the words he had spoken – how his reassurances had sounded false and shallow, and yet how deeply distressed he had been.

She had done as he had said. Mistress Barker had been very good to her, as usual. She had let her have a chamber at the front so she could watch over her own house. Rebecca had heard people passing several times, and knocking on the door. But if Henry had returned he was not answering their calls.

She tried to remember happier times. The day she married Henry: it had been a bright January morning, nearly fifteen years ago. But every memory of that day led inexorably to the first terrible memory of her marriage. Mary lying there, eighteen months old, for ever motionless in the cot. The stillness of death. It was as if, in dying, the child had become a cruel hoax played upon her by the Devil – as if the child had never really had life but only the appearance of it. And then Katherine at the same age. An object in the cot, with its eyes open. No longer hers. No longer female or even human.

How good Henry had been to her then. How understanding. The third time it had happened – three years ago – she had wanted to die herself. To be with her babies, to open the door to heaven for them. *If it hadn't been for Henry, I would have done it. I would have thrown myself off the bridge. Only he stopped me. Wise Henry. He knew. He had lost four of his five children by Joan, his first wife, and then Joan herself had died. My three girls were not even half of his sorrow. He still prays for her and for all seven of his dead children. He does not deserve even more grief.*

Outside, men were talking in low voices. She turned again on the straw mattress, her cheek lying on the wet pillow.

9

Clarenceux gasped, sodden and cold. His face was soaked with rain. He was shaking.

Here is the street, Little Trinity Lane. Machyn's house is on the left, about forty yards down the road. The first-floor jetty is lower than those on either side.

He walked on. At full stretch he could touch the projecting beams of the houses with his fingertips. He ran his hand along and felt the jetties, until he found one that was lower. He felt a wooden beam, plaster, a wooden doorframe, a door . . .

He drew the knife that hung from his belt and struck with the hilt against the door three times, just as Machyn had knocked on his door earlier.

No answer came, nor was there any sound except the raindrops in the puddles. *If Henry is not at home, I'll speak to his wife or his son.*

Again, he knocked.

As he waited the doubts came upon him. And then the fear grew again. This time he knew he had reason to be afraid. He heard footsteps somewhere, splashing through puddles.

Suddenly a gloved hand clamped down on his neck, and forced his face hard against the door. A shoulder shoved him in the back, so that one of the iron studs bruised his ribs. Held there, with an arm across his throat, he dropped the lantern. He felt a stranger's gloved hand searching him, pulling apart his fingers.

40

'Drop the knife.' The voice was rough and deep, the uneducated growl of a soldier from the north.

Clarenceux did not drop the knife. 'I am William Harley, Clarenceux King of Arms, herald to her majesty Queen Elizabeth, by divine grace Queen of England, France and Wales and Lord of Ireland,' he shouted into the darkness. 'Take your hands off me!'

'Drop the knife,' said the man holding him, 'or I'll stick it in your groin.'

Clarenceux sensed several men around him. 'Give your name!' he shouted back, letting go of the knife.

'What are you doing here, herald? And without a light?'

'Had you a light yourself, you would see that I do have a lantern. It went out some time ago in this accursed rain. It is on the ground at my feet.'

The stranger's hand let go. Clarenceux turned. Suddenly a brilliant, intense light burst in his face. It burnt into his eyes, making him flinch. One of his interrogator's companions had opened the aperture of a mirrored lantern and was holding it up. Clarenceux could only blink as the light rose and swept down to the doorstep and mud where his own cold lantern lay.

There were six of them. He saw the circle of their hats and faces briefly. Then the light disappeared, and he was once more in darkness.

'Pick up your knife and put it away.'

Clarenceux bent down and slotted the blade into the sheath on his belt. 'I demand to know who is addressing me in this manner.'

'I am Richard Crackenthorpe, one of her majesty's sergeants-at-arms. These men are warders of the city, acting under my orders. And now, herald, tell me what you are doing here.' An arm reached forward and started to push him against Machyn's front door.

Clarenceux knocked it away. 'Address me with civility. I am Mr Clarenceux to you, Cracken—'

A hand shoved his head back hard against the door, and held him there by the throat.

'I don't care about your title or you. All I care about is why you are here. Getting to the marrow of truth within your bones, even if I have to snap them. Do you understand?'

Clarenceux struggled to speak. 'My business ... is my own. And I will have you ... hauled before the mayor ... for this outrage.'

'You will regret that comment. Lord Paget was your patron. A dead man. And I piss on you for threatening me.'

The man who had been holding him withdrew and punched him in the stomach. However, Clarenceux had anticipated the blow, and had braced himself in advance. It did not wind him. There was a moment's silence.

Clarenceux swallowed, and wiped the water from his face angrily. *Crackenthorpe must have spent time in the army. That is how he knows about Paget.*

'I will drive a chisel between your ribs,' said Crackenthorpe. 'I ask you again, what are you doing here?'

Clarenceux shook his head. He did not understand the danger he was facing but he knew he would gain nothing by backing down now. 'Where is Henry Machyn? What have you done with him?'

'Damn your eyes! Why are you calling on him?'

'For the sake of Him who died for us. For the sake of mercy – and because of my duty. I am an officer in the queen's service!'

'And so am I, Mr Clarenceux. Performing my duty.'

'But are you about her majesty's business? Or your own?'

'Don't waste my time, herald. I am investigating a case of treason against the Crown. Do you think I want to be out, getting my boots and hose sodden? Do you think I like this wind and rain? So, I have told you my business. You tell me yours. You are not designing shields in this darkness. Or researching the history of some noble family. Speak.'

Clarenceux wiped the rain from his face. Now he realised why no one had answered the door. Crackenthorpe had been watching the house.

'I am going to return home now.'

'You are going to answer my questions first.'

'Your questions are no concern of mine,' shouted Clarenceux, knowing people nearby would be listening in their bedchambers. 'I am not only a herald. I am a freeman of this city. I am a warden of a livery company. I have the right to go about the city after curfew, with a lantern. There is no crime in knocking on the door of an old friend – whose declining health is of deep concern to me – whatever the hour of the night.'

'I am warning you, Mr Clarenceux . . .'

'No, Crackenthorpe. I am warning *you*. I am also a member of her majesty's household. I can bully and cajole and throw my weight around, like you. But I have more weight. It bears more heavily in higher places. What would her majesty's Secretary of State think of your accusing me of treason without due cause, just for being out at night and calling on an old friend?'

'You fool. You don't know . . .'

'Listen to me. Whom will Sir William Cecil trust more – you or me? The last time I spoke to him, at my daughter's christening, he urged me to look out for abuses of royal authority. Do you want to keep your position? Or do you want to end up running a tavern in some run-down tenement, with shit and vomit in the sewer outside the front door and a stinking tanyard out back? That seems to be the only other line of occupation open to old soldiers in this city.'

Crackenthorpe put his face close to Clarenceux's. 'I too have friends in power: friends who will persuade her majesty to grant me a pardon for your death. And I know you did not come here to enquire after that man's health.'

'Then I presume you have some evidence, and some reason for this harassment. If so, the magistrates will listen to you. But you do not.'

'I know about Sir Dagonet,' hissed Crackenthorpe, trying to keep his voice down. 'He talked.'

'And who, I pray your accursed soul, is Sir Dagonet?'

Clarenceux sensed a shifting among the men. No one spoke. He bent down and felt around on the ground for his hat and lantern. The ring of his hat was cold when he put it on. 'Now, as I said, I am going to return to my own house.'

'And how will you get past the gate? Perhaps the same way you came in?' There was a sneer in Crackenthorpe's voice.

Clarenceux paused. To mention the Cripplegate entrance would be to betray Machyn. 'I was going to ask the watch on Ludgate if they would kindly allow me through.'

'I know all the ways in and out of this city by night. Perhaps it was along the ditch on the back of the Ludgate tenements you came in? Or over the top of one of them, on to the walls? Maybe you took a small boat to the wharf at Dowgate, or somewhere else along that stretch of the river. Yes?'

'Sergeant Crackenthorpe, you are not speaking to some petty thief. I would be grateful if you would accompany me to Ludgate. I need hardly remind you that my lantern has gone out.'

'Mr Clarenceux, I will accompany you back to your house. I would like to know exactly where it is.'

Clarenceux leant against his front door. 'Here.'

'Good,' growled Crackenthorpe, holding up his lantern to see as much of the house as he could. 'We will know where to come. Goodbye, Mr Clarenceux. I have no doubt that we will meet again.'

Clarenceux said nothing but turned and walked down the alley beside his house. He felt for the handle on the back door and went in. He took off his hat, hearing the splatter of drips on the floor, and walked along the passage past the kitchen. He fumbled for the latch on the door to the buttery, smelling the sweet scent of ale and wine. He was shivering. He cursed the night under his breath, throwing down his hat and untying his cope, letting it fall. He undid the laces to his sopping ruff and unfastened his soaked doublet: these too he left where they fell, together with his hose. In darkness he undressed down to his shirt and braies, and in these wet underclothes he stepped out of the buttery and walked up the stairs.

His legs ached. He paused on the landing, with the door into the hall on his left. Directly opposite were the doors to the parlour and the guest chamber. He considered sleeping in the empty guest bed. But no, he wanted to find his own room. And see his wife.

A faint light reached him as he neared the second floor. He could see the door to his elder daughter's chamber. It was shut; there was no light around the edges. He nodded quietly in the darkness. *God bless you, Annie. Stay safe, my sweet.* Then he turned round, and looked at the door to his own chamber. It was ajar, candlelight coming from within.

He pushed the door. It creaked as it swung.

The candle was burning in the alcove above the bed. His wife Awdrey was asleep, half propped up on a bolster. She had obviously been waiting for him. She stirred at the sound of the door but did not wake. Their younger daughter was asleep in her cot on Awdrey's side of the bed, wrapped up well against the cold. Clarenceux smiled. Awdrey was a good mother, so dutiful to both their daughters. The candlelight cast a glow over both of them, allowing him to see his daughter's face and the gold of his wife's hair; she had fallen asleep without her nightcap. She looked at her most beautiful like that, when asleep and natural, he thought. Still not twenty-five. He liked to say her name in Latin, *Etheldreda*, and in Old English, Aethelfrith. She was his Saxon princess. When he looked at her he knew he was a lucky man.

It would be light in three hours. Then the serious questions would begin.

10

Henry Machyn stirred at the sound of the stable door opening. For a moment he thought he heard the stable boy, coming to see to the horses. Suddenly he was fully awake, his body rigid. Four or five men were down in the yard. He could hear voices. Through the opening where the ladder was, he saw a light. One of them had a lantern.

His heart was beating with fear and disbelief. How could anyone know he was here? But they were looking for him.

Clarenceux must have betrayed me.

The realisation brought shock to his heart and tears to his eyes. He had trusted the man. He had given him his book. *The* book. Everything he still hoped for and cherished now lay in ruins. Twenty-six years of keeping a secret, wasted.

How could Clarenceux have done this?

He heard feet on the rungs of the ladder. A second later, he saw a man's hat and the shadow of a head. The man lifted a lantern. A gold brilliance touched the harness hanging there, the piles of hay, several old apple barrels and the stacked hemp sacks full of oats.

The man saw Machyn and smiled, revealing yellow teeth. 'Sergeant Crackenthorpe,' he called down. 'He's here!'

11

Saturday, 11 December

Clarenceux was sitting in his candlelit study, with his robe close around him. He was alone again but for Henry Machyn's chronicle, smelling the wood smoke of his study. He heard footsteps on the stairs. A moment later his daughter Annie appeared, holding an orange. Her brown hair was tied back, showing off her high forehead.

'Annie, you should be asleep. It's very late,' he said, welcoming her into his arms.

'Yes, but Mother said I could show you this,' she replied, thrusting out the orange, and smiling. 'We buyed it in the market. It was priced a shilling.'

'You *bought* it in the market,' he corrected. 'Not *buyed* it.' He took the orange and held it up, examining it. 'A whole shilling? Do you know why it was so much?'

'Why?'

'Oranges grow on trees in a country far away, called Spain, where the sun shines all day long. Then they are picked and packed in barrels . . .'

Annie was not listening. She was looking at the chronicle that lay open on the table board. 'What is this?' she asked.

'A book. A chronicle.'

'What does it say?'

'It says, "December the eleventh. On this day did Ann daughter of Mr Clarenceux—"'

47

Clarenceux stopped suddenly. The next words read: *dye from her ateing of an orange fruyte.*

'Go. Go downstairs, now,' he commanded.

He watched her go. She left the door open. He knew she would be crying; he had been too abrupt. But he had had reason: this was outrageous. How dare Machyn write such things! Did the man not hope to win his favour? How far had his wits wandered?

He turned back to the chronicle. The next entry read: *Ye following daye dyed his wyfe Awdrey from the poysoninge appel gyven unto her by Mr Clarenshux because hee dyd not anymoore love her.*

He swept the book off the table board, sending his visitation, two other volumes, inkwell and paper flying across the chamber. As it fell he stood up, rage filling his body, and turned the board itself over. Did he not love her? He bent down and lifted the chronicle, and threw it with all his force across the room. Did he not love them both? His daughter? His wife? The mother of his children? How could anyone have written . . .

'William, William!' he heard his wife shout. 'William, stop it!'

He opened his eyes. It was light, the shutters were open. Awdrey was leaning over him, a loose strand of blonde hair hanging down.

Clarenceux rubbed his hand over his face, feeling his brow soaked with sweat. He lay back in his bed, warm and fresh, where the study in his dream had been smoky and cold. It seemed to him as if the malevolence of the previous night had come back with him, into his house.

That book . . .

It had been a prophetic dream, he knew. He had to give the book back to Machyn. But today was the day that Machyn had foretold was the day of his death.

'You've been thrashing about in your sleep like a man possessed,' said Awdrey, her voice tinged with fear. 'Where were you last night? I waited after all that knocking on the door, but you didn't come to bed. Thomas told me this morning that you went out. And now you are shouting in your sleep, shouting about me, and about Annie, like a man gone mad, and beating your arms about. What happened? Where did you go?'

He sat upright and breathed deeply. Calmer now, he swung his legs out of the bed and sat in his shirt, looking at the open window.

Blue sky. The rain had stopped. He looked at the crucifix on the wall.

'Did Thomas tell you who called last night?'

'He said it was Goodman Machyn.'

'Yes, it was Machyn,' he replied, glancing at her. 'He is in trouble.'

'Trouble? What sort of trouble?'

'He is in fear of his life. He was terrified. I didn't realise at first how serious his situation was. It only occurred to me later, after he had gone. So I went after him. A royal sergeant-at-arms stopped me.'

'William, that was not sensible.'

Clarenceux gazed out of the window. 'I thought at the time I could help him.'

Awdrey said nothing.

Clarenceux stood up. 'Will you fetch me some water?'

Awdrey slipped off the bed and picked up the jug. With it, she filled the brass basin on the floor, draped a towel over her arm, and then lifted the basin and carried it to her husband. He nodded his thanks and splashed cold water over his face, wetting his shirt.

'There is some sort of conspiracy afoot,' he said. 'Machyn is involved. He believes he will be killed today.'

He took the towel from her arm and wiped his face. He threw it on the bed and stood, looking into her blue eyes. 'I didn't realise it was treason. I still don't think it is. I thought ...' He searched her frightened eyes. 'I don't know what I thought. I felt that whatever trouble he might be in, he is a good man, and so I had no choice but to try to help him.'

'How?' she asked, a little coldly. 'In what way could you have helped?'

Clarenceux shook his head. 'I cannot tell you, my love.' He looked away. He let go of her and went over to his clothes chest. He lifted the lid, and pulled out a folded shirt. It smelled strongly of lavender and cloves, like the rest of his clean linen. 'All I know is that ... I have to find out more. I am going to go and look for him this morning.'

'You still intend to? Even though he is a traitor? And you mean to go by yourself?'

'Goodman Machyn is not a traitor. I'll take Thomas with me.'

'Go with friends. No one argues with you when you have your heralds and pursuivants about you.'

Clarenceux lifted a clean pair of hose from his clothes chest. 'I will take Thomas,' he repeated. 'All I need to do is ask Machyn one thing.'

12

Clarenceux stood on his doorstep and looked up and down Fleet Street. The sky was clear blue; he could see his breath in the cold morning air. A few people were coming into the city from the west. A man in an old green coat was leading a mule pulling a cart full of wooden crates. A woman in a white headdress was carrying two barrels of water suspended from a yoke over her shoulders, hurrying back to her house. Two well-dressed merchants were talking to each other as they rode along side by side. There was nothing unusual in the scene.

But something was not right.

He stepped casually into the street, waiting for Thomas to come out of the house.

On the same side of the road as his house, further towards the Strand, a young man was leaning against the side of a passageway. He immediately drew back, out of sight, as Clarenceux looked in his direction.

'Thomas, finally, you are ready,' Clarenceux said loudly, seeing his manservant emerge. His breath rose in the cold air. He clapped his hands and rubbed them together. 'Let us go.'

The street was a churned-up quagmire. The morning sun reflected off the ripples of mud and puddles that led all the way along to the River Fleet and the road to Ludgate beyond. But the air was fresh, after the rain. Thomas followed a few feet behind his master's right shoulder. A cart went by, spraying mud into the air, causing them to hold back until it had passed.

'Thomas, tell me something.'

'Yes, Mr Clarenceux.'

'Whom else have you told about Henry Machyn's visit?'

'Only Mistress Harley. Your wife was most insistent that I tell her who knocked so late, and why you did not come to bed. She feared the worst.'

'The worst?'

'Your being arrested, sir.'

They approached the bridge over the Fleet. The water was still in full spate, rushing and pouring over the refuse and broken rubbish. It seemed cleansing, the rank smell of putrefied food and debris less pervasive. A small dead branch swept past them. Clarenceux paused, watching it being carried away in the swirling torrent.

'Thomas, look back along the way we have come. Tell me if you see a young man in a russet jerkin.'

Thomas glanced back. 'He's looking this way, shielding his eyes from the sun.'

Clarenceux continued to stare at the river. 'It's better that he's following us. It means he's not waiting to search the house.'

They walked along the street and passed under the decrepit arch of Ludgate. A horse and rider came past them, the hooves echoing on the cobbles under the stone vault of the gatehouse. Clarenceux looked at the tower of St Paul's Cathedral – shamefully reduced of its tall spire since being struck by lightning the year before last – and glanced over his shoulder, noting that the young man in the russet jerkin was about a hundred yards behind.

'He must be one of Crackenthorpe's men. Last night Sergeant Crackenthorpe and I exchanged words.'

'Words, Mr Clarenceux?'

'When I reached Machyn's house, there was no one there. Only Crackenthorpe and his companions. He was watching the place, waiting for Machyn to return, despite the atrocious weather.'

They continued around the cathedral yard, past the stationers' shops and the booksellers.

'I need to ask you another thing, Thomas. Did you tell anyone about the book? Anyone – I mean, even Mistress Harley?'

'No, Mr Clarenceux. I only told her about Goodman Machyn's coming and your going after him.'

Clarenceux placed a hand on Thomas's shoulder as they walked. He spoke quietly, looking ahead to a bakers' row and the people queuing. 'I want you to forget that that book was left in my house. I want you to remember something else: that I refused to accept it, and that Machyn took it away with him again.'

'Now I recall, sir, that is exactly what happened. I remember distinctly holding the book for him as he donned his cope.'

'Good. Thank you.'

The two men walked on in silence. Clarenceux's thoughts occupied him so totally that he forgot about the man following them. *What drove Machyn to come out in such weather to pass on his chronicle? Fear of Crackenthorpe? Yes, but that can't be all. Why was he so fearful? What is it about that book? I must read it more closely when I get home. It feels different, looking at these houses, to know there is a secret society here, behind these shop fronts, if that is what the Knights of the Round Table really is. Lancelot Heath has to be one of the knights, with that Christian name. Perhaps Sir Arthur Darcy was one too. But he died many years ago. Have the Knights been going many years? Has this conspiracy existed all this time, spying on me? Did Machyn have a role in that group – was he discovered by Crackenthorpe? What else is going on here, behind these houses' shutters?*

'A city has so many secrets.'

Thomas looked at him.

'I was just thinking, Thomas, about all the things going on in this city that we don't know about. All the intrigues, the plots, the schemes, the conspiracies. Sometimes I wonder – sometimes another revolution seems possible.'

'Revolution?'

Clarenceux gestured along the road. 'Left here, and then right, into Little Trinity Lane. I mean an uprising against the queen, to return the country to the Catholic faith.'

They turned the corner, avoiding a large puddle in the middle of the street. 'I felt happier with the old ways, I confess,' said Thomas wistfully, 'but I can't believe that it will happen. Not now. No one wants to go back to the days of burning people alive. Do you remember the dead cur?'

Clarenceux nodded. Some years ago a tonsured dead dog dressed in a priest's dalmatic had been thrown into Queen Mary's presence chamber, after she had forced Parliament to ban the Protestant service.

'Mind you,' continued Thomas, 'if there were to be another uprising, we would see more processions in the city.'

Clarenceux smiled. 'Would that cheer you, Thomas? The Lord Mayor and the masters of the companies all decked out in their finery?'

'I mean for the lads and lasses. When I was a boy, it was like a holiday. The wardens of the companies would throw us pennies. The baker in our street would give us pies. My father, God rest his—'

Thomas stopped. Before them, in the street, a crowd of about twenty people were staring at a door. Henry Machyn's door.

'I don't believe it,' whispered Clarenceux.

They were looking at the house with the low jetty. The door and ground-floor window were both barricaded with planks, and over them were painted large red crosses. A young man with a breastplate, helmet and sword stood by the door.

'Not possible,' muttered Thomas, frowning.

'The last plague victim was buried three weeks ago,' agreed Clarenceux. He looked up and down Little Trinity Lane. He half expected to see Crackenthorpe, but did not. He could see no sign of the man who, until a few moments ago, had been following them. 'Thomas,' he said quietly, looking around. 'Go back to my house and fetch a crowbar. I believe there is one in the loft above the stable. Wrap it in some cloth and bring it here.'

'Yes, Mr Clarenceux. Shall I fetch help?'

'No, Thomas. These people want information. They won't hurt us. Not without orders, anyway.'

13

alsingham sat writing at a table by a window in his parlour, the morning light shining on to the page. A fire burnt in the large decorated hearth. He dipped his quill into the inkwell and paused, looking out of the window at the water in the Tower moat. It was not that he was unsure of his facts, but rather that he doubted whether he should commit this particular piece of information to paper. Perhaps it was safer to send a messenger? He could carry a double message: one real piece of news and one false, in case of capture.

There was a knock at the door.

'Yes?'

'Mr Walsingham, there is a man to see you. He says his name is Crackenthorpe.'

'With a scar?'

'Over his right eye, sir.'

'Allow him in.'

Crackenthorpe entered, holding his hat. He bowed.

Walsingham looked up at him. *If Crackenthorpe had not found his niche working for me, he would have been hanged by now. It is understandable that soldiers in battle kill men and rape women; such are the natural consequences of war. But Crackenthorpe sees no difference between war and peace. If he were sent back to the north, his own people would kill him sooner than the Scots.*

'I have arrested Henry Machyn.'

Walsingham's eyes opened a fraction wider. 'Arrested? Good. Where is he now?'

'He's under guard at the brick house in Bishopsgate.'

'In the cellars, I presume?'

'In leg irons.'

Walsingham set down his quill and got up from the table. He went to the far side of the room and ran his fingers over a plate of sweetmeats. He took one and started walking back, biting it with his front teeth. *Excellent. Trap the man's legs. Crackenthorpe is learning. Men take the ability to walk too much for granted.*

He saw the large man watching him chew and gestured for him to help himself. 'Where was he? How did you find him?'

Crackenthorpe raised a sweetmeat to his lips. 'I watched Machyn's house all night, as you instructed.' He placed the morsel in his mouth, and tried to speak and chew at once. 'Very late . . . a man arrived and started . . . knocking hard on the door.'

'Who?'

'He said he was William Harley, a herald.'

Walsingham smiled. 'Well, well. Yes, he is a herald. Clarenceux King of Arms, no less.' He saw Crackenthorpe glance back again at the sweetmeat tray, 'Go on, Sergeant Crackenthorpe. Have as many as you want. Tell me more.'

Crackenthorpe took two sweetmeats. He chewed and spoke at the same time. 'I escorted Clarenceux . . . back to Ludgate. He asked the guard there . . . to let us through. He said he had done it before but . . . I didn't believe him. We crossed the bridge and went to his house . . .' He swallowed, looking at Walsingham, and wiped his mouth on his sleeve. 'We waited. He went in by an alleyway along one side. I continued to wait, in the rain, for a further quarter of an hour. Then I left one man at the front and led the rest down the same alley, hoping to learn more of the layout of his house and yard, in case I needed to order that the house be watched. The back door was closed, but by the lantern light I noticed the stable door was ajar. One of my men found Machyn upstairs, in the hayloft.'

Walsingham picked up the piece of paper he had been writing on when Crackenthorpe had arrived. He took it to the fireplace, and let it drift into the flames, like a leaf. He knew his next message to Cecil had to be spoken. He would go and see him in person.

'Her majesty will be pleased. Have you started questioning Machyn yet?'

'No, sir. But I did leave a guard at his house.'

'And what about Clarenceux's house? Have you searched it?'

There was a pause. 'No, sir. I thought it best to report back to you for further instructions.'

Walsingham saw the blackened fragments of the paper drift up the chimney. 'It needs to be done,' he said, turning to face Crackenthorpe. 'But first, tell me everything you know about Clarenceux, everything he said last night. I want to know every word.'

14

Clarenceux stood amid the crowd. There were about forty people now in Little Trinity Lane, their breath visible in the sunlight as they whispered to one another. They were looking at the red crosses on the barricaded door. The plague that summer had been horrendous but people had begun to believe it was over. These crosses spelled doom not just for the occupant but for everyone else in the neighbourhood.

Clarenceux looked up the street. Now he spotted the spy who had followed them from Fleet Street; he was lurking fifty yards away, in the opening of a passageway. Thomas was walking towards him, carrying the crowbar. He had wrapped it in a horse's sweat pad. Clarenceux waited. Sunlight sparkled off the puddles. In some places the mud had been churned up, like the ground around a cattle trough in winter.

He took the crowbar from Thomas and felt its weight, examined one end, and then pressed it back into Thomas's hand. 'Stay with the crowd.'

'Mr Clarenceux, you ought to know, someone's been in your stable.'

Clarenceux paused. 'Who? Not one of the lads?'

'I do not know who, sir. But there's a lot of hay scattered in the loft and more at the foot of the ladder. Looks like there was a fight, or a scuffle at the least.'

Clarenceux remembered the open gate in the night. He glanced at the guard, then at the spy, and put a hand on Thomas's shoulder. 'Show me later,' he said, and stepped up to the door of Machyn's house.

The guard was young and scrawny, about eighteen. He had a freckled face and a thin ginger beard. He was dressed in no particular livery, but the helmet, sword and breastplate marked him out from the usual guards to be seen outside plague-infected houses.

'Godspeed,' said Clarenceux cheerfully. 'What's your name?'

The guard looked warily at Clarenceux. 'My name is Grey,' he replied, rising to his full height as the crowd fell silent.

'Goodman Grey,' Clarenceux continued, in a loud and confident voice, 'I have a question for you. How is it that a man who was in good health last night is now pronounced plague-stricken this morning?'

'The house is closed by order of the constable, sir.'

'Of course it is. But which constable? And when did he send in the women to do the searching of the sick bodies?'

'That I cannot tell you, sir,' replied Grey. He shifted a hand on the hilt of his sword for reassurance, looking from Clarenceux to the crowd, which was growing.

'No, of course you cannot tell me. And I dare say that neither can the constable. For I was here but six hours ago, and there was no cross on the door then. Did you know that?'

Grey looked worried. 'No, sir.'

Clarenceux turned to the crowd. In the voice of his office, he called, 'Has anyone seen the searchers enter this house this morning?'

The words echoed off the buildings opposite. One or two windows opened. Faces looked out and there was muttering among those in the crowd, but no one responded.

There were over fifty people in Little Trinity Lane now and more were approaching. Clarenceux turned back to the young guard and stared at him, saying nothing.

'Sir, what do you want?'

'I want to know if there is anyone actually in that house.'

'Goodman Machyn and his household are in there, I presume, sir.'

'You presume? You mean you do not know?'

Grey said nothing.

Clarenceux breathed the fresh air of the morning again, and looked around him. 'Then let me put it this way,' he said in his loud voice. 'There is no one in that house, young Grey. There was no one in there last night and there is no one in there now.' He paused, watching, listening to the mood of the crowd. 'Let me tell you something. When a plague house is marked out, *if* it is necessary to leave a guard – and it is not always so – he serves two functions. The first is to make sure the inhabitants do not leave. The second is to make sure they are fed. Through which window, exactly, are you meaning to feed Henry Machyn and his family?' Clarenceux pointed upwards to the first floor. 'Through that window? The only one you have left unblocked?'

Grey remained silent.

'Thomas,' called Clarenceux, not taking his eyes off the guard.

Thomas stepped forward. Clarenceux took the crowbar and unwrapped it.

'Sir!' Grey shouted, drawing his sword, 'I must caution you not to try to open—'

Clarenceux put a firm hand on Grey's arm and pushed him backwards. The lad stumbled.

'Sir, I have orders to arrest anyone who tries to make contact with those inside.'

'Anyone?' demanded Clarenceux, taking his hand off the young man. 'Anyone? What about the apothecary's man who will bring them dragonwater and methridatum? What about the women who will nurse them in their final agony? What about the priest? Have you no pity? You would arrest such God-fearing good people, would you?'

'Yes, sir, I would.'

'Well then, you'll have to arrest me too,' Clarenceux declared, stepping right up into Grey's face and grabbing his sword wrist. He toyed with the idea of forcing the lad to drop his blade but then decided that would only injure his pride. He let go, carefully. If the guard had been serious, he would have gone for his dagger by now. He was too young, too worried.

Clarenceux saw he had silenced the boy and lifted the crowbar. He turned to the door. He fixed it under the topmost plank, and began to lever it away.

'Sir, I order you to desist,' said Grey.

Clarenceux did not even turn round. 'Thomas!' he shouted, continuing to pull at the plank. Thomas stepped forward, looked the guard in the eye, and slowly raised a finger to his lips. Grey saw Thomas's lined old face, and the iron determination plainly visible beneath the wry smile.

The first plank came away easily and soon Clarenceux was levering the second. A couple of sharp wrenches, and soon that too was joined to the frame only by a single nail. Soon all four planks were lying in the street and the door was clear.

Clarenceux took the crowbar and swung it against the oak door. It thudded.

'Henry Machyn! Goodwife Machyn! John!' he yelled up at the front of the house. 'Are any of you at home?'

No answer.

Again Clarenceux hammered on the door with the crowbar, and shouted. More shutters and windows up and down the street opened.

He set the edge of the crowbar in the door frame, and pulled. It did not give way. He pulled harder, and harder, testing his weight against the wood, putting his foot against the timber frame of the door. After a few seconds there was a loud crack and the nails holding one of the oak timbers of the door came out, allowing the plank to break out of the frame, into the house. He quickly moved the crowbar to the split and pressed the loosened plank further back inside.

He had to work fast. The crowd behind him was growing.

They would attract the attention of the authorities. He pushed the head of his crowbar through the gap in the door, and shoved the split plank to one side.

He looked through the gap: there was nothing to be seen inside, just the shadowy entrance corridor. He put his mouth to the gap in the door and shouted.

'Henry! Goodwife Machyn! This is William Harley, Clarenceux King of Arms. If you are within, reply. Tell me if you are here.'

Nothing.

Clarenceux turned. Thomas was still standing between him and the guard. People were leaning out of the windows, watching. More were arriving. The spy was there too, standing at the edge of the crowd. Including the people in the houses, Clarenceux had now about a hundred witnesses.

He stepped towards the guard. 'Tell me: do you answer to a man called Richard Crackenthorpe?'

The guard did not reply.

'Tell him Godspeed from me, Goodman Grey,' said Clarenceux, putting a friendly hand on the boy's shoulder before he walked away.

15

Noon had passed. Clarenceux had been poring over the chronicle for several hours. He rested his head in his hands, elbows on the table board, so very tired. Awdrey had brought him some ale, bread and cheese on a wooden trencher an hour earlier but he had barely touched it. He was determined to find out why this book was more valuable to Machyn than his life.

He started again at the beginning and leafed through. Here and there entries caught his attention. On 28 April 1556 two gentlemen were taken from the Tower to Tyburn and hanged, cut down and quartered, and their heads set up on London Bridge. The following day a whoremaster was pilloried for delivering prostitutes to London merchants' apprentices, the said apprentices paying with goods stolen from their masters. And on 2 May a man and a woman were placed in the pillory for perjury, the man's ears being nailed to the wood but the woman's not. It was all vividly related: London described in more detail than perhaps any other chronicler had managed. Machyn had every right to be proud of his work. But Clarenceux knew it was all a cover, a means to an end, and the end remained hidden.

His own name rang out repeatedly through the pages. Under the entry for 2 December 1562 he read about the burial of his sister, and the dinner at his house afterwards. *Was that a year ago already?* He had spoken to Machyn several times that afternoon. It was a peculiar thought: that Machyn had been taking notes on that occasion. His name appeared again in the next entry, at the funeral of the wife of Lord Justice Browne. A few pages earlier there was that long entry about his daughter's baptism. He read it again, aloud, to make sense of the phonetic spelling.

'The twenty-eighth day of July was christened the daughter of William Harley alias Clarenceux King of Arms in the parish of St Bride's, the godfather Mr Cordall, Master of the Rolls, Knight, and the godmothers my Lady Bacon, my lord keeper's wife, and my Lady Cecil, wife of Sir William Cecil. And after unto Mr Clarenceux's house and there was as great a banquet as I have seen, and wassail of hippocras, French wine, Gascon wine and Rhenish wine in great plenty, and all their servants had a banquet in the hall with divers dishes.'

He remembered the day well. Indeed, it had been a day to remember, with the important guests dining in the parlour and the servants all arrayed at two long tables in the hall. It had been a particular honour to have Mildred, Lady Cecil, as godmother to his younger daughter. Not only was she reputed to be the most intelligent woman in the realm; her husband, Sir William Cecil, was her majesty's Principal Secretary. He was Elizabeth's most trusted adviser and the most powerful individual in the country, notwithstanding his rivalry with her favourite, Robert Dudley. Awdrey had decided that they should have the baby baptised Mildred, in Lady Cecil's honour.

He sighed, got up and went over to the trencher of food. The bread was already beginning to go stale. He ate it anyway, with a piece of strongly flavoured cheese, staring vacantly at his table board as he did so.

Searching the chronicle would take too long. Machyn was possibly facing death at that very moment. He had no option now but to follow the one clear instruction that Machyn had given him.

Find Lancelot Heath.

16

ir William Cecil strode through the Painted Chamber in the Palace of Westminster. Scenes of battles fought in Old Testament times were visible in the gloomy shadows high on unseen walls, the paints faded now from their ancient glory. He held the fur of his robe close to his chest as he walked – the palace was empty and cold. Once parliaments used to gather in this vast chamber. Not any more.

'Have you dined?' he called out to Francis Walsingham, who was waiting at the far end, seated on a bench. His voice echoed.

Walsingham quickly got to his feet. 'Godspeed, Sir William. No, when I work my diet is meagre.'

Cecil held up a finger over his lips to indicate that Walsingham should say nothing. Walsingham's eyes narrowed a little as he walked towards him. Cecil waited for Walsingham to catch up with him and then led him down the stairs, out into the great court.

The sun earlier in the day had given way to a cloudy afternoon. In the absence of the court there were very few servants to be seen. A light breeze chilled their faces. 'Tell me your news,' Cecil said, walking across the wide yard.

'Machyn has been found.'

Cecil's pace did not alter. 'Has he talked?'

'Not yet. He denies everything. Says he only knows Draper as a fellow merchant taylor.'

'So? What have you got?'

Walsingham looked around, and nodded to the windows. 'Will it matter if we are seen?'

Cecil understood his caution. Despite the cold, two windows were open. 'We are discussing your parliamentary instructions, of course. But you're right.' He pointed to a gate that led towards one of the more private yards of the palace and began to walk in that direction. The sun unexpectedly broke out and cast a shadow across the quadrangle.

Walsingham cleared his throat and spoke quietly. 'Machyn was found hiding in the stable of a house in St Bride's. The house belongs to your wife's friend, William Harley, the Clarenceux herald. You might recall that your wife and her sister stood as godmothers to . . .'

'. . . his daughter, last year. Yes, thank you, Francis. When I forget the details of my own family connections, I will ask you to pray for me.' Cecil began to walk along the edge of a small courtyard, in line with a high wall. There were no overlooking windows. 'This does not mean he is involved, of course.'

'No, not by itself,' agreed Walsingham, behind Cecil's shoulder. 'But Clarenceux was found knocking on the door of Machyn's house half an hour earlier, in the middle of the night, despite the bad weather. He visited the house again this morning. I had given my man orders to shut up Machyn's house after we found him. Unfortunately the fool made the mistake of closing up the house as if the inhabitants had plague.'

'What did Clarenceux do?'

'He took a crowbar to the door.'

Cecil came to the corner of the courtyard and stopped. 'Did he enter?'

'No. But he opened the door far enough to be sure that Machyn and his wife were not at home.'

Cecil fell quiet, looking at the cobbles. *If Clarenceux was protecting Machyn he would hardly have needed to break down the door to find out if he was there. He would have known he was in his stable. Still, such matters are best left for Francis to sort out. He wins all his battles – in the end.*

'You appreciate that this complicates matters for us,' Walsingham said.

'I was not born yesterday, Francis.'

'Both for you personally and for the investigation,' he continued. 'It suggests that your wife's friend is one of Machyn's Knights of the Round Table. This is not just a conspiracy of a few London merchants. Gentlemen of rank are involved.'

'Indeed,' said Cecil. 'He is certainly an intelligent man, our Mr Clarenceux. An honest one too. I gather he is not popular among the other heralds; they dislike him for refusing to accept bribes. They also dislike him because he understands the troops – having been a soldier himself, I understand. In the late Lord Paget's company. I like him because he has no time for selfish men on the make who would never lift a sword for their queen but nevertheless want a coat of arms to parade above their garden gates.' He stopped, and paused, thinking. 'Where are Machyn's wife and son? Is Clarenceux also harbouring them?'

'John Machyn is a mariner, gone abroad. He sailed for France last week. As for Machyn's wife, I do not know. I have yet to order a thorough search of Clarenceux's house.' Walsingham hesitated. 'I wanted first to ensure that he would cause you no embarrassment when he comes to you for protection.'

Cecil stared at Walsingham. 'You know you do not need to come to me to authorise searches for information.'

'But a man like Clarenceux ...'

'If he comes to me for protection from you ... that's no concern of yours. You search and you search diligently. If your men enter his house, and find nothing, all well and good. No harm done. But if there is guilt, we need to know. We need to root it out.'

'But this man's personal connections with you made me think that I—'

'Personal connections?' exclaimed Cecil. He immediately lowered his voice, hearing the echo in the courtyard. But he spoke with no less urgency. 'How many friends of mine do you think I would permit to be traitors? Do you think I am a hypocrite, prepared to overlook treason when it is perpetrated by a friend? Mr Walsingham, I suggest you do some hard thinking over the next day or so. There is no friend of mine more important to me than the State. If you do not think the same way, I suggest you consider where your loyalties really lie.'

Walsingham swallowed. But he looked Cecil steadily in the eye as Sir William continued.

'Remember what is at stake, Francis. I know at times I appear to you to be a bit of a fool – unaware of your nuances, your subtle conniving. Your talent for searching out the one man who can lead you to three more traitors is admired by everyone who knows what you have done. Your ability to second-guess their movements is uncanny. Your talent for applying pressure goes without saying. You might be right in this matter too – perhaps your instinct not to intervene yet has been inspired by divine providence. But let me remind you of one thing. You are responsible for finding information. I decide what to do with it, on behalf of her majesty. You are responsible for uncovering plots but I am responsible for suppressing them. These matters are not games. They concern the stability of the ship of the State, the very vessel of England. Nothing is more important than its safety and security. If a mariner falls overboard, we do not turn the whole ship round. I would rather that innocent men drown than the ship be unsteadied.'

'With what I—'

'No, enough. You have already wasted time, coming to see me. When Clarenceux discovers that Machyn is no longer hiding in his stable, he will be alarmed. What did his stable lads tell him? They surely told him who took Machyn?'

'Machyn was alone in the stable. Apparently Clarenceux lets his stable boys sleep in the house in winter.'

'That's just luck.'

'Yes,' replied a chastened Walsingham.

Cecil took a deep breath. 'Let me remind you, Francis, that we know very little as yet about this plot. But we know how dangerous it is. It thus has something of the character of a mad dog about it. If you see a wild dog barking and frothing at the mouth, do you wait until it has bitten someone before you take action? No, you kill it straight away. Without a second thought. Do you understand?'

Walsingham nodded.

'Well then. Proceed on the basis that Clarenceux is guilty. It will be interesting to see what the herald has to say for himself.'

17

𝕮larenceux looked up and down Skinners Lane. The clouds in the western sky were pink and golden with late afternoon sunlight. A man was standing on a ladder nearby, repainting the knife-shaped sign above a cutler's shop. Some boys were playing a chasing game, calling out to one another with sudden shrieks of excitement as they dashed from one side of the road to the other. Three people were approaching from the eastern end of the road, leading a group of packhorses and looking down to keep the glare out of their eyes. They passed, ambling along with their heavy loads. No one seemed to be paying any attention to him.

Clarenceux walked up to the iron-hinged oak door, knocked and stepped back, waiting.

The mud was particularly thick around the puddles. In summer, when it was dry, London was beset with flies, and you could smell the basement cesspits wherever you went. In late autumn and winter it was the puddles that were most prominent; the smell of wet clay and ordure hung in the air.

The door opened a little. A woman with a small round face and an old-fashioned linen headdress looked out. She was in her mid-forties, dressed in a plain smock. Her sleeves were loose, as if she had earlier rolled them up to clean something and had quickly unrolled them in order to be decent when she answered the door.

'Godspeed, madam. My name is William Harley, Clarenceux King of Arms. I need to speak to Lancelot Heath on a very urgent matter.'

'He's not here,' the woman replied abruptly. He noticed she had bags under her slightly bloodshot eyes.

'Well, in that case, could you tell me when he might return?'

'No. He's gone away. On business.'

'Well, my good woman, I have no wish to pry into his affairs. But I do believe that he, like another friend of mine, Henry Machyn, might be in considerable danger.'

Mentioning Machyn's name caused the woman to begin to close the door. 'I'll give him your message when he's back. Now . . .'

'Wait,' he said. 'Tell him that I bear the name King Clariance of Northumberland. Clariance, like Clarenceux, from Sir Urry's tale.'

'I'll tell him,' she said suddenly. 'He knows where to find you. Now, be gone.' She closed the door in Clarenceux's face.

18

The anticipated knock came later that afternoon. Clarenceux was in the hall with a mercer from a provincial town who wanted to commission a coat of arms. Clarenceux was in no mood to humour him. When he heard the knocking on the door, he seized the chance to put an arm round the mercer's shoulders and usher him to the stairs, telling him he would consider aspects of the design but now he had to attend to another client.

Thomas opened the door. The mercer donned his hat and brusquely nodded to the woman in a travelling cope and an undyed nurse's shawl who was waiting on the doorstep.

'Who is that?' demanded Clarenceux from the middle of the stairs, disappointed not to see Lancelot Heath. Before Thomas could answer the woman stepped forward and entered the house. She pushed her hood back and her dark hair fell loose about her shoulders – shockingly so. Married women were expected to dress their hair, or cover it with a coif. She looked up at Clarenceux, her eyes meeting his directly, with obvious determination.

'Please, Mr Clarenceux, may I beg you close the door quickly?'

'Goodwife Machyn, I . . . Yes. Of course. Come upstairs straight away. Thomas, bolt the door. Take Goodwife Machyn's hood and shawl.'

She was much younger than her husband – in her late thirties – with sad but beautiful brown eyes. Her most distinctive mark was a large brown mole on the side of her jaw. When Clarenceux had first met her he had regarded it as a cruel blemish, but over the years, as he had come to regard her with greater affection – albeit always from a respectful distance – it had begun to amuse him. It seemed utterly absurd that such a woman could be considered marred by such a tiny speck, a third of the size of his thumbnail. He saw it as the opposite of an imperfection; a sign of distinctiveness. But even so, there was always an air of tragedy about her. Her smile was a little wistful, as if the true delights of life were things she would never know.

'I heard you at the house last night,' she began. 'I heard Sergeant Crackenthorpe talking to you. And I saw you there again today, when you called for me and Henry.'

'It was nothing. I was only—'

'No, Mr Clarenceux. It was something. When you are in our position, it is the most blessed relief just to know that someone else has sufficient heart and goodwill to open his mouth and to shout out, "What has happened to these people?" But I did not come here just to say thank you. I came to talk to you.'

'About Henry?'

She began to walk towards the elm table. 'He told me yesterday evening that he had made a decision. He would not tell me what; but he told me to go to Mistress Barker's house. That was the last time I saw him.'

Clarenceux noticed that his maidservant, Emily, was about to enter the hall with some logs for the fire. She hesitated outside the door, uncertain whether to proceed. He gestured silently for her not to disturb them.

'What do you know of Henry's chronicle?'

'It was his most precious possession. He would not let anyone else touch it, or even look at it. That is why I am so worried. Last night, when he said goodbye to me, he shed tears. He kissed me over and over again. He picked that book up reverently, as if it were the Holy Bible. He looked at it solemnly, then turned to me. He told me to wait a short while after he left the house, and then go to the house of Mistress Barker and stay there. I did as I was told, of course. But I was very anxious. I could not sleep. I heard men outside, knocking on doors and arguing. When I went out early this morning, I saw the plague crosses on our house. I was shocked, too frightened to do anything. I ran back inside. I watched from an upstairs window as you broke open our front door.'

'Do you know where Henry is now?'

'I wondered if he had come here.'

Clarenceux glanced down the length of the hall to the door. He could see Emily in the doorway, speaking to Awdrey. He wondered how much of his conversation Awdrey had heard.

'Come with me,' he said quietly. 'It is better that we talk about this upstairs.'

He went to the front staircase, climbed the stairs and pushed open the door to his study. Having drawn his seat forward for Goodwife Machyn, he made a pile of large books near her on which to sit himself. The light was dim; it was nearly dusk.

'Listen, I do not want Awdrey to know this. All she knows is that your husband came here late last night. The truth is that he left me his chronicle ...'

'He left it here?'

'He also said he has bequeathed it to me in his will.'

'That cannot ... I have not seen or heard of any will of my husband's.'

'Really?'

'Truly.'

He paused. 'Now I understand why your house has been boarded up. They hope to find the chronicle there. And if they do not, they hope to find clues to its possible location. It isn't Crackenthorpe behind this. He is just an instrument.'

'I am sorry, I don't understand. I know Sergeant Crackenthorpe was at our house last night, but who *is* he? Do you know where Henry is now?'

Clarenceux stood up and went to the book press on the far side of the room. Two books were lying on their sides. He looked back at her. 'Can you read?'

75

'A little. Henry taught me.'

He set aside the Gospels and took down the chronicle. He passed it to her.

'Look at the final entry.'

She took the volume and turned back the blank pages at the end one by one until she came to the last section of text. She sat hunched over it.

Clarenceux stood, watching her.

She did not move. She remained in exactly the same position, as if still reading, long after Clarenceux knew she had finished. He bit his lip. He heard a tear fall on to the page. She wiped it away, carefully, with the edge of her sleeve.

'They sound like his final words,' she said, not looking up.

Clarenceux remembered the fond old man's imploring face, the tears running down his cheeks into his white beard. His enormous distress.

'I'm sorry,' she said, wiping her eyes with her hands.

'You've nothing to be sorry about. We're all in danger. Henry and you. Me too. That book contains a secret. When Henry was here, he told me that if I needed to know what it meant, I would find out. He gave me the name of Lancelot Heath, a painter-stainer, on whom I called this morning. I left a message with a discontented woman who answered the door.'

She closed the book gently and passed it back to Clarenceux with both hands.

'Do you know who the Knights of the Round Table are?' he asked.

She wiped her eyes again. 'Only the heroes of old romances.'

'When Henry was here, he said that when the Knights of the Round Table are gathered together, the way to understand that book will become apparent to me. And he was very particular on this point, that the secret will become apparent to *me*, to no one else.' He paused. 'I think the Knights of the Round Table is a fraternity, a Catholic brotherhood. Lancelot Heath – do you know if Lancelot Heath is a follower of the old ways?'

'He is, fervently so. He often comes to our house, and will even kneel down and pray in our hall. He and Henry work together on funeral trappings. Henry provides the black cloth for funerals and drapes the hearse with the colours of the dead person's heraldry. Lancelot paints the funeral boards with the coats of arms.'

'In that case I probably know him by sight.' Clarenceux tapped his finger on the book. 'Does the name King Clariance of Northumberland mean anything to you?'

She shook her head.

Clarenceux opened the chronicle and found the entry for 20 June 1557. 'And this?'

He passed her the book again. She read the entry concerning the sermon preached by the abbot of Westminster at St Paul's Cross. 'No,' she whispered.

'Henry gave me that date. He said it was important that I remember it.'

He went back across the room and replaced the book on the shelf. He turned and glanced at her as the last rays of sunlight caught the side of her face. Sounds of playing children entered from the street. She smiled, and returned his gaze. Distracted for an instant, he forced himself to look down and consider the important questions. *Why that date? Why St Paul's Cross? Why me? Why King Clariance?*

'I suppose there are several Knights of the Round Table,' she said.

'And it would be reasonable to assume that your husband knows who they are. But what does that date mean? The Arthurian King Clariance appears in *The Tale of Sir Urry*: at first he was a rebel against King Arthur; only later did he join with him to fight the Saxons. But that has little to do with a date in June 1557, or the inscription in that book. All I can guess is that the date Henry gave me relates to the abbot of Westminster, and that each Knight has a date connected to someone else in the chronicle, or something else. Or maybe several things, or places.'

She looked at him, her hands resting in her lap, and shrugged.

'The message of the book will probably only become clear when we know all the Knights, as Henry said. But John Howman, the last abbot of Westminster, has been in the Tower for the last three years – he is the arch-Catholic in England and even now he refuses to recant – so how are we supposed to get word to him, let alone in a private manner? We do not know what we are looking for, or whom. I do not even know how many Knights of the Round Table there are. All I know is that the fate of two queens depends on the safekeeping of this book.'

'There *are* only two queens in these islands.'

'Quite. And your husband is a Catholic, like the Queen of Scots. But I cannot see how anything that Henry could have known would affect the fate of either queen, let alone both ...'

Clarenceux stopped. *Not 'fates' but 'fate'. Henry Machyn definitely said 'the fate of two queens'. One fate, two queens ... O Lord Saviour, sweet and merciful Jesus does this mean what I think it means, that their individual destinies are combined into one fate? Within our grasp?*

'What is the matter?' she asked.

Clarenceux looked at her. 'In the event of Queen Elizabeth's death, Mary Queen of Scots could become Queen of England – queen of both countries. So you see: two queens, one fate. In the last parliament Elizabeth refused to name her heir. The only hereditary alternative to the Queen of Scots is Elizabeth's cousin, Lady Catherine Grey, younger sister of Lady Jane – but that is hardly likely now, not since Elizabeth found out about Lady Catherine's secret marriage. She was absolutely furious with her; she annulled the marriage and sent her husband abroad, effectively punishing him with exile. Elizabeth has no other recognised heir, and there is no other popular claimant except the Queen of Scots, who is favoured by all of those who prefer the old religion. If Elizabeth dies without naming an heir, then England will become a Catholic country once more.'

Clarenceux recognised a sense of foreboding and importance

combined in what he was saying. He had felt it before, once particularly, in June 1557, when he had stood in the centre of the great hall at Rheims, surrounded by the nobility of France, and announced in his loudest, proudest voice that England and France were henceforth at war. But then he had been merely a spokesman, a messenger. No one was telling him what to say now.

'In the event of the queen's death?' Goodwife Machyn looked up at Clarenceux.

'I know: it is far-fetched. But that does not mean Henry has not ...' He broke off. Looking towards the dying light of day through the window, he felt a chill breeze. It would soon be time to close the shutters. 'Crackenthorpe told me last night that it was a case of high treason he is investigating. That, I suspect, was a slip of the tongue: an honest one. I doubt he would have closed your house like that without some higher authority. To go over the constable's head and declare a house plague-infected ... it risks causing panic.'

Rebecca Machyn closed her eyes. 'Oh, husband,' she muttered, 'what have you got yourself into? What have you got *us* into?' She stood up and walked to the fireplace. 'I do not know what he has been doing. I have no real wish to know. It is none of my business. All I really want is to be safe, and for Henry to be safe too.'

Clarenceux thought. *Crackenthorpe will know by now about my breaking open the door this morning. Whoever is giving him orders will also know about our argument at Machyn's house last night. I have been dragged into this, even though I do not understand what is going on.*

He glanced at her. 'That book contains something treasonable. The fact we do not know what it is doesn't make us any safer.'

'But let us say that the book is discovered, and that you and I are questioned by some judge. Surely we can deny any knowledge of what is written there? Anything Henry actually wrote could be described as just his work, and wrong-headed.'

'Treated as a mistake? Goodwife Machyn, we're talking about the queen's paid killers – men who have fought in the wars and have not been able to get used to the peace. Sergeant Crackenthorpe – or whoever is giving him orders – believes something in this chronicle presents a threat to the queen. Henry has been keeping it secret. You yourself said he never lets anyone even touch it.'

'Are you saying that Henry might have been planning an attempt on the queen's life? That is ridiculous. He is but a poor merchant and a parish clerk. And sixty-six years old.'

Clarenceux stood up and took a couple of paces, pushing his fingers against his forehead, willing himself to think. 'Crackenthorpe knows that some information – something treasonable – is here, in this book, in this house. After today's events he will know I am involved with your husband. He will come here, without doubt. He will search this house, looking for your husband. Looking for the chronicle and you too.'

He looked up. *It will be dark soon. It will not be long before the city bells will ring for the end of the day and the closing of the city gates. But Goodwife Machyn cannot go home; her house is being watched.*

And so is mine.

Clarenceux went to the window. He hesitated for a moment, then looked out. In the fading light he could see no sign of men loitering or acting suspiciously. *But that means nothing. Crackenthorpe thinks like a soldier: he's going to come tonight, when I am off guard and he has the town watch at his command.*

'Goodwife Machyn, listen,' he said, turning round. 'This is important. We have the book. No one trying to stop this plot will have any idea what we do know and what we don't. It probably won't make any difference even if we give the book up, for no one will know for certain whether we have read it. My name appears on nearly every page: no one is going to think me innocent. If, on the other hand, we *do* learn what this is all about, then we are in a bargaining position. I have important friends whom I can ask for protection.'

'But what about my husband?'

He took a deep breath. 'Henry is in great danger. As long as he remains alive he will be considered a threat. Giving up the book will not be enough to save him.'

'So what should we do?'

Clarenceux shook his head. 'I had hoped Lancelot Heath would have come here by now, or at least sent word. But the more I think about it ...' Clarenceux glanced at the window. He could hardly see her face in the gloom of the darkening room.

'Yes?'

'It is only a matter of time. And when they find us, and find the book, well, I do not expect I will get away with merely having my ears nailed to the pillory.'

'Can we not just hide it somewhere?'

'We've got to leave this house. And remove the book.'

'But if no one finds it, how will they know it has been in your possession?'

Clarenceux did not answer. He went across the room and picked up the chronicle. 'Crackenthorpe is a sergeant-at-arms, a royal enforcer. A killer. If his political masters want someone to cut a throat, he does it. If they order him to find a book, he will do it. I have been foolish. I should never have accepted this chronicle. I should never have gone to your house last night. But having—'

Suddenly a loud knocking at the front door rang out.

Clarenceux looked towards her. He knew that she was thinking the same thing as he was. The next few instants might be their last moments of freedom.

'What now?' she whispered.

'It could be Lancelot Heath,' he said. He turned back to the window and leant out. Although the house projected over the street, he could just see the backs of two men at the door below.

'Oh, Christ in heaven. It is them. And they are armed.'

'Then we must try to hide the book in here,' she said.

Clarenceux ignored her. 'Go downstairs. Tell my servant Thomas not to answer the door immediately. Tell him to delay, to say anything to give me a few moments more.'

The knocking came again, harder, more insistent.

Clarenceux did not say another word. Putting the chronicle under his arm, he followed Rebecca to the door, ran down the stairs behind her and hurried across the candlelit hall. He flung open the door at the end and went down the back stairs. A little light seeped through from the kitchen at the end of the corridor. He opened the door to the buttery; it was totally dark within. The pungent smell of ale wafted around him. He felt for the first barrel, and placed the book on top of it. He strode to a large wine cask in the far corner, took hold of it, and pulled it towards him, tipping it on to its rim, and moving it sideways.

He heard the knocking again, from the front of the house.

He went down on his knees, and felt around on the floor for the loose floorboard that he knew was there. He could not find it. Panicking now, he gave up looking and felt his way back to the barrel where he had left the book, and picked it up.

Then he stopped. *If Crackenthorpe boards up this house and marks it with red crosses, it will only be a matter of time before his men find the book. There has to be a solution – something more subtle.*

But it was already too late. He could hear the bolts being pulled back on the front door. And footsteps. He cursed, and hurried through to the kitchen. The kitchen boy, Thomas's great-nephew Will Terry, was holding a glowing taper, lighting rush-lights. He watched as Clarenceux plunged the book into an open sack of oats, burying it beneath the surface, pushing it right to the bottom. Clarenceux turned to the boy, who had paused.

'This is important, Will,' he said hurriedly. 'No one must know it is there, do you understand?'

The fair-haired lad nodded in alarm and watched as Clarenceux ran from the kitchen and along the corridor. *That was foolish.*

The boy is only eleven. I hope that he has the sense to confide in Thomas and ask him for advice.

Clarenceux hurried up the back stairs and entered the hall. Awdrey was with Goodwife Machyn: they were standing together, having just embraced to comfort one another. He could hear the bells ringing out all over the city. Soon the gates would shut for the night.

'You have a summons,' said Awdrey anxiously, stepping quickly towards him. 'A Mr Walsingham wants to see you.'

'When?' he asked, turning from one woman to the other.

But at that moment he heard many footsteps echoing on the stairs from the front door.

He looked at Goodwife Machyn. He began to mouth the word 'Hide' and pointed to the stairs; but she had already grasped his meaning, seeing it instantly in his eyes. She turned and hurried to the door that led to the stairs up to his study.

A moment later a tall, dark-haired man entered. He had a long scar across the right-hand side of his face. He strode into the room, followed by three other armed men, and looked around the hall at the panelling, the paintings, the mirror, the plaster ceiling. Clarenceux did not recognise him at first. But when he spoke, he knew exactly who had walked into his house.

'Mr Clarenceux,' said Crackenthorpe. 'You will come with me.'

'Where to? For what reason?'

'To the house of the Secretary's chief counsellor, Mr Francis Walsingham, the Member of Parliament for Lyme Regis.'

'I protest. Why?'

'Because Mr Walsingham would like to ask you some questions. If you refuse, I will arrest you in the name of her majesty. And then you will be taken to Mr Walsingham's house in chains.'

Clarenceux glanced from Crackenthorpe to the other men. One was very tall, with lank brown hair hanging on either side of his face and an expression like a slow-witted dog. Another was small and weasel-like, prim and ready for action. The third was medium height, with a narrow face, a thin goatee beard and cruel eyes. All four were staring at him. There was no hope of escape.

'The choice is yours, Mr Clarenceux. Choose now.'

In an upstairs chamber his younger daughter Mildred began to cry. He turned to his wife, and saw the tears welling in her eyes. He himself felt sick with nerves, too anxious to be sad. He moved closer to her, put his hands on her cheeks and wiped her tears away with his thumbs. Their daughter's crying and the thought of departure tore at him, a final moment. Time was passing so slowly, and yet there was so little left.

'Now, I said, Mr Claren—'

'For heaven's sake, be patient!'

He took a deep breath, looking into his wife's blue eyes. Then he spoke in a calmer voice, but not so quiet that no one could hear him. 'I am going to accompany these men now, my love. If I do not return by morning, send a message to our friends, telling them what has happened. Tell them that I have been arrested, without charge or warrant, by a sergeant at-arms, one Richard Crackenthorpe, on the instructions of a Mr Walsingham. Tell them to press immediately for a case of unlawful distraint, contrary to the terms of Magna Carta, even if it be the queen's will . . .' he turned to look at Crackenthorpe, 'and contrary to the common law if it be merely Mr Walsingham's.'

19

ebecca sat in the chair in Clarenceux's study, hunched, her hands turning over and over in her lap. It was almost dark. She wiped her eyes, feeling a trembling sickness in the pit of her stomach. She took a deep breath, and another. And another. Her hands were still shaking.

What is going to happen to us?

She looked at the dark room. She could just make out the book press along one side. A moment ago, when there had been more light, the books had seemed naturally a part of Clarenceux's world, the instruments of his profession: they had been reassuring. Now, suddenly, they were abandoned in the dark, and useless. It seemed that Mr Clarenceux was dead – as dead as a never-read book. And Henry too was dead. Both men taken by this Sergeant Crackenthorpe. How she hated the thought of him, from the heels of his leather boots to the scar above his eye. His name sounded like the breaking of a stick underfoot. She wished she could break *him*.

She heard footsteps on the stairs. *O Heavenly Father, is this it? Are they searching the house now?* The creak of the wood sent shivers through her body, through her mind. She wanted to get up and scream, for all this darkness to go away, for her husband to be back, for Mr Clarenceux to walk into the room, to tell her everything was going to be all right.

'Goodwife Machyn?' whispered a woman's voice.

She tried to answer, but she found there was no sound when she opened her mouth to speak. The sudden shock of her inability to utter a syllable only made things worse.

'Gooodwife Machyn?' She saw the flicker of a candle flame.

Awdrey came into the room. She set down the candle on the table board and came to put a hand on her shoulder.

'Is ... is Mildred asleep?' Rebecca asked, wiping her eyes, growing calmer.

'Yes. And Annie is going to bed now. Nurse Brown has her.'

Rebecca began to pull herself together. 'So that's it then. We are in the same rudderless boat, you and me. Both our husbands stolen from us by Sergeant Crackenthorpe.'

Awdrey fingered the ruby ring she was wearing. 'It seems we are indeed in the same boat,' she said after a little delay.

'It's going to happen tonight, you know,' said Rebecca, pushing her hair back, out of her face. 'The search, I mean.'

'The search?'

'They'll find the book.'

Awdrey took the candle and held it close to Rebecca's tear-streaked face. 'What book?'

Rebecca was surprised. Then she remembered. *Clarenceux said he did not want Awdrey to know.* She searched Awdrey's face: all she found was an expression of alarm.

She looked briefly into the flame, and shut her eyes. 'Do you really not know?'

'No. Why will they search this house? They will find nothing of interest if they do.'

'That is not true.'

'Why do you say that? What do you know that I do not?'

'You know my husband was here last night?'

'Yes, of course. Thomas told me – and William too.'

'Do you know why he was here?'

'Because ...' Awdrey paused, trying to remember. 'William said that he was in trouble. He believed he would be murdered today.'

It was a harsh reminder. Rebecca had not expected to be so affected now. She looked down, trying to compose herself.

'Forgive me. I . . . didn't mean . . .'

'No, no.' Rebecca shook her head. 'You're quite right. Only that was not the reason why my husband came here.'

Awdrey did not move. She felt hollow, set aside. 'Then why?'

For a moment the two women looked at each other.

'There is a book,' Rebecca said, almost forcing the words out of her mouth. 'A book which Henry has written over many years. It contains a secret. Last night, in that terrible storm, he said goodbye to me as if he would never see me again and brought it here. He gave it to your husband.'

'What sort of book?'

'A chronicle.'

Awdrey sighed. 'We must get it out of the house,' she announced, moving away from Rebecca, still holding the candle. Rebecca was left in shadows.

'It is not going to be that easy.'

'So, we'll burn it then,' Awdry said, glancing at the cold fire-place.

'But do you know where it is hidden?'

Awdrey paused. 'We'll *say* we burnt it. That way we can have no knowledge of it.'

Rebecca shook her head. 'They will come and search this house from top to bottom. They will pull the place apart. And when they find the book – for they will find it – they will look at your denial as a sign of complicity. Unless I am much mistaken, Mistress Harley, that will be enough to send your husband to the gallows.

'Your husband explained it to me,' she continued. 'Burning the book will solve nothing. No one will ever be sure we have not read it and discovered its secret. So . . . you are right. We have got to find it quickly and get it out of the house, secretly.'

Awdrey nodded. She held the candle up a little higher and looked around the room. 'It's probably in here somewhere. William keeps all his books in here.'

Rebecca looked at the dark doorway. *Poor woman. She has done nothing to deserve this. Henry has brought disaster on her simply through trusting her husband. And she is not even aware of what is going on in her own household. Someone has got to do something, and with Clarenceux arrested, and my husband disappeared, and this proud woman so ill-informed, that someone can only be me.*

20

It was dark by the time Clarenceux arrived at Walsingham's house. Two of the guards carried flaming torches. In addition to the three men who had been with Crackenthorpe when he arrested Clarenceux, two more had been waiting outside. All six men had surrounded him as he was led through the streets, but at the door of the mansion they fell back and Crackenthorpe alone conducted him inside and up the stairs.

The great chamber on the first floor was panelled in an exotic imported wood. There was an elaborate plaster ceiling. The oak floorboards were bare. Several sets of silver candlesticks around the room brightened it; the candles themselves were wax, not tallow. It was a touch of refinement and, in this environment, that meant control. The room was clean – even the sturdy oak table was tidy. Several folded pieces of paper and parchment were arranged along one edge of the table in a neat line: a far cry from Clarenceux's own table board in his relatively cramped second-floor study, laden with books and documents. Clarenceux entered, and waited, scratching his left palm with his right thumbnail.

Anxiety. How often have I known it. Before an assembly, waiting for the moment to speak. Worried lest I make a mistake. Aware of the potential for disgrace if I should say something at the wrong moment on a matter of international importance, before some frowning prince or head of state. Steeling myself to do and

*say exactly what my mind says is right, and yet to act naturally.
Above all, to put thought before fear. If I am to control myself
now, I must remember what I am, as well as who I am.*

He could hear Crackenthorpe, just outside the room, speaking
to someone in a low voice. A boy came in and put logs on the
fire, then looked at the table and saw some dirt which needed
removing. He brushed it into his hand and threw it in the fireplace. Before he left, he closed the internal shutters over the
windows. He glanced furtively at Clarenceux and then made his
way soundlessly from the room.

A moment later, Clarenceux understood the reason for the
boy's furtive glance. There was someone else in the chamber.
Behind him.

The door closed and a lock clicked. He turned round.

Walsingham stood there, in a black cloak and doublet, holding
a key. He was almost a foot shorter than Clarenceux. Their eyes
met. Walsingham turned away and put the key in a small pouch
hanging from his belt.

'You are Mr Walsingham?'

'I am,' said the small man, looking Clarenceux up and down,
and walking slowly across the room towards the table.
Clarenceux's eyes followed him.

'What have you done with Henry Machyn?'

'I'll ask the questions, thank you, Mr Harley.' Walsingham
paused, then went to a cupboard and picked up his silver tray
of sweetmeats. He offered it to Clarenceux. Clarenceux did not
even bother to shake his head.

'Do you understand why you are here?' Walsingham replaced
the silver tray, and chewed his sweetmeat as he went round to
the far side of the table.

Clarenceux did not respond. He watched Walsingham as he
tried to dislodge a morsel trapped behind his teeth. The man's
jaw moved, his tongue running around the inside of his cheek.
He accomplished the dislodgement.

'I presume that your silence means yes, in some degree or other.'

'Presume what you will.' Clarenceux stood still and tall as Walsingham leant over the table, his knuckles and thumbs pressing down on the wooden surface.

'You are here because you were found at Henry Machyn's house on the night that he went missing.'

'Do you think I had something to do with his disappearance?'

Walsingham shook his head. 'Of course not.'

'No. Because it was on your orders that he was arrested. What have you and that murderous sergeant done with him?'

Walsingham walked over to the wall, and operated a device unseen by Clarenceux. A panel slid aside, revealing a concealed wine store behind. He took out two plain silver cups and a squat, flat-bottomed leather bottle. He placed the cups on the table, filled them with red wine and held one out to Clarenceux.

Clarenceux did not move. After a second or two, Walsingham withdrew the cup and replaced it on the table.

'Who is to say I have your Henry Machyn? Do you have any evidence?'

'Lack of evidence is never enough to remove suspicion.'

Walsingham drank, looking towards Clarenceux. 'Fine. Be suspicious. It will do you no good.'

'Mr Walsingham,' said Clarenceux, feeling anger rising within him. 'I have been arrested and brought here against my will. To imprison someone without reason is contrary to the terms of Magna Carta. And I am an officer of her majesty the queen. You have no right to arrest—'

Walsingham held up a hand. 'Stop there, Mr Harley. I did not arrest you. Sergeant Crackenthorpe did. He too is one of her majesty's officers. If you wish to take issue, the proper process is to enter a plea in the Court of Queen's Bench.'

'Damn Queen's Bench! What am I to be charged with?'

'Tell me what you are guilty of—' Walsingham stopped abruptly and smiled at the irony of what he was about to say. 'In fact, no. Tell me what you are guilty of, and you will *not* be charged. I am more interested in your information than your punishment.'

Clarenceux stared at the little man. 'It would be unwise to play games with me. I demand to be released. Or, if you have something to hold against me, tell me.'

Walsingham stepped closer to Clarenceux, looking up at him. 'Unwise? *Me?* Who, might I ask, is your patron? If not a dead man?'

Clarenceux struggled to make sense of the situation. As far as he could see, Walsingham had simply decided to rip up the laws of the land – laws that had proved their worth for three hundred years or more – on no authority but his own.

'As you have seen, Mr Harley, I have royal officers at my command. Do you suppose I have no idea what is wise and what is unwise? Do you not realise that I too have a patron, and a protector?'

Clarenceux bit his lip. The pain helped him concentrate. *Thought over fear.*

'Now you are wondering who it is, this patron?' continued Walsingham. 'You are thinking, "Who protects Francis Walsingham? Is he a more powerful protector than *my* protector?" That is what you are thinking, is it not, Mr Harley? And what is your conclusion?'

Clarenceux could see where this was going.

'You are asking yourself, is it someone who has the ear of her majesty?' Walsingham was almost sneering. 'Is it Dudley, you wonder? Perhaps; there are few more loyal protectors than the hero of Protestant England, though there are many better men. But what about the one man who is undoubtedly as strong, and who is a good man? What about her majesty's Secretary, Sir William Cecil?'

Walsingham wiped his sleeve across his face. 'And if you are not a fool you will already be thinking: "What if Mr Walsingham's protector and mine are the same man? The one whose wife and sister-in-law attended the baptism of my daughter in July last year?"'

Clarenceux felt as if he were falling. The rope to which he had been clinging had snapped. The word *betrayal* hit him and fastened itself in his mind. Cecil's betrayal. Not only had the trap been set, but he had fallen into it without realising it was there.

'You see, Mr Harley, knowledge is a powerful thing. Friendship is even more powerful. And when you have both – knowledge and friends – you are invincible.' Walsingham drank the rest of his wine.

Clarenceux saw now how much he had been relying on the thought that he could call on Cecil for help and security. That thought, even though untested, had cushioned him from his worst fears. Now that cushion was gone. *Walsingham is right. If he and I both need Cecil's help, whom will Cecil choose? He cannot choose us both. If Walsingham enjoys Cecil's protection as much as he implies, then I am not just friendless, I am lost.*

'Tell me, Mr Harley,' began Walsingham, 'have you ever—'

'Clarenceux! I am Clarenceux, for God's sake,' he snapped.

'Mr Harley, you have a—'

'MY TITLE IS CLARENCEUX!' he shouted, his voice echoing in the chamber.

'I don't pay much attention to heraldic titles, Mr Harley. Especially when they are claimed by traitors trying to dignify themselves.'

'You do not have the right to call me . . .' He broke off, too angry to reason. Instead he warned him, 'I still have friends.'

'Not as many as the queen.'

'I have fewer enemies.'

Walsingham shook his head. 'I would not count on that, if I were you. You do not even know who your enemies are.'

Clarenceux breathed deeply. There had been a moment, on the way here, when he had wondered why he was being taken to Walsingham's house and not simply to some cellar to be beaten up and questioned. Now he knew. Threats work better when they are not just physical. And it was not over yet. The only good thing was that Walsingham was also talking.

'I'll have that wine now,' he said, feeling sweat on his brow.

93

Walsingham hesitated. He set his own cup down and steadily refilled it before passing the other one, still untasted, to Clarenceux.

'You want to talk about friends. Tell me about your friend Henry Machyn.'

'He is a ... merchant taylor and an old man. A good man, too. He does not deserve to be ill-treated.'

'Is he your friend?'

'I have known him for many years.'

'But is he your friend?'

'It depends ...'

'Will you allow him to destroy you?'

'Why would he do that?'

'So you do acknowledge that he has the power to destroy you?'

'You are too hasty. And you infer too much.'

'Do I? What have I inferred in particular?'

Clarenceux said nothing.

'I will tell you what I infer. From your reluctance to help me with my inquiries, I infer that you are a party to the plot involving a secret fraternity which calls itself the Knights of the Round Table. I will continue to believe this until you persuade me otherwise. And the only way you will be able to do that is to hand over the book that was written by Henry Machyn, the one that has the character and title of a chronicle. Do you understand? The only way you can convince me of your innocence in this matter is to betray your friends, because I *know* they are guilty.'

Clarenceux breathed deeply, trying to control himself. 'I am not in possession of such a book. Nor have I heard of the society you mention.'

'But you have seen it?'

'Seen what?'

'The book, Henry Machyn's chronicle. Have you seen it?'

Clarenceux realised he was at the point of a crucial decision. *If I deny that I have seen it, and Walsingham's men question Thomas too, my statement will clash with his. Maybe even the*

94

other servants' too. Will Terry won't be able to hold his tongue. I have no choice.

'So you *have* seen it.'

Clarenceux raised the cup of wine to his lips and sipped. But he said nothing.

'Well?'

'Mr Walsingham, you seem to be very determined on this point. But I am not part of any plot. Nor any conspiracy. I just want to see that my friends are safe – safe from people like you. It is true that Goodman Machyn showed me his chronicle. In all truth, I had no idea that it was anything more than a work of historical record. I looked at the first few pages. I saw it was very poorly written, very badly spelled. I told him, as kindly as I could, that I did not want it. I said it would be a great loss to his son if he were to give away such a treasure after working on it for so many years. I gave the chronicle back – ask my servant Thomas if you do not believe me.'

Walsingham looked at him for a long time.

Something I have just said was enough to disrupt him. Clarenceux took another sip of wine.

Walsingham took the key out of his pouch and walked slowly towards the door. 'Very good, Mr Harley,' he said, not glancing in his direction. 'We are making progress. At least you are now prepared to admit a modicum of truth. That you have seen the chronicle . . .' He opened the door, and Clarenceux, turning, saw two men enter. 'Yes, Machyn did bring you the book. I know he did. But the rest of your story is invented. Spurious. Lies. Machyn did not remove his book, did he? It is still in your house.'

Walsingham moved back to the other side of the table. Once more he leant forward over it, resting his hands on the surface. 'All I want is that book. It really is that simple.'

Clarenceux forced himself to respond calmly. 'I do not have it. Machyn took it, I swear.'

'Do not swear, Mr Harley. I would not wish your eternal soul to be as damned as your mortal body.' Then, looking at one of the guards, he pointed at Clarenceux's legs and gave an abrupt command. 'The right.'

An instant later Clarenceux felt excruciating pain as something struck his right knee. He lay on the floorboards, writhing, his wine cup rolling away, his breath coming in spasms.

'I do not like having to repeat myself, Mr Harley. Nor do I like it when people lie to me. Lies are hostages to the truth – remember that. They will betray you in the end. So every time you try to mislead me with a tedious little falsehood, I will take out my displeasure on you. So, let us begin again. Where is—'

'For heaven's sake, Walsingham!' roared Clarenceux from the floor. 'I told you the truth. What more do you want?'

'Answers,' said Walsingham coldly.

Clarenceux forced himself to look round. One of the men had been standing behind him. He was holding a metal bar.

'It is strange how often people overlook the legs as a means of effective control,' said Walsingham. 'We rely on them to move us swiftly away from danger. We trust them to carry us in both peace and war, on foot and on horseback. What better way to make a man feel vulnerable than to damage his legs?'

Clarenceux winced as the waves of pain surged in his knee.

Walsingham walked across to the tray of sweetmeats. He set it down on the table and ate another morsel, looking at Clarenceux on the floor.

'You seem to me very complacent, Mr Harley. You think we do not realise how serious this matter is. I can think of nothing of greater importance to her majesty at this moment than the location of that book. Do you understand? Nothing. Not even France.' He paused, allowing the message to sink in.

'Let me illustrate. Imagine being suspended above the ground by your hands. Not high up, just eight or nine inches. And then imagine a guard, not unlike your assailant here, breaking your lower legs. One leg strapped to a stool, and a sudden blow with an iron bar. Then the other. As you swing there, with both your legs broken, in agony, you may scream and do other time-wasting things. Eventually, however, you will stop. Then I might ask you again where Machyn's chronicle is. If you tell me, you will be let down gently, and I will have the bonesetter see to your injuries. But if you choose to remain silent, I might well decide to cut that rope, and let you fall . . . The damage would be irreparable. And that would not be the end of the pain but rather the start – for I would just leave you there, where you fell.'

Walsingham gestured for the guards to raise Clarenceux to his feet.

'You are a . . .' began Clarenceux, but he broke off. The pain surged in his knee as the guards lifted him upright, forcing him to stand. He put his weight on his left leg. 'We have a . . . law against torture.'

Walsingham calmly placed his palms flat on the table. He leant forward again. 'I will repeat what I said a moment ago. You seem to me to be very complacent. Until just five years ago we burnt men and women for heresy. Forty years ago we boiled women alive for poisoning at the king's court. Some crimes will never deserve anything other than the most extreme punishment. Heresy is one. Treason is another. The festering wound of religious division must be cauterised. If not with fire, then with something equally efficient.'

'Hence . . . your damned searches,' hissed Clarenceux, still grimacing against the pain.

'So, you *do* understand. Good.' Walsingham ate another sweet-meat. 'Now, what I said about breaking your legs will not happen to you tonight. And if you tell me where Machyn's book is, it will not happen to you at all. That knock on your knee will do no lasting damage.'

'No?' said Clarenceux, still feeling it.

'Of course not,' snapped Walsingham. 'I need you to stand in the pillory first, with your ears bleeding. Then I want you to be seen walking through the streets to the Tower. In chains, in procession. To show the Catholics what they can expect, so more of them are minded to bow before the power of her majesty and inform on their fellow plotters.'

Clarenceux said nothing.

'Where is Machyn's book?' Walsingham demanded.

'I do not know.'

'Again, where is Machyn's book?'

Clarenceux wanted to shout, to give vent to his anger, but he knew that that was what he was expected to do. Instead he concentrated on the pain in his leg.

'Mr Harley, you are being very foolish. Or . . . what was it you said earlier? "Unwise". I know you have that book.'

'Then send your men to find it.'

'The search is under way as we speak. And I have given Sergeant Crackenthorpe every liberty to be as thorough as necessary. Every chest, every floorboard, every nook. He will search every hole in every wall and every floor. Every barrel, full or empty, every keg in your kitchen, every piece of furniture will be upended, every fireplace unblocked . . . He will find it.'

'So why are you asking me for it?'

'Have you not worked that out for yourself?'

Clarenceux stared at him. *What does he mean? Surely I am being interrogated . . . pleading for myself, my own case. Is this not a battle between the information I have and the punishment he can inflict?*

'You disappoint me, Mr Harley. I had hoped you would be honest, and save me a lot of trouble. But I suppose it does not matter. Mr Secretary Cecil will forgo his kind memories of you, I am sure, when I tell him why you are to be sent to the gallows.'

Clarenceux closed his eyes. *Maybe this is not about me . . . If I have already been pronounced guilty, I am being interrogated to see if I will confess. To see whom I might implicate in Machyn's plot.*

He opened his eyes: Walsingham was smiling. He tried to set aside the man's confidence, to reassure himself. *I have admitted many things since coming into this room, but very few that Walsingham did not already know. I have learnt far more than he has.*

'Are you going to tell me about the book, Mr Harley? Or do you want to feel the iron bar against your other knee?'

'Even if I had the book, I could not help you. I did not realise it was more than a very poor chronicle. That is the honest truth. I have no idea how it might be—'

'I do not believe you.'

'It is true!' exploded Clarenceux suddenly. 'It is true, true, TRUE, I tell you! If that is a secret document, only Henry Machyn can tell you how to use it. I cannot help you.'

Walsingham poured himself another cup of wine and walked over to his sweetmeat tray. 'Still not good enough, Mr Harley. You see, I know that you are lying. Do you not understand?'

A slight draught caught the candles, and they guttered together. Tears were rolling down Clarenceux's face.

'Do you not know where Machyn was arrested?'

'Of course I don't.'

'In your stable loft.'

'What?' At first Clarenceux did not believe what he had just heard. Then he remembered Thomas telling him that there were signs of a fight in the stable. He himself had found the gate unlocked when he went out in the night.

Walsingham nodded. 'When you were taken home, after your little interlude with Sergeant Crackenthorpe, your friend Machyn was found on your premises.'

'No. No!'

'Left knee.'

'No!' As he turned to look at the man with the iron bar, he lost his balance on his one good leg and fell. He hit the floor hard, and found himself sobbing, terrified by the thought of his imminent torture and hanging. He felt sick. He tried to wipe the tears from his face. He backed into the table, attempting to shield himself from his attacker. But the man with the bar did not strike him.

Walsingham was leaving the room. There had been a knock on the door. He was talking to someone outside in a low voice.

Minutes passed. He remembered Machyn's tears. *That was only last night. After Machyn left my house, he must have hidden in the stable loft through the worst of the storm. Fool! Why did he not stay inside when I offered? Then I would not have left the house, never have been caught by Crackenthorpe . . .*

A different thought suddenly occurred to him. *How did Machyn know Crackenthorpe would kill him by the end of the day? How did he know that Crackenthorpe would find him there, in that stable loft? Was it just a guess? Or had he planned it? Was that last line in the chronicle written simply to stir me into action? Is this all an elaborate trap?*

Walsingham walked back into the room.

'You will be put in the cellar overnight. Tomorrow you will be taken over to the Tower.' Walsingham lifted his cup to his lips. 'No one outside those walls will hear you.'

Clarenceux was motionless, numb. 'Am I to have no trial?'

Walsingham frowned. 'Mr Harley, do you still not see? This *was* your trial. It is over.'

21

Awdrey tucked the blankets around her daughter in her cot and, looking at her sleeping face, whispered a prayer. She set the candle on the floor, and wiped her eyes. The handkerchief was already sodden. She put it down, and looked around the room again, trying to take in what she had lost.

They had been ruthless. They had destroyed her clothes chest, smashed it to pieces with an axe. They had even ripped up the clothes. Here was a linen sleeve from a chemise; there a bodice from a favourite blue dress she had had for years. Why did they need to do that? Machyn's book could not be hidden in the seams.

She picked up a linen shift. It had a huge tear across the breast. She wiped her eyes again. Lifting the candle, she could see that William's chest had had one side smashed in and the top wrenched off. The candlestick in the recess above the bed was broken. The mattress and pillows had been slashed. Feathers lay all over the floor, shifting in the air of the room. Even the rocker under the child's cot had been broken off. The front of the cupboard in the wall was nothing more than splintered wood. The brass basin she had proffered to William that morning lay upside down, dented by a boot.

William. What has happened to him?

She crossed herself, unsure whether to be angry at him for bringing this on them, or fearful lest he be injured or imprisoned.

William had said that he feared that Henry Machyn would be killed. But it had been Rebecca who had told her about the book. It had also been Rebecca who had taken it from the house in the minutes before Sergeant Crackenthorpe had returned. Why hadn't William given it to her? Why had he not told her where it was? Now everything they owned was destroyed. They had even slashed open Annie's mattress. She was sleeping on a makeshift mattress of blankets.

This is William's fault. If they indict him, he will have brought that fate on himself. In a moment of madness. He should have known better: he is experienced enough. No doubt they have destroyed all the books in his study too.

She crossed herself again. She would go in the morning down to her sister's house in Devon to get away from this horror, which she had once cherished as her home.

She looked at her sleeping daughter, and made the sign of the cross over her. Then she left the room quietly.

Holding the candle, she went down the stairs. When she glanced in the parlour, the glow of the candle revealed broken wood and plaster across the floor just inside the door. She turned away. She would leave first thing in the morning. Take nothing with her to remind her of this. Just the children.

But where was everyone? Where was Thomas? Emily? Nurse Brown? The boys? She had been told to go upstairs and stay there with her daughters after they had ransacked and destroyed her bedchamber. She had not seen what had happened down here.

In the silence she looked around the hall. The elm table was almost the only thing that had not been broken. The silver candlesticks too were intact. She bent down and picked one up, setting it on the table. To her left, William's prized round mirror was smashed, lying in pieces on the floor where a soldier had stamped on it. The carpet over the chest had had a knife driven through it.

As she moved along, bringing her small light to bear on each minute sadness, she felt that much more had been destroyed than her possessions. Her trust in the place had been destroyed too. Her husband's protection had been found wanting. And more than that: she was walking in dead, empty space. There was no one, no sound from anywhere in the house.

Could they have arrested them all?

She walked, almost in a daze, down the dark back stairs. The lake of liquid across the floorboards in the corridor told her that they had broken the barrels. The buttery door was open; inside the kegs were on their sides.

She carried her candle through to the kitchen. Apples and vegetables were everywhere, having been stamped underfoot, and kicked together with corn strewn from the sacks that used to be propped against the wall. Joints of meat that had been hanging in the rafters had been cut down and thrown on the fire. The remains of several legs of salted pork sizzled quietly in the ash and embers. There too lay several blackened meat bones and a trivet, upturned. A skillet nearby had been thrown on to the fire so its handle had burned away.

She felt the tears welling up in her eyes again. There was nothing for her here now. She lifted the candle for a final look and turned to go. At that moment she realised that an old brown blanket had been hanging almost directly above her. It was suspended from one of the kitchen roof beams. It was odd, she thought, for them to throw a blanket up into the beams. She raised the candle and looked up. The blanket was damp at one corner, and a few spots of glistening water were dripping from the damp edge. But that damp edge enclosed a dirty foot. She looked higher, into the shadows, and saw the torn shirt with the blood on it, and the jerkin covered in sawdust. Only then did she see the white face of Will Terry – and his lifeless eyes staring into the infinite void.

22

The door to the cellar slammed shut and Clarenceux was left in darkness. He heard the bolts being fastened. All he had managed to see of his accommodation for this, the last night of his life, were the stone steps leading down into the blackness. It was damp and very cold. It stank of urine and decomposing excrement. It must be a large cellar, he thought, and the shutes of the privies on the floors above must empty into barrels stored down here.

He reached for the wall. The smell made him feel sick. He already felt queasy from his interrogation and now he felt worse. The pain in his right knee had slightly abated, and he could walk. But it was still difficult to put weight on it.

He took a step down in the darkness, keeping his hand on the wall. A small stone or piece of plaster, dislodged, fell from the steps and splashed into the water that covered the cellar floor.

Clarenceux stopped. At this time of year, in this temperature, everything would be damp. His own house had no cellars but those of his neighbours were often flooded. His neighbours said the flooding was a benefit, for the urine that fell into the barrels rotted the wood so that the liquid seeped out and was dissolved in the water. But Clarenceux was sure the water did not go anywhere. It just sat there in winter: cold, stagnant and stinking.

Still touching the cold wall, he carefully eased himself down on to the step. His knee ached terribly. He heard shouts from upstairs, and a few men walking about. Then nothing.

A rat scampered through the water in the darkness.

He ran a hand over the velvet of his doublet. By now they would have found the book. And they had Henry Machyn. They would torture Machyn until he confessed everything. And when he did so – whatever it was that he confessed – he, Clarenceux, would be deemed guilty of all the same offences. He too would be tortured, and even though his confession would hardly tally with Machyn's, they would both be condemned. His name was everywhere in the book. He was Machyn's social superior, so Machyn would be considered just a foot soldier in whatever battle he was fighting. Clarenceux would be judged the leader.

He remembered Awdrey's face and her golden hair as she had lain in bed the previous night. And Annie, in her bright-eyed innocence, sitting on his knee a few days ago and talking to him about things she had seen in the city.

What were they doing to his house? He hoped they would be restrained. And Awdrey – was she too in prison somewhere? How were they treating her? And what about Goodwife Machyn? If they had arrested her husband they were bound to want to question her too. He imagined her being arrested, those sad, brown eyes shocked and fearful. O God, he prayed, please do not let any harm befall either of them.

He wiped his eyes on his sleeve, feeling the anger rise. It was Machyn's fault. That was the truth. What was it he had said about his recognising a sentence from the book of Job? What could he remember of Job? Should a wise man speak vain knowledge, and fill his belly with the wind from the east? Should he reason with words of no value? Or make pointless speeches? You cast off fear, and fail to pray before God, for you have confessed your sins with your own mouth, you choose the way of cunning. It is your own mouth that condemns you, and not mine. It is your own lips that testify against you.

Machyn was probably testifying at this moment. Are the conso-

lations of the Lord small for you? Is there any secret in you?

Is there any secret? Clarenceux clenched his fist and pressed it against the stone wall. Machyn had overestimated him. The man had had too high a regard for his learning and his influence. And he himself should have known better. A lesser man had taken advantage of him, and he in his vanity had succumbed.

Walsingham had been right in one respect. He had been complacent. He had been naive. And now he was going to die.

'I AM INNOCENT!' he yelled, the sudden words like colour across the darkness. 'I AM AN INNOCENT MAN!'

What would it feel like, the rope around his neck? But no, he did not need to fear that. He was going to be tortured to death. Would he fear death if he felt only pain?

What would they use to bring it about? He shivered in the cold. He had heard about a contraption they used in France. They called it the rack. He had read about it in his copy of Sir John Fortescue's *De Laudibus Legum Angliae* Fortescue had been so horrified by the very idea of the rack that he had not described the instrument in his book. Instead he had described the anguish, worse than death, experienced by guiltless knights who were tortured until they confessed to treasons so they might be killed quickly rather than be subjected to further torment.

There was nothing he could do now but wait and pray.

Where was God in this? Could this, in any possible way, be His will? That a man should be tortured to death for a crime of which he was completely ignorant?

This cellar had been deserted by God. He was already entering the kingdom of the dead.

23

In the darkness of the stable, lying in the dung on the floor, Thomas managed to slip his right hand out of the rope knot. He had been struggling for hours to free himself. His shoulder ached; his skin was chafed and painful with the rope burns. Will had been just eleven years old. He had told them all he knew. And then they had killed him anyway.

He had died screaming for his mother.

The men had demanded to know where the book was and no one could tell them anything. The other servant boy in Clarenceux's household, John Wrightson, had shouted out, weeping, that it was no longer in the house, so they beat him, making him watch as they hanged Will. And despite Thomas's shouts and pleadings, they had hoisted the boy higher and higher, as his legs kicked frantically and he tried to breathe.

He had died slowly. The moment he went limp, Thomas felt his heart break. Until that instant he had not believed they would kill him. He thought about his nephew, Will's father, and the day Thomas had proudly told him he had found his son a position in Clarenceux's household. How happy they had been. They had gone to drink wine at a tavern.

Thomas gasped, tears rolling down his face as he released his left hand from the rope. *Wherever my master is, if he still be alive, please let him return. And may he take revenge on these killers.*

24

Sunday, 12 December

Clarenceux was on his knees in the darkness, where he had been for hours, praying even after he had lost all feeling in his body.

Anxiety was simply a cloud he had flown through. A golden chariot, pulled by six white swans, was taking him up into a blue sky and showing him the world laid out beneath him. He could see the thousands of churches across Europe, all tiny, far below, as if he were an angel choosing which one he would visit. There were many more Catholic ones than Protestant, he realised. The sickness of faith lay here in England.

No, the woman who was holding the swans' reins seemed to say, pointing to his own parish church, St Bride's, and all the people coming out of its doors. *It is not a matter of which faith. All faith is righteous. It is unbelief that is the sin, warring against faith. This is the pattern of death: you will be lifted up into heaven; we will sing in the heavens. And those who choose not to be lifted – who choose to oppose God – will remain on earth, nothing but rotting food for worms.*

They began to descend. Peering between the clouds he could see the River Thames, with its hundreds of boats moored on the sparkling water. The gatehouse on the bridge was opening for the day. The bells were ringing. And among the people leaving their houses early in the morning air was Goodwife Machyn, striding purposefully along the street to the market, which was just beginning to gather in Cheapside. Outside his own house a cart was passing. His family were all still indoors. They were happy there, even though they were without him. God's blessing had come upon them all. They knew he had passed, or was passing, into heaven.

At that moment, as he turned to the beautiful driver of the swan chariot, he could not look at her. He did not dare. She was the Holy Ghost. She had been sent to guide him.

A shout somewhere in the house above jerked him out of his reverie. He felt the cold again, and was in more pain than before.

Men were running upstairs. Perhaps it was the servants at daybreak? But if it was daybreak, then he had only a few hours to live. The creature inside him shrivelled up, his fingers frozen, curled. He buried his face in his arms, and placed one wrist across the other, making the sign of the cross with his arms.

Even though he could see nothing, he could feel the sign there, made with his own body. He raised his arms, keeping them hard against each other. This was the emblem of the faith. *His* faith. It was a dark sun that shone even in the deepest night.

The rebirth of the light. Despite his pain, he felt reborn. As sure as life was life itself, he knew that he, not Walsingham, was in the right. And nothing could ever make it any other way.

25

The sound of a bolt being shot broke the silence on this, the day of his execution.

'You. Harley,' the man called. He came down the steps and nudged him firmly with the side of his foot. 'Get up,' he commanded. He pulled the collar of Clarenceux's doublet, attempting to drag him to his feet.

Clarenceux forced his legs to straighten. He was still kneeling on the stone step, both legs numb.

'Get up, God damn you!'

The man was almost strangling him. Clarenceux reached out and gripped the man's arm.

'Leave off me,' the stranger commanded.

'Give me an arm, then, for pity's sake,' croaked Clarenceux. His voice surprised him. Parched with lack of drink, sleep and food, it sounded somehow different. Transformed. Capable of understanding power: absolute and immense power.

The guard said nothing, but gave him his hand and helped him to his feet.

Clarenceux stumbled up the cellar stairs, staring into the light, placing one hand on each step. He could not help but stare: he simply felt drawn to the light, leaving the cellar, leaving the darkness of the cold night.

Suddenly he felt the pain of a fist against his jaw. The blow sent him sprawling down the passageway. He heard

Crackenthorpe's voice. 'Mr Walsingham is going to give you one chance to redeem yourself. If you fail, you will be put to death.'

Clarenceux's head was swimming. He felt sick. He stayed where he was on the floor, with the dust on the floorboards before his eyes, his head pounding with pain. *What chance is this?* He heard footsteps elsewhere in the house – men running down stairs. *Are they coming for me too?* He could see the legs of just two men: Crackenthorpe and the man sent into the foul cellar to fetch him.

'The bells have just rung seven of the clock. You have until this evening, at eight of the clock, to produce Henry Machyn's chronicle. If you do not, you know what will happen.'

Clarenceux lifted his head and stared at the uneven white-wash on the stone wall. So he was not going to be killed straight away . . . His mind moved slowly through the realisation. They were letting him go home so he could fetch the book and give it to them. That meant they did not find it themselves.

The thought of what it might mean made Clarenceux's head spin more, and he retched. He tasted bitter bile in his mouth. Crackenthorpe took a quick step and kicked him in the stomach.

'Do not spew on Mr Walsingham's floor.'

Clarenceux turned to face him. 'You do not need to do this. No master would require it of a servant.'

Crackenthorpe tensed at the word, but said nothing. He looked away, impatient for Clarenceux to get to his feet. Clarenceux reached out and put one hand on the wall, and pushed himself up off the floor with the other.

'Eight of the clock?'

Crackenthorpe nodded. 'You heard me.' He gestured to his accomplice to move Clarenceux outside, and he followed as the soldier put Clarenceux's arm over his shoulder and manhandled him along the corridor. They turned a corner and Clarenceux could see the freedom of the door.

Never in his life before had sunshine looked so good. It seemed heavenly.

26

It was over a mile back to his own house in St Bride's from Walsingham's, near the Tower. It was a slow journey. The pain in his knee forced him to stop regularly, and his arms and head ached. Along Lombard Street he felt weak, and had to sit down on a step. A member of the Skinners Company caught his eye – a man he knew by sight but not by name. Nevertheless, the other man's awareness that they belonged to the same livery company was enough; he offered to have Clarenceux carried back in a chair to his house. Clarenceux declined: he wanted to keep his thoughts to himself, and to keep thinking them through. So he borrowed a shilling from the man for an eel pie and thanked him for his kindness.

The pie tasted wonderful. Normally he would have said an eel pie from a street vendor was not worth giving to a pig, but at that moment he felt touched by grace. He was free, and the taste of over-salted eels was blissful in his mouth. A few minutes later, when he reached the conduit in Cornhill, he drank water – the most blessed water his lips had ever touched.

A miracle had taken place. That was the only way it could be described. As he leant over the conduit trough and rinsed his face, he reflected on his extraordinary turn of luck. He had prayed and prayed; he had prepared himself to be tortured and killed; and God had saved him. Divine providence must have stayed the hands of the men searching his house, and protected the kitchen boy who had not revealed the whereabouts of the chronicle, so that it remained a secret. Was the miracle his decision to put the book in the sack of oats, or the turning of the eyes of the men searching his house? It did not matter. It was beautiful, however it had taken place. It brought tears to his eyes.

Although Clarenceux was standing before the conduit, in the middle of a wide street, surrounded by the chatter of people coming to and going from the market, he lifted his hands to heaven. He closed his eyes and gave thanks. After savouring the moment he opened his eyes and walked on. With the sun shining, he felt he was recovering, with God's help.

Crossing the Fleet Bridge he glanced at the weight of water rushing through, swirling as it made its way into the Thames. That gave him an idea: he too would travel south. He would take Awdrey and the children down into Kent, to the house of his good friend Julius Fawcett, who had a small estate near Chislehurst. Julius would shelter them, at least until all this misunderstanding could be cleared away. There too he could give thanks for his safe delivery from Walsingham and Crackenthorpe.

He walked on to his house.

The front door was slightly open. Clarenceux pushed it and saw the rushes from the hall strewn on the stairs and a broken bench in the passage leading to the service rooms on the ground floor. The bottom of a painted earthenware jug lay on its side on the stone flagstones inside the front door, a few fragments on the stairs where it had been cast down. Otherwise there was silence.

Clarenceux climbed the stairs one by one, feeling the pain in his knee as he lifted his right leg but anxious to see the state of his hall. Clearly Walsingham's men had been ruthless in their search. So how was it they had not found the chronicle?

At the top of the stairs he noted the cresset lamp was untouched, its wick and oil still in place. But as he lifted his eyes to the room, the destruction shocked him. He could see the pieces of his mirror on the floor, the candles where the soldiers had stamped on them, even the smashed plasterwork above the fireplace. The paintings were broken: the wooden panels had been knocked out of their frames and splintered. Someone had placed an unbroken candlestick on the elm table, as if to try to reclaim something civilised from the wreckage. But apart from that, everything was in disarray.

'Awdrey,' he called. 'Awdrey!'

His voice echoed in the cold house. He glanced at the fireplace; only the slightest wisp of smoke rose from the hearth. They had smashed the plasterwork but they had not gone so far as to burn the house, or to scatter the burning embers. They could easily have done so, and set light to the rushes and the whole street. This destruction had not been without care; it had been controlled.

Clarenceux stepped slowly down the back stairs towards the wine puddle across the flagstones outside the buttery. He stopped. He could hear something.

'Is there anyone here?' he called, hearing the fear in his voice.

There was no reply. Only a distant choking sound from someone in one of the rooms ahead.

Clarenceux bit his teeth hard against each other. Overcoming the pain in his knee, he continued down the stairs and approached the buttery. He came to the door and looked in. As his eyes grew accustomed to the darkness within he began to recognise smashed kegs and barrels.

This had not been a search; this had been an exercise in intimidation.

He heard the choking noise again. He turned away from the buttery and came to the door that led to the kitchen. Thomas was sitting with his back against the wall, the body of his fair-haired great-nephew in his lap. His face was soaked with tears, his shirt pulled out of his breeches, his jerkin torn and his doublet ripped down one sleeve. There was blood on his face and on one arm, and he was sobbing.

At first Clarenceux just saw Thomas, rocking and crying over the boy. It took some moments for him to understand that the lad was dead.

A sickening feeling rose through his body – far worse than Crackenthorpe's kick to his belly, for it rose from within himself. He was responsible for this. He had entrusted Will Terry with a secret too great for his safety. He steadied himself with a hand on the frame of the door.

'They killed him,' said Thomas, staring at his great-nephew's face. 'They hanged him, in this kitchen. There was nothing any of us could do. They would not listen.'

Clarenceux felt as if all the blood pulsing in his body had turned to regret. He looked around for the barrel of oats and saw it lying on its side, its contents spread on the floor. Clearly the book had gone.

'Mr Clarenceux, I feel . . .' Thomas looked up at him, struggling for the words. 'I . . . I must – *must* have revenge. If I do not . . . I will be a broken man. Will was like my own son. He was a good lad. He served you well. And they killed him. Why could they not have chosen me?'

'Thomas, we are not broken men. We will take revenge. I swear it. Tell me what happened.'

Thomas shook his head, trying to control himself. 'It was chaos, after you were arrested. Goodwife Machyn came down from your room and said you must have hidden the chronicle in the service rooms, as you had come from that way. She insisted that she remove the book from the house. Your wife was in agreement. Will . . .' He broke off, clutching the dead boy in his lap.

'Go on.'

Thomas sighed again, and ran his hand over the boy's cheek. 'Will was terrified of Goodwife Machyn: she was shouting and her hair was flowing all over her face, like a wanton woman. But when Mistress Harley told him to obey, he showed Goodwife Machyn where the book was. She took it and fled, not saying where she was going. And then, hardly ten minutes later, the soldiers came. They were led by that man with the scar.'

'Crackenthorpe.'

'Him. He and his men rounded up everyone in the house. They held us in the hall while they searched the upper chambers. They left us just one candle. Mistress Harley was with us, and the children were crying. Emily was crying too. Nurse Brown was doing her best to comfort the girls. Will and John were terrified. I stood with a hand on each of their shoulders. Then the soldiers came down, angry because they had found nothing. Their captain – Crackenthorpe – told Mistress Harley to take your daughters upstairs, and she tried to object but he threatened to force her, and she complied. We heard her shriek when she went upstairs; I don't know why. Some of the soldiers laughed, and one tried to lift up Nurse Brown's skirts. Crackenthorpe then asked how old Emily was, and on being told she was not yet eleven, ordered that no one was to touch her; but the one who found the chronicle would be the first to lie with Nurse Brown.'

'So they resorted to hanging a young boy,' said Clarenceux. He felt the anger rising within him.

'When they had looked everywhere and destroyed everything, they led us down here, into the kitchen. But not the mistress and your daughters: they stayed upstairs. The captain slung a rope over the beam and told us what he was going to do. He said he was going to hang one of us unless we told him where the chronicle was hidden. At this John, who was fearing they might hang him, yelled out that it was not in the house any more. The scarred man did not believe him: he thought he was trying to fool them. So he pointed to Will and told John he was going to hang him ...'

Thomas's voice gave way to a howl. Clarenceux felt pity burning in his breast. Thomas had no children of his own and had taken charge of his great-nephew. No more would there be a bright-eyed lad in his life.

'The boy died screaming, struggling and terrified. For mercy's sake, Mr Clarenceux. He was shouting for his mother, and imploring me to save him. And one of the bastards held a knife at my throat all the time; I could do nothing.'

'I feel for you, Thomas. But where are the others? Where are my daughters now?'

Thomas wiped his face. 'Mistress Harley has taken them to her sister's house, in Devon.' He paused, looking up at Clarenceux, for a moment regaining his servant's intuition. 'They were not harmed. I think Mr Walsingham must have given very precise orders concerning the women.'

Clarenceux nodded. Walsingham had probably ordered that his wife and daughters not be harmed because of their connection with Lady Cecil. Even so, he knew they must have been terrified. He shut his eyes and said a prayer for them. When he opened them again, his eyes were wet with tears. Stepping forward, he knelt down, put a palm on the cold brow of the dead boy, and silently said a prayer for him too. When he had finished, he crossed himself and said, 'We must go and tell his father.'

Thomas reached out and gripped Clarenceux's wrist firmly. 'Mr Clarenceux, we must have our revenge.'

'We will, Thomas. I will do what it takes, whatever it takes.'

Thomas looked into Clarenceux's wet eyes. 'You are a good man, Mr Clarenceux. I will tell Will's father you are a good man.'

'I try to be. But I have failed.'

Thomas held his gaze. 'No, Mr Clarenceux. You are a good man. And I must tell you, there is a message for you. You must find out where Sir Arthur was on June the thirteenth, 1550. Before the soldiers left, they took me into the stables. They tied me up in there. They said they were going to burn me and the horses alive – they seemed to think I knew where the chronicle had gone, even though I said I did not. But they didn't burn anything. After some hours I worked my bonds loose and escaped. And when I came out of the stable there was a woman in the yard. She asked me to give you a message. "Tell him Sir Lancelot will meet him where Sir Arthur was on June the thirteenth, 1550." That was all.'

Clarenceux stared at Thomas, struggling to take in this news. The death of the boy, the chaos of his home and now these threats of burning had shocked him so much that he did not realise straightaway that the woman in the yard must have been the wife of Sir Lancelot. Then, slowly, the various names fell into place. He pictured her. He remembered that the first entry of the chronicle had mentioned a meeting on or about that date, between Machyn and one John Heath – perhaps some kin of Lancelot Heath. But still his mind was unclear. Where had they met? He could not recall.

'Thomas, are you sure you have no clue as to where Goodwife Machyn has gone?'

Thomas shook his head.

Clarenceux tried to get up. It was difficult, as his knee could not take the weight and he had to steady himself against the wall. 'I'll do what I can. But I cannot promise things that are not in my power to deliver.' As he said the words, he looked down at the face of his old servant. Leaning over, he put a sympathetic hand on the man's shoulder. Thomas looked up.

'You do not know what lies in your power and what does not, Mr Clarenceux. You do not know how much grace God will give you, what trust He will place in you. If you are a man of God, what you promise will happen. I know it.'

Clarenceux took a deep breath and placed his hands over his face momentarily. Then he looked down at the boy's broken body. 'I have done nothing wrong, I have committed no treason, and yet I have had my servant killed, my house wrecked and my family cast out. Believe me, Thomas: I will make them pay for this. Even if I have to commit a crime to end this tyranny, I will commit it again and again. I am not going to let Will's death go unpunished. In my mind I have cut out their tongues and put out their eyes. I will let the Devil have their souls and dogs eat their hearts. They have made an enemy of me. I no longer want to be innocent.'

27

ebecca knelt on the floor of the small chamber, resting her forehead on the frame of the bed. She was quietly humming a tune to herself – not a tune that she had heard anywhere in recent years but notes that seemed to go together in a comforting way: a sort of rhythmic lullaby. At the same time she ran the beads of a rosary through her fingers. The notes of her tune were her prayer.

She heard shouts from the house across the road. A man was hammering against the wood of a door. Men had been coming and going there since last night. They had given up all pretence of it being a plague-infected house; the boards had been removed and the door left open, guarded by one or two soldiers.

She did not stir. It hardly felt like her house now. It was a place in the past, where once she had lived. It had become a place for soldiers, not her. Nor Henry. *Mary, mother of God, save him from the men who are searching for him, protect him from them – and from all adversity, suffering, fear and pain.*

She stopped, and crossed herself. She had been fortunate, getting back here to Mistress Barker's house. She had been almost the last person allowed back into the city by the watchmen on the gate. She had been lucky that they had not recognised her in the fading light. She had been even luckier to have found the chronicle in Clarenceux's house. Most of all she had been lucky that Mistress Barker had welcomed her back into the house. She could have kept the door shut, for fear of being caught; but she had not. She was a kind and loyal friend.

The chronicle lay on the bed. It had been important to get it out of Clarenceux's house. She had understood that only she could save him and his family. Mistress Harley wanted to do everything *her* way, but she would not have had the wit to find the chronicle; she was too much taken up with fearing for her daughters. As for old Thomas, he would have waited for orders.

It had been the right thing to do, bringing it here.

28

Henry Machyn did not know where he was. The dimly lit brick cellar could have been anywhere. He could hear a slow drip into a puddle – a drop falling every eight or nine seconds. It seemed the water clung to the brick for as long as it could before falling. That was like his soul now: clinging on for as long as it could, just waiting for the final release.

He remembered his grandfather's death. He and his brothers had been very young at the time, playing on the riverbank upstream from the mill. Their father had arrived unexpectedly and told them all to come quickly. The old man was dying, he said. It seemed that the next moment they were all standing formally at the foot of their grandfather's bed as he gave them his blessing. Henry had thought to himself, *How does he know he is dying?* They had said their goodbyes in all politeness, and kissed him; and they had gone back out to play by the river. An hour later their mother appeared to tell them the old man had gone to heaven.

Heaven. All his life he had hoped to see heaven. All his life he had feared that he would be cursed for his sins and not allowed by St Peter to pass those gates. But in these last hours he had seen how cruel men could be. Nothing he had ever done in his life compared with this torture. God would see in his heart that he had never meant to hurt another man – and yet these vile animals were capable of enjoying a man's scream as they cut strips off his flesh and poured salt into his wounds, or took pliers and pulled off his fingernails. Or tied him on to a gridiron and placed it over a fire. Through all these things, one thought alone had comforted him: that he had betrayed no one. As long as he said nothing, his path to heaven was assured, even though that path led through a valley of fire and darkness.

When he was arrested by Crackenthorpe, he had believed Clarenceux had betrayed him; but as soon as they started questioning him, and slicing the skin off his back, he knew that he had been wrong. Clarenceux was not to blame. They wanted to know where his chronicle was and they would not have asked that if Clarenceux had told them. They wanted to know where Rebecca was; she too must have stayed in hiding. Now all that remained to be done was to let them break this frail mortal body and release his soul.

He heard footsteps outside the door. And took a deep breath. Still the anxiety was there, even after all this pain. But this time the soldier would suspend him from a rope and break his legs. That was what he had been told. Like his grandfather, he knew his time had come. True, there would be no one standing at the foot of his bed. His brothers were long since dead, his son abroad, his wife in hiding. But he was about to die. And it was good. God would see it happen – and see that it was an honest departure from the world. In its own small way, his passing would be triumphant.

The door opened. The warder entered with a coil of rope. Henry Machyn crossed himself. 'Go with God, my Knights of the Round Table, and King Clariance,' he whispered. 'My son, John, my wife, dear Rebecca, go with God. Harry Machyn, be bold.' Then, with a trembling voice, and tears in his eyes, he began to sing.

29

Amid the scattered pages and split wood, Clarenceux lifted the broken spine of a leather-bound volume and looked at its desecrated contents. He put it down. So many folios had simply been pulled from his books . . .

The portrait of his father was missing. He searched the debris and found a corner of the frame under a torn piece of printed text. Pulling at it, he realised the painting had gone. A flash of red on the floor nearby caught his eye, however, and he moved a volume that was covering it. His father's scarlet robe, right eye and the right-hand side of his face looked back at him. The cut in the top of the wood showed that they had forced the painting out of its frame and split it in two.

Clarenceux turned to the window. Practically the only thing in this place they had not broken was the glass.

He thought about Awdrey. She had clearly had no hesitation in leaving London. He was not surprised: she was not running away, she was simply protecting their daughters. She must have taken money from the house, and presumably she had Nurse Brown to help her; but nevertheless it was a brave step for a woman to set out to travel a long distance without male company. The highway inns were never comfortable. Women travelling alone were vulnerable. Local constables did not want to deal with the pleas of strangers, especially when they were directed against men they knew. If a crime took place, constables often empanelled a jury of the accused man's friends, who would acquit him as being of good character. Landlords tended to charge women higher rates, too, to make up for the fact that a woman could not be expected to share a bed with other travellers.

That was the first thing he needed to do: to make sure Awdrey was safe and well. For a moment he thought of going after her himself. *But it is impossible; I cannot search for the chronicle and Lancelot Heath while travelling, down to Devon. I will have to send Thomas, as soon as he has attended to his family duties. Riding hard, he will be able to catch up with her in two days. A neighbour's boy can look after the other horses while he and I are away. I presume the other servants will not return until they know this house is safe.*

Clarenceux saw one of his own manuscripts on the floor, its leaves partly torn out of their binding. He lifted it and set it carefully on what remained of the table board.

But what about money? From the looks of things, Crackenthorpe's men have taken all there is. I cannot even sell anything, for everything I possess is broken.

He went to a small overturned wooden box in the corner of the room. There was no sign of the coins that it formerly contained. A few minutes searching revealed a single gold half-sovereign that had escaped the attention of Crackenthorpe's men, concealed by a loose vellum deed. *That will suffice for Thomas's expenses while he rides after Awdrey. I myself will have to rely on friends ...*

But what friends will support me?

Clarenceux caught a glimpse of the rawness of his position. He would not return to Walsingham with the chronicle: he could not, even if he wanted to. But he would not return empty-handed either. He would have to go about the city in hiding from now on. Crackenthorpe would have to find him.

He stood and breathed heavily, concentrating, trying to form a plan. *I need to find the chronicle: that has to be the first thing. Goodwife Machyn will have hidden in a place where she knows*

I will find her. She will want me to find her, to protect both her and her husband. She has no other protector . . . except Mistress Barker.

He remembered her face, and imagined her running through his house with the book under her arm. She was an intelligent and strong woman, despite her air of sadness.

I will find her and, when I have the chronicle, I will go down to Chislehurst. It will be safest to leave the city. Julius will provide me with food and some money. Then I can return to the city and seek revenge for the killing of Will Terry and the disappearance of Henry Machyn, as well as the destruction of my home.

He looked at the door and saw the splintered edge of the wood, its cold reality, and felt that this was not his house any longer. He no longer had any possessions or any place of comfort. From now on, nothing could be taken for granted.

30

Walsingham walked briskly along the corridor to his parlour. He was angry. The journey back from Westminster had irritated him – and he had already been annoyed with Cecil. Now there was Crackenthorpe's latest failure. Further explanations would be necessary.

He flung open the door and sat down at his writing table near the window. After a few seconds he got up again, walked over to his plate of sweetmeats, took one and then put the plate back down. The sweet tasted bad; he took it out of his mouth and flung it into the fireplace. It hissed in the burning logs.

He turned to the mirror and began to stare at himself, to interrogate himself, as he often did. He looked at each garment he was wearing: black doublet, black jerkin, small ruff with a high collar, black skullcap. Then he looked into his own eyes. He concentrated hard to see what lay behind them, inside the skull.

Walsingham frowned. He *was* the queen's purpose. And Cecil's too. That was his life. *He* was the method. His whole being – from his intuition to his imagination – was the tool that kept Cecil safe. He had drive, cunning and intelligence. The great entity that was the divine queen, Elizabeth of England, was not just a woman: it was him, and Cecil, and thousands of other men who made Elizabeth great and all-seeing, all-powerful and favoured by God. Just because Crackenthorpe could not find the chronicle did not mean that Clarenceux was not hiding it somewhere.

He, Walsingham, would find it. He would show Clarenceux that he was the controller of his fate.

He stared deeper. *But what if I am wrong? What if it was a coincidence that Machyn was found in Clarenceux's stable? No, it cannot have been a coincidence. Clarenceux was at Machyn's house – both in the night and the next morning. And between those two events Machyn was found.*

Then where is that damned chronicle?

'Mr Walsingham,' came a voice from the door, 'Sergeant Crackenthorpe has returned. He wishes to see you.'

'About time. Tell him to come in.'

Before Crackenthorpe even entered the room – even before he saw the short figure of Walsingham standing there by the mirror – he heard the stark accusation in the small man's cold, quiet voice.

'You failed me.'

'Mr Walsingham, I am—'

'Stay silent! I will not be interrupted. To say I am angry does not begin to state the case. Machyn's book was in Clarenceux's house and you let it slip away. You are like a cannon too large and powerful to be of any use, too heavy to move or direct against a target, too cumbersome, too stupid. How many mistakes have you made? First you killed that Scotsman – and, before you say anything, I know he was about to kill Draper; but he would have been much more valuable if you had kept him alive, if you had struck his hand with your sword, not his neck. Then you pretended that Machyn's house was suddenly somehow infected with plague, in December – after a whole summer of the fearful visitation – bringing all London to look at it. Now you have failed to find the chronicle.'

'But in my judgement . . .'

'No! You will not answer, you will listen. I had to order you to release Clarenceux because you failed to find that book. How am I to locate it without him? Heavens! My enemies are more useful to me than you are! Traitors are more compliant, more obedient. In fact, your incompetence is so great that I am sorely tempted to charge you with treason.'

Crackenthorpe listened and said nothing. All of this was unfair. Nevertheless, he would get his revenge before the end of the conversation. He would let Walsingham speak himself out and then he would make him eat his words. He had the means to do it tucked inside his doublet.

Walsingham continued. 'Machyn was at Clarenceux's house the night before last. If he did not give him the chronicle at that time, then he did so on some earlier occasion – it was not in Machyn's house when you started searching and yet Clarenceux has admitted he has seen it. So, at some point between Machyn's arrival and the search of Clarenceux's house, the chronicle was moved. Where to? Were any of the servants missing when you went back to Clarenceux's house, after escorting him here?'

'No. There were two boy servants, a maid, the old man and—'

'If one of them had taken the chronicle elsewhere, they had returned to the house. I take it you interrogated them all?'

Crackenthorpe glared at him. 'Machyn's wife took the chronicle. My men are still searching for her.'

'Machyn's wife? So where are Clarenceux's family and servants now? I presume you are keeping a watch on the house.'

'They do not have the chronicle. As I said, Rebecca Machyn took it. I turned over everything in that house that could have contained it.'

'But they know where it is, Sergeant Crackenthorpe. Or they know where she is. One of them must. What did you do to find out what they knew?'

'God damn you, Francis Walsingham, I hanged one of them!'

There was a long pause. 'You what?'

Crackenthorpe looked around the room, as if seeking some refuge. Seconds passed. He turned to face his accuser. 'I hanged one of the boys. I was as sure as you are that they knew where the chronicle was. So when one of the boys said that Machyn's wife had taken it, I decided to force him to speak. I strung up the other boy from a rafter in the kitchen. They all shouted, screamed and raved, and yet no one said a thing about the chronicle, even when the boy was at the point of death. If any of them had known, they would have talked.'

Walsingham stared at him.

Crackenthorpe continued. 'It is clear that Machyn's wife must have been in the house between the time I arrested Clarenceux and my return to search the building. She was the one who removed it. The old man told me when the boy was nearing death.'

'Did you have to hang him? It is very difficult to pass a hanging off as accidental. Or self-defence – especially a boy.'

Crackenthorpe shrugged. 'You should not complain. This way you win twice over. *You* have the information and *they* will not forget that I am prepared to kill in pursuit of the truth.'

'You fool! There were witnesses. You could be arraigned before the justices. And then I will have to step in and save you again. Only this time I think I am not going to bother. It will save me a lot of trouble just to let you go to the Devil.'

Walsingham took a deep breath and walked across the room to the window overlooking the Tower. He stared at the grim walls. They were like a mirror to his mind. His eyes saw the crenellated stone but his thoughts saw his soul.

Crackenthorpe enjoyed the silence. This was the moment he had been waiting for. He had weathered the storm and now he could advance. 'As I said, I do not know where Machyn's wife is. The servants did not know. But they knew it was she who took the book. I tried to get the old man to tell me where she was but when the boy died the old man became more difficult. I hit him and bloodied his face, and threatened to burn him alive in the stables – he still said nothing. But if she is hiding with someone, I know where to start looking.'

'You do?' Walsingham was suddenly interested.

Crackenthorpe reached inside his doublet and pulled out a

folded piece of paper. He unfolded it, stepped forward and placed it on the table. Walsingham picked it up and took it nearer to the window. One glance over the badly formed letters told him exactly what it was: Machyn's will, written in his own untrained hand on the eighth of November, just one month ago.

It was much more than just a will, however. It was evidence, beautiful evidence. It mentioned several bequests to his wife Rebecca and his son John. Then it read:

I do give and bequeath unto Master Clarenshux all my skochyns and my Cronacle and the rest of all my goodes Cattelles Debtes plate jewelles Readie money after my Debtes paid my funeralles Discharged and Donne.

Walsingham looked at Crackenthorpe. 'He left Clarenceux his chronicle. That comes as no surprise. But his escutcheons? His plate and jewels? And all goods and chattels? It is most strange that he did not leave his silverware and jewels to his wife or his son. Instead he left them to a herald – a man not only wealthier than him but of a wholly superior class.'

Crackenthorpe felt a deep satisfaction. 'Read the rest.'

Walsingham looked back at the paper. A few lines later, after a bequest to his wife, Machyn had written: *I make ordaine and name Lancelott heth Citizen and paynter stayner myne oversear.*

'Lancelot Heath,' muttered Walsingham. He continued. The last passage read:

In witnes hereof I the said Henrie Machyn to this my present Testament and Last will have sett my hande and seale dated the Daie and yere firste aboue written Witnesses to this will both at the ensealing and Delyvering of ye same.

Walsingham almost hesitated to read the names, such was his sudden pleasure at this discovery. Crackenthorpe watched him:

this was clearly what Walsingham liked best – the thrill of the chase, a new clue.

Walsingham cleared his throat. 'Here are the names of the witnesses: Lancelot Heath, William Draper merchant taylor, Nicholas Hill ironmonger, Michael Hill merchant taylor, and Daniel Gyttens.' Walsingham nodded towards Crackenthorpe. He paused, considering the man who had given him the document. 'You have done well. I still maintain you should not have let the chronicle slip through your fingers. You certainly should not have killed a boy. But this goes a long way to making up for your miscalculations.'

'I think those are the names of the Knights of the Round Table.'

'Yes, I would not be surprised. Including Clarenceux and Machyn himself, that amounts to seven men. Rather more than William Draper was prepared to let on. He mentioned only four: himself, Machyn, James Emery and Lancelot Heath.' Walsingham set the will down on the table. 'I thought he had told us all he knew. But there was more.'

'In my experience, Mr Walsingham, there always is.'

Walsingham looked at Crackenthorpe. 'I believe that is the nearest thing to a profound statement you have ever made.' He went over and lifted the tray of sweetmeats and carried it to Crackenthorpe. 'Here, take them all. A small reward. Later you and I are going to visit Mr Draper and have words with him. You will speak to his mortal body. And I will speak to his immortal soul.'

31

Clarenceux rested against the bridge over the Fleet and looked towards the city wall and the gatehouse. It was a cloudy day, and he wished for his furred robe. And he felt cold in another way, like water splashing on a newly made steel blade.

Someone will pay for Will's murder.

He looked down at the swirling water and reflected that he owed Goodwife Machyn his life. *If she had not removed the chronicle when she did, I would never have seen the light of day. Walsingham would have had me beaten to a pulp, and then hanged – or worse.*

He looked at the grey skies, glad to be alive, and started to walk alongside the city wall. A breeze ruffled his hair as he passed beneath the arch of Ludgate. He was not sure how he would identify Mistress Barker's house but it had to be within sight of Henry Machyn's. He could ask people in the street for directions. *That might be dangerous. If Walsingham discovers that I have been asking for Mistress Barker, she too will be in danger.*

He pressed on. Every time he felt the pain he commanded himself to overcome it. He cut through St Paul's Churchyard and made directly for Maidenhead Lane, thinking all the while about what he would do to Crackenthorpe if he could get hold of him.

In Maidenhead Lane he stopped and pulled himself to his senses. He knew he was losing himself in bitter feelings of revenge. And all for what? His purpose was to find Goodwife Machyn.

If he did so he could find out where Sir Lancelot was and call together the Knights of the Round Table. Then he would discover what all this chaos was about.

When he came to the corner of the street where Machyn lived, he paused. The house was no longer boarded up. No one appeared to be guarding it. He was anxious to go ahead and knock on some doors, looking for Mistress Barker; but at the same time he was worried that he might have been followed. Although he had checked several times and could see no one obviously following him, he was not certain he was not being watched by Walsingham's spies. After all, Walsingham had taken a big risk in letting him go. He was trusting him to return with the book. But surely he must suspect he was not going to return? Walsingham would not be so foolish as to let him out of the sight of his spies.

The sky was heavy with grey clouds; it was about to rain. A maid reached out of an upstairs window and closed the shutter with a bang. There was a dog barking in a back yard. Two servant women were chatting as they swept the street outside their adjacent houses. A linen-coifed woman with a basket on her arm and a concentrated frown on her face was approaching at a fast pace. When he saw that the basket contained many fish, Clarenceux made a quick assessment. The fish suggested she was catering for a substantial household. Her fast pace told him she was a dutiful servant. It seemed a risk worth taking.

'Godspeed, my good woman. Can you tell me which house hereabouts is that of Mistress Barker?'

'Can't say I've heard of her,' she replied, hardly slowing her step. 'I'm not from this parish. Good day, sir.'

Clarenceux looked about but could see no one else whom he felt comfortable asking. The servants sweeping the street would be too easily questioned by Walsingham's men. He turned back to Machyn's house. He walked past to the next residence. The front door had a solid bronze handle for pulling the door to. He pushed it. Locked. He reached for his knife and found it missing. Cursing, he lifted his arm and hammered on the door with his elbow. Although he waited, and repeated the knocking, no answer came.

Nervous, he looked back up the street. He could not see any sign of anyone watching him. He turned round, about to cross to the neighbour on the other side of Machyn's house – a taller, more handsome building with a carved cherub's head on its corner post. But at that moment he heard the click of a key turning in the lock in the door.

A soldier stepped out from Machyn's house: very tall – taller even than Clarenceux – with lank brown hair and slow, heavy-lidded eyes. Clarenceux recognised him as one of the men who had come with Crackenthorpe to arrest him the previous evening.

Clarenceux froze, aware that he was unarmed and in a weakened state. The soldier was surprised to see a tall man, whose face he could not immediately place, standing right in front of him, staring at him strangely. A moment later he remembered both the face and the previous night, and recalled what had happened to the boy in the kitchen.

Clarenceux threw himself forward, reaching for the man's side-sword. The soldier instinctively put his hand down to protect it but Clarenceux was half a second faster. As he drew the blade he sliced through two of the soldier's clutching fingers. The soldier twisted and yelled in pain and rage, then turned and swung his arm at Clarenceux. He missed and lunged, trying to grab Clarenceux's throat. Clarenceux stumbled backwards, looking for space to wield the sword; but the man was already on top of him. He heard a woman's scream, and the sound of running feet, and then he was suddenly falling backwards, the soldier tumbling with him. Only the instinct not to land flat on his back made him turn as he came down, forcing himself away from the soldier by pushing at him with the sword, trying to twist in the air and thrusting the sharp blade through the soft flesh of the man's groin and against the bone.

Clarenceux hit the ground hard with his shoulder. The pain in his knee, which was jolted by the fall, made him grit his teeth.

Out of the corner of his eye he saw a second man – the man who must have tripped him – swinging an iron-rimmed wooden pail. Clarenceux lifted himself, trying to regain his feet. The man swung the pail with force and connected with the side of his head. The blow made Clarenceux cry out, laying him back on the ground. The man swung the bucket again and brought it down towards his head; but Clarenceux saw it coming and rolled sideways. He looked upwards as the man threw the pail hard towards him. Instinctively he raised an arm to break the force of the throw and the bucket hit his elbow, jarring the bone. He tried to get to his feet, feeling the pain in his knee, but before he could rise the man drew a long dagger and lunged forward, the point towards his throat. It was all Clarenceux could do to throw himself out of the way, guarding against the thrust with the sword in his own hand. The man immediately turned and came after him again, jabbing forward at Clarenceux's face as he scrambled about in the mud of the street, trying to use his left leg to force himself to his feet. Clarenceux crawled backwards, using both hands behind him to move, unable to wield the sword. Again the man jabbed the dagger towards him. Clarenceux kicked out with his left leg. As he did so he felt a doorstep with his elbow, and used it to lift himself into a crouching position while he brought his sword forward. Two, three thrusts he parried, and then he finally was back up on his feet.

The man delayed, hesitant at losing the advantage. Clarenceux watched him, his back against the wall, waiting for him to strike. His assailant would come at him with a sudden movement, he could anticipate that. He remembered a lesson he had learnt on his sole military campaign, at the siege of Boulogne. *You can tell more about a man from a minute in a fight than from a year in conversation.* He knew he was not as good a fighter as this man. He had been lucky to wound his first opponent as they fell. He was unpractised.

Suddenly there was an almighty scream from the soldier away to his left. A moment ago the man had been lying in the mud, rolling around, clutching his guts and cursing in pain. There were about a dozen people in the street, huddled on the far side, but they were only watching; no one was helping the wounded man. Now, however, he was on his feet and shouting, bloody, stumbling towards Clarenceux. Clarenceux waited, then darted a glance to him, knowing that the knife fighter would choose that instant to lunge again.

When the blow came, Clarenceux was already moving. He slashed back with the sword as he shifted his body to his left. The blade sliced the knife fighter straight across the middle of his face as Clarenceux threw his weight behind his shoulder and hit the advancing soldier in his bloody belly. He paid no attention to the scream of the knife fighter; he did not even hear him. All he heard was his own panic as he drove the sword home under the wounded soldier's ribs as he fell with him, twisting the blade, ripping it out, frantic. He fell on top of the dying man, then pushed the palm of his left hand into his face, lifted the sword and stabbed him again through the chest. Only after he had plunged the blade into the man for a third time did he turn to look for the knife fighter. He was already twenty yards up the street, and stumbling blindly, his bloody face in his hands.

Clarenceux stared at the blood on his own hands. He saw the glistening blood soaking the soldier's tunic and spreading in the mud. The stab wound in the man's groin revealed the glistening intestine.

Clarenceux felt sick. He tried to get to his feet but could not. The world was closing in on him, his head pounding with the pain of the blow from the bucket, his body aching. Suddenly the nausea rose within him and, unable to stop himself, he vomited beside the corpse, letting himself fall into the mud, beyond prayer, hearing his own panting, tasting bitter bile and staring at the grey skies.

It started to rain. For a few seconds he lay still, feeling the cold droplets fall on to his face.

'My mistress bids me tell you come quickly, if you want to live.'

Clarenceux looked up and saw the sharp features of a boy, about twelve years old.

'For all our sakes, Mr Clarenceux, please get up. Come quickly!'

Clarenceux was suddenly alert. He got to his knees, cursed the pain, then pushed himself unsteadily to his feet. The people in the street were watching him. They had seen him attack the tall soldier for no apparent reason. He had committed a hanging crime in front of all these witnesses – a whole jury's worth.

The rain started to come down harder.

'Please, Mr Clarenceux!' He looked in the direction the boy was urging him to go. There was a door open on the other side of the street.

He took a look at the dead man and removed the sword from his chest. He threw it down beside the body, feeling disgusted, a stranger to himself. *I should say a prayer for his soul. But I do not even know his name.* He crossed himself, said 'Rest in peace. Amen,' and turned to follow the boy.

Only when he had gone did the witnesses send for the constable, as the raindrops continued to fall on the bloodied corpse of John Crackenthorpe, Richard Crackenthorpe's brother.

Clarenceux followed the boy into the house and along a passage that led to a walled yard at the rear. Here was a small gate opening into the courtyard of the adjacent house, and that in turn led to the yard of the neighbouring property. None of the gates was locked: the boy knew exactly where he was going and how to open each one.

Clarenceux followed in the rain. In the fourth and last yard was a ladder, propped against a wall. The boy climbed up it without hesitating and waited. Clarenceux went up step by step and balanced precariously on the top of the wall as the boy pulled the ladder up then let it down on the other side, and scurried to the ground. Clarenceux descended more slowly.

He stepped off the ladder and looked up. He was facing the elaborately carved rear wooden jetties of a handsome town house. Many glazed windows let in light to the rooms on the upper floors. Large lead cisterns around the cobbled courtyard caught the rainwater running off the roof of the main house and its wing. To one side was a stable and a gate leading through to the street. To the rear, beyond the curtilage wall, was a large old building that Clarenceux recognised as Painter-Stainers' Hall.

Goodwife Machyn approached from the back door of the house, her fear and resolve both showing in her face. She had white linen towels on one arm. Clarenceux wanted to embrace her, to feel her warmth; but he knew he could not touch her. He could not touch anyone. It was not just the blood, it was the uncleanness. He had killed a man – it was not right that he share in any human warmth.

He realised he was trembling. *I need to make a confession.*

'Put this round your head.' Rebecca reached up and wrapped a linen towel around him. 'Hold it in place. There.'

'I am in grave trouble, Goodwife Machyn,' he said as he followed her indoors.

'I know. I watched from a window. Is that man dead?'

'I believe so.'

'Let us not talk here. Let us get away as quickly as possible.' She led him into the house. They walked down a dark corridor.

'Where's the chronicle?'

'Hidden.' She turned and silently pointed up in the dimness. She put a finger on her lips.

'I need to see it,' he whispered. 'As soon as possible.'

They entered a high stone-walled room with enormous fireplaces on either side. Steam curled in the light of the windows high above them. The late morning dinner was being cooked: pike for the lady of the house and her companions, pottage for the servants. Clarenceux could smell fried onions and garlic. Two kitchen boys attended to the fires, the spit and the cauldrons while the cook recorded what had been spent in an account book. He glanced first at Rebecca and then at Clarenceux, who was still holding the linen towel to his head.

Rebecca led Clarenceux down a flight of steps into a cold room full of large barrels on their sides. The pungent smell of old ale was heavy in the air. Putting her hand on his shoulder, she spoke with her mouth close to his ear, quietly. 'Mistress Barker's servants take in deliveries here: outside is an alleyway that leads to Huggin Lane. That door at the far end of the room is locked; but I will get a key. At the other end of Huggin Lane, beyond Thames Street, is a warehouse. It used to belong to Henry's brother, Christopher, and now is owned by his daughter, but she doesn't use it; Mistress Barker does. We will be as safe there as anywhere. You must wait here while I go and fetch the chronicle and the keys.'

Clarenceux watched her leave the buttery, then took the linen from his head. It was heavily stained. In this dim light the blood looked black against the white linen. He was shaking. He was very cold. He had killed a man and a part of himself too. The soft part, the innocence – that was what had died. He remembered his rage on seeing Will's body; he remembered saying to Thomas that he no longer wanted to be innocent. That wish to take arms and seek revenge still gripped him. But how little he had known about loss of innocence. It was not like being a soldier, when he had killed men at someone else's order.

His shivering grew worse. The bitter taste of vomit in his mouth, the smell of the ale, the pain in his head. He felt with his hand and looked at his fingers; they were dark with blood. He held the cloth to his head again, and wondered whether he would have been in such a frenzy to kill that soldier if he had not been hit on the head.

Yes. The decision had already been made. I made it when I put my hand on Will's cold forehead.

Noises came from the kitchen, pots being banged together. *Was that a warning?* He felt nervous, on edge, as if any moment Sergeant Crackenthorpe might appear. He wondered whether he had actually blinded the second assailant. Undoubtedly the man would return to Crackenthorpe and tell him what had happened. And Crackenthorpe would not risk coming with just a few men to arrest him a second time. He would bring a whole army.

He heard footsteps and looked up to see Rebecca. She was wearing a long mulberry travelling cape and a felt hat decorated with an ostrich feather. Under one arm she had the chronicle; over the other she was carrying an old brown robe that had once been of fine quality, with fur trimmings and long sleeves, and a wide black velvet cap.

She held the robe out to him. 'You will need this.'

Clarenceux wiped his head once more and put the linen cloth on an upended barrel. He took the robe and put it on. It smelled musty and vaguely perfumed but it was warm. It would also conceal the blood.

Rebecca put down the chronicle and hat on the barrel and came close to look at his head. She touched with her fingers, and saw the dark, fresh blood. She picked up the linen cloth, ripped off a portion, folded it and placed it over the wound.

'It is only a short distance but we cannot risk you being seen,' she said, passing him the velvet cap. He put it on. 'Good,' she added, looking at him. She handed him the chronicle.

'You take it,' he said. 'They will be after me for murder. If they see me you can still get away.'

'No. Women with books attract attention – it means we can read. Besides, you are the only one who can make sense of it.'

With that, Rebecca went to the far side of the cellar and inserted the key in the lock. Clarenceux followed with the book under his arm, watching her from behind. In the shadows he saw her shoulders rise and fall as she took a deep breath, and then turned the key. She opened the door and stepped out.

It was still raining. She looked down the alley and beckoned Clarenceux out, locking the door behind him. Then she started walking fast. He followed her, struggling to keep up, watching the heels of her shoes splash in the mud and puddles as she turned into Huggin Lane.

'Goodwife Machyn, slow down a little,' he gasped.

She turned to look at him but immediately saw his gaze shift to the end of the street. A watchman of the city was riding fast, straight towards them.

'Walk on,' said Clarenceux suddenly. 'Here, take my arm. Keep walking,' he urged. He made himself look away from the rider, and gathered himself for the shout and the attack. Was he prepared for another fight? No. But he would fight anyway.

I no longer want to be innocent.

The rider was almost upon them and not slowing down. Clarenceux expected to hear the command for them to halt. He tensed his body, held Rebecca's arm close and whispered a prayer under his breath.

The rider galloped past. Clarenceux glanced back and saw the man turn the corner of the lane behind them.

'Did you recognise him?' Rebecca asked.

'No, and thankfully he did not recognise us. But I would lay a bet that he was acting on Crackenthorpe's orders.'

They continued down to Thames Street. Clarenceux followed Rebecca as she walked quickly across and went round the back of the row of facing buildings. Here the wide prospect of the Thames and the masts of the ships on the quay came into sight, as well as dozens of porters, labourers and mariners, together with a few clerks, merchants and customs officials. Rebecca turned her back on the crowd and opened a gate between two tenements; a small quiet yard lay beyond. She walked to the door on the opposite side, produced a key from her dress and opened it. Clarenceux followed, feeling the solidity of the oak door, thinking of refuge.

Inside the warehouse was a wide space, the nearer part open to the roof beams. Chinks of light came through in two or three places, where tiles were missing; water dripped here and there into puddles on the ground. The further half was divided into three floors – two open-sided platforms with a pulley along one side. Stacked on the windowless ground floor were sawn planks of Scandinavian pine and large oak tuns. Above, arranged in rows, there were huge sacks of the sort that traders used for transporting wool fells.

A ladder led to the first-floor platform. Rebecca went straight up and Clarenceux followed, looking around. On this side the roof had not been allowed to decay. A pair of rough doors opened out above the wharf on the far side. Although they were closed, daylight crept in around the edges, allowing a little light into the warehouse.

He sank down on the bare floorboards between two large woolsacks, resting his back on one. He was glad of the robe. He took off the velvet cap and looked at the blood otained linen cloth. He touched his wound: the bleeding seemed to have stopped.

'I don't know where that second man came from. If there had been only one, I would not have needed to kill him. But two . . .'

'He was walking in front of you. I saw him from the window. I had been waiting all day for you to come. I knew where you were going; he did too.'

He watched her taking off the travelling cape. She held up the hat, showing him the bedraggled ostrich feather. She smiled briefly, then pulled the feather off and threw it to one side.

'Goodwife Machyn, I have something to tell you. Something serious. Your husband was arrested by Sergeant Crackenthorpe the night before last. He was hiding in my stable loft – he must have gone there after he saw me. Walsingham told me so himself.'

'Where did you see Walsingham?'

'At a house near the Tower.'

'And he let you go?'

'Only because his agents did not find the chronicle. Crackenthorpe returned to search my house. He would have found the book if you hadn't taken it. They were thorough – they destroyed everything.'

'I am sorry. Are your wife and daughters . . . holding up?'

Clarenceux looked into her eyes. 'Awdrey has gone down to Devon with my daughters. The house is uninhabitable.' He straightened his right leg slowly and reached for the chronicle.

'There is something you are not telling me.'

He hesitated. There were several things he was not telling her. He was not telling her that there was no hope for her husband. He was not telling her how glad he was to see her, and how much she touched him with her presence. He was not telling her about Will.

'What made you attack the guard at my house?' she asked. 'You are not a violent man by nature. At least I have not detected that in you before now.'

'You remember the boy – the one who told you the chronicle was hidden in the barrel?'

'Of course.'

'They hanged him. In front of the others, including Thomas, who was his great-uncle.'

Rebecca remembered the boy's terrified face. 'I am truly sorry. It seemed the only way. It seemed I . . . I had to take the chronicle.'

'If you had not taken it, maybe they would have killed him anyway. They would certainly have killed me. But as it happened, you did take it, and I am glad that you did.'

Rebecca managed a weak smile, as if to express recognition of a small mercy.

The sounds of labourers calling to one another on the quay reached them. Clarenceux looked down through the gaps in the timber at the boats moored by Queenhithe.

'What do we do now?' Rebecca asked.

'Lancelot Heath's wife sent a message. Apparently he will meet us where Sir Arthur was on June the thirteenth, 1550. I recall that as being one of the first entries in your husband's chronicle. So, let us put our regrets to one side. We shall pray for Will's soul later. First let us do what we can to make amends.'

He opened the book and read Machyn's first entry quickly and silently. Then he passed the open book to her and watched her as she read the unpunctuated words slowly and aloud. 'The thirteenth day of June 1550 did Sir Arthur Darcy knight John Heath painter and Harry Machyn merchant meet dining upstairs at the sign of the Bull's Head by London Stone there setting everything straight and ordered fair in the green night room and after to Paul's Cross where we heard a goodly sermon by the good bishop of Durham.'

'I am going to the Bull's Head alone. I am no longer the man I was two days ago. I am set on a path now and I cannot turn back. But you, you still have your innocence. I would urge you to go back to Mistress Barker's house and stay there quietly for as long as it takes – until this horror has passed.'

Rebecca shook her head. 'Mr Clarenceux, you and I both know that Walsingham is not going to let my husband go. If Henry's secret concerns the fate of the queen – *two* queens – and is so grave that a royal soldier thinks nothing of hanging your servant, then he is not going to be released. He is not a well man; I would not be surprised if he is dead already. And if he dies, then what have I got left? I am alone. I have no money, no income.'

She looked away. 'If . . . if Henry is dead then what do I have but his memory? Nothing but the knowledge that I will not forget him, that I will never do anything that would displease him, and that I will always honour him.' She wiped her eyes. 'And since he gave that book to you, and was so insistent that you are his true heir, rather than his son, I have to help you, for my own sake as well as Henry's. And for your sake too. Look at you. You are bloody and covered in mud, you can only run with great difficulty. When was the last time you ate?'

'This morning. An eel pie.'

'Hardly enough. You haven't slept and you're not thinking straight. You killed a man in the street and you expect just to walk away. I would not be fulfilling my promises to my husband if I were to go back to Mistress Barker's now and abandon you, the man he entrusted with his legacy.'

Clarenceux looked at her. She was firm in her conviction, and brave. She held his gaze: her sad eyes looked deeply into his and allowed him freely to look into her.

'You know that Crackenthorpe is protected by Walsingham?'

'It does not surprise me.'

'Walsingham also has a protector: none other than Sir William Cecil, the Secretary and the queen's chief adviser. We are up against the full power of the kingdom, with all its ruthless weaponry.'

'God will protect us,' she said.

Clarenceux nodded. 'Well, so be it. We must find our way now to the tavern of the Bull's Head by London Stone, where Lancelot Heath is waiting. I suggest that we leave the key to this refuge somewhere where we can both find it. This will be as good a place as any to hide, if need be.'

32

❧

The young man pulled on the reins to avoid riding into a cart of hay which was crossing the street. He was impatient. The task he had been given might have been awful – to pass the most distressing news to the most violent of men – but there was one thing even worse: to deliver it late.

He urged his horse on and started again to canter down Thames Street. He noted that there was a great deal of activity on the wharves; he had expected most people to be at their dinner by now, or sheltering from the drizzle that had settled on the city. But there were clusters of people at Dowgate, and he had to ride through the puddles to go round them, splashing them in his hurry. They shouted after him but he went on. At Queenhithe there were several large vessels moored. Labourers were carrying off sacks of spices and craning off tuns of wine for storage in the quayside warehouses. He took one look at the conglomeration of workers and cut off up Huggin Lane. Even here he was not alone; a tall man in a brown robe and velvet cap was walking beside a woman in an ostrich-feather hat. They seemed startled as he galloped up the otherwise deserted lane.

He finally caught sight of Crackenthorpe and his three companions from the top of Ludgate Hill. Kicking his heels into the horse's flanks, he urged the beast to a gallop. Crackenthorpe was not riding fast, and the messenger came within shouting distance as they rode along Fleet Street, near Fetter Lane.

'Sergeant Crackenthorpe,' he called. 'Wait, I have news.'

Crackenthorpe gave a command and they all reined in their horses and waited, the horses' breaths and snorts punctuating the silence.

'I have the gravest news,' the rider said as he came to a standstill alongside them. He remembered what the constable had told him. *Break it to him as if it is an order. He is going to be angry and distressed; he may even be violent, but Sergeant Crackenthorpe understands orders, and he respects those who do their duty.* 'It concerns the traitor Clarenceux. He has killed your brother. He attacked him at Machyn's house and killed him in the street, in front of witnesses.'

Crackenthorpe's horse stirred, sensing its rider's change of mood. He pulled on the reins to control it, and looked at the messenger. 'How did it happen?'

'Apparently Clarenceux seized John's sword and stabbed him with it.'

'Was no one watching him? I gave instructions for both Clarenceux and his house to be watched. Did those men not help?'

'Ralph French was watching but Clarenceux put out one of his eyes.'

'Holy Mary! When did all this happen?'

'About three-quarters of an hour ago.'

Crackenthorpe clenched his fist. He was expected at Whitehall soon. Walsingham had gone on ahead to report to Cecil. He could not fail in that duty. His instinct was to go back to the city, to start looking for Clarenceux. But it might take hours.

'You three, return with this boy to the constable of the ward. Tell him to have watchmen on every street corner. Tell him that I want to hear everything about this incident when I return. Then go to the mayor and the sheriffs. Tell them that Clarenceux is plotting to kill the queen. He is armed and has already killed a royal officer. Have a warrant issued to all the constables for him to be arrested on sight. Tell them to hold Machyn's widow too.

No doubt she is with him. When you have done that, go to Clarenceux's house and take the horses from his stables. Sell them to pay for my brother's funeral. If anyone tries to stop you, arrest them.'

'What about you, sergeant?' asked one of the men with him.

'I must see Walsingham before he meets Cecil this afternoon. I have promised to do so, and I will not break a promise. And likewise I promise I will make Clarenceux suffer for killing my brother. I swear it. I am going to do to him and his manservant what they used to do to traitors in the past: cut his guts out and burn them in front of him. You four are my witnesses.'

The messenger had been expecting a violent reaction – shouting, accusations, recriminations. Instead he watched as Crackenthorpe kicked his horse's flanks and started to gallop towards Whitehall.

The violence, he realised, was yet to come.

33

There were two rooms on the ground floor of the Bull's Head Tavern. Clarenceux and Rebecca entered through a low oak door and found themselves in what had once been a long hall but had now been divided by a partition with a large fireplace on either side. In this first room a man was playing a fiddle while a woman beat time with a tambourine; several men and women stood watching, holding wooden mugs and pewter tankards of ale, tapping their fingers. Dogs scampered, chasing each other among the watchers' legs. In a corner there were four men playing cards, sitting on low stools and casting their cards on to the rushes on the floor; two women were with them, cradling their cups, helping to shoo away the dogs when they came too close. A couple of bronze cooking pots were lying on their sides by the fireplace, waiting to be taken out and washed up. A boy attended a spit loaded with a hunk of roasting meat in the fireplace, despite it being Advent. The boy turned to play with a small puppy after every turn.

Clarenceux frowned at the smell of the meat and led Rebecca through to the next room. Here were three tables with linen cloths. A group of men were seated at one, leaving their shop work in the hands of their apprentices. A woman in a bright red bodice, with a young child on her lap, sat at the next table; as Clarenceux watched she passed the child to a much older woman seated on the other side of the table and went to speak to one of the two men standing by the fireplace with mugs of ale. Above them joints of salted meat, branches of bay leaves and baskets of fruit hung from the beams.

Clarenceux looked around for the taverner. After a short while he emerged from an inner door, dressed in a leather apron. He was about forty and bearded, with a wide ruddy face and a thick mop of golden hair that curled above his ears. He held a linen towel over one arm and spoke amiably to his customers.

'My good man,' said Clarenceux, stepping towards him. 'I am led to believe you have an upstairs room here.'

'That depends, sir. I do have an upstairs room, but it is let to a gentleman. I don't believe I can oblige you – unless you are a friend of the gentleman.'

'We are looking for a man called Hoath.'

The taverner was unmoved. 'What sort of night are you expecting, you and your lady wife?'

'We are not married,' interjected Rebecca.

Clarenceux suddenly understood. 'A Green one.'

The taverner looked at Clarenceux. In a low voice he asked, 'You are with Henry Machyn?'

Rebecca broke in, 'I am Rebecca Machyn, Henry's wife. This is Mr Harley, Clarenceux King of Arms.'

The taverner nodded and threw the towel down on a nearby bench. 'Lancelot is expecting you. Follow me.'

They went out of the tavern hall into a passage and up a narrow stone staircase. In places there was barely enough light to see that the plaster walls were flaking. At the top of the stairs was a small landing: two doors faced them. The floor creaked as the taverner walked towards the right-hand one. He knocked three times and waited. Then he knocked once more. Almost immediately there was the sound of a key in a lock and the door opened to a warm chamber.

A dishevelled golden-haired man with blue eyes bearing a strong resemblance to the taverner stood there. His bearing was awkward and ill-at-ease; he seemed to be struggling to cope with his strait-ened circumstances.

'Mr Clarenceux is here.'

Lancelot Heath clapped the taverner on the shoulder. 'Thank you,' he muttered. 'Heartily you are welcome, Mr Clarenceux. And you too, Goodwife Machyn.' He beckoned all three of them into the room and locked the door. 'Please forgive the precau-tions. You know how dangerous things are.' He indicated the tavern-keeper. 'This is my brother, Gawain. A trustworthy soul.'

The room was stone-walled, part of an older building. It was heated by a large fireplace above which was an old rack intended for longbows and muskets. Just one bow lay there now. To the right was an imposing old tapestry of Sir Gawain and the Green Knight. The rest was plain whitewashed plaster. There was a small bed on one side, a couple of chests and a table and seat. The remains of a meal lay on a pewter plate on the table. An old stone-framed window overlooked the roof of the tavern, invis-ible from the street.

Clarenceux bowed politely to both men. 'Greetings and well met. An Arthurian family indeed – Lancelot, Gawain. Are there other knights in your family?'

'My father, the late John Heath, was a lover of the old romances. We have a sister Iseult in Mile End. Another sister, who died some years ago, was called Guinevere. Hence the tapestry and, of course, the Knights. I presume you have come to talk about the latter.'

'I was rather expecting you to inform me. Henry Machyn gave me his chronicle and the name King Clariance of Northumberland. He also gave me a date. He told me to find you and ask you to summon the Knights of the Round Table.'

'I thought he would. But it is not possible, not now. All the old plans are in disarray. They were laid down years ago, by my father, together with Henry and Sir Arthur Darcy. Gathering the Knights is no longer so straightforward. I do not know them all, or where they all are.'

'But who are they?' asked Rebecca. 'And what did they have to do with my husband? What was the purpose? To me it seems like a game, an indulgence.'

Gawain Heath caught his brother's eye. 'At this point I will leave you,' he said. 'I will do what I can to help, Lancelot, but the less I know about our father's business in this respect, the better for all concerned. Good day, Mr Clarenceux, Good-wife ...'

'Before you go, Goodman Heath, I want to ask you, is it with your blessing that the meat is roasting in the hall downstairs? Given that your brother is a fighter for the old religion, I am surprised you do not observe the Advent fast.'

'No doubt you are, Mr Clarenceux. But my customers want it and I do not believe the new religion condemns it. Besides, it is a perfect cover for my brother here. Is it not a most un-Catholic smell?' He smiled, bowed, and went to the door, unlocked it and left the room, shutting the door behind him.

Lancelot waited until his brother had gone and then went over and locked the door once more, leaving the key in the lock. 'Be seated,' he said, turning and gesturing to the bed. He himself took the bench from the table, set it in the middle of the room, and sat down.

'Where to begin? It is difficult, because I was not the first generation, as you are aware. My father and your husband held some great secret – a document. I think it concerned our present queen and her brother Edward, the then king. They talked to Sir Arthur Darcy about it, and it was agreed that they should form a fraternity, the Knights of the Round Table, to guard the document and to use it when the time was right. They hid it and encoded the means to find it in a chronicle. There were to be nine knights guarding it, and each one had an Arthurian name and a date. No one was to reveal their date to anyone else except when they were all gathered together. I have the name Lancelot by baptism, as you know, and my father chose the name Sir Lancelot for himself. His idea was that, if he died, I would be the bearer of that name. Henry Machyn always intended you, Mr Clarenceux, to be the inheritor of his name; and so he chose the name King Clariance, which I believe he has passed on to you.'

'He gave it to me, yes. Go on.'

'There is not much more to tell. The last time all the Knights met together was shortly after my father's death, ten years ago, just after Queen Mary came to the throne. My father left money in his will for a dinner at my brother-in-law's tavern at Mile End – you will find it mentioned in Henry's chronicle – but since then the Knights who have died have not done the same. I think they have lost interest. Although Henry has urged them to protect the document, it is not important to them. When he called the Knights together to witness his will recently, only five of us attended. I myself was not particularly concerned, although I understood that the event was connected with the document, and the chronicle might yet become important. Then some soldiers came looking for me a few days ago, asking questions about Henry. They tore everything in my house apart in their search for the chronicle.'

Clarenceux nodded. Now he knew why Lancelot's wife had been so keen to be rid of him the day before yesterday. 'Who were the Knights who witnessed Henry's will?'

'Myself, Michael Hill and his son Nicholas, Daniel Gyttens, and William Draper, the merchant taylor. The strange thing was that Henry had written that he was of sound mind but ill in body. But he seemed to me to be as hale and hearty as ever.'

'These men, what are their Arthurian names?'

Heath shook his head. 'William Draper was Sir Dagonet, but the rest I do not know.'

Clarenceux remembered the night in the rain when Crackenthorpe had mentioned Sir Dagonet. 'Where do they live?'

'Nicholas Hill lives in St Dionis Backchurch and his father in St Mary Woolnoth, opposite the church. Draper's house is that big brick one on the left as you go up Basinghall Street. Gyttens – I don't know.'

'And the others?'

'Again, I do not know. You must understand that I did not agree to witness Henry's will because I was one of the Knights but because he and my father were old friends. It was only in the course of the meeting that Henry told me that all of us present were Knights. He added that it was important that we observe the clause in his will concerning the chronicle. He willed it to *you*, you see. That dinner at the sign of the Rising Sun in Mile End ten years ago remains the only time I have met all the Knights. I cannot now remember which names I heard that day and which I simply know from being surrounded by Arthurian things. I do know that one Knight was special – Henry said he was not even to repeat his name. I think I heard someone call himself Sir Reynold, but I can't be sure. The only name I can be sure of besides my own is Sir Dagonet. I remembered that one because it was so unusual – I had never heard of a Sir Dagonet.'

'He was the jester at Arthur's court,' Clarenceux said with an uneasy, sickening feeling rising in his stomach. He had assumed that finding Lancelot Heath would relieve him of the burden of responsibility, at least in part. Lancelot would summon the Knights and they would go into action, for better or for worse; he would join them or not as he saw fit. But now he saw the whole set-up was chaotic.

He rose from where he was sitting and went to the window. 'This is impossible,' he said, looking out. 'We have all had our lives upturned. Your house has been ransacked. Mine has been rendered uninhabitable. Henry Machyn has gone missing, my servant has been murdered and I have killed a royal officer. We can hardly leave things as they are. What do we do now?'

'Mr Clarenceux, you know as much as I do.'

'Tell me the date. Your Arthurian date.'

'Henry said not to reveal—'

'Goodman Heath, someone has got to find out what is going on here. We are not playing boyish games any more. Our lives are at risk. We need to share what we know. The date he gave me was the twentieth of June 1557. It relates to a date in his chronicle but the entry doesn't make sense. Something about a sermon by the abbot of Westminster at St Paul's Cross.'

Lancelot still hesitated. He looked from Clarenceux to Rebecca.

'Mr Clarenceux is right,' she said. 'We need to work together. Our lives are already at risk – sharing this information will not help our enemies but it might help us.'

Lancelot stood up and went to the wall, thinking. 'It's the date I told you, the first entry in the book. June the thirteenth, 1550. There. Now what do we do?'

Clarenceux nodded. 'Thank you.' He glanced at Rebecca, disappointed. 'Had it been any other date, I would suggest that we go and look it up in the chronicle, but seeing that we already know what that entry says, it is hardly necessary. We have two dates and three or four names. And I am at a loss.'

Rebecca broke the silence. 'Can we get some food here, Goodman Heath? And some hot water? Mr Clarenceux has a nasty wound to his head that needs cleaning.'

'Of course. Gawain's wife is in the next room. I will ask her.'

'We are going to need money too,' added Clarenceux. 'Everything I had in my house has gone. I don't know whether my wife took it or Sergeant Crackenthorpe's men. But I have nothing. I don't even have an eating knife.'

Lancelot paused at the door. 'Money I can help you with. In fact, it's your own money,' he said, looking at Rebecca. 'Henry deposited a sum in gold – twenty pounds, I believe – with Iseult and her husband, John Crawley, in Mile End, to be collected at an unspecified time by King Clariance of Northumberland.' He went out of the room.

Rebecca lay back on the bed and yawned. 'I could go to sleep here, it's so quiet and warm.'

Clarenceux listened to the vague sounds from the tavern downstairs. The high notes of the fiddle came to him, and distant laughter. But even though it was not silent, she was right. It was quiet.

'Don't,' he said.

'What are we going to do?'

Clarenceux felt his bruised knee, and flexed it. 'What do you think we should do?'

'We are not safe here. We would not be safe anywhere in the city. All I know is that I must do what I can to find Henry. And save ourselves. That is all we can do.'

Lancelot came back into the room carrying a knife, a pail of warm water and a sponge. Clarenceux looked at the pail. 'It was one of those that did the damage in the first place,' he muttered. Lancelot handed the knife to Clarenceux and placed the bucket beside the bench. Clarenceux sat down and Rebecca began washing his head around the wound.

'Some pottage, cheese and bread will be coming up in a minute,' Lancelot said.

Clarenceux felt the warmth of the water, and its sting on his scalp. He felt Rebecca's firm but careful touch. She had saved him by removing the chronicle – an act which, although it had had disastrous consequences, was well meant. She had led him to safety after the fight. And she needed him to help her find her husband. He could not abandon her and go down to Devon now – no more than she could abandon Henry.

'We will go to Mile End,' he said. 'We will pick up the money left with your sister and take the ferry across to Greenwich. There we can hire horses to take us to a place in Kent where I am known.'

'When you say "we", I take it that you do not mean all of us,' said Lancelot. 'I intend to go my own way as soon as you have left this place. I will return to London when everything has settled down.'

Clarenceux looked at him warily, considering Heath's position. After a long delay he said, 'I agree. The more of us there are, the more conspicuous we will be.'

'Why not let Goodwife Machyn come with me?'

Clarenceux felt the sponge pause on his scalp. He said nothing.

'I will go with Mr Clarenceux. I need his help to find my husband.'

'In that case, may I make a suggestion?' Lancelot said. 'Or, rather, two. First: when you travel, go on foot. At least in town. People always look to see who is riding; they assume that people on foot are of no consequence, and ignore them. The second is that you travel as man and wife. People will be less suspicious of a woman travelling out of town with her husband than a woman in a man's company.'

Clarenceux looked up at Rebecca. She caught his eye momentarily. 'Gawain Heath thought we were man and wife when we arrived,' she said. 'It makes sense.'

'What was your maiden name?' Clarenceux asked.

'Lowe.'

'We shall travel as Mr and Mistress Lowe. After we have supped here, I will fetch the chronicle from where it is hidden – alone. Mistress Lowe, you will go to the sign of the Rising Sun in Mile End and wait there for me. I will join you as soon as I have recovered the chron—'

Suddenly there was a creak of the floorboards outside. All three stopped and looked at the door. There came one knock, then another, and a third.

Clarenceux felt himself tense, holding his breath as he waited.

Eventually the last knock came. Lancelot exhaled and went over to the door to unlock it. He took the bowl of pottage that Gawain had brought for them, and the basket from under his arm. Clarenceux sniffed the air suspiciously but the pottage did not contain meat.

Rebecca noticed him inhaling but mistook his purpose. She squeezed out the sponge and dabbed once more at Clarenceux's wound. 'Smells good, doesn't it?' she asked.

34

Cecil was sitting beside the fire when Walsingham arrived. He had just been handed a letter in code and was about to read it. He gestured to Walsingham to seat himself on the wide wooden seat on the other side of the fire.

Walsingham was impatient. He was annoyed at finding Cecil more intent on reading a letter than listening to him; he wanted to tell him the news. He suspected that Cecil was trying to annoy him, but did not rise to the bait. Instead he raised his eyes to the ceiling to look at the newly completed plasterwork, and the frieze. The panelling was fine, too – he approved of the red and gold highlights on the edges of the panels.

Then his impatience got the better of him.

'Sir William, I have news that I think you should hear sooner rather than later.'

Cecil set down the letter. 'Come then, Francis, tell me. What is it?'

'Several things. The first is that Clarenceux has confessed to having seen Machyn's chronicle. I did arrest him, and was interrogating him while his house was searched. However, in an unguarded moment when the house was left unwatched, Machyn's widow took the book away. She has not yet been found ...'

'Machyn's *widow*?'

Walsingham shifted uneasily on the seat. 'Under interrogation ...'

'He was in his sixties.'

'He confessed to entering and leaving the city by way of a blacksmith's house – a man by the name of Mason, he said. I have not yet identified the exact house. However, a search of Machyn's premises did reveal his will. In addition to William Draper, it names Lancelot Heath – the man about whom Draper spoke. It was also witnessed by two men by the name of Hill and one Daniel Gyttens – men whom Draper failed to mention in his confession. We are searching for them now.'

Cecil pondered. 'This news is hardly earth-shatteringly important, Francis. In fact I would go back to reading my letter but for the fact that you said you had interrogated Clarenceux. What did he tell you?'

'He said nothing about the plot except that Machyn was a friend of his and he had seen the chronicle. He pretended not to know that Machyn was in his stable. He was lying, of course. He said nothing about William Draper or Heath.'

'What did he say about me?'

'Only that he believed you would protect him.'

'And did you say that you were working for me?'

'No.' Walsingham hesitated slightly. 'Of course not.'

'Is he still in custody?'

'No. I released him in the hope that he would lead me to the chronicle.'

'And did he?'

Walsingham realised he had walked straight into one of Cecil's traps. How had it happened? Talking to Cecil was like rowing along a mountain river: suddenly you realised you were in white water, struggling to stay afloat as you were swept along between the rocks of his knowledge, until you were becalmed in a pool, having inadvertently said something that was both secret and true.

'There are other factors, Sir William. In the course of searching Clarenceux's house, Sergeant Crackenthorpe unfortunately killed one of the servants. It seems that in revenge Clarenceux sought out Crackenthorpe's own brother and killed him, blinding another of Crackenthorpe's men in one eye at the same time.'

Cecil's voice betrayed his surprise. 'Quite the soldier, our herald.' *Especially considering the man has not been under arms for nearly twenty years. Lord Paget did tell me once that Clarenceux was the best herald because he was the only one who understood how soldiers think, having been one himself.* 'Where is he now?'

'That I do not know, Sir William.'

Cecil stood up. 'That is the real news, isn't it, Francis? You have allowed the man whom you suspect to be the chief architect of this plot to go free, having failed to secure the chronicle. And you have seen to it that he has put himself outside the law. He is hardly likely to come to me for help now. We have lost him.'

'But we have the names in Machyn's will . . .'

'And so does he, if he is the protagonist you think he is. He has all he needs. He can go into the north and proclaim a rising in the name of Mary of Scotland, and he has whatever secret this damned chronicle holds as well.'

'He is under instructions to deliver the chronicle to me by curfew.'

'He will not. Killing Crackenthorpe's brother puts the matter beyond doubt. *I'd* be scared to show my face at your house if I'd killed Crackenthorpe's brother. What about Machyn's body?'

'I've told the gaolers to bury him in a plague pit, befitting his state as the late owner of a plague-infested house.'

'Foolish. Give him the dignity he deserves. He was an old man and he buried many members of the gentry and aristocracy with lavish and kindly displays. He deserves better than a plague pit. And Clarenceux?'

'What about him?'

'No. What are *you* going to do about him?'

'I am going to continue looking for him. Crackenthorpe has posted guards on every street corner in Queenhithe ward. He is desperate for revenge.'

'If he finds Clarenceux first, you'll be interrogating a corpse.' Cecil paused. 'What time did you release him?'

'About seven of the clock. Why?'

'I want to know. Is there anything else you need to report?'

'No, Sir William.'

'Not even where Lancelot Heath might be?'

'I regret to say I have no information on that matter, Sir William.'

'I regret it too. I expect you to do all you can. And more. He may be as important as Clarenceux. Together they may be more important to this plot than the chronicle itself. Go now, and good luck.'

Cecil watched Walsingham leave the chamber. He turned and looked into the fire.

Francis released Clarenceux eight hours ago. If he had interrogated him the previous evening, and said nothing about me, why did Clarenceux not come to me as soon as he was released?

He stood up and walked the length of the chamber. He tapped his fingers on the panel at the far end, then turned and walked back to his table.

There are two possible reasons. One is that he now knows Walsingham has my protection, and is working under my direction. The other is that he really is guilty.

Cecil stopped walking.

Perhaps both are true.

35

~

In his velvet cap and old robe Clarenceux left the tavern to return to the warehouse. He looked up at the old church of St Swithin's on the other side of the road and glanced both ways along Candlewick Street. No one seemed to be looking for him. He decided to walk towards Dowgate, where Skinners' Hall was situated, and then along past the church of St Thomas the Apostle. He pulled his robe tight, wishing the cold was not so extreme.

The thought occurred to him that, as a warden of the company, he was well known by those coming and going from Skinners' Hall. Walsingham might have bribed his fellow liverymen to watch out for him. But the fact that he had to get to Queenhithe forced him in that direction. Caution was necessary – fear a mere hindrance.

He looked into the faces of those he passed, quickly shifting his gaze if they made eye contact. He glanced ahead and saw a man loitering by St John's Church, rubbing his hands against the cold. He was not tall but small-framed, ill-at-ease, and wearing a side-sword. Was he one of Crackenthorpe's men? And the armed man, on the other side of the street – was he?

Clarenceux turned and walked swiftly into Dowgate, as if going to the hall. He could turn off right and head along the back street past St Michael's Church, then cut through to Little Trinity by the alleys in Garlickhithe. He felt his breathing becoming faster. Turning into the lane he saw another two men, on the corner of the road opposite the church. *They are guarding the boundaries of the ward.*

He stopped. Instantly he realised that he might alert them by the very act of stopping. He hurriedly bent down as if to refasten the buckle on his shoe and looked back to the Skinners' Hall. The sweat on his brow chilled his face. If he went on, he would have to walk past the waiting men. He could not do that: they were looking for him and the risk of being caught was too great. But if he went back, how was he going to get to Queenhithe?

He retraced his steps, breathing hurriedly, expecting the men at St Michael's to come after him at any moment. There were more people in the street, and a couple of carts too. But the men guarding the ward would not care who saw them make an arrest; no one would intervene. He felt the pain in his knee and wondered if he could run. Not fast enough. Back in Dowgate he turned for the safety of the hall, walking as fast as his stiffness would allow. He turned in through the entrance alleyway.

'Good day, Mr Clarenceux,' said one of the porters, stationed in one of the chambers beside the entrance.

'Hoskins, my good man,' said Clarenceux, relieved to see a friendly face.

'Watch out, Mr Clarenceux. Behind you.' Hoskins put out an arm to guard Clarenceux from a cart entering the alley.

Clarenceux drew in close to the door to the porter's chamber and watched the cart trundle past. The rider was wearing a huge rainproof cape and hat; on the cart behind him were several barrels of wine. Clarenceux noted that the man's face could not be seen. *Perhaps I could change clothes and positions with him? But that in itself is bound to arouse suspicion – what if he should betray . . .*

And then he hit upon a far simpler plan.

'Hoskins, do you know anyone with a boat who would be prepared to take me a short distance along the river, from Dowgate to Queenhithe, and then on to the Isle of Dogs?'

'Why, Mr Clarenceux, I might well. It depends when you want to go. My cousin is a bargemaster, but he is at Southwark this afternoon.'

'No, Hoskins, I need to go now. This very moment.'

'Then what about young John Gotobed, the court clerk's nephew? He was here just this morning and will be returning shortly with a consignment of paint. Shall I tell him when he appears?'

'Hoskins, I would be very grateful. Tell him he may find me in the wardens' chamber.'

36

*It was almost dark by the time Clarenceux arrived at Mile End. He entered the inn and found the hall lit by a fire and many candles, and thronged with men and women, children and dogs. At one table a family party were eating together; at another three merchant travellers in fine doublets and stylish flounced hose were discussing their journey. At one end of a long table some farmers were drinking; next to them a bailiff and a letter-carrier were playing cards. Two travelling musicians were occupying the same table, laughing as they fended off the calls of a group of young men and their wives to play some music so they might dance. Standing around the hall were the tradesmen of the area – a blacksmith and his wife, a surgeon, a brewer, a butcher, and clerks who kept accounts for their masters, or for the church.

Clarenceux, holding the chronicle under his robe, pushed through the people standing in the centre of the large room. He was looking for the tell-tale leather apron of the landlord. It was not to be seen; but a weary-looking woman in a faded red gown, laced bodice and apron did catch his eye as she carried a large flagon to the long table.

'I'm looking for Mistress Lowe,' he said to her over the noise of the crowd, adding the explanatory 'my wife', embarrassed at the necessary lie.

The woman shouted her reply as she poured ale from the

leather flagon into a wooden cup and pocketed a silver penny in return. 'Good day to you, Mr Lowe. I had to move three men from that room, seeing as a married couple would be paying for the bed, so 'tis good you've arrived.'

She beckoned Clarenceux away from the hall through to the screens passage at the far end, and out into the courtyard. The cold air and near-darkness was a shock after the warmth and light of the hall. The woman carried no candle. Clarenceux followed her as she started to climb the outside staircase to the gallery, where she opened the second of three doors. He saw the light of a single flame within, a lamp fixed to the wall.

'Mistress Lowe, your husband's here,' she called.

There was very little furniture in the room: just a bed lacking its curtains, a stool, a washing basin, a ewer, and an oak chest. There was no fireplace. Clarenceux saw Rebecca rise from the far side of the bed and turn towards them. He could not see her face, silhouetted by the lamp behind her. He made a small bow.

'Good evening,' he said, looking at her.

She nodded a reply and whispered 'Good evening' back to him. He noted her voice was weak. He also could see she was wearing a fashionable and expensive dress with elaborate shoulders and upper sleeves – she must have been back to Mistress Barker's house.

He turned to the innkeeper's wife. 'I presume you are Goodwife Crawley?'

'Sir, I am.'

'Come inside, please.' He closed the door behind her. 'Has my wife asked you about a sum of money left here for us some years ago? It was deposited by a man called Henry Machyn.'

She seemed anxious. 'Sir, I don't know that such a sum was ever left here. Maybe my husband knows . . .'

'Your brother Lancelot told us of the money. Maybe it would help if I reminded you it was left here for collection by King Clariance of Northumberland.'

'Lancelot says a lot of fanciful things. Comes of our having such a father. If he put himself to a hard day's work, as myself and my husband do, he would have less time for dreaming about knights and kings.'

Clarenceux glanced at Rebecca. She had moved out of silhouette and he could see the material of her dress, a rich velvet. She was even wearing a small ruff. But he was shocked to see that her face was wet with tears, reflected in the candlelight.

'I do not wish to discuss your late father but the money that was left here. Lancelot said it amounted to twenty pounds. Are you telling me that your brother was lying to us?'

She stiffened and her voice grew defensive. 'If ever there was such a sum, it was not so great as twenty pounds. And it may already have been repaid. You will forgive me, but I should be getting back to my drinkers. I will ask my husband to speak to you in the morning.'

She left the chamber abruptly. Clarenceux let her go. He shut the door and sat down on the bed.

'As soon as something good seems to happen, something else comes along to set us back again.' He sighed, took off his robe and cap and placed them on the chest beside the bed.

Rebecca had not spoken. He turned to her.

'Tell me,' he said gently.

The words tumbled down, dropped like heavy stones from her soul. 'Henry's dead.' Tears rolled freely down her cheeks, and she broke into a moan.

Clarenceux's heart fell. He got up and moved to hold her, putting his arms around her, feeling her shoulders rising and falling with her grief. He held her tight. It was all he could do.

He remembered his conversation with Henry two nights earlier, and the moment he had read Henry's prediction of his own death in the chronicle. He recalled all the occasions when Henry had come to receptions at his house, or had been at other gatherings. He thought of the many times he had seen him following a funeral cortège, head bowed, dignified, correct and respectful.

'I went to Mistress Barker's house after leaving the Bull's Head,' she said, wiping away her tears. 'I was thinking that, if I was going to pretend to be the wife of a gentleman, then I should dress like a gentlewoman. There were soldiers everywhere, as I am sure you saw for yourself; but I walked straight past them. I decided that if you were bold enough to do it, Mr Clarenceux, then I should be too. But Mistress Barker was solemn when I arrived. She told me the news. She had heard it from an acquaintance of Henry's, called James Emery, who had been told by a friend of his that he had seen Henry's body being taken to the plague pit.'

'The plague pit?'

'They didn't even give him a proper burial.'

Clarenceux let her cry into his shoulder. *She has now lost everything precious to her: her husband, her daughters and her home. Perhaps that is why she was so bold as to walk past the guards in Queenhithe and I was not.*

'Goodwife Machyn,' he said, 'there will be a time for mourning. But first we must have some food. We must eat to keep up our strength. If they are not going to give us the money we came for, then they can put our debt in a shopbook. I will pay at a later date.'

Rebecca broke away from Clarenceux and looked down at the sleeves of the elaborate dress.

'I feel ashamed.'

'Ashamed? Why?'

'Because I have no right to wear these clothes. And I am ashamed not to have been with my husband when he died. Ashamed to be here with you, pretending to be your wife when your real wife is riding down to Devon, no doubt in great fear. You should be with her. You should go after her.'

Clarenceux shook his head. The whole notion of Rebecca's shame left him confused. 'My wife – I know. I agree. I feel it, believe me. But I cannot properly look after her until this matter of the chronicle is resolved. She would not be safe and nor would my daughters. As for your shame . . . It is just the shock that has made you feel this way.'

'Maybe. I don't know what has made me feel so ... empty of pride.'

He searched for something to say to make her feel proud.

'You look beautiful in that dress. But you look no less beautiful in your own daily clothes. It is simply a finer frame for a lovely picture. So let us not say another word about shame. You are a fine woman and I am proud that you are prepared to pretend that I might be your husband.'

'Honeyed words, Mr Clarenceux. But you do not need to flatter me.'

'Let us go down to the hall and take some supper.'

She nodded. 'You had better put the robe back on.'

'The robe? Why?'

She wiped the tears from her face with her hand. 'Look at your doublet. You can still see the dried blood.'

37

hey were both quiet during the meal. The musicians struck up late in the evening and people started dancing; but neither Clarenceux nor Rebecca did more than look sadly at the jollity. She cried several times, trying to conceal her tears from both Clarenceux and the other guests at the inn. She drank three mazers of wine, reaching for her cup each time she found herself failing to control her nerves. Then she would smile nervously at Clarenceux and look away.

As they made their way from the hall into the half-light of the screens passage and out into the cold darkness, he took her hand in his. He did it almost without thinking; and Rebecca accepted it. He led the way up to the gallery, feeling for the door with his other hand. He lifted the latch and they entered.

The candle was still burning in its holder on the wall, casting a small gold glow across the room. Neither of them spoke. Clarenceux sat down on the near side of the bed. He assumed that the far side was her preferred place of sleeping, as that was where he had seen her earlier. She knelt down by the washing bowl and rinsed her hands and face, drying them on a linen towel draped over the stool. He watched her for a moment, then directed his gaze at his feet. He took off his robe and laid it across the end of the bed. He unfastened his belt and shoes, placing both on the chest beside the bed. He removed his doublet and ruff, seeing the bloodstains and remembering the fight. It made him feel sick, and he forced his mind away from the memory. Looking away, and taking a deep breath, he closed his eyes. Then he felt the cold as he stood in his shirt and hose. He pulled back the sheets and blankets and got into the bed. He turned on his side, facing away from Rebecca so she would see that he was not watching her.

Rebecca had to remove her dress. No one could have slept in a garment with upper sleeves so stiff with braid and brocade. She started to unfasten it behind her back, and then found herself struggling with the ties which were too high for her to reach.

Clarenceux listened to her movements. *That is a gentlewoman's dress. Gentlewomen are dressed by their servants; they do not dress themselves. What Goodwife Machyn is trying to do is impossible.* He felt sorry for her.

Rebecca stood still, silent and cold – and growing colder.

'Is everything all right?' he asked quietly.

'I was thinking, did you look in the chronicle for the dinner which took place here? The dinner that Lancelot Heath mentioned, when all the Knights met together.'

'I did. It gives no names. In fact, it says very little: only that it took place.'

She fell silent again, struggling with the dress. Eventually she gave in to the inevitable.

'Mr Clarenceux, I cannot unfasten this dress. Mistress Barker's maid helped me into it. I am very sorry, but could I prevail upon you ...'

Clarenceux slipped out of the bed and went round to her side. She turned her back to him, and bent her head. He looked at her pale neck in the candlelight, and then dropped his eyes to the fastening. It was quickly undone. He glanced at her neck again, and her back as the dress parted, and turned away.

'Do you leave the candle alight?' she asked as he climbed back into bed and lay down again, facing away from her.

'Yes. Let it burn down.'

He felt the ropes supporting the mattress shift with her weight.

They were loose, and had begun to lose their strength, with the result that the mattress sagged greatly in the centre. He could sense that she was rigid, on her back, struggling not to roll towards him. He too was holding himself from rolling towards her.

'Mr Clarenceux,' she whispered.

'Yes?'

'This is very awkward. I fear we are bound to touch one another.'

'I think that is a great likelihood, Goodwife Machyn. I apologise if I keep you awake.'

'No, Mr Clarenceux, it is I who should apologise to you. I would have taken the servant's bed, if there had been one.'

Clarenceux turned over and propped himself with an arm to prevent himself rolling into the middle. He saw her tear-streaked face in the light of the candle and lifted his other hand from under the sheets to put it on her shoulder.

'I feel for you,' he whispered.

She looked at him, shivering now. Cold and nerves – combined, they made her tremble all the more. 'Mr Clarenceux, I know we are only here together out of necessity, but I am grateful ...'

'You do not need to keep calling me by my title.'

'Sir, I am only pretending to be a gentlewoman. I am a merchant taylor's wife – I would not presume to address you in any other way.'

He was silent. He did not want to be the one who corrected her, to use the word 'widow'.

'Everything I do is false,' she went on. 'Every movement I make seems to be ungentle; every word I say is that of someone lower in class than you ...'

'Goodwife Machyn, this anxiety is not going to help you sleep. We must rest. Try to stop shivering.'

She nodded. After a short while she swallowed. More tears fell on the pillow. 'Will you ... will you hold me for a moment, Mr Clarenceux?'

Clarenceux put his arms round her shoulders awkwardly, trying to embrace her and yet not draw her close. But she came nearer, nestling against his body in the middle of the bed, resting her head on his shoulder.

'I am sorry,' she whispered. 'I just feel so ... so lost.'

'Goodwife Machyn, you are not lost. I owe you my life, for removing the chronicle.' He closed his eyes, remembering seeing Will Terry's body in Thomas's arms and Thomas's tear-covered, lined face.

'You owe me nothing, Mr Clarenceux. But thank you. Thank you for your understanding. Thank you for your warmth.'

38

Clarenceux was drifting in and out of consciousness. The scratching of rats in the walls kept him awake. So did Rebecca, shifting restlessly through the night. There were moments in his half-sleep when he thought he was lying at home, beside Awdrey, and the warmth of the woman beside him made him think of love. But then he would remember where he was, and he would turn both his body and his mind away from Rebecca and the dip in the bed to think about his wife. He thought about the chronicle, too, and as soon as he did that his mind fastened on to a whirling wheel, and went round and round, trying to sort out the Knights' names and dates. He kept pondering 13 June 1550 and 20 June 1557, searching for something that might connect them.

It would not be long until dawn. The candle had burnt down; it was completely dark. He felt Rebecca move again.

'Are you awake?' he whispered.

'Yes.'

'What are you thinking?'

She said nothing for a long while. 'I was wondering where we are going to go.'

'We will cross the river and go down to Chislehurst. A friend of mine lives there, a gentleman and an antiquary by the name of Julius Fawcett. He is a little outlandish, and very old-fashioned, but he is a good Catholic. He will be able to protect us for a few days.'

Rebecca moved her hand to his shoulder. 'And you?' she asked. 'What were you thinking?'

He shifted away from her and sat up, with his back against the tester. 'I was wondering what connects the two dates we know – the thirteenth of June 1550 and the twentieth of June 1557. A saint's day? Or some other commemoration or anniversary? I don't know. Henry said that he was sure I would recognise a quotation from the book of Job, if I saw one. But what can the Bible have to do with those dates?'

'Both entries in Henry's chronicle mention St Paul's Cross.'

'Yes, the abbot of Westminster and the bishop of Durham both preached there. It is the place where prelates deliver their most important sermons. But beyond that . . .'

The mattress undulated as she raised herself on to one elbow in the darkness. 'What if the other Knights' dates all relate to sermons preached by powerful men there?'

Clarenceux pictured the cross in London, in the cathedral yard. It was a large timber pulpit with a stone base and a lead roof, surmounted by a gilt cross, and probably the single most visited spot in the whole city. Huge crowds flocked there to listen to preachers: there were dozens of references to it in the chronicle. But there was no writing on it, no inscription. It was just a preaching place. 'I can't see that the cross can tell us anything,' he said.

'Perhaps Henry meant it to be a marker. Maybe all the Knights' dates relate to a different man preaching at that cross. Maybe the Knights we are seeking are just decoys and the real agents are the people who preached at that place? Maybe it is them we need to see.'

Clarenceux thought about it. *If Henry wanted to start a revolution he certainly would have needed the help of important people, such as the abbot of Westminster and the bishop of Durham. But Goodwife Machyn cannot be right.* 'The bishop of Durham in 1550 was Cuthbert Tunstall. He died four years ago. And the abbot of Westminster is locked in the Tower.'

'Even so, that might have been what Henry intended when he and the others established the Knights.'

'No. He would not have been so insistent that I contact Heath if the chronicle was simply going to lead us to dead and imprisoned men. What we need are more Arthurian names and dates. Henry said that when all the Knights were gathered, the secret would become apparent to *me*, no one else. He must have written something into it that only I would know.'

'If we are going to go into Kent,' Rebecca asked, lying down in the warmth of the bed again, 'does that not take us further from the other Knights?'

'Do you want to stay in London and be arrested?'

'Where is your courage, Mr Clarenceux?'

He swung his legs out of the bed and sat on the edge. 'I left it behind, years ago, when the duke of Suffolk marched out of Boulogne.'

'I don't believe you.'

For a long time he said nothing. 'I want to make sure you are safe first. I will come back to London and find the other Knights afterwards.'

Now it was her turn to be silent. He heard her move and felt the mattress shift.

'Are you well, Goodwife Machyn?'

'Yes, Mr Clarenceux. I was just reflecting on how lucky I was. To be married to Henry, for so many years. He was a considerate man too.'

39

Monday, 13 December

It was a bright mid-afternoon when Clarenceux and Rebecca arrived in Chislehurst, and approached Summerhill, the estate of Julius Fawcett. The wintry sun was going down, casting bright contrasts of shadow and light through the trees at the side of the road. They were riding horses that they had hired at Greenwich with money obtained from Crawley, the innkeeper at Mile End. Crawley had relented and admitted that he and his wife had been given a sum by Henry Machyn. Hard times had forced them to borrow from it and eventually it had all been spent. They had not expected that anyone would ask for it after so many years. In the end he gave Clarenceux fifty-six shillings, which he claimed was all the money he had in hand, and waived the three shillings and elevenpence of their bill. Clarenceux saw that the money was more than enough to pay for the ferry and horse hire, and respected the man for his honesty too. He took just forty shillings.

As they rode through Kent, Clarenceux imagined that Summerhill would be to them as a castle was to a medieval knight. It would be their refuge, where they could keep the chronicle safe. There they could take the time to plan their actions and from there they could make sorties. A medieval army did this to impose control on the neighbourhood; Clarenceux's vision was that they would ride to London, enter the city secretly by way of the blacksmith's gate, and find their way to the houses of the

Knights. They could use Machyn's niece's warehouse for shelter or, in the north of the city, there were some houses that he knew well near Aldersgate. He had received a royal grant of the income from them when first he had been appointed a herald, fifteen years ago; and he had taken it upon himself to inspect them regularly.

Clarenceux's thoughts kept him occupied for much of the journey. Rebecca too was silent. She found it difficult to understand all that had happened in the last three days. On Friday morning she had woken up as usual with Henry beside her. Later that day he had told her to go to Mistress Barker's house, and had left with a tearful goodbye that evening. And now he was dead. She was in hiding, her future bound to Henry's friend. She had even shared a bed with the man, and he had held her, at her request. She could not have predicted any of these things, nor any of the feelings she had had since first calling on Clarenceux. She had met him many times over the years, and even though she had only occasionally spoken to him herself, she listened with admiration to his conversation. His self-confidence and intelligence were very attractive; but she had always seen him as different from her. He was important, a gentleman, educated and well connected. He was barely a part of the world that she and Henry shared. Or, rather, they were barely a part of his.

Poor Henry. He had worshipped Clarenceux. 'The most noble man of my acquaintance' was how he used to describe him when talking about him. Henry was in awe of his learning and his social position. Clarenceux had been a soldier yet disapproved of war. He spoke with lords and knights yet valued his acquaintances among the lower classes. Never did Henry fail to mention that Clarenceux had been the herald who declared war on France. In Henry's mind, that portentous moment made Clarenceux's the voice of England, and the man himself the spokesman of the throne. It was too much – that her fate and his should suddenly have been woven into one, and her husband killed.

'There it is,' said Clarenceux, surprising her out of her reverie.

Rebecca looked ahead and saw an ancient stone mansion between the leafless trees. It was positioned on a ridge, looking out over the Thames valley to the north, with woods around it. She could see the lead roof of the great hall adjacent to a large crenellated tower, and buildings round a courtyard in front, with more buildings behind the hall. There was ivy in places: it was like a castle that time itself had chosen to defend. She could imagine men-at-arms riding out from the gatehouse to tilt at one another. Perhaps their ghosts still did. It was a picturesque but crumbling testimony to the distant century in which it had been built.

The view of the courtyard from under the gatehouse arch confirmed her initial impression of antiquity. The old windows looking outwards from the house had been small, barely larger than arrow slits, but those overlooking the courtyard were much larger. The house had been built defensively, in an age before guns were common. Large stone cisterns caught rainwater from the roof. To one side of the courtyard a spiral stone staircase in a ruined tower led nowhere – or, rather, it ascended into the past. The chamber to which it once had given access had long since vanished: the space in which men and women had talked, argued, fought, loved and died was now graced only with walls of air.

A servant boy ran over to take the reins of their horses as they dismounted in the grass-fringed outer court. There seemed to be a large number of servants carrying wood, or buckets of water. Clarenceux led Rebecca across the courtyard and through a tall arch into a wide passage. When they turned into the hall she was confronted with a lofty space, sixty feet long and forty feet high. It appeared even more ancient than the exterior, for the walls were decorated with heraldic banners and moth-eaten tapestries, all overlapping with old swords, pikes and bows. Long trestle tables indicated that the household ate together still, in the old fashion. On the dais was a table, as was usual; but above it was an old baldaquin, a canopy projecting out above the lord's seat in the centre. She had once been in the Guildhall in London and seen something similar, and it seemed like a relic from a remote age. Here was an old aumbry against the wall, its wood dented and dark, close to an old iron-bound chest. It was as if a magic spell had suddenly been broken and she had walked into a house from two hundred years ago, which had been forgotten by the rest of the world.

There was a sound from a doorway to the left. A short man with a kind, round face appeared. 'Good day to you, sir. I am James Hopton, chamberlain to . . .' He stopped himself and smiled. 'Why, it's Mr Harley. I haven't seen you for a long time. To think I was about to welcome you formally as a stranger. I humbly apologise. Here I am: chamberlain, steward, marshal and general groom to Mr Julius Fawcett, as I ever was. Sir, it is good to see you again.'

'Thank you, Hopton. And where is Julius? In his chamber?'

'No, coming fast to welcome an old friend,' called a voice from the dais. 'William Harley, herald of the meritorious and fellow champion of the ancient and glorious dead, I spied you coming from afar. Welcome to you and your companion!'

Julius was somewhere between fifty and sixty years of age – it was difficult to tell. Long black hair streaked with grey emanated wildly from his scalp in all directions. It was almost a surprise to see that a man with such outlandish hair was clean shaven. He was slim, and wore a fur-trimmed black robe over a green velvet doublet trimmed with gold brocade. He was quick on his feet for his age, walking with neat, precise footsteps towards Clarenceux and Rebecca. As he approached she noticed that his eyes were brown and full of sparkle, and his fingers were long and thin, with a gold ring on each one.

'Julius, heartily I greet you,' said Clarenceux, as he met his old friend with an embrace. 'Allow me to introduce Rebecca Machyn, whose husband has produced an antiquarian work of especial interest. Goodwife Machyn, this is Julius Fawcett, gentleman and antiquary, direct descendant of the famous Sir John Fawcett who built this house in the reign of Edward the Third.'

Julius noticed Clarenceux's head. The expansive style was set aside in an instant. 'You've been bleeding.'

'Julius, I will be straight with you. Perhaps even blunt. Goodwife Machyn and I are trying to evade a royal sergeant-at-arms called Richard Crackenthorpe. He is an agent of Francis Walsingham, who is attempting to uncover a scheme that involved Goodwife Machyn's husband, Henry Machyn, a man of the old religion. We have reason to believe Crackenthorpe has murdered Henry. He has certainly killed one of my servant boys and destroyed everything in my house. There was a fight, in the course of which I killed one of his soldiers. My wife has fled to her sister's house in Devon, not far from Exeter, with the children. I come here begging for safety, food, the use of your horses and advice. If I cannot rely on your support – and, as God is my witness, I can understand why you would not want to shelter us – then just say so, and we will be gone from here and leave you in peace.'

Julius shook his head. 'William, you cannot do me the honour of seeking my protection and then insult me by suggesting I am so inconstant as not to stand by you in your hour of need. If anything were to happen to you, I would not forgive myself. You must stay here. Money is in short supply, as well you know; but I can afford to feed you and shelter you. My noble progenitor, Sir John Fawcett, did not build thirty-five chambers in this house for the sake of my servants.'

Clarenceux embraced his friend again. 'You are a good man, Julius. I knew you would stand by me. Thank you.'

Julius waited a moment while Clarenceux recovered his composure. 'Actually, I have my own reasons for wanting to thwart Francis Walsingham. Did you know he grew up at Scadbury Park, the next manor? I've hated the devious little runt since he was ten years old. But let us go up to my study. I have spiced wine and Naples biscuits to warm you. It is chilly in this old hall, when it is empty. Warming to the soul but cold to the fingers.'

*

Rebecca learnt much about Julius and Clarenceux that afternoon. Both were animated: there was never a lull in their conversation or a moment of idle talk; everything they discussed was a matter of importance. She reflected on how much Henry would have liked to be there, to see his hero talking so earnestly with a man he clearly respected, trusted and considered his equal in every way.

They were sitting at a table in the centre of a room full of books. She had been impressed by the number of volumes in Clarenceux's study; but this upstairs chamber was both lined with books and stacked with them. Piles of them lay on the floor. Some were left open, heaped on one another. Each wall was lined with book presses. Late afternoon sunlight entered the chamber through a courtyard window and she watched the dust twisting and drifting in the air, hearing Clarenceux explain to his antiquarian friend everything that had happened over the last three days.

She learnt how many adversities Clarenceux had kept to himself. He spoke freely with Julius about recent events – about Henry's visit, the chronicle, his journey across London by night and his first meeting with Crackenthorpe. The account of his interrogation and subsequent sufferings in the cellar of Walsingham's house disturbed her. His emotion when describing to Julius the religious conviction he had felt in the cellar moved her. His tears on describing the sight of his dead servant boy in his manservant's lap made her own heart weep. She had not realised before how guarded he had been in speaking to her.

Through all the conversation Julius listened intently, asking questions and clarifying details. Attention turned to the chronicle: both men pored over her husband's uneven handwriting. Julius had no more idea than Clarenceux about the meaning of the Arthurian names and the dates. But as he remarked, at best they had just four of the nine names and only two dates.

'I should point out,' said Julius, 'if Henry Machyn said that only you will understand the secret of his chronicle, then I have to presume that my knowledge will not help you. All I can really offer you is a safe harbour.'

'That is something. There must be a hundred hiding places in this old house.'

'Oh, indeed there are. Although I am sure your enemies are used to searching old houses. But as it happens . . .' Julius drained the last of his wine. 'William, I am going to show you something that you have not seen before. Something I have never even told you about. I must swear you to secrecy.'

'Of course. And Goodwife Machyn?'

Julius paused and looked at her. He gave Clarenceux an enquiring look.

'She has already saved my life once, as you have heard.'

'Yes, I was listening. But I wanted to hear you say it.' Julius got up from his seat. He took down a large volume from a shelf nearby and placed it on the table. He opened it, so they could see it was a Bible.

'Both of you, place your hands on it.'

Clarenceux and Rebecca did so, their two hands side by side on the holy page.

'Do you both swear never to breathe a word of what you are about to see to anyone else, at the peril of your immortal soul and the judgement of almighty God?'

'I do,' they both said.

There was a moment's silence.

'Good. Follow me.'

Julius led them out of his library and through a series of three chambers with interconnecting doors. The fourth was a small antechamber with a fireplace: Julius's writing room. Flames quietly flickered around several thick pieces of oak on a pile of ash and embers. The room was warm and light, with a large window facing the courtyard and a large faded tapestry covering much of the walls. There was a chest and a single chair and table here, together with quill and ink and pen holder, and several piles of dusty books.

Julius lifted the lid of the chest, took out a couple of lanterns and removed the candles. Having lit the first candle at the fire, he reinserted it and passed it to Clarenceux. Then he lit his own.

'Follow me, and be careful on the steps.'

He lifted a corner of the tapestry and pushed back a piece of oak panelling. Inserting his hand, he turned a handle on the other side and a small, concealed door opened – no more than four feet high. With the candle before him, he bent down and went through. Clarenceux gestured for Rebecca to go before him.

Beyond the secret door was a straight stone staircase leading down, built within the wall of the tower. It was cold, dank and dark, and smelled musty. Rebecca and Clarenceux both trod anxiously, feeling the unevenness of the stone steps, running their hands along the cold wall. One storey below, there was a chink of light where a second secret door led into a ground-floor chamber: Clarenceux peered through and saw a disused room, the floor piled with papers and rusted horse armour, a shield, and a chest of tarnished pewter plates.

They continued down, below ground. Here was an undercroft, wholly devoid of natural light. Clarenceux pushed the door and saw by his candle that the room was vaulted and empty apart from a couple of old broken barrels. He turned back to the staircase. From here on down it was a spiral; Julius was still descending.

'Where does this lead?' Clarenceux asked, hearing the echo of his voice.

'You'll soon see.'

They continued down for another forty or fifty steps. At the bottom the stairs ended at the mouth of a passage. Clarenceux rubbed his knee, which hurt after the long descent. He lifted his lantern and inspected the rock but he could not identify it in the candlelight. He scraped the surface with his knife: it was soft and, where he had scratched it, white. It was chalk.

The passage sloped gently. At the upper end, far away, was a vague spot of greenish daylight. The descending tunnel led into complete darkness.

'There are miles of passages under the house,' said Julius, his voice echoing. He held his lantern aloft, illuminating his face as well as the passage. 'They are the remains of an ancient quarry.

The people who built them were probably looking for flints for their houses, but in so doing they created a labyrinth. When my ancestor, Sir John Fawcett, bought the manor he decided to build a fortified house on top and to fortify the passages beneath. The house and passages work together in a most subtle way. Up there, where you see that light, is an opening in the side of the hill, about forty feet beyond the corner of the outer courtyard, and thinly covered in ivy. Now, come and look at this. Mind, do not walk in front of my lantern. Keep back behind me.'

He led them up the passage towards the distant daylight. At first he walked at a normal pace but gradually he slowed. 'Careful,' he warned. 'There. Stop.'

At first neither Clarenceux nor Rebecca could see anything. The hillside opening was still almost a hundred yards away, and the floor looked as dark and as uneven as the rest of the passage. But then something caught his eye, something not quite right. And as he looked at it, he began to see that the chalk he was looking at was not horizontal, or nearly so, as the floor would be, but vertical, dropping down from the level he stood on. In fact, it was the far side of a shaft, about twelve feet long, and running the entire width of the passage.

'Take two steps further forward and you would fall into that chasm. It is forty-eight feet and three inches deep – I know because I measured it with a rope when I was a boy. You would land on a series of jagged rocks, placed there by Sir John to break bones, I imagine. And just supposing you managed to survive that, you would have to crawl in complete darkness through the tunnels for about half a mile – *if* you knew the way out.'

Clarenceux looked up at the opening. 'But why have the entrance outside the house? Why not inside where it would be better protected?'

'Ah. He was a clever man, Sir John. If he was already in the house, he could just escape into the tunnels the way we came down, by the stairs. But the tunnels allowed him to think differently from his contemporaries. Most castles, you see, had a sally port so their occupants could *escape* quickly and safely. Using these tunnels Sir John constructed a means whereby he could *enter* his house quickly and safely, even if being pursued. As you come into the tunnel from the daylight you are blinded – it takes your eyes time to adjust. Of course he knew where he was going and would run on into the darkness for sixty-seven paces. Then he would stop and feel for a stone jutting out on the right-hand side of the wall at head height. One step beyond that is a concealed passage to the right, which goes through the chalk there and comes out just to your left. His pursuers would not know about the passage; you can't see it, even with a lantern, as it's concealed by the rock. And coming from that direction the shaft resembles the rock floor, just as it does from here. If you are carrying a lantern, you do not even see a shadow. You do not realise there is a gap here until you step and feel nothing beneath your feet, and fall into the darkness.'

Clarenceux shuddered at the thought of falling so far underground – and not knowing what lay below.

'Did he often need to kill his pursuers, your ancestor?' Rebecca asked.

'Oh, yes. He was the sort of man who would grow bored in a castle during a siege and attack the enemy for his own amusement. He made enemies easily. A number of them ended up down there. Some of the bones I inspected as a boy might have belonged to wild animals but I expect most were human. Elsewhere in the tunnels there are three or four skeletons of men who died trying to find the way out.'

'Who else knows their way through the passages?'

'Outside the family, no one. Only the older servants know there are tunnels here, and that the secret passage from my study leads to them. After twenty years' service they are told. But, even then, they are strictly forbidden to come here. A few other people have been let into the secret from time to time – I sheltered a couple of priests down here last year. But otherwise this underworld is my family's own. That is why we have held on to this manor when all our others have been taken or disposed of. And that is why I swore both of you to secrecy. Now, come this way.'

Julius led them back down the long sloping tunnel to a large cavern, from which several passages led off in various directions. He made one turn then another, his lantern guiding them through the labyrinth. The temperature was warmer than above – warmer even than the hall had been. The air was still and dead. Apart from their footfall, there was no sound at all – except once, when Clarenceux thought he heard the dripping of water.

After five minutes they came to what seemed to be a long chapel cut out of the chalk: a nave with columns supporting the roof, and side aisles too. Glints of silver sparkled on the walls. At the end was an altar, covered with an ancient gold-embroidered cloth. Six candles and a gilt-silver crucifix were set upon it. Julius lit the candles, and a golden glow filled the cave.

Clarenceux was astonished. There were jewelled crosses on the walls, and reliquaries in carved niches in the columns. Books were piled high in one of the aisles, next to vellum documents in barrels. He could see a chest full of silver pattens, gilt-silver chalices and more crosses.

'Julius, you said money was in short supply.'

'This is not my property. It belongs to the Church; I simply protect it. Much of it came from the abbeys, taken by abbots, priors and monastic treasurers to stop it falling into the hands of the old king. Several monastic libraries are here, and their archives. As you can see, your chronicle will be safe.'

'There are no locks,' Rebecca observed. 'Anyone could come down here.'

Julius gave a little laugh. 'Exactly. If I had told you that I would place the chronicle somewhere without a lock on it, you would have thought me foolish or mad. But locks tell you where secrets are hidden. Down here the hidden and the secret are one. There is no need to lock things away – only almighty God and my sons and I know how to find this place. And God and we have an agreement. He won't tell anyone if we don't.'

40

'You have left a trail of devastation across the city,' shouted Walsingham. 'I thought when we spoke yesterday, in this very chamber, that the worst you had done was kill a servant boy.'

'What are you accusing me of?' retorted Crackenthorpe, facing the small man on the other side of the table.

'It's not me accusing you. It's Clarenceux's manservant, and he has a host of witnesses. Not only did you hang the boy but you also stole Clarenceux's horses.'

'I did not steal them. I took them as compensation for the murder of my brother.'

'You had no right simply to appropriate another man's property just because you felt aggrieved. There are courts—'

'I don't give a damn about courts. No one kills a member of my family, or blinds one of my men in one eye, and lives to brag about it. No one.'

'Don't be a fool, Crackenthorpe. It is not a personal matter. Regard it as such and you will get yourself killed. You'll betray me. You failed to keep Clarenceux in your sight – that is what matters most. That he killed one of your men is not my failing but yours. You should have posted more guards. You should have followed him yourself.'

Crackenthorpe suddenly kicked over the chair in front of him and stamped on it, splitting the struts. He stamped again, then pulled off one of the legs and held it like a cudgel. He pointed it at Walsingham. 'So it's my fault that Clarenceux killed my brother? My fault that Ralph French was blinded? I have a good mind to beat your brains out, here and now.'

Walsingham stared him down. 'Yes, it's your fault. And beating me won't change what you've done. It will remove your only protector – the only man who will save you from the gallows. You are responsible for the death of that servant boy. And Machyn's. And that of the Scottish assassin. And the theft of the horses. And the fact that Clarenceux is at large. You have failed on almost every count. If the course of the law were to run freely, you would draw your final breath this very day.'

Crackenthorpe gripped the chair leg more firmly. 'I found Machyn's will. Not you. And I found Machyn himself too. No one else stayed out that godforsaken night. I waited for hours in the cold and the rain – and not only did I find Machyn but I discovered that Clarenceux was part of the plot. You had not even imagined that he was involved. I protected Draper from the Scots assassin and I found out about the Knights of the Round Table. Don't tell me I have failed on every count. I have paid a very high price, in your service. And I have succeeded in ways you did not foresee.'

Walsingham stepped round the table until he stood barely five feet from the taller man. His voice was calm. 'Do not presume you can speak to me in this manner.'

There was silence. Suddenly Crackenthorpe smashed the leg of the chair down on the edge of Walsingham's table, breaking the leg in two. He threw the piece into the fireplace. 'I'll speak how I see things, Mr Walsingham. I'll do things my way. I will kill Clarenceux. I have sworn it and I will do it. And if you try to stop me, I will kill you too.'

'Don't even think of it. I could crush you.'

Crackenthorpe laughed. 'You? Look at the size of you!'

'Exactly, Crackenthorpe. Look at the size of me. I am the State. I am the force of law. If you kill the body of Francis Walsingham, you have not even begun to touch me. I am just one of the many instruments of her majesty. I hang men like you every day by the hundred – all across the country – and I glory in those hangings, the true measure of my power.'

Crackenthorpe stared at Walsingham, the black skull cap, the relentless will. 'All right. I have made mistakes. But I swear that what I said is true. I will kill Clarenceux. And I will kill anyone who tries to stop me.'

'First you must find him. Then you must let me interrogate him. Afterwards you can do what you want.'

'I will find him, be certain of it.'

'And the other Knights of the Round Table – you will find them too.'

'Draper we have already seen. Nicholas Hill was found in Queenhithe ward by the guards I had posted looking for Clarenceux. He ran as far as the Guildhall before they brought him down.'

'Has he talked?'

'He will soon.'

'I don't care about his welfare, as well you know, but I don't want to offer the authorities any more reasons to indict you. Their interference will just make our problems worse. Don't kill him. What about the others, Michael Hill and Daniel Gyttens?'

'No sign of them. Yet.'

'And the blacksmith's house, the one by which Machyn came and went. Have you identified it?'

'There are no houses on the walls owned by anyone called Mason. But there are only a limited number of ways into the city. I will know by this time tomorrow.'

41

At Summerhill, Julius's wife Lychorus joined them for supper. She was a pleasant, round-faced woman who wore a wide ruff, elegant gold-embroidered clothes and a radiant smile. It was difficult for Clarenceux and Rebecca to make a meaningful contribution to the conversation, or even to answer all her questions fully and openly. The principal topic was the two Fawcett sons, one of whom was at Oxford and the other in Venice. Rebecca smiled at Lychorus and spoke occasionally but felt awkward, knowing she was behaving falsely, like a woman acting above her station. They retired early, Rebecca to go to bed, Clarenceux to drink wine with Julius.

Rebecca and Clarenceux were assigned adjacent chambers in the great tower. Hers was as comfortable a room as she could imagine. There was a fire already alight when she was shown to her bed, and the maid helped her undress in front of it. The walls were panelled and covered with bright red, blue and gold tapestries. The shutters were closed, and the hangings around the bed were clean – newer than almost everything she had seen in the house. The silver ewer was full of fresh water, the basin recently polished. The candles on the table made everything in the room glow in the winter dark. She undressed, snuffed the candles out as was her custom, and got into bed. She lay between clean sheets, listening to the crackle of the fire.

Clarenceux stayed up drinking sack with Julius until late. The drink made him vulnerable to his sadness. His entire life lay in ruins, he explained. He had lost his home and his wife, his children and his friends. He began to lose himself in wine-soaked self-recrimination.

'William, I know why you are talking like this. I can see that these are your honest feelings. But I must be honest with you too. You sound full of self-pity. Tomorrow I want you to reflect on this moment and to realise that this was when you were at your lowest – lower even than when you believed you were going to be killed, for then you did not know what you had lost. I am prepared to shelter you, and to guard your chronicle. But you must be yourself: your bold, intelligent, well-meaning self. I have no desire to shelter a self-pitying wreck, or to risk myself for the sake of a traitor awaiting his own betrayal. But a man who has lost almost everything and is still fighting a holy Catholic war because he truly believes he is in the right – he has my respect and my unquestioning service.'

Clarenceux was left speechless. Julius was exhorting him to be himself, but that now seemed impossible. What Julius was referring to was a man he had been in the past, not the man he was now. He felt hollow. He mumbled a reply: 'Believe me, Julius, I *am* willing to fight ...' but his voice trailed off. It was not that he was lying – it was simply that he could see that Julius was right. He was becoming a self-pitying wreck – if he had not already become it.

Julius gently urged him to go to bed. He stood up, embraced his friend, and walked unsteadily towards the stairs.

As Clarenceux climbed to his chamber, Rebecca sighed in her bed, trying to breathe deeply. A heavy weight seemed to have settled on her chest. She put back the blankets and tried to breathe again. Nerves racked her body. Or, rather, the feeling of being so alone. Her life was like a street with houses on either side, and every house was someone else's home. She just had to carry on walking until she came to the end of that long street, when there would be no more houses, no more people.

She heard the sound of footsteps on the tower staircase.

Clarenceux lifted the candle and crossed to the door of his chamber, the old floorboards creaking as he walked. He looked at the door on his left, which he knew was Rebecca's. He stared at it for some few minutes.

Inside, she listened, aware of his presence.

In his mind he saw her looking at him, speaking to him with her eyes. Gradually the outward reminders of his life came back: Will's dead body, the smashed furniture of his house, Crackenthorpe's scarred face, the man he had killed in the street. He thought of Awdrey's vulnerability and Rebecca's need for his protection ... His life was being torn between the opposites of fear and love. He wished he had been able to see it when Julius had spoken to him but then he had been too dismayed to see anything clearly. Julius had been right to castigate him – but he had been looking from the outside. On the inside, his life was simply a matter of fear and love. And he could embrace either all his fears ... or everything he loved.

Rebecca heard him take another two steps, lift the latch to the adjacent chamber, and close the door.

42

Tuesday, 14 December

It was a bitterly cold morning. A harsh frost had whitened the landscape, touching the fallen leaves of the autumn with ice and freezing solid the puddles in the road. As Clarenceux and Rebecca rode back to Greenwich on their hired horses, leading two more borrowed from Julius, they saw the crests of the hills behind them powdered with snow. Long icicles hung down from the thatched roofs of cottages. The rooks in the trees on either side of the road *caw-cawed* in their gathering, anxious at the hardness of the ground.

There were few people on the road and none who regarded the travellers with any suspicion. None the less, Clarenceux rode with his velvet cap pulled down low and the collar of his robe pulled high. At Greenwich they returned the horses and set out to ride along the south bank to Southwark. The tower of the old abbey church came into view, as did the spires and towers of the churches north of the river and the houses on London Bridge. They fell into silent thoughtfulness. The nearer they came to London, the greater the danger.

'Are you worried?' Clarenceux asked.

She did not grace his question with an answer.

'We need not both go into the city. You could stay in Southwark.'

Rebecca brought her horse to a standstill. 'If one of us should go alone, it should be me. I will arouse less suspicion.'

Clarenceux rode on. He was wearing gloves that Julius had given him but, holding the reins, his hands were fists. Rebecca could see that the leather across his knuckles was taut. She urged her horse on.

'Well?' she asked after a minute more of his silence.

Clarenceux stared straight ahead at the tower of the abbey. 'When Daniel entered the lions' den, it was a test of faith. And when the king went to the lions' den in the morning and called out to Daniel, asking him if God had protected him, Daniel replied, "God has sent an angel who has shut the lions' mouths."' He rode on in silence for a few paces. 'It is your choice,' he added, glancing at her. 'I hope you will come with me. Your company is a support to me. You keep me mindful of my duty. You give me strength. But ultimately, our fate is in God's hands. If He wants us to succeed, then He will protect us. He will send an angel to cover the eyes of those watching.'

'Mr Clarenceux, do you think you can presume so much? Did almighty God save you from that man at my house when you went there, the one you killed? Did God shield you from the other man who was watching you?'

'Perhaps He did.'

'If He did, then you should be thankful and humble, and not so proud as to think He will protect you a second time. Do not put the Lord to the test.'

Clarenceux stopped and turned to her. 'Do you believe we are doing His work, Goodwife Machyn? In your heart, do we have a choice?'

'Yes, I do believe we are doing His work,' she said, looking him in the eye. 'But we do have a choice. We could choose to run.'

'I am too angry to run. I am ashamed of what has happened to my family – I have brought ruin on them. I am ashamed that I did not protect your husband. I am ashamed that I killed a man. I am ashamed that I believed that God had performed a miracle for me when I was in the cellar of Walsingham's house.

There were things that Julius said to me last night, as well, that made me feel ashamed. That was my weakest moment ...'

He could not bring himself to say more.

The bell of Southwark Abbey rang out. Twelve long chimes touched the icy eaves of houses near and far.

'God will protect us, Mr Clarenceux. I believe that. Because He is angry too.'

43

They left Julius's horses at the Bell Inn in Southwark as the clock struck one. From there it was a short walk to London Bridge. The tall houses on either side of the bridge peered over them and darkened the thoroughfare so that it felt more like a narrow alley than a river crossing. The crowds intensified the feeling of being hemmed in: carts and wagons were being driven across, as well as cattle and sheep. Some wealthy men and women were visiting the small jewellers' shops that proliferated here. The way was too narrow for so many people and vehicles; Rebecca took Clarenceux's arm and once again pretended they were man and wife, avoiding the women with baskets on their arms and the men leading packhorses.

Clarenceux walked fast despite his bruised knee, which worried her. There were bound to be watchmen at the gatehouse on the north side of the bridge.

'Slow down a little,' she muttered as they stepped around another slow-moving cart. 'You are drawing attention to yourself.'

Clarenceux slowed. His gait fell into line with Rebecca's as they reached the middle of the bridge. His attention remained fixed on the far end.

Rebecca tried to look ahead to the three men waiting there. Had they been warned to watch out for them? She could see them now: they were armed with side-swords and halberds and wearing breastplates. A fourth man appeared, holding a pike and inspecting a cart that was making its way out of the city.

'What shall we do?' she whispered anxiously.

Clarenceux said nothing. He kept walking.

It is as if he is going into battle, so purposefully he walks. Perhaps the watchmen are less wary of those coming in, expecting that we are still inside the city and more likely to be trying to escape than re-entering it? If we have to run, what will we do? We cannot jump into the river – our limbs would freeze stiff in the cold.

She turned to Clarenceux and saw his mouth moving. She caught only a few whispered words: '. . . in our hour . . . Lord, bless thy humble . . .'

They were twenty paces away, fifteen, ten. A feeling of desperation was growing, threatening to take hold of her. She knew that she had to do something. Clarenceux was so certain, walking so determinedly, that she was sure he was going to confront the guards, and try to fight all four of them. And they were armed. But what could she do? She held on to his arm.

One of the guards saw them approaching and held up his hand.

'Your name, sir?'

'My name?'

Rebecca's heart was pounding. She looked beyond the guard to his three companions: two were not paying attention but one was watching them.

'My name?' repeated Clarenceux in the declamatory tone of his profession. 'You need to ask me my name? This would not happen in Cambridge. It would not happen in Norwich. Just because I am not riding a horse into the city, you want to know my name, as if I am someone you might haul before a justice of the peace. Well, I am a justice of the peace myself. My name, my good man, is George Courtenay, of Moreton Courtenay in Devonshire, cousin to the late earl of Devon. And this is my wife. What, pray, is your name?'

The watchman glanced at his fellow guardsmen. 'My name is no matter, Mr Courtenay. I am sorry I had to bother you.'

'I am sure you are just doing your duty,' Clarenceux replied.

'Indeed, perhaps this is fortuitous. We are newly arrived and unfamiliar with all the lanes and streets. Can you please direct us to the parish of St Dionis Backchurch?'

The watchman nodded, and turned to point the way. Rebecca wanted to run. The second guard lost interest and looked away.

'Yes, Mr Courtenay, it is an easy walk. The bridge leads directly into New Fish Street and then Gracechurch Street. At the crossing with Fenchurch Street you need to turn right. You'll see St Dionis on the other side of the road, about a hundred yards further on.'

'Thank you, I am much obliged,' said Clarenceux, making a polite bow as if he were indeed a foreigner from the southwest of the country.

'I thought we were Mr and Mistress Lowe,' said Rebecca as they walked up Gracechurch Street.

'It came into my mind to say something grandiose,' explained Clarenceux.

'Will you warn me next time?'

Clarenceux stopped and looked round. 'Let us turn left here, rather than go where they think we were heading. We can call first on Michael Hill, opposite St Mary Woolnoth. But I think it might be better if we were not to walk together. If Crackenthorpe sees me there is no need for you to be arrested and tortured too. If they take me, you can slip down an alley and get away. And if that happens, go back to Julius.'

The house was a modest two-storey building but had glazed windows: a mark of comfort denoting a reasonably prosperous owner. Clarenceux told Rebecca to wait further down the street in case there were soldiers inside.

He knocked hard on the door with his gloved hand. There was no answer.

He turned and looked around: a few snowflakes were falling. Two young men in wide-brimmed, tall black hats and smart velvet doublets walked by at a pace, both laughing at their conversation. A water-carrier's cart trundled past on solid oak wheels, a large water butt on the back. A moment later a woman in a long brown dress and a white cap appeared. She was carrying a baby and held a toddler by the hand. The child stamped to break the ice in a small puddle as he passed Clarenceux but the mother hauled him on, glancing nervously at the stranger.

Clarenceux turned and knocked again, firmly. Still there was no answer. He continued to wait.

Rebecca came over. 'That woman, with the children – did you see her?'

'I did.'

'She was looking at you all the time. She has gone into the house behind this one, in the next street.'

Clarenceux knocked again and waited for a few seconds more. There was no sound from within.

'Very well, let us call there, then.'

They went round to the house that Rebecca indicated. She stood back and allowed Clarenceux to knock. A shutter opened upstairs and the woman appeared.

'What?'

Clarenceux looked up and was about to speak when Rebecca held up a hand to silence him.

'We need to speak to Mr Hill,' she called. 'He is in danger.'

'Don't I know that,' replied the woman. 'Soldiers been here all last night and all morning. Wait there.' And with that she shut the window.

Clarenceux looked at Rebecca.

'Woman to woman, it's sometimes better,' she said. 'People like you frighten people like her.'

A minute later the door opened a fraction and the woman in the white cap peered out. 'Come in,' she said, looking up and down the street behind them. Clarenceux and Rebecca entered. The woman shut the door.

'This is Mr William Harley, Clarenceux King of Arms,' explained Rebecca, adding 'a herald' when she saw the blank look on the woman's face. 'My name is Rebecca Machyn. We know that soldiers are looking for Mr Hill. They have already killed one of Mr Hill's friends.'

'Killed a man, you say? The soldiers – they came yesterday afternoon. And then again in the evening. Mr Hill, he didn't come back home. Mistress Hill was in such a state, not knowing where he was or who had taken him. She is staying with Goodman Sansom and his wife across the way.'

Clarenceux asked, 'Do you know if anyone visited him recently – apart from the soldiers?'

'But of course, sir. All the time there are comings and goings from that house. Mr Hill is very well thought of.'

'Can you direct us to Goodman Sansom's house?' asked Rebecca.

'Out of this door, turn right and then turn left; go past the lane by the church and it's the third house on the right.'

'We are much obliged to you,' said Clarenceux, lifting his cap a fraction and turning to the door.

Rebecca caught up with him in the street, lifting the hem of her skirt to hurry along at his rapid pace.

'They've started rounding them up already,' she said.

'Without question.'

'But even if they arrest just two or three Knights, we are never going to unlock the secret. We need all the names and dates.'

'And Crackenthorpe has many men,' agreed Clarenceux. 'There are just the two of us.'

It only took them a brisk minute's walk to reach Sansom's house. The door was promptly opened by the householder himself. He led them through the front parlour – where piles of sawn wood lay in mute witness to his work fitting wainscoting – to a rear room, newly panelled and warm. There were five triangular chairs – two of them occupied – and a trestle table. In the fireplace a small pot of vegetables was simmering on a trivet placed among the embers on a large pile of ashes.

Two women sat beside the fireplace. The older one, facing them, was about sixty, white-haired and very pale. This seemed to be Mistress Hill, judging by her hollow cheeks and reddened eyes. When Clarenceux asked her about her husband she seemed almost unable to reply, she was so weak.

'I don't know where he is or how he is,' she whispered. 'I just wish he would come back. And that the soldiers would go away and stay away.'

'But is there anything you can tell us that would help us find him? His life is at stake, and so are the lives of others. It will help him and us if we can find him soon. Who has been to visit him recently?'

'Mistress Hill,' Rebecca interjected, 'the men who are hunting your husband have already killed mine. I am a widow because of them. Don't let it happen to you. If you can help us find him quickly then maybe we can save him. Please.'

The hesitation showed. 'Your husband was Henry Machyn? The man who did the black sheets in the churches at funerals?'

'Yes.'

'James Emery called yesterday morning. He had heard that Henry Machyn was dead at the plague pit, and had arranged with my husband to collect the body and give it a proper burial. They left straight away, and that was the last I saw of him.'

'He left with James Emery?' Clarenceux asked.

'That's right.'

'Where does James Emery live?'

Clarenceux had directed the question to Mistress Hill but it was Rebecca who answered. 'Near my house, in Huggin Alley. We've got to go back into Queenhithe ward. Thank you, Mistress Hill, for your help. Mr Clarenceux and I will do all we can to find your husband and make sure he is safe.'

'One last thing,' asked Clarenceux. 'Do you know where your son Nicholas is?'

The woman shook her head. 'I have not heard from him for several days.'

'Thank you again,' said Rebecca, turning to Clarenceux. He nodded to her, made a polite bow to the women and left the room.

44

⚜

The two watchmen were very cold as they waited on Garlick Hill, at the junction on the northeast of Queenhithe ward. They had been told to keep warm by walking between the two crossroads: the one on Garlick Hill and the other at the top of Little Trinity Lane. That short exercise was not enough, though. Rubbing their hands together was not much good either. Even the one who had a travelling cape was cold. And now it was snowing. Large flakes the size of silver pennies were falling slowly through the London chill on to the frozen mud of the street.

Their instructions were to remain there until dusk. Another two and a half hours. The one without the travelling cape had taken to putting his hands under his arms to keep them warm. But Sergeant Crackenthorpe had walked past only five minutes ago and shouted at him for not attending to his duty.

'At least it will be another hour before he barks at you again,' muttered his companion after Crackenthorpe had gone.

They watched the people coming and going. They had been given a list of names, which only one of them could read; but they had been told to look in particular for a tall man in his mid forties with short dark hair and a trimmed beard, and a woman in her late thirties, of average height, with long brown hair. No one they could see at that moment matched either the man or the woman. There was a servant boy, probably delivering a message, and three women coming back from the markets.

None of them were like the description of Goodwife Machyn. A man in a tall hat with a proud demeanour was the nearest to the description of Clarenceux in the street, but he had no beard. The unguarded confidence with which he walked made it very unlikely that he was their man. Otherwise there was no one but the old water-carrier, driving his emaciated horse.

The watchman with the cape decided that he would stop and question the man in the hat, if only to relieve the boredom. As he did so the other watchman leant against the wall of a house. The water-carrier's cart trundled past and turned into Great Trinity. The watchman looked at the water butt and the solid wooden wheels, but saw nothing suspicious. He shifted his attention to the women walking towards him from the market.

Clarenceux, pressed against the barrel on the far side of the cart, let himself slip back to the ground and started walking again, his legs shielded by the cartwheels and his body by the huge barrel. He signalled to the water-carrier.

'Next left, into Little Trinity Lane. Then first right, into the alley.'

The water-carrier obediently turned right into the alley that ran opposite Henry Machyn's house and came to a halt. Clarenceux tapped on the barrel. 'We're here.'

Rebecca stood up cautiously in the empty butt and looked around.

'Hurry,' he urged.

'Help me out then.'

Clarenceux climbed up on to the cart, feeling a twinge in his knee, and held out his arms to help her, placing his hands on either side of her body and lifting her so she could put a foot on the top of the barrel and climb out. He stepped back down and fished in his pocket for a coin, which he held up between his thumb and forefinger as he spoke to the water-carrier. 'Here's an extra shilling. Head down to the river and go along Thames Street. Take note of whom you see there – how many men are loitering. Then come back to this point. It should take you about twenty minutes, and there will be an extra shilling for you when you come back. Have you got that?'

The water-carrier nodded and drove on.

Rebecca led the way past her house and past Mistress Barker's on the corner, and round the front of Painter-Stainers' Hall into Huggin Alley. She walked briskly and silently across to a modest merchant's house and knocked on the door. Clarenceux held back, on the north side of Huggin Alley, watching all around.

No one answered.

She knocked again. Clarenceux noticed movement in an upstairs window, as if someone was trying to see who was calling. But still there was no answer.

There were men riding up Little Trinity Lane towards them. At first he thought nothing of them – he had grown easier in his mind since they had entered the city. But then he noticed that there was a very tall dark-haired man riding in the centre of the group.

Clarenceux edged away from the corner. As soon as he was out of sight, he hurried across the road. 'Crackenthorpe is coming.'

At that moment the door opened. Rebecca started to speak to the elderly manservant who held it but Clarenceux pushed past him and dragged Rebecca inside, closing it behind them.

'My apologies, my good man, but desperate situations call for desperate measures. I must speak to your master now – it is a matter of life and death. We have little time: perhaps only a minute.'

'Sir, your manner of entering is most shocking – rude, I say. If my master were here no doubt he would . . .'

'He is not here?' said Rebecca.

'Don't tell me,' added Clarenceux. 'He hasn't been here all night.'

'Not since he went out late yesterday afternoon, no, sir. Now, will you leave.'

'Yesterday afternoon? So . . . Is Michael Hill here?'

The servant froze. Confusion showed in his face. 'Sir, I ask you again to leave . . .'

Clarenceux heard footsteps and looked up. A man was standing at the top of the stairs – about sixty and white-haired, but with a handsome manly face, dressed in a furred winter robe. He took two steps down and stood there, levelling a long-barrelled pistol at the intruder.

Clarenceux held up a hand. 'Shooting me would be a mistake, Mr Hill. I know you are one of the Knights of the Round Table, and that is why I must speak to you. There is a man outside at this very moment who would probably torture you if he knew you were here.' He took a step forward and stood on the bottom step. 'We are friends of Henry Machyn – this is Rebecca Machyn, his wife. Is James Emery with you?'

'No.' The man's expression did not waver. Nor did the aim of the pistol.

'I have no time to explain, Mr Hill. The man outside – if he finds me, he will kill me. He will probably kill you too, and Goodwife Machyn. Everything that the Knights of the Round Table stand for hangs by a thread. May I come up?'

Michael Hill let the gun down slowly. Clarenceux and Rebecca quickly ascended and followed him into a wide, comfortable chamber at the front of the house. The large windows let in plenty of light and a fire was burning on the hearth. There was a settle and a bench there, gathering the heat. Hill positioned himself with arthritic slowness on the settle. Rebecca sat on the bench. Clarenceux went straight to the window.

'I am sorry,' said Hill. 'When I heard the knock at the door, I was afraid.'

'I have been in a similar position,' said Clarenceux. The street below was clear. He turned back to face the others. 'I understand.'

Hill continued. 'I am sorry about your husband, Goodwife Machyn. He was a kind man. I knew him for many years: a very gentle soul.'

'James Emery told you?'

'Yes. On Sunday a message arrived here: one of the gravediggers is a man of our acquaintance and a follower of the old religion. He knew Henry Machyn by sight, and knew that we were his friends. Having realised that Machyn did not die of plague, he thought we would want to know.'

'What did Henry die of?' Rebecca asked. 'I mean, how did the gravedigger know?'

Michael Hill said nothing. He looked into the flames of the fire. Clarenceux was tense, listening for the sounds of men outside, hearing only the crackling of the fresh logs. Rebecca too was inwardly frantic, the tears close to her eyes.

'Mr Hill, I *have* to know.'

Hill shook his head. 'If you want the truth, his legs were broken. Both of them. Below the knee.'

'Christ have mercy!' exclaimed Clarenceux.

Rebecca made the sign of the cross on her breast.

'We made plans to bring the body back to Little Trinity for burial but when we arrived there were soldiers everywhere – a watchman placed to guard Henry's house had been killed. So we agreed to meet the following day. Yesterday morning we met, and saw the priest, and James went in the afternoon to fetch the body while I waited here. He did not return. That is all I can tell you.'

Clarenceux looked at Rebecca: she was sitting forward on the bench, looking down. *It must be bitterly hard news. But the truth is that that is what is likely to happen to us too. This is not the time or place for compassion. This is the time to meet steel with steel.*

He turned again towards the window to see if anyone was in the street. It was still clear; but the knowledge that Crackenthorpe was in the area was worrying. 'I presume James Emery is also one of the Knights?' he asked.

'Yes. Sir Yvain.'

Clarenceux turned round. 'And you are?'

Hill was seated with his hands on his knees. No less anxiety showed in his face. 'Sir Ector,' he said after a while.

'Good, we're getting somewhere. How many more names do

you know? I need to know everything about the Knights of the Round Table.'

'Whom else have you seen?'

'Only Lancelot.'

Hill looked back into the fire. 'There were nine of us originally. Sir Arthur Darcy, Henry and John Heath were the founders. They agreed on the scheme: each man would have a date and a name, and when all the names and dates were gathered together they would reveal the key to the book that Henry Machyn was writing. It was a sort of chronicle, which would give us the knowledge to overthrow the queen. Only the three founders knew exactly how, though. John Heath died long ago. Darcy died two years ago. And now Henry.'

'What other names and dates are there?' asked Rebecca, wiping her face and trying to recover her composure. 'We know of King Clariance of Northumberland. Lancelot told us his own name and also remembered hearing the names of Sir Reynold and Sir Dagonet – though he could not remember who Sir Reynold was. Now you have told us two more, Yvain and Ector. That's six. What are the others?'

'When Sir Arthur Darcy died, my son, Nicholas, took the name of Sir Reynold. As to the other three – I do not know.'

'What about dates?' Clarenceux asked, walking over to stand by the settle. 'Lancelot told us his: the thirteenth of June 1550. Henry gave me the twentieth of June 1557. Both of those appear in the chronicle in relation to sermons preached at St Paul's Cross. What is your date?'

Michael Hill shook his head. 'We are all under strict instructions not to reveal our dates except when gathered together.'

Clarenceux looked the old man in the eye. 'With respect, if James Emery has been arrested, he will not be gathering with us. Not here or anywhere. Lancelot Heath is in hiding too – he will not be joining us. The last of the founders is dead. Unless we work together we will each go to the grave with our secret dates. And much good they will have done us.'

'I swore an oath. It feels like a betrayal.'

'How many dates do you know?' asked Rebecca, leaning forward on the bench. 'Do you know your son's? And Mr Emery's?'

'If it helps at all, think of this as a different sort of gathering,' said Clarenceux. 'We are gathering the Knights' names and dates. It is all we can do – with the streets being watched and our numbers being reduced through fear and murder.'

Hill was silent for a while. Then he said, 'I know two. My son's and my own.'

'Tell us,' said Clarenceux, who had walked back to the window. Snow was falling thickly now. 'We have the chronicle in a safe place. We can begin to make this work . . .'

Rebecca nodded. 'If James Emery has been arrested, as looks likely – and if your son has also been arrested – we will need something with which to bargain for their release. If we understand the code, then maybe we can talk to Walsingham. God knows that my skin crawls at the very thought, but it might be our only option.'

Hill remained silent.

Clarenceux looked out of the window again. Still no watchmen or guards were in sight. The snow showed that no one had walked that way since they had arrived. 'Goodwife Machyn is right. This nightmare is not going to be over until we understand this code. For any of us – you included.'

Hill put his face in his hands, and thought. 'The eighteenth of June, 1555,' he said eventually.

Rebecca nodded. 'And your son's?'

'The fifteenth of June, 1552. God curse you if you betray him and me.'

'You have my most solemn oath,' Clarenceux responded, coming away from the window. 'But what of the other Knights? We know about William Draper and Daniel Gyttens – although we are not quite sure where Gyttens lives.'

'I don't know the names of the others. One has no name – or at least he is not allowed to repeat it. But you'll find Gyttens on

Paternoster Row. Ask the bookseller there, Francis Colwell. Tell him that you wish to buy a book of sonnets by Gyttens. That's the code. Otherwise he'll deny all knowledge of the man.'

'We will. Thank you for that too.' Clarenceux looked at Rebecca. 'We must go now.' Turning back to Hill, he added, 'I want you to know this: Walsingham searched Heath's house some days ago. He has subsequently searched both mine and Henry Machyn's. If James Emery has been arrested, they must know who he is and where he lives. I guarantee you: men will search this house this evening or tonight. I strongly recommend that you change your lodgings – and soon.'

'I hear what you are saying, Mr Clarenceux. And I respect your reasons for saying it. But I feel I must remain here, out of loyalty to Mr Emery. I said I would, and I intend to stand by my word. There are hiding places.'

Rebecca was astonished at his complacency. 'Mr Hill, listen to Mr Clarenceux. His advice is urgent and important. They will destroy everything in this house and they will torture you. You must do as he says.'

'What threat could I possibly be to them?'

'They killed my husband – and he was sixty-six years old.'

Clarenceux agreed. 'It's not a matter of whether you are a threat or not, it's enough simply to know a threat exists. Your knowledge is their weakness. If you don't understand that, you are in grave peril.'

45

Clarenceux and Rebecca had to wait for several minutes for the water-carrier to return. Rebecca insisted that it was Clarenceux's turn to ride inside the water butt. He had accepted this quietly at first, being distracted with his thoughts of the chronicle; but as the time passed and the snow continued to fall he began to argue. Why should he travel in a water butt? True, it was capacious – it was more than four feet in diameter – but it was simply an indignity. He would walk beside the cart. Rebecca could travel safely in the butt.

She protested. 'You are the one to whom Henry entrusted the chronicle. We must keep you safe.'

'I have no intention of hiding in a barrel while you risk yourself.'

'I cannot quite fathom your excessive pride, Mr Clarenceux. You tell other people to be practical, and yet here you are, sought by a royal sergeant-at-arms who has placed watchmen to find you, and you won't even get into a barrel. You know Sergeant Crackenthorpe is riding around this area. It is dangerous for you.'

'It is no less dangerous for you, Widow Machyn.'

The word hit home. It hurt.

Rebecca walked away. Clarenceux feared she was about to turn into Little Trinity Lane, in full view of the watchmen; but at the end of the alley she stopped, turned round and came back.

'I know I should not be upset, because all you did was tell the truth. I am Widow Machyn now. But it does upset me – because you intended it to hurt me. You just made a speech to Michael Hill about his knowledge being our enemies' weakness. Well, your knowledge is my weakness. Please be careful what you say, Mr Clarenceux, because a hurtful word from you could destroy me.'

Clarenceux bowed his head. 'I apologise, Goodwife Machyn.'

They heard the sound of the water-carrier's cart. Clarenceux looked up to see the old man shaking his head. 'Thames Street is a busy place this afternoon, sir. I wouldn't like to take your lady wife along that way. Not in the barrel nor out of it. Not even for another shilling.'

'You don't have to, my good man. All you have to do is drive north from here. We will walk beside you, both of us. I will walk by your front wheel and my wife . . .' he glanced at Rebecca, 'will walk beside the rear. I do believe we can avoid the men in Garlick Hill that way.'

'Awdrey must have the patience of a saint,' muttered Rebecca.

46

aniel Gyttens was, like Michael Hill, a once-handsome man of about sixty, with high cheekbones and a pugnacious jaw. But he was dressed shabbily in an old doublet and jerkin, both of which he allowed to hang loose. 'I daren't go out,' he explained, and Clarenceux could see from the fact that he wore his side-sword in the upper rooms of the bookseller's house that he was indeed too nervous to go anywhere. Instead he ate, drank and read books borrowed from the bookseller below. When they entered his room there was a plate of bread and cheese on the table and an open copy of Edward Hall's *Vnion of the Two Noble and Illustrate Famelies of Lancastre and Yorke.*

After the formal introductions, it soon appeared that Clarenceux and Gyttens had much in common. Both had been at the attack on Boulogne in the reign of Henry the Eighth, and both considered that that king's strategy had been as deplorable and misguided as his religious policy. Clarenceux remarked on the book Gyttens was reading, a Protestant work. 'One should know one's enemies,' replied Gyttens, 'and a bad historian is the most steadfast enemy of the truth.'

Clarenceux smiled. 'Turning to the Knights of the Round Table, we need the names and dates of each Knight. The dates we believe all correspond with entries in Henry Machyn's chronicle. There is no hope of gathering all the Knights together, but if we can collect all the names and the dates, and then find the dates in the chronicle, we should be able to discover Henry's secret. Then we can start to bargain with those in power.'

Gyttens refilled his wine goblet. 'That is easy enough. My name is Sir Reynold.'

Rebecca and Clarenceux looked at one another.

'No,' said Rebecca, worried.

'Well, it is.'

'But Sir Reynold is the name carried by Nicholas Hill.'

Gyttens shrugged. 'I've met Nicholas Hill – he's a son of Michael Hill. I would be surprised if he had the same Arthurian name as me. That would not make sense.'

'It might,' Clarenceux mused. 'We were told that Nicholas Hill took Sir Arthur Darcy's place as Sir Reynold.'

'Who by?'

'Michael Hill.'

That seemed to cause Daniel Gyttens some discomfort. He lifted his wine glass to his lips and drank.

'Were you one of the founders of the fellowship?' asked Rebecca. 'Do you remember what happened in 1550, the year of the foundation?'

Gyttens took another swig of wine. 'No, no, you've got it all wrong. It was many years before that. After the Pilgrimage of Grace had failed and all those northern lords were hanged for daring to stand up for the true faith. You'll get a different explanation from Edward Hall, of course, but it's in there too.'

Clarenceux remembered the horror. Twenty-six years ago, more than two hundred men had been executed by the king, including abbots, priors, lords and members of the gentry. It had been one of the bloodiest stains upon that bloody king's character. Man after man of distinction had gone to the gallows, the king's officers mercilessly killing them for speaking the truth.

Rebecca was confused. 'But the chronicle begins on the thirteenth of June 1550, when my husband, Sir Arthur Darcy and John Heath dined together at the Bull's Head. We have assumed the fellowship was founded then. Are you saying that that was not the case?'

'Well, when I say it was after the Pilgrimage of Grace, that was when we started to meet. We didn't have Arthurian names then, but we were angry. And we wanted revenge on the king.'

'What date did Henry give you?' asked Clarenceux.

'June the nineteenth, 1556.'

Clarenceux nodded, satisfied. 'So there are indeed two Sir Reynolds. You have one date and Nicholas Hill has another, June the fifteenth, 1552. But *why* have two Sir Reynolds? It is hardly the most auspicious of Arthurian names. Why no Sir Bedivere? Galahad? Gawain? Kay? King Uther – even Merlin?'

'Maybe those are the names we don't know?' Rebecca speculated.

'We know seven now – King Clariance, Lancelot, Dagonet, Reynold – twice – Ector, and Yvain. There are only two more. That leaves several famous Arthurian names unused.' He turned to Gyttens. 'Do you know any more dates?'

'No. Only my own. We were all instructed never to let anyone else know them. It is only because you are Henry Machyn's friend that I feel I can trust you. Obviously others have trusted you too.'

Rebecca turned to Clarenceux. 'We need the chronicle. We need to return to Summerhill ...'

Clarenceux suddenly frowned at her and shook his head. She gave him an enquiring glance, and then was mortified, realising the meaning of his expression. *If Crackenthorpe finds Gyttens, he will be interrogated. A man who wears a side-sword by day in his lodgings is hardly a man with the strength of mind to resist torture: he is torturing himself.*

'We do need to see the chronicle, you are right. But first let us go and see Draper,' he said. 'We have that one last lead to follow up. Let us do that now, before dark. We know his Arthurian name but we must get the date too. After we have seen him we will have done as much as we can for the time being.'

'Can we eat something before we go?' asked Rebecca. 'I am

desperately hungry.' She looked down at the bread and cheese on the table. 'I am so famished I can't think clearly.'

'Help yourself,' said Gyttens with a slightly drunken flourish of his hand. 'Christian bodies need sustenance as much as Christian souls.'

47

The light was fading as they left the house in Paternoster Row. A blanket of snow lay across the street, trampled into hard paths by pedestrians. Never did the city look so pure and clean, thought Rebecca – the perpetual mud had been frozen solid and concealed by a layer of white. The roofs were similarly pristine. The footsteps of a hundred thousand citizens and visitors to the city packed the snow down hard on the ice and made the ground slippery. The air was full of the smell of wood smoke. Some boys by the gate to the cathedral yard were sliding on a smooth patch – a long frozen puddle now covered in compacted snow. They laughed as one fell over and carried on skidding on his back.

Clarenceux looked up as he put on his gloves and watched the heavy snowflakes falling against the backdrop of the tower of St Paul's. The cathedral still looked broken to him. All his life he had known the tall spire – one of the tallest in Christendom – and then one day, as he had been sitting in his study, Awdrey had run up the stairs to tell him it had fallen. He had not believed her until he had seen it with his own eyes – something so magnificent and holy reduced to a gaping hole, a mass of splintered oak and smashed stone. Now just the stunted tower stood there, gaunt against the grey sky, snowflakes falling like sad blessings all around it.

Something had broken in London that day. Since then nothing

had been wholly good or perfect. England was struggling on, like the cathedral, damaged in spite of the prayers of the faithful. It was as if the faithful were drinking wine from a broken cup.

He walked in a sombre mood beside Rebecca through the wide street of Cheapside. The last market stalls were still doing business but most had now closed up. The purchasers had departed, unable to confirm the quality of the goods in the dim light and driven away by the snow. Traders were loading their panniers and baskets on to carts or loading up packhorses, calling out to one another as they worked. Some were warming their hands over a fire of broken-up wooden boxes that they had lit in the street.

One of the market traders recognised Clarenceux and waved a greeting. Clarenceux nodded perfunctorily in reply.

'Do you think this is safe?' asked Rebecca.

'Crackenthorpe has been searching for me since Sunday. He has probably been looking even longer for you. Do you think they imagine we are walking through the middle of the main market street in London?'

'They might.'

'We are hidden by people. If we were in an alley and ran into Crackenthorpe, we would be the only ones present – he'd recognise us instantly. At least, he would recognise me. But here there are too many distractions.'

They turned off left, along Ironmongers Lane, following a crowd of hooded and hatted men and women heading in the same direction, all hunched up against the cold. The chill wind sent the snowflakes swirling for a moment between the houses, and blowing them into their faces. A dog padded along behind its master, leaving claw marks in the compacted snow. A broken sign above a tavern hung at an angle, its design almost invisible against the darkening sky, while below it men and women were queuing up to go inside, into the warmth. The music of a lute, a tambourine and a man's voice could be heard as they passed the open door. A cart stood on one side of the road, the snow on its wheel rim undisturbed until a boy ran his hand over it, gathering the snow to throw at another boy who was chasing him.

'Not much further now,' Clarenceux said, looking around warily.

They crossed quickly into Basinghall Street, both of them watchful. But even here they were surrounded by people going home. An old woman came towards them dragging a handcart loaded with firewood, struggling against the flow of pedestrians. A younger woman on a grey horse rode behind her, with a large faded blue blanket wrapped around her shoulders. Snow was piled thickly on the rungs of a ladder propped against the side of a house, and the barrel at the foot was frozen over, with snow across the surface of the ice and heaped over the rim.

Clarenceux pointed to the large red-brick house on their left, rising proudly above the snow. Its tall windows were filled with many small panes of glass, some with armorial designs. Two of the windows on the first floor projected out in a semicircle above the street and rose through to the second floor. This new-built house, three bays wide, shouted of fashion, money, authority and distinction.

Clarenceux climbed up the three steps to the front door, which was intricately decorated with ironwork, and knocked hard. He looked around – across the street, past the snow-piled ladder, back to the crossroads – but there were no obvious signs of watchmen.

The door opened. It was dark within but they could see the servant's bald pate.

'Greetings to you and your master. I have come to speak to Mr Draper on the most urgent business. My name is William Harley, Clarenceux King of Arms. This is Goodwife Machyn.'

The bald man was dour. 'Is Mr Draper expecting you?'

'In a manner of speaking,' replied Clarenceux. 'May we come in?'

'It is very cold out here,' Rebecca added with a smile.

The bald man did not smile back. 'If Mr Draper is expecting you, you had best wait in the hall.' He held the door open while

Clarenceux and Rebecca shook the snow from their feet on the doorstep and stepped inside. 'This way,' he said, leading them into a dark passageway.

A moment later they emerged into a spacious hall lit by candles. The ceiling was in shadow, about forty feet above them. One wall was largely composed of glass from head height upwards: windows twelve feet high. On the opposite side there were benches piled with coloured cushions. Halfway along was an elaborate fireplace, where a fire burnt slowly, hissing with new wood. Candles flickered silently, fixed to the wall, and above the fireplace was a frieze of plasterwork that seemed to be painted with bare-breasted black women. Portraits hung on either side of the fire-place, and an Arras tapestry at the far end, above a table on a dais, showed an army besieging a town beside the sea.

'Wait here,' the servant commanded, and disappeared up a small staircase that led from the far corner of the dais.

'Draper certainly has money,' commented Rebecca, looking up at the carved wooden ceiling in the shadows, noticing the gold leaf on the beams in the candlelight.

Clarenceux lifted his eyes to follow Rebecca's line of sight, and caught the curve of her neck in the light of the candles before he looked away and up into the beams. He did not care for the quantity of gold leaf on display. He looked back at Rebecca and saw the mole on the side of her face. *There can be beauty in imperfection, and imperfection in something as beautiful as this hall.*

He turned away again, wondering what could be taking the servant such a long time, and looked up at the tapestry. It was difficult to make anything out. *Perhaps it is supposed to represent Calais? The supposedly impregnable English town on the French coast. It took the great king Edward the Third nearly a year to capture it, two hundred years ago. And England held on to it for all that time – until Queen Mary let it slip through her fingers five years ago. She might have been a Catholic but she was still a bad ruler. The burnings, the neglect of duty, her fear*

*and the resultant oppression, the concentration on herself and
her royal will . . . Even Catholic queens have their faults.*

Rebecca looked at him. She came closer, and spoke in a very
low voice. 'How comes it that Mr Draper is the only one of the
Knights whom we have found in his own house?'

Clarenceux did not understand why she was asking the question. Why should they not find a rich merchant in his own house?

'I am worried, Mr Clarenceux. Mr Hill was so fearful he pointed
pistols at us. You had to leave your house. I had to too. Lancelot
Heath is in hiding. Everyone is in hiding. But not Mr Draper.'

As she stopped speaking, he heard again the voice of her husband
in his ears. *I trusted the wrong man. Everything is gone. It is
over for me.*

'What can they be discussing up there?' he asked aloud, realising the only possible answer as he said the words.

Nothing.

The blood in his face turned to cold fear. 'You're right. We've
walked into a trap,' he whispered.

'Do you think he's with Walsingham?'

'I don't know. But I'm going to find Draper now, before it's
too late . . .'

Even before he finished the sentence, Clarenceux started
moving. By the time he was at the staircase he was in a run. His
knee hurt but he was not going to let it stop him. He put his
foot on the first step and realised the need for stealth, and slowed.
He turned around: Rebecca was following. He raised a finger to
his lips, then turned and crept up the stairs.

At the top, on the landing, a candle burnt on a small table
under a picture of the Virgin on the wall. He crossed himself and
then looked at the door in front of him. There was a latch. He
put his hand forward, enclosing the metal, said a small prayer,
and opened the door.

It took Clarenceux barely two seconds to understand the geog-
raphy of the betrayal. He saw the long panelled room, the two
fireplaces, the candles on the walls and the writing table at one

end. He saw the door directly opposite and the curtain on the inside – still drawn back. The servant had not closed it behind him when he left. He saw the narrow-faced grey-bearded man at the desk at the far end of the room – with a look of surprise on his face – and he saw the pistol on the desk. But in those two seconds, without any fear at all, he worked out exactly what he would do.

When Draper saw Clarenceux enter, he realised that he had underestimated the herald. He had hoped the man would wait obediently in the hall. He was too shocked for his mind and body to respond. He reached out a hand for the pistol but he fumbled, and by the time his finger found the trigger Clarenceux was already at the fireplace. He looked on in fear as a gloved hand reached for one of the hot silver-headed firedogs, lifted it, and threw it straight at him. He ducked, trying to avoid the spinning hot metal, but he was too slow: the edge of the foot caught him on the side of the head. An instant later Clarenceux was on him, pulling the pistol away and throwing it across the room with one hand while wrenching his hair out of his scalp with the other as he dragged him away from his desk. Draper was stumbling, head low, yelling with pain as Clarenceux ripped his hair out in tufts.

'This is for Henry Machyn!' roared Clarenceux, grabbing Draper's beard in his fingers. He punched him in the face as hard as he could, breaking his nose. Draper's head jolted back and he fell, blood leaking across the floor. 'And this is for Will Terry, an innocent boy who never did a wrong deed.' Draper's body contorted as Clarenceux's boot broke a rib.

Clarenceux bent down and seized Draper's hair again, and twisted his face upwards so he could look at him. 'Now, I have one question for you. I know your Arthurian name is Sir Dagonet. The buffoon whom King Arthur knighted in jest. What is your date? Tell me.'

'May your soul burn in hell and your body rot ...' gasped Draper.

Clarenceux glanced at Rebecca. She was standing by the door as if she wanted to run. He listened: as yet there was no noise from below.

He turned back to Draper. 'One last chance.'

Draper said nothing.

Clarenceux took the knife from his belt and held the blade directly in front of Draper's right eye, half an inch away. 'I said, one last chance. Or I am going to cut out your eyes.'

'The . . . sixteenth of June.'

'The year?'

'1559.'

Clarenceux took the knife away and sheathed it. 'You are a proud man, Mr Draper. You must have once believed in the cause or Henry Machyn would not have chosen you. But you would rather give your soul to your mortal enemies than stand by your friends in Christ. As disciples go, you are Judas.'

He stood up and looked across at Draper's writing table. He saw a large leather pouch, walked over and took it. It contained three gold sovereigns, several gold half-sovereigns and angels, ten large new silver crowns and a few silver shillings, groats and pennies. He hesitated for a moment, then remembered the money taken from the box in his own house, and the gold leaf on display in the hall. He pulled the pouch strings closed and tucked it into a pocket of his doublet, then glanced back at the figure of Draper.

'Men have died because of your faithlessness. Remember that.'

Then, with a final look around the room, he strode to the door opposite the one by which they had come in, and beckoned to Rebecca.

'The servant will think we don't know about this route, so he will enter with Crackenthorpe by the front door. Come, quickly.'

It was cold and dark on the narrow winding stairs. Clarenceux found himself reaching out for the walls, steadying himself as he descended, not knowing where they would come out. When the stairs stopped he found himself in blackness, uncertain whether he was at the foot of the stairs or on a landing.

'I can hear someone – footsteps running,' whispered Rebecca.

Clarenceux knew there was no time. He dropped on to all fours, cursed the bruising of his knee, and felt around. A moment later he felt a wall, and then steps going down. *They could lead to a cellar.*

There were voices above. Clarenceux could hear his own hurried breathing, and sensed Rebecca's anxiety. A faint light caught his eye, level with his feet. *It is grey light, not candlelight. It has to be the bottom of an outside door. I just pray that the servant left it unlocked.*

'Goodwife Machyn,' he whispered, standing up and reaching out for her. He touched the wall first, and then her outstretched hand. He held it. 'Be careful, there are steps here,' he said, guiding her past them.

A flickering torchlight appeared behind them on the spiral stairs.

'Don't fear them,' he urged, finding the door and fumbling for the latch.

The door was unlocked. Clarenceux opened it. The shadows of the chill night revealed that they were in a brick courtyard at the side of the house. There was only one obvious way out: through a gate ahead of them, beneath an arch. It was the only thing they could see – it was too dark to see any other doorway. But the gate was wide enough to allow delivery carts, and that meant it had to lead to the street. Clarenceux pulled Rebecca towards it.

'Hold there!' yelled a voice behind. The light of a flaming torch fell on the gate. But Clarenceux was not turning back now. By the torchlight he saw the handle in the centre of the gate, grabbed it and turned it, and pulled the left-hand side open to allow Rebecca through. He followed her as the pursuers rushed towards them, shouting, and slammed the gate shut behind him, holding the metal ring of the handle on the outside of the door.

'Go down the lane,' he gasped, holding the door firmly shut despite the attempts of the men within to open it. 'Turn right and keep going. I'll see you at the back of St Michael's Church.'

Rebecca hesitated. There were people all around them in the street, hooded shadows moving here and there, a few with lanterns but most simply returning from the markets.

'Go on! Run!' he shouted as he fought to hold the handle of the door.

Rebecca turned and ran.

He had only seconds now to make up his mind what to do next. A sudden forceful effort from those within pulled the door open a couple of inches; Clarenceux hauled it back but could not shut it. He could see the flickering of a torch through the narrow opening, like the flames of a pyre, and the light that was cast on his gloves. *Crackenthorpe's men are probably running through the house now, about to come round from the front and trap me.* Again there was a great pull from those inside. Clarenceux turned and frantically looked for somewhere to hide, knowing he could not outrun the guards. But there was nothing to see – it was far too dark. But as he looked at an approaching group of hooded figures, their faces invisible in the near-darkness, he realised what he had to do. He waited another moment, and another, as several lanterns came towards him, and then let go.

Holding a flaming torch in his left hand, the huge figure of Richard Crackenthorpe yanked open the front door with his right and jumped down the steps into the snowy street. He drew his sword as he turned to the outer gate, expecting it to be closed, and to see Clarenceux there. But there was no one. The door was open, yet there was no fighting. There were just the shadows of his men.

'Where is he?' yelled Crackenthorpe to the crowd in the street. A woman screamed when she saw the sword, and all the figures in the lane backed away from him as he swirled between them, pushing back the hats and hoods of those nearest him. 'Where is he?' he shouted into the faces of the three watchmen who had come out through the gate. 'He cannot simply have disappeared.'

'We could not see,' explained the man who had passed through first. 'When we pulled the door open it was too dark to recognise anyone. And then you appeared, and the torchlight reflected on the snow.'

'The pox and the bloody flux upon you.' Crackenthorpe took a deep breath. 'Damn you! I want you to pursue ... No.' He stuck the sword in the snow. 'No. The city gates are shut now. They will try to leave the city through the blacksmith's yard by Cripplegate. Two of you will stay here to guard Draper – I do not trust him. You two, come with me.'

'Why bother guarding Draper? Didn't you see? Clarenceux bloodied his face.'

'But he left him alive. If Draper had betrayed me like that, I would have slit his throat.'

48

Clarenceux ran on in the darkness for as long as he could. His whole body had taken too many blows – not just his bruised knee. He ached; he just wanted to lie down and sleep.

But he was alive and free.

On he went, pushing hard on his leg. *It will not defeat me. Today, nothing will defeat me. A left turn, then a right, and I will be heading straight for St Michael's Church in Wood Street. Where will Rebecca be? At the back, I said. In the churchyard.*

Clarenceux slowed. Another group was approaching with a lantern, and they were not on their way home: they were official watchmen. For a moment he felt the irony of escaping from one danger because he had no light and then being arrested for nightwalking. He stopped, and backed into the side of the street as the swinging light and shadows passed.

He felt the still falling snowflakes cold against his neck, and the wet fur of his collar. He pulled the robe closer and limped on, bumping occasionally into carts, barrels and the other jetsam of the back streets of the city. Soon the tower of St Michael's Church showed against the dark sky. Coming to the wall of the cemetery, he felt with his hand all the way round to the lych-gate, and went through.

His cap was soaked now and melted snow was running down the inside of his shirt. The city was almost silent. Only the occasional shout of watchmen in neighbouring streets disturbed the peace, or a father shouting at his children behind the shutters of a nearby house. He heard the screeching of cats fighting not far away. Then it was silent again.

'Goodwife Machyn?' he called quietly. But there was only silence in the churchyard.

Where is she? I said the back of the church. Surely she must have understood that to be the churchyard? The church itself will be locked at this hour.

'Goodwife Machyn?' he said, a little louder. 'Rebecca?'

His shoe caught on a recently dug mound of earth: he stumbled forward, his gloved hand burying itself in fresh snow. He got up, shook it, and moved on.

Nothing. Just cold silence. And the smell of wood smoke. The church rose in stone before him.

She is not here.

What if they caught her? Clarenceux's thoughts began to gnaw at him. *If she has been arrested, what should I do? I have no way of finding her. If I go and take shelter in the stable lofts of the tenements near Aldersgate, she will never find me.*

The thoughts turned in his mind, leaving it as cold as a bone beneath the stars. *I cannot lose her now, not when we have come so far.*

'Rebecca?'

Only the snowy silence answered, and the barking of a dog in the next street.

Clarenceux waited for twenty minutes, leaning against the wall of the church. His robe was soaking wet. He turned and placed his hands flat upon the cold stones. Holy though they were, he could find no consolation in them. All he could see in his mind was Rebecca. Somehow he had lost her. He rested his forehead against the stones and remembered his father's words, years ago, a few days after his sister had died. *Gold, fame and fine horses mean very little: this is what we learn when we lose a loved one.* His sister had been sixteen and he fourteen: all the laughter they had shared had vanished, never to come back. In the years since he had come to think of his faith as a consolation. Faith did not diminish with the loss of a mortal soul. But now he was not so sure. *Where is faith now? What is God's consolation? If a man loses someone he holds dear yet can find consolation in God alone, surely that person never meant that much to him?*

And then he shocked himself, profoundly. *If the spiritual world is as real as the material world, then one is meaningless without the other.*

'God alone is not enough,' he whispered to himself.

Suddenly he was swimming in deep pools of truth. He felt sick as he started to walk alongside the church, steadying himself on the stones. He made the sign of the cross in the darkness.

God alone is not enough. Not enough.

Someone moved nearby.

'Is that you?' a woman's voice whispered.

'Goodwife Machyn?' He could hear the weakness of his voice.

A hand touched his arm. 'It is me. Rebecca.'

'Rebecca.'

He held her hand in his and recognised the feel of her, and put his arm round her, clasping her tightly and holding her cheek to his own.

'For a moment, I thought God had been cruel,' he said.

'God is never cruel. Only we are vulnerable. How did you escape?'

'I will tell you, but not here. First we must find somewhere to hide. I know a place not far away.'

He took her hand in his and led her through the darkness.

The stable felt warm as they came in from the cold. The smell and the heat of the horses was welcome after the ice and snow of the lanes. Clarenceux knew where to feel for the ladder in the darkness, and they climbed into the stable loft and lay upon a pile of soft hay, fragrant of a now-forgotten summer. They lay near each other and were quiet for a long time.

'So how did you escape?'

'The soldiers' eyes were used to the torchlight – I realised they would be plunged into darkness when they came out. Like moths, their eyes were bound to be drawn to the first lights they saw in the street. I guessed it would be two or three seconds before they could make out a human shape. That's enough time for a man in a dark robe and a black velvet cap to disappear in the shadows.'

'I was so worried. I went back to look for you – I thought that if you were caught, I needed to know. To try to find out where they took you, so I could tell Julius. But by the time I got there you had vanished.'

'All is well now, though.' Clarenceux leant back in the hay and looked up into the darkness. 'I think we have done all we can in the city. We know who the traitor is. No one has breathed a word about the last two Knights – not even their Arthurian names. It is time to go and check what dates we have against the chronicle, to find out what they mean.'

'Why do you think one of the Knights' names cannot be mentioned?'

'You knew Henry better than anyone else; why do you think?'

Rebecca was silent.

'Rebecca?'

She sighed – not with relief but with unease. 'Why did they break Henry's legs?'

Clarenceux knew the answer would hurt her. It was an image which deeply troubled him too. 'They have various methods of torture. It could be any one of several. But he is at peace now. It is over for him.'

'What he started we must finish.'

'I feel as you do. We are resolved.'

'So the next thing is to get back to the chronicle,' she said, resting her head on his chest. 'There's no point in leaving here before dawn. We cannot pick up the horses until after the inn opens.'

'No, but it might be easier to leave the city by night than during the day. Crackenthorpe knows we are still within the walls. He will have guards on every gate.'

'What do you suggest? Another exit?'

'Indeed. There is a gate in the back yard of a blacksmith by Cripplegate. Henry told me about it – I used it the night I called on your house.'

'I know it. The blacksmith is my brother, Robert.'

Clarenceux had not made the connection. 'Of course. You said your maiden name was Lowe. I did not know you had a brother. You've never mentioned him.'

'We're not close. But Henry liked him.'

'Well, in that case you know the place. From there we can find our way to my house and wait there until dawn. No one is going to imagine it needs searching again, not after the damage they did. And no one will be watching it: there is no one there.'

'Let's rest here first,' she said. 'It will be safer in the streets in the middle of the night, and both of us are tired.'

As he lay there, feeling her head on his chest, he was glad. *God alone is not enough.*

After a while she asked, 'What do you know about the Pilgrimage of Grace?'

'Why?'

'Because Gyttens said it was the reason why the Knights started to meet. It was long before 1550, wasn't it? I remember people talking about a Catholic rebellion in the north, and a large number of men being executed – but I was only nine or ten, I think.'

'There was a rising of discontented followers of the old religion in Lincolnshire. It was in October 1536, after Henry the Eighth had broken from Rome and was determined to impose his will upon the English Church – as if its lands were his own to dispose of. The lords and gentry of the county, like the common folk, all agreed that what the king was doing amounted to heresy as well as tyranny. Their forefathers had founded monasteries and endowed them so priests would sing Masses for their souls;

what right had the king to dissolve them and sell off the land? What right had the king to make the break with Rome and declare himself spiritual head of the Church in England? As for the nobles, what right had the king to sell off the very abbeys in which their predecessors had been laid to rest, as if their honourable bones had been buried in any common kitchen? In this they found common cause with the people who looked at the altars of their country churches and could not believe that the figures of the saints to whom they had prayed last week were now to be destroyed. We forget what a shock it was, even those of us who look back on their struggle and believe they were right and good people. Remember the old days: when your horse broke a leg or your mother broke an arm, you would place a clay or wax figure on the altar, make a donation and pray. The old king forbade that. To many people it seemed that he had made it a heresy even to pray for good health. Add to that the physical destruction of the rood in every church and the implementation of a new prayer book, and you can begin to see why the people of Lincolnshire rose as one. Rich and poor, young and old, they all did exactly what the king had forbidden them to do: they went on a pilgrimage to Lincoln. Forty thousand of them. They wanted their saints back, they wanted to be able to go on pilgrim-ages and make offerings. They wanted to pray in their own way, to do what they knew was dutiful in God's eyes.'

'That was the Pilgrimage of Grace?'

'No, that was just the start. The king responded by sending the blood-stained duke of Suffolk against the pilgrims. He threat-ened the faithful with death if they refused to give up the pilgrimage and go home. The king himself had expressly ordered that no mercy was to be shown them, the duke said. As a result, the men of Yorkshire began their own protest, under the leadership of a lawyer, Robert Aske. He was a pious man; he did not want to provoke a conflict, nor even to threaten the king's forces. He led nine thousand men into York and restored the monasteries there. He was a good leader too: he took Pontefract Castle without a single casualty and kept his followers under control, so there was no looting or theft. He even managed to control the more political demands of his fellow gentlemen. But the king was duplicitous. He accepted a list of demands sent to him by Aske but never responded. When pressed, the king pretended to accede and Aske, realising his pilgrims could not remain mobilised indefinitely, disbanded them. In January 1537, after a rebellion in Cumberland, the king gave orders that all those who had taken part in the events at York should be rounded up and executed. More than two hundred knights, abbots, priests and clergymen were hanged. Aske himself was dragged back to York and hanged there in chains.'

Clarenceux shook his head, his voice cracking with emotion. 'When people ask me about my religion, what I mean when I say I am *Catholic* in my faith, I think of the men trying to protect the burial places of their families, and their honest ways of praying, and their desperate hopes in the saints, and I applaud them for fighting to preserve the Church from the monster that was Henry the Eighth. And yet what did I do? I fought for that despicable, unholy king at Boulogne. I fought for him, in Lord Paget's company, under the command of the same duke of Suffolk. To the end of my days I will regret that. And to the end of my days I will believe that what Henry did in the north was the work of the Devil. Kings should not pretend to be men of the Church or to rule the Church; nor should they condemn men simply because of their faith.'

Rebecca was quiet for a long time. 'That is what we are getting ourselves involved in, isn't it? You are a new Robert Aske.'

Clarenceux rested his head in his hands. *They begged Aske to be their leader; Henry begged me to take the chronicle. Like Aske, I am prepared to fight for what I believe is right. For both of us it is a matter of freedom. But there is a difference: Aske knew what he was up against.*

'If I am, does that matter to you?'

'Yes. It means that I believe in you.'

*

They left the stable loft about three o'clock in the morning. The sky had cleared, and the new moon had not yet appeared, so the stars were the only light. It was just enough to show the whiteness of the snow; they could see the streets and alleys and did not have to feel their way.

They walked carefully nonetheless. The deeper cold meant that the snow had frozen harder; but at the edge of the lanes it had not compacted as much, and so crunched under their feet. Clarenceux led the way, stopping here and there to check for the night watch in this ward. No one seemed to be about. There was just starlit stillness.

It occurred to Clarenceux that the door to which they were heading might be locked. For a long time he did not whisper this to Rebecca; but when he did, she reassured him that Henry had told her that her brother rarely locked the gate. Still, his mind was not at ease.

On they went. Despite the dimness Clarenceux saw a rat scurry across the white of the street, and then two more. He realised that the rats were used to the streets at night.

'We're nearly there,' he whispered.

'I know,' she whispered back. 'Why have you stopped?'

'If this is your brother's house . . .' He did not need to finish the sentence.

'Don't worry. Not many people know.'

'All the same. If something happens, and we get separated, let us meet back at the stable loft.'

'Nothing is going to happen,' she said.

They moved on. Now he could see Robert Lowe's house. There was the white of the lane outside his yard: the gate was in the shadow of the wall, twenty feet away.

'Wait here. I am going ahead to check. If it is clear, I will come back directly. If not, retrace your steps. I need to be sure you will do that, Rebecca. Do you understand?'

'Yes, I do.'

'God be with you,' he said.

He crossed the last few yards to the house in the darkness and reached out to feel the walls – first the wall of the house, then the wall of the yard. He took two more steps in the snow and his fingers touched wood. He pushed: the gate was shut. He fumbled in the dark for the latch, found it, and went through.

49

Francis Walsingham could not sleep. He threw back the covers, pulled open the bed curtains and sat on the edge of the mattress in his nightgown and cap. He noticed that the candle was guttering, and about to burn itself out. He pulled on a heavy robe, took a wax candle from a small pile in a recess in the wall and lit it from the old candle before setting it in its place. The new flame flickered and rose into a perfect small tongue of light. Feeling the cold, he got back into bed, and sat there.

Six Knights had been arrested. Machyn had died – that had been a god-awful scene, and a mess from start to finish – but otherwise Crackenthorpe had done well. Robert Lowe and Michael Hill had only been seized that evening. But Emery and Nicholas Hill had talked. Draper had yielded more at the second time of asking. Indeed, he had been so fearful at the thought of what they would do to him for having been circumspect first time around that he had told them everything he knew. And his new evidence this evening provided conclusive proof that Clarenceux and Rebecca Machyn were working together.

The dates were important, that was clear. So far he only had three: Draper's, June the sixteenth, 1559; Nicholas Hill's, June the fifteenth, 1552; and Emery's, June the twenty-first, 1558. But there were nine in total. If Lowe and Michael Hill also talked, then he would still need four more in order to understand the chronicle, as Draper had explained.

Six Knights taken into custody or dead. And I know the names of the other three: Gyttens, Heath and Clarenceux himself.

He lay on his side, sure that there was something very obvious that he was missing. It was impossible for Clarenceux to gather all the Knights together, but it was not impossible for him, Walsingham, to learn all the dates. *If I do not find Gyttens and Heath, it does not matter. All I need to do is find Clarenceux – for he will know them. He probably drew them up.*

He turned in his bed. *If only I could see the chronicle. Do the dates relate to false entries? That makes the most sense: a chronicle full of true facts but with a series of false descriptions of events that together tell people how to foment a rebellion. Brilliant. If our spy had not sent word from Edinburgh in time for Crackenthorpe to save Draper from the assassin, we would never have known.*

He turned over again. *But who is the woman whom Draper described as 'her ladyship'? It couldn't be the Machyn woman, could it?*

50

※

ebecca was waiting in the cold blackness beside her brother's front door when the shout rang out: 'Hold fast!' She almost fell with the shock; her arms and legs felt suddenly heavy. She did not know what to do.

There was a fight going on. Something metal hit stone. A man yelled 'Get him down!' and then there was just silence punctuated with the occasional crashing sound.

Christ help me! Mr Clarenceux made me promise to retrace my steps. But what if he needs me? Where is Robert? I must wake him – he can help. Only then did it dawn on her that her brother was not in a position to help. He had not left the house even to investigate the noises in his own yard. Whatever they had done to him, whether they had killed him or tied him up somewhere, she was on her own.

Another minute passed and Rebecca remained motionless, half expecting Clarenceux to come limping out of the fight. But all was quiet now. *Retrace your steps,* she told herself. *It is all you can do. You promised you would.* But still she did not move. *Go back – for what? To wait and starve until Clarenceux is hauled off to … I don't know where. The Tower. Or Walsingham's house. I must wait and find out where they take him.*

Suddenly the gate of the yard banged open. There were hurried footsteps on the snow and shadows moving towards her. She pressed herself against the house, praying that the men would not see her.

And then they were gone, running westwards across the snowy lane.

Eventually she felt her way back to the stable loft, shivering, with her arms wrapped around herself for warmth. As she found the ladder and started to climb she carried a hope that somehow Clarenceux would have escaped and be here. But he was not. There was nothing of comfort except the hay where they had so recently lain.

51

The first sign of danger that Clarenceux noticed was the smell of coal smoke in the darkness. He paused. Suddenly someone grabbed him from behind, and pressed a knife to his throat.

'Don't move. There are four of us,' his assailant hissed.

Clarenceux did not try to struggle, feeling the blade against his windpipe. He sensed other men gathering around him, coming from the workshop at the back of the yard. Out of the corner of his eye he noticed a glow: they had the forge burning.

'The woman?'

'She ran from the house in Basinghall Street. I have not seen her since.'

'Liar,' growled the voice. But short of actually cutting Clarenceux's throat there was little he could do to force him to speak the truth. 'Tie him up. We'll take him to the sergeant straight away.'

Clarenceux sensed that his last opportunity to escape was about to disappear. He tried to remember the layout of the yard, when he had felt his way around here before. He could remember the gate in the wall and the low roof of the forge. And there had been a stone cistern, full of water. He felt the knife blade sharp against his throat and a second man trying to tie his hands. If he succeeded, then Clarenceux was as good as dead, with only the agony of torture in a dank cellar between him and the gallows.

'For God's sake, man, hold your hands steady.'

Clarenceux sensed that they were tired and nervous. He twisted again in the darkness and his fingers brushed the exposed hilt of a weapon. *O Lord, help me now.*

One instant he was standing with his chin up and a blade against his throat. The next he had dropped and turned his body suddenly: he felt the knife cut into his cheek as he grabbed the hand holding it and twisted the man's arm. He threw himself against the man holding the rope and seized the hilt he had touched – it turned out to be a long dagger, not the sword he had hoped for – and slashed down in the darkness, striking an unseen arm and causing a man to scream in pain. For a moment he was off balance, stumbling, with two men reaching forward; but in his falling he managed to push himself away from them, towards the forge. By the faint red light he could see the silhouettes of the cistern and the low roof. He placed a foot on the cistern, hauled himself up on to the roof and scrambled across the snow-covered shingles to the centre, where the snow had melted with the heat coming from the forge below.

'Get him down!' yelled one of the men as Clarenceux strained to look around. Behind, two shadows were hauling themselves up in pursuit across the dim white of the roof. Ahead there was a rim of ice round the dilapidated walkway of the city wall. He decided that that would be his means of escape – until he had to turn and fight.

I will not be taken. I am not going to be a prisoner again. They will need to overpower me if they want me alive.

They were not far behind. He stepped unsteadily across the slippery shingles, hurrying to the wall. There he placed his gloved hands on the edge of the wall-walk and tried to haul himself up, but he failed to lock his arms, and fell back. He kicked out, knocking the first pursuer off balance, sending him tumbling from the roof in the darkness. But two men remained: he could see their shadowy figures against the snow, advancing towards him. He turned and prepared to meet them, the dagger drawn.

He had the advantage of the wall behind him, to steady himself. But they might have swords. The dagger in his hand was anything but reassuring.

They hesitated. They felt precarious, on an icy sloping roof, facing a man whom they knew to be armed. *The wall is behind me – they cannot see me at all, not even an outline.* He fumbled with his left hand for a better grip, searching with his fingers for a gap in the stones where the exterior mortar was weak. *O God, please! They will attack soon.* His hand touched a projecting, rigid nail. It was perfect.

It was more than perfect.

Without waiting a second more Clarenceux turned and jumped, stamping his left foot on to the nail at the same time as placing his hands on the wall-walk. The nail held. The soldiers heard him – and suddenly saw his shadow against the thick ice piled on the walkway. 'He's on the wall,' shouted one, running forward with a blade and stabbing at him as Clarenceux pushed himself to his feet and started to run. 'He's heading to Aldersgate.'

It took the men behind some time to find the projecting nail; when they had, Clarenceux was already thirty seconds ahead, gasping as he scrambled over the old walkway. The surface was broken and uneven beneath the snow. He slid the dagger into his belt, needing both his hands free to balance. Several times he stumbled before he reached the corner and turned southward with the wall. No one walked along here these days. Cracked stones and split surfaces constantly tripped him. In some places the flat stones of the wall-walk had simply been removed, leaving a snow-covered gap into which Clarenceux's foot plunged. He cursed as his foot fell into another deep fissure and the ragged stones tore at his shin. *At this rate I am going to break a leg.* He struggled back to his feet.

On he went, soaked, gasping now for breath in the night's cold air. After a minute he looked behind. At first he could not see his pursuers but then realised that they had waited for one of their number to fetch a lantern: he could see its small light in the distance coming along the wall-walk about a hundred yards behind.

After nine or ten minutes of struggling along the snow-covered rubble of the walkway he paused and looked ahead, panting for breath. He saw the kink in the snow-covered wall near Noble Street. Beyond rose the dark spire of St Anne's Church. He heard a shout from Aldersgate and then saw torches appear on the wall-walk, coming from the gatehouse ahead. His heart sank. *One of the men from the blacksmith's house must have taken a message. I am trapped here. I must get down.*

Clarenceux hurried ahead to the kink in the corner of the wall: a right angle where it turned west for about fifteen feet before turning southward again. *If I wait, they will see where I fall.* He crossed himself, and then got down into a sitting position on the edge of the wall. He knew the drop here was about twenty feet: he placed one hand on either side of the right angle made by the stones and began to lower himself. But then he heard his pursuers. He remained, hanging by his hands as the men from the black-smith's house came closer. *If I drop now, they will surely hear me.* But he could not hang on – already his gloves were slipping on the ice.

He fell.

Clarenceux had intended to roll on hitting the ground, but not being able to judge the drop he winded himself. He lay in the soft snow in the back yard of a house, choking, trying desperately to regain his breath, and praying that he would be able to get out into the street. He looked up. The torches were coming along the wall, there were men above him: he had to move. He pushed himself to his feet and stumbled across the unseen obstacles in the yard to the fence.

'There! See him against the snow, down there!'

Clarenceux started striking the fence with his hand, hoping to find a gate or a door. It seemed there was none. But the fence itself was only six feet high. Now, breathing again, he placed his hands on the top of it, and jumped. He straightened his arms and swung his legs over, one after the other, letting himself drop on the other side just as the first man fell to the ground from the wall-walk behind him.

Clarenceux ran forward across the second yard. The vague whiteness of the snow was marked by the dark ruts of a cart – there had to be a gate somewhere. He came to a stone wall and felt around in the darkness. Here it was – locked, yes, but the bolt had to be on this side somewhere ... *somewhere ... where?* He found it at head height, opened it and rushed out into Noble Street as the pursuing soldiers clambered over the fence behind.

He knew where he was now, crossing the street into a narrow alley and running as fast as he could along one side. He was not far from the stable loft where he had been with Rebecca. *But she must be back there by now – I must lead them away, in another direction.*

He turned right down another alley, and slipped on some ice. The first man pursuing came to the corner and saw his shape clearly outlined against the snow. Clarenceux scrambled to his feet and pushed himself on, drawing the dagger from his belt and holding it ready for the strike, when it should come. The man was almost on him when Clarenceux suddenly turned, thrust once with the dagger, caught the man's arm with the point and slashed through the air in front of his face, just catching his nose. He started to run again, down another turning, aiming to get back to Wood Street.

The blow had gained him a few seconds, that was all. The sudden stopping and twisting had weakened his knee further and he knew he was going to have to rest soon. Then they would surround him. *I have to hide somewhere. Use the darkness: I am wearing a dark robe. Disappear.*

A church loomed in the darkness: there was a lighter patch of ground just this side. Clarenceux knew it was St Peter's, and that the lighter patch was the churchyard on the north side of the church. He turned down the alley that ran alongside it and, after about ten yards, pressed himself flat against the dark front of a house overlooking the snow-covered open space. He held the dagger at the ready.

He edged along the wall but then froze, hearing his pursuers come to the turning.

'He turned right here,' said one man.

Clarenceux could hear himself breathing heavily, and realised there were two men walking towards him. They were bound to sense his presence. He edged away into the darkness, as silently as he could, biting his lip, trying to quieten the heaving of his chest. The wall behind him seemed to give way to a gap, and he inched around it. This second alley was even darker, for the upper storeys of the houses projected out and closed over the passageway so that there was barely any starlight visible. Less snow had fallen here, and what had fallen had been churned to mud over the past day.

He backed down the alley a little further, and his hand touched wood. There was a tub of frozen water behind him. If he moved around it, the men at the end of the alley might see him. He saw their shapes silhouetted in the starlight of the alley's opening, just fifteen feet away. They were coming towards him – one feeling in the shadows with his sword.

Very slowly, Clarenceux crouched down, with his back to the barrel.

'What do you think?' whispered one of the men to the other.

'He's here,' replied the man with the sword. 'You take the left-hand side, I'll take the right.'

Clarenceux strained his eyes to see in the darkness. The man with the sword was waving it along the gutter, feeling for Clarenceux in the dark shadows at the edge of the road. Clarenceux knew he could not be seen. But the man with the sword was coming straight for him. He heard the point scrape the wall and stab the stones on the ground. He saw the man's shadow come closer, and closer – and he knew he had no choice.

This was where he had to fight.

He waited. As the sword swung towards him he stood, took

one silent step forward and thrust upwards with the dagger, hard, puncturing the man's windpipe at the top of his throat. The long blade skewered his tongue as Clarenceux drove the point through the top of his mouth into his skull. The man had no chance to cry out, not even to draw a breath; half a second after realising Clarenceux was there he was dying, the blood flooding his brain and frothing out of his mouth and out through the cut in his neck. Clarenceux twisted the dagger and withdrew it as the blood spurted. He tried to catch the body; but it was heavy and already falling away from him. The sword fell silently into the icy mud and snow but the man's body thumped on to the ice.

'Roger?' called the other man, alarmed.

Clarenceux slowly bent down and felt for the sword. He picked it up, swapping the dagger to his left hand. He could see nothing against the shadows of the houses on the other side of the alley. He heard the other man's footsteps crunch on the frozen mud. Then they stopped.

'He's here,' he shouted to the men still in the churchyard, backing away from the corpse. 'He's here somewhere.'

Clarenceux watched the man and saw him move into the blackness on the far side of the alley. He listened carefully, to sense if he moved. He did not. But nor was he coming to look for Clarenceux.

If he shouts again, I will have three of them to contend with. If I fight this one, I have just the one.

Clarenceux had no choice. Staying hidden was unsafe when his location was known. They could simply seal off the alley and wait until dawn. He crept along, knowing the other man could not see him, until he was ten feet further away, and then darted across to the other side of the alley and waited, listening.

After a minute he edged slowly and silently back towards the opening of the alley. Soon he could see the vague outline of the second man, hunched low, directly adjacent to the dead figure in the snow. He watched as he too crossed the alley, placing himself again on the opposite side from Clarenceux.

'Quickly. He's here,' the man shouted again.

The man was a coward; his strategy was simply to call for help. He was also blind to Clarenceux's movements, so there was a chance of escape. Clarenceux began to back away down the alley, watching in case the other men appeared. Then he turned and made his way quickly and quietly to the far end, leaving his pursuers to search the dark corners of the empty alley in fear of their lives, while he made his escape.

52

It was about an hour and a half before dawn when Clarenceux opened the door to the stables. He listened. No sound came from above. He felt his way to the ladder and climbed, stopping halfway to whisper, 'Are you here?'

He heard Rebecca move. 'Oh, Christ be praised! I heard the fight in the yard and came back here, as you said. Are you hurt?'

'I have more bruises, a cut to my face and another on my arm, and I am covered in blood – but most of the blood is not mine.'

'Whose is it?' she asked as he reached the top of the ladder.

'One of Crackenthorpe's men.' Clarenceux remembered the moment. It had been a cold-blooded, merciless killing. In terms of its execution, it had been perfect. But he felt sick with himself. He was a herald, not an executioner.

He bent down, felt the hay and let himself fall into its softness. 'Goodwife Machyn, we cannot continue like this. Crackenthorpe knows we are together. The Knights are in disarray; they can do nothing to help themselves. We have to get out of the city.'

She came near him in the darkness and lay down beside him. 'That is what we are trying to do, isn't it? That is why we went to my brother's house.'

'I suppose so. I just want to be away from this city, from . . . all this.'

Rebecca heard the note of despair in his voice, and was worried.

He had not previously sounded so weary, so despondent. If he had thought such things, he had not expressed them to her. He had always been strong for her. It was her turn now to be strong – to distract him from the abyss of dark doubts.

'I've been thinking while I have been waiting – about the names.'

'What have you found out?'

'Nothing – except I have an idea. Maybe the names of the Knights spell a word.'

'What makes you say that?'

'You asked why there were two Sir Reynolds and not one Galahad or Gawain. No Mordred. Well, maybe it's simply because the word that Henry intended required two R's.'

Clarenceux was sceptical. 'Is that what Henry might have thought? Does that sound like his way of thinking?'

'As much as anything else I can think of.'

'So, which letters have we got, if we put all seven together?'

'Lancelot Heath – L for Lancelot. You and Henry – C for Clariance. Michael and Nicholas Hill are Ector and Reynold, so E and R. There's D for Dagonet, another Reynold and Yvain. So . . .'

'L, C, E, R, D, R, Y,' he repeated. 'Only one vowel.'

'The other names could be vowels. A could be Arthur.'

'But it doesn't seem right that someone else should be King Arthur if Sir Arthur Darcy – one of the founders – was merely Sir Reynold.'

'So, if there's no A, what about U – for King Uther? Do you think we can dismiss that too?'

'I don't think we can guess things like this. If we had an M and an O we could make "Mercy, Lord". If there was an A, then one word might be "Darcy". But who knows? They might not actually be initials. We need to see the chronicle.'

53

Wednesday, 15 December

Dawn had broken: light now crept around the opening of the door to the stables, and in through the cracks under the eaves. One of the horses shifted her hooves and searched for fodder; her stablemate awoke and whinnied.

Above, lying on the hay, Clarenceux opened his eyes, blinked and looked around. He lifted himself on to one elbow. Rebecca was asleep beside him. He watched as she started to stir also, her deep slumber touched by the never-sleeping part of her mind that knew she was in danger, which even now was listening out for signs of alarm. But the sound of the horses was not enough to wake her; she had become accustomed to being in the stable.

He looked at her face: eyes closed, seemingly at peace. He looked at her brown hair upon her pale neck, the mole on the side of her face. He was struck by her beauty. Looking at her sleeping was an indulgence; he could gaze on her. And yet she was not the same woman as she was when awake. If she woke now, he would feel guilty.

Suddenly there was a cough outside. The door to the stable creaked open, the latch lifted by an uncareful hand.

Clarenceux was on his knees instantly, reaching for the sword that he had brought back in the early hours. He picked it up and crouched, ready, hearing the person in the stable below and Rebecca shifting as she woke. He moved forward, peering down through the open space where the ladder rested.

Rebecca gasped, and started breathing as if in shock. He turned to gesture to her to keep quiet and saw that she was looking at him.

'Holy Mother of God,' she whispered.

Clarenceux turned back to the stables, watching. A lad appeared, not more than twelve years old. He watched him pat the first horse and hand her some good oats.

'Mr Clarenceux, look at yourself,' Rebecca whispered, touching his arm.

Clarenceux looked down. His robe was streaked with the brown encrusted blood of the soldier. His hands were torn and bloodied. His clothes were ripped too, with seven or eight holes and gashes to his legs. As for his face, Rebecca's expression told him enough. *The boy will scream if he sees me like this.*

He moved away from the opening. 'The boy down there is called Philip,' he whispered. 'He's the son of Tom Griffiths, a dealer in hides and skins. Tell him I am here, and that I'm hurt. We need his help.'

When he heard the footsteps on the ladder, the boy was startled. He dropped a bucket he had been holding, and backed away. The sight of a woman only confused him further.

'Philip?' Rebecca asked, stepping cautiously down the ladder as he retreated to the far side of the stable. She could see he had fair, curly hair by the light of a small window.

The boy said nothing. He glanced at the door, but did not run. He was further from the door than she was.

'Don't worry,' she said. 'There is a friend of your father's upstairs in the hay loft. He is badly injured. Do you know him? He is an important man: his name is Mr William Harley, Clarenceux King of Arms.'

Again the boy glanced at the door. Rebecca felt he might bolt for it, and waited, watching him breathe.

'Is Mr Clarenceux in danger?' he asked at length.

Rebecca nodded. 'There are men chasing him who want to kill him. We need your help to get washed, and dressed in some spare clean clothes – they can be old, they don't have to be new – so we can get out of the city. Can you do that for us?'

The boy hesitated for a long time. Then he said, 'By your leave, madam, I will ask my father.'

This troubled Rebecca. But it was inevitable. She stood back as he walked self-consciously from the stable. Their fate was now in the hands of this boy's father, a stranger to her, a skinner by the name of Tom Griffiths. If he valued his safety more than Clarenceux's friendship, they were dead. They would be waiting there until the guards came.

No one came.

Rebecca went back up the ladder to Clarenceux. He was crouching by a chink of light, tending to his wounds as best he could. As she came up the stairs he looked up at her.

'He's gone to get his father.'

Clarenceux nodded, and looked down. He could not keep his worry hidden when he looked at her. She could see it in his face. And she knew it was reflected in her own.

The stable door opened again. They both heard heavy footsteps on the ladder. Clarenceux glanced at where he had hidden the sword, under the hay. If it came to the worst, he could make a fight for it here – perhaps hold them up while Rebecca escaped.

Another step, and another. The whiskered face of Tom Griffiths appeared at the top of the ladder. He caught sight of Clarenceux, crouched in the hay, and Rebecca standing beside him, and climbed the last rungs.

'My boy tells me you're in trouble.'

Clarenceux could not be sure how this meeting would turn out. He had no inkling of Griffiths's religion. He only knew him on two accounts: the tenement he rented and the Skinners Company. He could easily imagine the gruff and stoutly traditional Griffiths taking it into his head to turn him in to the authorities.

'Goodman Griffiths, I am in a desperate plight. A man of my acquaintance – this goodwife's husband – came to me one night last week and asked for my help. Naturally, I did what I could; but there is some business in which the man was involved that attracted the attention of a royal sergeant-at-arms. I don't know what that business is; I am trying to find out. Nevertheless, that same sergeant-at-arms wrecked my house the following day and killed one of my servants, a boy. The same man tortured this woman's husband to death. Last night there was an attempt to kill me. I fled here, in desperation. I need to leave the city and to stay away for a while. I need clean clothes and a basin of water.'

Griffiths thought for a moment. 'You left tracks. Not just footprints; bloody tracks. They lead straight to this stable.'

'For that, Goodman Griffiths, I am deeply sorry. I beg your forgiveness.'

Griffiths said nothing.

'We have trespassed on your time too much and will trouble you no more,' said Clarenceux suddenly, feeling that Griffiths was disinclined to help them. He started to get to his feet.

Griffiths did not budge. 'Hear me out, first, before you go. You are a good man, Mr Clarenceux. I know you don't have to come here and check these houses. The queen's bailiff would take the same two pounds and five shillings every quarter either way, and it would be delivered to you whether you cared about their condition or not. But you do come and look, and you do send men to repair them. You take far more care of us than the bailiff. Maybe you've only done all that so today you'd have a hiding place. But you're a good warden of the company too. So I'll do a deal with you. I have a young family, and we have little money. It is a struggle every quarter to pay the rent. If I don't give you clean clothes but take you out of the city in a pelterer's cart, how much is it worth?'

'A pelterer's cart?' Clarenceux almost laughed at the repulsive thought. But then he realised that it was perfect. Who would suspect anyone would hide in a cart of stinking hides and skins?

'We need to go across the bridge, to Southwark.'

'Then I'll take you across the bridge. There's a threepenny toll for a full cart.'

Clarenceux looked up at Rebecca. She looked nervous, but shrugged her shoulders. *What alternative have we got?*

He felt in his pocket for the purse he had taken from the table in Draper's study and looked at the coins. 'Half a year's rent. Four pounds ten shillings.'

'Make it five pounds.'

'Payable when you get us safely to the stable yard of the Bell Inn, in Southwark.'

'Mr Clarenceux, you and I have an agreement.'

54

Lady Percy, the dowager countess of Northumberland, was about sixty years of age. She had a permanent frown upon her deeply lined, very pale face. She was motionless, seated on a massive horse in the park of Sheffield Manor, which was slightly frosted after the recent cold weather. Her small bright eyes were fixed on the dead rabbit in front of her. The goshawk had dropped it on the ground and, being allowed to peck, had broken open the skull and eaten the brains first. Then it had eaten the rest of the head and the top half of the body. Next it had upended the remains, so the legs were in the air, and pulled the fur out in tufts, scattering it all around the carcass. Now it was gorging on the thigh muscles. Every so often it would look up and its bright red eye would switch from point to point in the landscape.

Her ladyship remained motionless. Fascinated.

She had seen the rider out of the corner of her eye but he could wait. Her servants had instructions not to disturb her. If she guessed rightly, she knew who the caller was, and what his mission was.

Today her hawk was not hungry and quickly lost interest. With a sudden great beating of its wings, it flew off. Her ladyship waved a hand at her falconer and turned her horse back to the manor, to see the visitor.

*

No one spoke to her until she had dismounted and entered the house. The servants knew better; the visitor understood, and bided his time as he watched her stride into the lofty hall, then turn to receive him formally.

'My lady, this man announces himself as Sir Percival.'

'Well he might,' she responded. Looking at him she said, 'Your arrival means bad news.'

'Indeed, my lady,' replied Sir Percival, bowing and removing his travelling cope. He was a tall thin man of forty years, with a neat brown beard and sharp, concentrated features that suggested he was a shrewd man, which indeed he was. His eyes were not unkind but nor were they forgiving; his lips were pursed as if permanently considering a grave matter.

'When did you leave London?'

'On Sunday morning, not long before midday.'

'We must converse in private.' Turning to the various servants who had now gathered in the hall, she declared, 'There is no need for any of you to be present. Come, sir.'

And with that she turned and marched up to the dais, stepped on to it, and went through the wide doorway and up the broad sweeping stairs beyond.

They were alone in the privy chamber, next to her bedchamber. There was only the one seat: a large wooden throne, on which Lady Percy sat. Apart from the tapestries on the walls, and a chest behind the throne, there was no other furniture in the room.

'What time did he die?'

'That I do not know, my lady. I left London as soon as I had had confirmation from Mistress Barker's contacts.'

'But he definitely passed over the chronicle? To its intended recipient?'

'Yes, my lady. To the new King Clariance.'

'Well, that is something, at least.'

Lady Percy tapped the arm of her throne. The man before her was the linchpin, the Knight whose name was not known to the others and whose principal purpose was to announce to her when the chronicle changed hands. In line with the original plan he should now return to London and make his identity known to the new King Clariance. But if the plot had been discovered, this was dangerous.

'I presume you have not yet revealed your identity?'

'No.' Sir Percival looked her in the eye. 'The new King Clariance knows nothing.'

Lady Percy got up from the chair and walked to the window. 'It is difficult to know what to do. The plan was all about the right time to act, not about how to cope with betrayal. I take it you understand what has happened?'

'Not entirely, my lady.'

She continued walking, considering her words carefully. 'One of the Knights – Sir Dagonet, whose real name I understand is William Draper – was heard discussing the Knights' fraternity with representatives of Queen Mary of Scots, at Holyrood. He was heard by a number of men, one of whom was a spy for Elizabeth of England, a man called Wood. Apparently Draper spoke about Henry Machyn's chronicle. As you are aware, there is not much damage a Knight can do by himself; that is why the fraternity exists. But when I made further inquiries, it turned out that Wood had left Scotland immediately and Draper was following him back to London. As it was certain that Wood would tell the authorities, I decided to eliminate Draper, to stop them from interrogating him further. There was little time to spare but I judged the mission essential. I sent a good man with instructions: he was to return a certain pistol when Draper was dead. That was nine days ago. Needless to say I have not received the pistol.'

Sir Percival nodded, understanding now what had thrown the whole scheme into jeopardy. 'Henry Machyn told me on Friday he was planning to hand over the chronicle that night – he knew Draper had talked. He said he had been told by a royal sergeant-at-arms that he had twenty-four hours to surrender the chronicle or he would be killed. But he was resolute. He sent his wife to Mistress Barker's, telling her to stay with her. I waited for those twenty-four hours, and was preparing to come north on Sunday when a message came to Mistress Barker's that Henry Machyn's corpse had been seen at the plague pit.'

'Is Mistress Barker still in London?'

'Yes.'

'And her identity is still a secret?'

'As far as I know.'

'Good. She is a brave woman, my sister. If the new King Clariance can act on the instructions he has received, we may still have a chance.'

55

The journey to Julius's house was decidedly uncomfortable. Clarenceux and Rebecca felt every jolt of the cart as they travelled across the frozen streets of the city. With many skins piled over them they were not cold, but the weight made it difficult to breathe. Then there was the stench. Tanyards smelled bad at the best of times but having to travel in a cart full of skins, furs and pelts was perpetually nauseating. Regularly Clarenceux found himself retching, his stomach too empty to vomit. He listened to Rebecca undergoing a similar ordeal as her body also revolted against the smell.

But comfort was not their highest priority, safety was, and in this respect the journey was perfect. They travelled through the city and crossed London Bridge without being questioned or bothered by the guards. Rebecca had waited in the yard of the Bell Inn while Clarenceux went inside, stinking of dead animals' skins, and paid for their horses' fodder and stabling. Tom Griffiths had thanked Clarenceux for the money, wished him well, and driven off briskly with the cart; and Clarenceux and Rebecca began the ride down to Chislehurst. They arrived back at Summerhill just as it was beginning to get dark.

Julius met them in the hall – and insisted that they both take a bath immediately, in that same place. The bathtub, six feet in diameter – like half of an enormous barrel – was brought out and placed in front of the dais, by the fire. Half an hour later it was steaming, filled with rose petals and hot water from the kitchens, poured into the tub by all the servants working as a team. Two large standing candelabra, each with a dozen candles, were placed on either side. Clarenceux and Rebecca were each handed two sponges: one large one on which to sit and a small one with which to wash themselves. They watched as one of the servants added some milk and the appropriate herbs for a skin-cleansing bath: feverfew, nettles, violet leaves, fennel and rose-mary. Julius sat at the table on the dais, poring over the chronicle. Another servant laid out clean clothes on a bench nearby.

Clarenceux bathed first. He took off his stinking clothes and left them in a pile on the flagstones. His hose he threw on to the fire. The hot water stung his wounded legs as he stepped in, and tingled on his skin. He soaked the larger sponge, placed it on the bottom of the tub, and sat on it. Then he began to scrub with the other sponge.

Julius was staring at the chronicle. 'The first two dates both refer to St Paul's Cross. Give me a third.'

'Try Nicholas Hill's date, the fifteenth of June 1552,' said Rebecca, who had been discreetly watching Clarenceux.

Julius cleared his throat. 'It says, "The fifteenth day of June was buried Baptyst Borow the milliner without Cripplegate in St Giles's Parish, with a penon, a cote armour, and a herald, and with twenty-three staff-torches, and so twenty-three poor men bore them, and many mourners in black; and the company of Clerks were there, and this place was hanged with black and arms six dozen."'

Clarenceux looked up at Rebecca and saw the puzzled expression on her face. He turned to Julius, who was also staring at him. 'I have no idea,' he said. 'Try another date. The eighteenth of June 1555.'

Julius turned the pages. 'It's difficult to work out which year is which ... Here, I think this is the one. Yes, it must be.'

He said nothing, reading silently.

'What does it say?' asked Rebecca as she touched a servant

on the arm and took from him the brass basin and small jug of
scented lye he was carrying. Clarenceux ducked his head into the
bath and came up again. Rebecca went over to him and surprised
him by pouring a little of the lye into his hair. He started to turn,
then realised what she was doing and relaxed as she started
rubbing his scalp.

'It doesn't say anything,' said Julius.

'What?' asked Clarenceux, turning. Rebecca paused.

'There is no entry for that day.'

'Try looking on the adjacent pages – the dates are not all in
order,' Clarenceux urged as Rebecca began to rub in the lye again.

Julius looked. 'No, there still doesn't seem to be a day with
that title. It goes from the third of June – lots of entries for that
day – to the tenth, the eleventh, the seventeenth and the fourteenth. Then we're into July.'

Clarenceux stopped Rebecca with his hand. 'Are you sure that
there isn't a leaf missing?' He waited a moment then ducked his
head under the water to wash away the lye, and stood up, naked,
to take a towel from a servant.

Julius inspected the spine. 'Quite certain. There isn't an entry
for that date. That is all I can say.'

'What about Gyttens's date, the nineteenth of June 1556,'
Clarenceux said, stepping out of the tub and drying himself,
glancing suddenly at Rebecca. Embarrassed to be caught looking
at his naked body, she turned away.

Julius searched the manuscript, carefully scrutinising the pages
as he turned them, making sure he did not miss any stray entries.
'I'm sorry, but there does not seem to be anything for that date
either. It goes from the ninth to the tenth, the fourteenth, the
fifteenth, the eighteenth. There it mentions three hangings: first
that of Thomas of Watheryng for robbing a cart, and then "the
same day was arraigned at the Guildhall, for a conspiracy, Master
Francis Varney and Captain Turner, and they cast to be drawn,
hanged and quartered". There is an entry for the twenty-seventh:
the burning of eleven men and two women between four posts

at Stratford le Bow, attended by twenty thousand people. Then there's another entry for the tenth and another for the last day of the month, the drawing, hanging and quartering of Lord de la Warre for treason. That's all for June 1556.'

Clarenceux took a shirt and pulled it over his head. He walked across to Julius and read the chronicle over his shoulder. 'I don't know. I don't know what it means. I don't know what to say. I wonder if Henry gave me the right book.'

Rebecca had removed her outer clothes and was rubbing lye into her hair over the basin. 'No, that is definitely the book,' she said, pausing but not looking up. 'He only had one like it.'

'But still, why all the fuss with the dates if they do not relate to the dates in the chronicle?'

'Maybe they have some other meaning?' she suggested, pulling off her chemise and stepping into the bathtub.

'Well, that's obvious,' said Julius, looking from her to Clarenceux and noticing that Clarenceux's attention was all on her. He nudged him and Clarenceux turned away and continued dressing, listening to the splashing of the water.

James Hopton entered at the lower end of the hall and bowed. 'Supper is ready when you require it, sir.'

'Good. Come now, William, let us leave Goodwife Machyn to soak in her bath in peace.'

They discussed the chronicle before, during and after supper. Julius took notes – seeming as interested in the social details as in the mystery it contained. Clarenceux wished he would stop reading out the entries that concerned men and women being burnt for heresy, or being drawn to the gallows on hurdles, then hanged, and quartered for treason.

'I do not understand why the dates do not relate to the chronicle,' he said again. 'Even the ones for which there are entries do not tell us anything.'

Rebecca tapped her fingers on the table. 'I suggest putting all the dates in order on a piece of paper. To see them all together.'

'What do you have in mind?' asked Clarenceux.

'I think there's a pattern.'

Julius shrugged, and pushed the candle nearer to Clarenceux, then handed him the pen, ink and a piece of paper. Clarenceux started with the first date, and wrote the name beside the entry in each case.

13 June 1550 – Sir Lancelot
15 June 1552 – Sir Reynold
18 June 1555 – Sir Ector
19 June 1556 – Sir Reynold
20 June 1557 – King Clariance
16 June 1559 – Sir Dagonet

He then added the name Sir Yvain, for which they did not have a date, at the bottom.

'Let me see,' said Rebecca, her face bright in the glow of the candle.

Clarenceux passed her the paper, and watched her studying it. Her attention to the document interested him. 'How much of it can you read?'

'I have difficulty writing but Henry taught me how to read. He thought everyone should be able to.' She paused, and then pushed the paper back towards Clarenceux. 'It is as I thought. William Draper lied to us. He gave us the wrong date.'

Julius leant forward. 'What? How do you know?'

Clarenceux looked at the list again.

'Look at the pattern,' said Rebecca. 'Look, the eighteenth of June, then the nineteenth – as the year increases by one, so too does the day. If you fill in the gaps, the fourteenth of June will relate to 1551. The sixteenth of June should be 1553, not 1559. Draper lied to us about the year.'

'He might have lied about the day,' Julius observed.

'Maybe. But I doubt it. Mr Clarenceux was holding a knife in front of his face at the time. And we know he got the month right – they're all June. In the circumstances, it would have been easier to lie about the year.'

Clarenceux raised his hands to his face, and then set them down on the table. 'I think you have it. These aren't dates – they're all one date, disguised.' He stared at the paper for a moment and then pointed to the dates before him. 'Henry said something about the date he gave me being "exactly like that". Now I can't remember for certain, but I think that by "exactly like that" he meant June *the twentieth* 1557, not the twentieth of June. I think the *twentieth* does not relate to the day but the year. Rebecca is right: Draper lied. They are all the same date: June 1537 or 1538.'

Julius placed his hands on the table. 'I do not follow you. Why 1537 or 1538?'

'Because "the twentieth" was 1557, "the nineteenth" was 1556, "the eighteenth" 1555, "the thirteenth" 1550, and so on; so the second was 1539 and the first 1538.'

'So why June 1537 or 1538? Why not just 1538?'

Clarenceux did not answer. He seemed deeply troubled. He suddenly got up and walked to the far side of the room and stood there, with his back to them.

It is so simple. It is not a code at all – it's an acrostic.

'Julius,' he said, 'when did the old earl of Northumberland die?'

Julius looked up at the ceiling. 'Oh, about fifteen thir—'

'No,' said Clarenceux suddenly. 'I need to know exactly when. The day and the month. You must have a book here that can tell us.'

Julius nodded, got up from his seat and went to a large folio volume at a nearby book press. He lifted it and set it down on the table beside Machyn's chronicle, then leant over and leafed through the pages.

Clarenceux said nothing. He just stood, watching.

Julius straightened and turned to Clarenceux. 'You're right,' he said solemnly.

'June 1537?'

'The last day of the month.'

Rebecca could not stand it any longer. 'For the sake of Mary, Mother of God!' she exclaimed. 'What is it?'

Clarenceux wiped his face with his hands and looked into the candle flame, thinking. 'These are not years, they're anniversaries. They mark the years that have passed since the death of Henry Percy, earl of Northumberland.'

'So?' asked Rebecca impatiently. 'How do you know? And what does it mean? Why have you both gone so ... so solemn, so quiet, so fearful? Who was this Henry Percy – apart from the earl of Northumberland?'

Clarenceux did not move. 'Goodwife Machyn, do you remember saying you suspected that the reason why there were two Sir Reynolds was because the first letters of the names of the Knights spelled out a message? Look what happens if you correct Draper's date and put his Arthurian name in its proper place.'

Clarenceux drew a line through Draper's name and date and wrote them again, interlining them between 1552 and 1555.

> 13 June 1550 – Sir Lancelot
> 15 June 1552 – Sir Reynold
> 16 June 1553 – Sir Dagonet
> 18 June 1555 – Sir Ector
> 19 June 1556 – Sir Reynold
> 20 June 1557 – King Clariance

'The missing dates show us the missing letters. So we have L then a gap, then R and D, then a gap, then E, R C. And we have a Y. That Y could be the second, fifth, or last letter. It happens to be the last. It is an acrostic: it spells LORD PERCY. He died in June 1537 – just after the executions following the Pilgrimage of Grace.'

Rebecca said nothing, trying to take it all in.

'No wonder our late friend declared that only you would be

able to understand it,' said Julius. 'It's a damn good thing he didn't entrust his revolution to me.'

Rebecca was worried. 'This doesn't tell us anything. As you say, Lord Percy has been dead since 1537. He can't help us now. Besides, why did Henry guard the book so carefully for so many years if the code merely refers to a dead earl?'

'A good point indeed,' said Clarenceux. 'The dates and names simply tell us where to go next, where to take the chronicle.'

'And that is?'

'Sheffield. Where Lord Percy's widow lives.'

Suddenly Julius picked up the volume he had consulted and slammed it shut. 'No, you will not . . .' he began. But something stopped him. 'Have you ever met the dowager countess? She is not so much a woman as a dragon – the sort of woman who causes the Devil to walk in fear.'

Clarenceux shook his head. 'Julius, may I take one of your horses?'

'No! For God's sake, you'll get yourself killed, William.'

'Oh, heavens above! What are you talking about?' Rebecca pleaded. 'What is it that is so serious that you suddenly can't talk openly in front of me? And you won't lend him a horse? Mr Clarenceux, not so long ago we lay side by side together in a bed. That speaks of a certain degree of trust, no? And yet you will not tell me something that makes your friend shout at you and refuse to lend you a horse. What is it? What makes you so fearful? Tell me.'

Clarenceux and Julius looked at one another. Julius shook his head.

Clarenceux began to speak. 'The man we are talking about, Lord Henry Percy – the man who seems to lie at the heart of this conspiracy, your husband's legacy, call it what you will – was widely believed to be the first husband of Anne Boleyn, mother of our present queen. Indeed, until the old king decided he wanted Anne for his own bedmate, it was said to be an open secret that Lord Percy and Anne Boleyn were man and wife. As

Lord Percy was still quite young, and in Cardinal Wolsey's household, they did not live together, although they were deeply in love. Then the king took an interest in Anne. He had no qualms about bedding another man's wife – and no man was so foolish as to stop the king from taking what he wanted – but Anne herself insisted on only sleeping with her husband. That was a challenge for King Henry. He put all his efforts – both charm and threats – into making *himself* her husband. He forced Wolsey to separate Lord Percy and Anne, and then he married Anne. And when he grew tired of her, and took a fancy to Jane Seymour instead, he had Anne beheaded. Her brutal killing was one of the reasons for the Pilgrimage of Grace – Aske himself petitioned Lord Percy to lead them in revolt against the king's tyranny.'

There was silence.

'What William is failing to make clear,' added Julius after a little while, 'is that there are those who believe that Lord Percy was not only the love of Anne's life but also the real father of our present queen. If proof of that relationship were to be found, it would naturally bar her from the throne.'

Clarenceux nodded. 'So a secret that will affect "the fate of two queens" and centres on Lord Percy points in that direction. Hence our concern for the—'

'Concern?' interjected Julius. 'You use a very slight word for it. You are talking about high treason – no, the very *highest* treason. If you get caught your fate will be the same as all traitors' – you will be drawn, hanged, and quartered. Except that they don't quarter women.'

'What do they do with them?' Rebecca asked.

'Need you ask?'

'They burn them alive,' said Clarenceux. He made up his mind. 'I will go alone to Sheffield. Rebecca, you will stay here. Thanks to you we understand the acrostic – your part is done. Now it is clear what I have to do.'

Rebecca looked up with shining eyes. 'You are not going alone,

Mr Clarenceux. Do not even think of it. I am coming with you even if I have to walk behind you all the way.'

Julius shook his head. 'Goodwife Machyn, you are talking about pursuing a line of inquiry that is sufficient in itself to send you to the stake. Neither of you should do this. William, you cannot risk being killed for a plot that does not concern you, especially when you have a wife and young children. And as for you, Goodwife Machyn, you cannot even think of inviting such a terrible fate. You know what it is like: we have all seen men and women burnt to death. You've heard the screams and smelled the burning flesh – and no doubt you've seen that people do not die immediately in the flames but can survive even after their skin has burnt away and the bloody fat is dripping from their legs. Nothing is worse than that.'

'Perhaps.' Rebecca looked defiantly at him. 'But death does come eventually, and the pain passes and the soul ascends to heaven. The chill of regret lasts much longer.'

'I will not allow it. Not for either of you.'

'Julius,' said Clarenceux gently, 'we are not asking for your permission. We are asking for your help. Neither of us will rest safely in our beds until this matter is ended. If you won't help us, then I will have to find someone else who will.'

Julius stared at Clarenceux. 'Would you help *me* into my grave, if I asked you?'

'No – but I would help you do God's work, even if it meant you put yourself in grave danger.'

'God's work?' said Julius, looking down at the table surface, and then the chronicle. 'You call it God's work. Others will call it treason.'

Once again Clarenceux and Julius stayed up talking and drinking sack after Rebecca had gone to bed. She was exhausted and was glad to lie down in the warmth. But then she could not sleep. Too much was happening around her. She was no longer in control of her own fate.

She heard a noise on the stairs, footsteps on the landing.

'Mr Clarenceux, is that you?'

There was a pause. 'Yes, Goodwife Machyn.'

'What are you doing, standing outside my door?'

He said nothing for a long time. She lay with her eyes open in the dark.

'Mr Clarenceux?'

'Yes?'

'Will you promise me something?'

'What?'

'That you will not leave without me in the morning.'

There was another long pause.

'Good night, Goodwife Machyn.'

56

Thursday, 16 December

Clarenceux woke at dawn. He felt the chill in the darkness as he pushed back the sheets and blankets. When he made his way across to the ewer and basin, the cold of the water was a shock.

He walked to the door and paused before putting his hand on the latch. *It is better that Rebecca stays here, for I will be travelling with the chronicle. Julius will look after her. Just as it is for the best that Awdrey and my daughters are far away. I must put distance between myself and everyone dear.*

He closed his eyes and said a prayer as he stood there – for his wife and family, for Rebecca, for Henry Machyn's soul and that of Will Terry. And he said a brief prayer too for the souls of the two men he had killed. He crossed himself, said 'Amen' quietly, and lifted the latch to go downstairs.

The door opened suddenly, seemingly pushed towards him. He looked down and saw, in the dim light, a figure lying on the floor. Rebecca had been sitting there, leaning against the door.

'Good morning,' she said wearily. 'I presume it is time?'

'Rebecca, it is time for *me* to leave.'

It took her only a couple of seconds to come to her senses. 'I know where you are going. Unless you are planning to lock me in irons, I am coming too.'

Clarenceux had no answer. He watched Rebecca get to her

feet and turn to face him, pushing her hair out of her face, struggling to see his expression.

'It's not what you think. I mean that ... It's just that I have no guarantee otherwise that I will see you again. You could just be running away, for all I know. Saving your own skin. Then what will I have? Fear. Fear of Walsingham and Cecil. They won't spare me; they will torture me and not even give a thought to my suffering.'

Clarenceux shook his head and made his way to the old stone staircase. He touched the wall to steady himself, his mind turning still between tiredness and bewilderment.

Rebecca followed him. 'Ask yourself this, Mr Clarenceux. If it is God's work that we do, what right have you to forbid me to assist?'

Clarenceux stopped at the foot of the stairs. *She is right. What right have I to appropriate God's work to myself? Is it rather fear of her that makes me say she should stay here?*

She was there behind him. 'You must follow your calling and I must follow mine,' she said. 'God puts these things into both our hearts. And though they may be dangerous, we are good Christians if we obey.' She paused, looking at his figure in the dim light, and added, 'It is a good thing too, for we understand each other's obeying.'

Clarenceux turned to face her. He remembered finding her in the graveyard, when he feared he had lost her. He remembered his realisation that *God alone is not enough.* His mind went back further too, to his suffering in Walsingham's cellar, and how he had realised that he would rather die as Clarenceux than live as Walsingham. And at that moment, standing there on the stairs of the tower, it did seem to be God's will that they should be together. If what they were doing was called treason by some men, it did not matter, for it was sacred.

'Very well, Goodwife Machyn,' he said. 'If you believe it is the will of God, then let us ride to Sheffield together.'

*

They took their leave of Julius and his wife later that morning. Julius had ordered his servants to pack extra clothes for them both the night before, having guessed that Rebecca would be travelling with Clarenceux. The chronicle was safely encased in wooden boards wrapped in canvas and bound firmly to Clarenceux's saddle. His sword was given an old scabbard and hidden among the travelling bags placed on a sumpter horse. As they prepared for the long journey in the stable yard, Julius handed him a leather purse.

'I wish I could spare more,' he said.

Clarenceux felt the weight. 'You are a kind man indeed, Julius, the most generous man I believe I have ever met.' He embraced his friend and held him firmly for a long moment before breaking away, and mounting the palfrey that the stable boy was holding ready for him, 'Thank you. With luck we'll be back to share roast beef with you on Christmas Day.'

Julius smiled but said nothing. He turned to Rebecca. He took her hand, drew it to his lips, and kissed it as he would the hand of a lady. 'Look after him, Goodwife Machyn,' he said. 'Go with God's speed.'

Both Clarenceux and Rebecca looked back several times before they passed out of sight of Summerhill, along the road towards Bromley.

The snow was beautiful at first – large flakes falling against the backdrop of trees on both sides of the road. The branches were soon laden so heavily with snow that they sagged, weighed down with the unexpected whiteness. But it quickly soaked their collars and clothes. It was difficult too for the horses to walk on the ice, and Clarenceux and Rebecca often had to dismount, to dislodge compressed snow from their horses' hooves. With less than five hours of daylight left, Clarenceux realised that even if they rode for an hour after dusk, the most they could hope to manage was twenty miles that day. Their journey was set to be a long, cold one.

Chislehurst was on the far side of London so, to travel north they could either cross the river at Greenwich or take the ferry between Putney and Fulham. Clarenceux deemed the second route safer, but it took a long time – far longer than he had imagined. The main problem was the unevenness of the frozen ground. Turning the corner in the middle of Beckenham, by a thatched inn crested with snow, they gazed down the wide street to see it wholly churned up: huge ruts in the mud that had frozen solid overnight and now were covered with snow. The last thing they wanted was a horse with a broken leg. Clarenceux deemed it sensible to dismount and walk, leading the animals by the reins. *At this rate we will be walking all the way to Sheffield*, he thought as they left Beckenham, cursing the cold wind and the snow that had looked so beautiful when it had begun to fall.

It was well after noon on that first day when they crossed the river, and an hour later it was beginning to grow dark. Clarenceux urged Rebecca on, telling her they needed to reach Barnet by nightfall, knowing that their chances of doing so were small. They were still four miles away when the last colour drained from the landscape and they were once more in a freezing world of dark and shadow. Rebecca said nothing but rode in silence, knowing that Clarenceux's frustration would probably cause him to argue with her whatever she said. It was a blessed relief when, as they neared the looming shadow of a wayside inn, he suggested stopping for the night. Hunched in his travelling cape, he was obviously suffering from the bitter wind as much as she was.

Once more pretending to be man and wife, they hired a private room and dined on a mess of good pea pottage, bread, ale and cheese. With a pair of candles burning and a fire on the hearth Rebecca felt comfortable. The change in Clarenceux's mood was also a relief. On the road he had been desperate to push on, silent and moody, irritated that their progress was so slow. She suspected that he blamed her, and that he regretted allowing her to accompany him. But all those fears and anxieties melted on entering the inn. The comfort of the fire was almost enough to make him smile too.

The clothes she had travelled in from Chislehurst were more practical than those she had worn last time she had stayed at an inn with Clarenceux, and she was able to undress herself that evening without having to ask for his assistance. Clarenceux divested himself of his clothes and retired wearing nothing but his shirt and a cap. Watching him out of the corner of her eye, Rebecca did likewise, and swiftly climbed under the sheets and blankets. With one candle left burning she curled up on her side, facing him as he lay on his back. They lay motionless for a long time, in silence.

At last, he turned to look at her in the candlelight.

Without thinking what he was doing, he reached forward and moved the dark hair away from the side of her face with one finger. Running the tip over her cheek to her mole, he touched it lightly. She said nothing and did not move.

The candle guttered, almost spent. It spoke of their being together: a companionship as they waited for the inevitable darkness. He looked away.

'Always waiting for the going out of the light,' she whispered.

The candle went out.

Now there was only the intimacy of speech and touch. But he dared not touch her, not in the darkness. In the light, intimacy was a sign of their closeness in the face of shared danger. In the darkness it was like a whisper of lust.

'Let us sleep now, Goodwife Machyn. Good night.'

He closed his eyes and lay still, seeing the two of them as small creatures in God's vast world.

The daylight hours were a hard trek, battling against the snow, ice and frozen ground. They pushed back the moment of stopping as far as it could go – even to the point of travelling by the thin moonlight that now was to be seen in the sky. The new moon had appeared on the fifteenth of December, the day before they set out; but such were the clouds that it gave them little help. On the evening of the seventeenth there was still enough light at dusk for them to ride on from the small town of Luton, confident that by following the snow-covered frozen road they could press on for another four or five miles. That left them in a quandary, for when it was properly night they found themselves freezing in a sharp wind on Luton Downs, with little idea of where the next inn might be. In the end they led their horses to the nearest house and begged shelter. Fortunately the spirit of hospitality was not yet dead in this corner of Bedfordshire, and the yeoman gave them a chamber and a meal of cold ham, bread and caudled ale in return for a few coins.

The following day they pressed on for another thirty miles, reaching Higham Ferrers in Northamptonshire by nightfall. Long icicles hung from the eaves of the roofs fronting the empty, snow-filled marketplace. Following their experience the previous evening they decided to stay at an inn rather than continue in the darkness.

Their second and third nights were like the first: anxious on account of the danger and cautiously intimate until the candle went out. Clarenceux began to wonder whether their increasing closeness made them more conscious of their vulnerability. To be together was a comfort, it was true; but it was also a reminder of the danger they faced.

The next morning they set out to travel to Oakham. It was warmer but blustery and overcast. Grey clouds swept across the sky and sent the piles of snow cascading from the boughs of trees. Not long after starting they came to a great oak that stood beside the road. One bough had been so heavily weighed with snow and ice that it had split and torn from the trunk, and now lay across the road in a wreck of splinters, twigs, leaves and mistletoe.

Then it began to rain.

Clarenceux fastened up his travelling cape against the weather and smiled at Rebecca. 'It will be good for us, the rain,' he shouted over the downpour. 'It will dissolve the snow. We will be able to ride faster.'

Rebecca looked at him askance, suspecting that he was being too optimistic. She was right. An hour later they were both utterly drenched, sheltering from the storm in a barn near the road. The rain was indeed dissolving the snow – and rapidly – but in its wake it left huge stretches of mud. Wide puddles emerged in the road, and the sludge kicked up by the horses' hooves soon had them dirty as well as wet. Far from allowing them to hasten ahead, three hours of rain left the ground too soft to ride fast, and too dark with mud to be followed by the scant moonlight. At Uppingham they decided they could go no further. They were wet, miserable, shivering – and still short of their destination by six miles.

Clarenceux was despondent as he took off all his clothes except his wet shirt in the cold, small chamber of yet another roadside inn. He did not speak as he hung them over an old rail.

'They won't dry quickly enough in here,' Rebecca observed.

'What else can we do?' he sighed. 'There is no fireplace.'

'I'll find one.'

Twenty minutes later she was back, with the innkeeper and two servants. The innkeeper bowed frequently and apologised profusely, and declared that had he known who Mr Clarenceux was, he would never have presumed to give him an unheated room. Clarenceux found himself being hurried along a corridor in nothing but his linen shirt, then up a staircase and across a landing to a fine panelled chamber in the main building of the inn, while the servants followed with their baggage. A fire was newly alight in the room and roaring magnificently, with a clothes rail placed before it. Four candles were burning around the room, and there was even a footbath of warm water ready.

Clarenceux sat on the bed in his shirt, and watched the last servant close the door behind him.

'You told them my name?'

Rebecca stared at him. 'Would you rather freeze to death in

wet clothes? Yes, I told the innkeeper who you are. I said that you are conducting a visitation of these parts; and although you are not a demanding man yourself, and are prepared to suffer hard beds and little comfort, the gentlemen whom you meet are bound to enquire as to your lodgings. In all honesty you could not say you were well lodged here, without a fire. Pardon me if I was wrong.'

She turned away from Clarenceux and began to remove her own wet clothes. Clarenceux sat on the edge of the bed and simply looked at her as she wrung them out over the basin and hung them on the rail. *She must have convinced the landlord that she really is the wife of a gentleman.*

'Don't waste the hot water of the footbath,' she said, not turning round. 'And take off that shirt so it can dry.'

Clarenceux did as he was told. He got into the bed naked and lay on his side, listening to her arranging their clothes around the room. After a few minutes he fell asleep. He did not feel her slip into the bed beside him, also naked.

57

Sunday, 19 December

'You have no idea how tired a man can be,' said Sir William Cecil as he sat at the wide table in the study of his house. 'Believe me, no one wants the queen to marry more than me. The country might want an heir, but I just want her to have a husband who takes her to bed at a decent hour and keeps her there until morning. I am exhausted. Policy until three hours beyond midnight, and then a messenger at dawn to tell me I am required at court immediately – two days running.'

'I am sorry to hear of your exertions,' said Walsingham, placing a sheet of paper on the table. 'I have some sympathy. This problem of the Knights of the Round Table has been commanding my sleeping hours as well as my waking ones in much the same way as the queen has been commanding yours.'

Cecil pulled a candle closer and studied the page that Walsingham had put in front of him. He squinted, reading the lines of secretary-hand. It contained Arthurian names, dates, and here and there a dotted line across the page. He put it down. 'I'm sorry, Francis, my wits are dull. You are going to have to explain.'

'Daniel Gyttens still refuses to speak. But we know his Arthurian name. We also know that Lancelot Heath is one of the Knights, and that the name for William Harley is King Clariance, as it was for Henry Machyn when he was alive. So we have the identities of eight of the nine knights, all but one of their Arthurian names, and five of their dates.'

'I presume none of them gave this information freely?'

Walsingham smiled briefly. He pointed to the sheet of paper.

'All the details are there, Sir William. I have laid them out to show the pattern in the dates: as the day increases by one, so too does the year. No doubt this relates to a series of hidden entries in the chronicle. It is a clever system: each date by itself appears innocuous but together they spell something potent and no doubt treasonable.'

'But – forgive me, Francis – you still don't have the chronicle. So you cannot hope to determine what those entries are.'

'No. But the pattern means we can establish what all the dates are – or are likely to be.'

Cecil looked at the paper again. 'The dotted lines show the missing dates in the sequence?'

'As I see it, yes.'

Cecil kept looking at the paper. In particular his eye concentrated on the first three names and dates.

Robert Lowe (Sir Owain) – 1551, June ye 14th
Nicholas Hill (Sir Reynold) – 1552, June ye 15th
William Draper (Sir Dagonet) – 1553, June ye 16th
----------------------- 1554, June y^{ye} 17th
Michael Hill (Sir Ector) – 1555, June ye 18th
----------------------- 1556, June ye 19th
----------------------- 1557, June ye 20th
James Emery (Sir Yvain) – 1558, June ye 21st
xxx
William Harley, Clarenceux (King Clariance of
    Northumberland)
Daniel Gyttens (Sir Reynold)
Lancelot Heath

'But there should be nine names and dates, you said?'

'According to Michael Hill, there is one Knight whose name

and identity is not known to any of the other Knights except the commander, King Clariance.'

Cecil stared longer at the paper. *So one of the dotted lines represents the ninth Knight. Or perhaps he has another date altogether, either at the start of the sequence or at the end.* He remained silent, thinking. Eventually he asked, 'Why do you suppose the name chosen for the king was King Clariance of Northumberland?'

Walsingham shrugged. 'I suspect Clarenceux adopted "Clariance" to match his heraldic title. Perhaps vanity played a part.'

Cecil looked at Walsingham. 'You are still presuming he is the instigator of this affair.'

'Clariance is the so-called "king" of these men. He is the only one who knows the identity of one of the Knights. And who else of rank is there to organise them? It is not Draper. He is rich and well connected but he is a coward. And his Arthurian name is that of a jester.'

'Yes, Francis, I know all that. But don't you think that the similarity of Clarenceux and Clariance is a little obvious? Clarenceux is no fool; he would rather go out of his way to conceal his identity than suggest it. I suspect that you think he is in command because he is a gentleman. If so, you are narrowing your mind.'

'How else should I think of him? He *is* a gentleman.'

Cecil got up from his seat. He walked across to the fireplace and rubbed his hands together, looking into the flames. 'Think of him as just a man. He might be a ringleader and he might not. You think in terms of hierarchy, that the most superior being always commands. But ideas are not the preserve of the richest or the socially elevated. Rebellious ideas rarely come from above. More often they come from lesser men ...' Cecil turned and looked into Walsingham's emotionless eyes. 'Even from women.'

'Are you referring to Rebecca Machyn?' Walsingham remembered his self-recriminations for overlooking her in the past.

'I am saying nothing, just suggesting possibilities. But consider this. If the title of King Clariance was previously used by Henry Machyn, it stands to reason that Clarenceux did not choose it to reflect his heraldic title. Quite obviously, he did not choose it at all.'

'Do you have a better theory?'

'Oh, come on, Francis. I am a tired man but my wits are not so slow as to agree that a theory is good simply because it is the only one you have. If we all thought like that, half of London would be locked up by now. But, as you ask, I do have a better one.'

'Well?'

'You pride yourself on solving this problem – you almost treat it as a game. So you tell me. I'll give you a clue. The key is not in the word "Clariance" but in "Northumberland".'

'The duke of Northumberland?'

'No. The earl.'

Walsingham looked away, his small eyes darting around the plasterwork and gold-painted corners of the great chamber, searching for some hint – something to trigger his thinking. But none was to be seen.

Cecil walked back over to him. 'My theory is this: there has to be some reason for King Clariance of Northumberland rather than simply King Arthur. Now, the family name of the earls of Northumberland is Percy. Let us presume – for the sake of experiment – that the name Lancelot is actually Lancelot Heath's Arthurian name. Put his name first in the sequence: the first four names spell LORD. I'm not saying that that is the correct interpretation but I do think we should consider it. Especially as the other two options don't make sense. So, if the pattern of the first letters of the name is indeed correct, then the remaining letters constitute a five-letter word with the second letter E and the last letter Y, including an R and a C somewhere. If the one unknown name begins with a P, then you have "Lord Percy".'

Walsingham was sceptical. 'The present earl, Thomas Percy, was made a Knight of the Garter earlier this year. Do you think he might turn traitor?'

'Do you believe he has turned to the new faith? I do not. Queen Mary restored the title to him just before she died, twenty years after the Pilgrimage of Grace, when his uncle and father had turned traitor. The question is: what connects Lord Percy and the chronicle?'

'Sir William, you are speculating without reason. We need evidence . . .'

'Calm yourself, Francis. You have the evidence before you. And sometimes you have to speculate to make sense of it. When was the last time Clarenceux was seen in the city?'

Walsingham took a deep breath. 'On Tuesday night. Five days ago. He tried to escape through the back yard of Robert Lowe's house.'

'And do you think he has been able to lie low for so long? While you have managed to round up almost all the other Knights?'

'No. But I do not see . . .'

'A different Lord Percy, perhaps?'

'Sir William, I do not follow you.'

'Well.' Cecil cast a glance into the fire. 'I am, as you say, just speculating. And I am tired. But Henry Machyn must have been writing his chronicle for some years to incorporate all these dates, yes? So, he must have woven this plot together over a long period of time. As the present Lord Percy has only been earl for six years, and some of these Arthurian Knights' dates are earlier than that, we might be talking about the *last* Lord Percy.'

'Henry Percy?'

'Yes, Henry Percy. Of course, Machyn might have retrospectively written false entries for all these dates.'

Walsingham was quiet for a long time. 'Henry Percy died at his house on Newington Green. He is buried in St Augustine's Church, Hackney.'

'Close to London, you see.' Cecil took his seat once more. 'I feel confident about the identification of Lord Percy, whichever one we are talking about. Have the present earl watched. Have the late earl's widow watched too – she resides at Sheffield Manor, one of the houses of her late brother, the earl of Shrewsbury. I will have a writ made out in the queen's name and sent to the sheriffs of the South Riding and Northumberland for every Percy house and castle to be searched. But just as importantly, if I am right with regard to Lancelot being the first in the sequence, then we have eight names and all nine dates. All we need now is the chronicle itself.'

'Sir William, with due respect, that is not all we need. We also need to bring the perpetrators of this Catholic obscenity to justice. The man who keeps the chronicle must be destroyed. You know that. Let not your fond heart dissuade you – he may surrender the chronicle and yet continue working to capsize the ship of State.'

58

Monday, 20 December

The fifth day of their journey was by far the hardest. The road was a muddy slush from the moment they set out from Uppingham. A strong wind sent the grey clouds scudding, and the wind blew the rain against the sides of their faces. The streams were swollen from the melted snow as well as the rain, and in several places rivers had burst their banks. Fields were often completely under water. As for the roads, they became even more difficult. Rather than solid frozen mud ruts there were deep puddles to watch out for. When the ground had been frozen their horses had been able to walk over these. Now that they had thawed, or were thawing, the larger puddles – some as much as two or three feet deep – proved a danger. Clarenceux and Rebecca took to leading their mounts and the packhorse around the wider ones.

When disaster struck, however, it was not due to a slip or a deep puddle. A carter trying to lead a heavy four-wheeled wagon loaded with oak trunks down a muddy slope had tethered his team of five horses behind it, to slow its descent, and was steering it carefully when the rearmost horse fell and broke its leg. Its anguished whinnying startled the other horses who began to skitter in fear – and the wagon picked up momentum through the mud, dragging the horses, which all lost their balance, one by one, as the heavy wagon thundered down the hill, faster and faster, to the corner where Clarenceux and Rebecca were riding, heads down against the weather.

They heard the sound of the horses' screams and the carter's shouts as he threw himself clear and looked up to see the wagon careering towards them. Instinctively Clarenceux spurred his horse out of the way of the wagon, and the packhorse went with him, not having a rider. But Rebecca's rouncey, seeing the packhorse turning suddenly in front, lifted its head, looking frantically for a safe way forward, and hesitated for a moment too long. The wheel of the heavy wagon struck its hind leg and sent it tumbling down, over and over, legs and neck thrusting, and Rebecca found herself thrown into the mud.

The wagon went on, plunging through the timber-frame and cob frontage of a cottage and smashing down the internal walls before it came to rest. Thatch hung limply, and then fell from the scarred front of the house. Clarenceux dismounted hurriedly and helped Rebecca to her feet. She was bruised but otherwise fine.

Her rouncey never got up. It made several frantic attempts, but its snapped leg bone only dragged a wider and wider gash in the skin. Clarenceux knelt beside its head, looking at its large, dark eye, seeing the resignation of a fatal wound as he stroked its neck. He turned and unpacked his sword and cut its throat himself; and afterwards tethered the corpse to his own horse to drag it out of the road. He left it on a grass verge and told the men of the village, who had gathered to survey the damage to the cottage, that they could do with its meat and hair as they saw fit.

The accident cost them dearly: three hours of precious daylight. Refusing all entreaties from the villagers to stay the night, they went on, with Rebecca riding the packhorse and their saddle bags stuffed with those necessities that they could not afford to leave behind. They were soaked, muddy and exhausted when they rode into Melton Mowbray. Clarenceux was tense too: so far it had taken them a full five days to travel a hundred and twenty miles. Normally a man could ride to Sheffield in four days from London. But then he reflected that almost all his long-distance travelling had been in summer, when forty or even fifty miles a day was possible, with twice the daylight and good roads. The weather had proved a formidable challenge.

That evening Rebecca insisted on having a bath at the inn, to scrub away the memory of the accident as well as the mud of the road. It was expensive, on account of the huge amount of water that had to be heated and the number of servants required to carry it; but Clarenceux was not going to deny her, not after such a horrendous day. She asked him to join her, and he did so, concerned lest she think him dirty by comparison. But he was preoccupied, and hardly spoke.

We still have two days' journey ahead of us. And what is it all for? What are we going to find out? Only something that will incriminate us further, and perhaps hasten our executions.

Where is Awdrey? How is she managing? Did Thomas find her in Devon? And how are my daughters, my Annie and little Mildred? How many babies do not survive their first cold winters – do I have two daughters now or just one? Is either of them still alive?

He thought of Walsingham and Crackenthorpe. *Have they caught Nicholas Hill and Michael Hill? Lancelot Heath and Daniel Gyttens? And the other Knights? If they have, and Crackenthorpe has interrogated them, what could they tell them? Their names. Their dates. Just as they told us.*

Rebecca saw the change in his expression. 'What is it?'

'If we can work out the pattern of the names, so can Walsingham. The longer we take, the greater the chance we will arrive at Sheffield Manor to find Crackenthorpe has got there first.'

59

Wednesday, 22 December

hey rode through the open gates of Sheffield Manor in the early afternoon. The previous day they had ridden hard for as many hours as they could, and covered no less than thirty-three miles. It had been a stoic effort from Rebecca, who had finally admitted her wrist was sprained from her fall. Today they had left at first light and covered the twenty-four miles at a similar pace.

As if in welcome, the clouds that had lowered over them for so much of the last week now parted and a weak winter sun shone through, gleaming off the wet bark of the trees that grew alongside the approach to the house. The parkland was a wide swathe of green grass dotted with oaks and elms. A herd of deer was feeding beneath the spreading boughs of a large oak. Further on a cart loaded with firewood was being hauled across the park. As they came in sight of the house both Clarenceux and Rebecca admired the impressive proportions of a substantial three-storey stone mansion with a large number of elegant mullioned windows and a tall entrance porch. The sun shone across the face of the building, reflecting off the panes of glass and giving the stone a welcoming, warm hue.

The gatekeeper approached and enquired who they were, and the nature of their business, and then led them to the front of the house. He ordered a boy to hold Rebecca's horse as they dismounted. Clarenceux untied the chronicle, still wrapped in its canvas-covered boards, and put it under his arm. As the boy led both horses away to the stables, the gatekeeper gestured for them to follow him through to the hall.

Servants were setting up two long trestle tables for supper, covering each table with white linen cloths. Tapestries surrounded the dais but were cut away to allow access to the doors that led to the private apartments. A fire was burning on the central hearth, grey-white smoke rising in the sunlight that entered by the tall windows on the south side. On the walls at the lower end of the hall were racks of bows and pikes, and a few long-barrelled guns. The arms of the earl of Shrewsbury were painted on a huge cloth that hung high on one wall.

A fresh-faced young gentleman in a high collar and smart narrow ruff came through one of the doorways on the dais and bowed to Clarenceux. 'God speed you, Mr Clarenceux, Goodwife Machyn. My name is Benedict Richardson, her ladyship's chamberlain. Her ladyship has consented to give you an audience immediately in the great chamber.'

Richardson led them along a corridor and up a handsome wooden staircase, well lit by the tall windows. At the top, on the first floor, the ceiling was high and the space light and airy. Through into the first chamber they went, and then into the next: a warm room, wrapped in brilliantly coloured tapestries, with a blazing fire.

Lady Percy, dowager countess of Northumberland, watched both of them from her chair as they entered. Behind her stood four gentlemen of her chamber. Her black silk dress was covered in jewels and fine brocade. Her tightly dressed hair was also bedecked with jewels, and her ruff was decorated with lace.

'Mr William Harley, Clarenceux King of Arms, and Goodwife Machyn,' Richardson said in a clear voice, bowing.

A strand of grey hair was loose, and she pushed it back out of the way as she studied them.

'You are a younger man than I was expecting,' she said.

Clarenceux stepped across to the middle of the room and knelt before her, putting his right knee all the way to the ground. Then, still holding the chronicle, he stood and looked her ladyship in the eye. 'My lady, right heartily I greet you, having travelled directly and as speedily as possible from London. If you were expecting me, then you will know me by the name of King Clariance of Northumberland. My companion is the widow of the last King Clariance, Henry Machyn, a member of the Merchant Taylors' Company. He was indeed older than me. He died for the cause.'

The dowager countess looked Clarenceux up and down. Then she turned her attention to Rebecca, noting her simple clothes, high cheekbones and determined expression. She guessed that she was nervous but making sure it did not show. The countess liked that. Self-control was a virtue – especially in a woman, and especially in political matters.

Lady Percy lifted her right arm and, with a wave of her hand, dismissed the men standing around the room. Benedict Richardson waited for them all to leave and then shut the door to the great chamber with a well-rehearsed formality. He alone remained with the three of them within the room, standing beside the door.

'Mr Clarenceux, I presume you have good reason to risk leading the authorities to my house?'

'You know the reason. I am holding it under my arm.'

'That would be a chronicle. Written by Goodman Machyn.'

'Indeed. The authorities in London have threatened to kill me if I do not hand it over to them.'

'Then why do you not do so?'

'Because they would kill me anyway, simply for having it.'

'You are a wise man, Mr Clarenceux. So, why have you come here?'

'With all respect for your ladyship, I need to know what the chronicle means.'

At first Rebecca had been overawed by the grandeur of the room, but she had quickly found her confidence and recovered her normal train of thought. Now she interjected, 'My lady, you

289

said you had been expecting King Clariance. How long have you been waiting?'

The countess looked at Rebecca. Suddenly, a small light crossed her face, a sense of recognition that nearly – but not quite – became a smile. 'How long indeed. That is a more difficult question than you realise. In some respects I have been waiting twenty-six years, since Lord Percy died. In others, only a few days. When Sir Percival discharged his duty exactly a week ago, and told me that your husband had been killed, I knew that this time the recipient of the chronicle would act. You would either come to me or use the chronicle directly.'

Rebecca was stunned. Clarenceux spoke in her stead. 'My lady, who is Sir Percival?'

'There are some things you must not ask – because my reluctance to answer might appear as rudeness, even though I conceal these things for your own good.'

Rebecca looked at Clarenceux and then at the dowager countess. 'But how did Sir Percival know my husband is dead?'

'That is another thing you must not ask.'

A silence followed. Clarenceux took the opportunity to speak. 'My lady, twenty-six years is a long time indeed. But the chronicle only covers the last thirteen. How does it come about that you have been kept waiting all this time? What have you been waiting for?'

Lady Percy's grey eyes rested on her chamberlain near the door. 'Mr Richardson, you may leave us. I will call if I need you.'

Richardson bowed, and left the chamber.

'What do you know of Lord Percy, Mr Clarenceux?'

Clarenceux looked at her. 'Henry Percy, earl of Northumberland – he was your husband. I know that he died shortly after the Pilgrimage of Grace. Rumour has it that he first married the old king's second wife, Anne Boleyn, but Cardinal Wolsey broke off their engagement.' He felt like adding that the earl was widely criticised for how much he spent, but thought better of it. It was dangerous enough to broach the subject of Anne Boleyn.

The countess nodded. 'It is still a bitterness, even after all these years. It will be until the day I die – and I cannot help but believe it will plague me in purgatory thereafter, for I will never be able to forgive her, even though I do feel sorry for her. What you call rumour is, in this case, common knowledge. But it is important that I tell you the whole story.

'My father was the earl of Shrewsbury, Lord Percy's the earl of Northumberland. In the way that powerful men do they sealed their friendship with a family betrothal. Lord Percy was fourteen at the time and I was twelve. We did not know one another; we had hardly ever spoken. Not long after our betrothal Lord Percy entered the household of Cardinal Wolsey; and on one journey to court, he met Anne Boleyn, who was then a maid of honour to Queen Catherine. They fell in love. They loved each other for years, exchanging secret kisses and small gifts on his visits to court. However, as far as the old earl of Northumberland was concerned, his son was betrothed to me. Knowing that he would never win his father's approval, my supposed husband married Anne in secret. They were both twenty-one and consummated the marriage shortly after the wedding – so it was fully legal in the eyes of the Church and the law. But they told no one. Not even me.'

Clarenceux noted the bitterness with which she said the last words. He let her continue.

'That was in the year 1522. Wolsey had noticed Henry's love for Anne and he disapproved. He knew that Lord Percy's father, the old earl of Northumberland, would be angry. Then it emerged that the king himself had his eye on Anne, and asked Wolsey to separate the two. Wolsey was pleased to obey, and dragged Lord Percy back to York, where he reminded him that he was betrothed to me. I knew none of this at the time, and simply saw the union of our two houses as being wholly sensible, for it was what my father wanted. At nineteen, it made no great difference to me that I did not know Lord Percy – what wife ever does really know her husband before marriage? I was assured by my mother that he and I would grow to love one another afterwards. But on my wedding night, as I lay nervously in bed – a maiden on the cusp of becoming a woman, or so I thought – my supposed husband came to me. It was the first time we had been alone together. He coldly declared that our wedding was none of his will and that it was invalid, for he was already married to Anne Boleyn. He added that he would never consummate our marriage for he loved his wife, and it would be sinful for him to come to my bed. He further declared that he would not give me money for my support and I should seek such sums as I required from my father, who was the architect of his misfortune and mine. And with that he left my bedchamber. He never came back.

'My father wrote to my so-called husband demanding that he make financial provision for me, but Lord Percy refused even to discuss it. My life was miserable – I was treated as an unwelcome visitor at Alnwick, Wressle and all the other Percy houses and castles. I was provided with a room and the necessities of hospitality, but that was all. He would not even give me sufficient money to clothe myself, protesting that I should return to my father or enter a nunnery. Obviously I could do neither because, in the eyes of the world, I was his wife. Besides, my father was reluctant to accept that his choice of husband was a bad one, even though he knew Lord Percy was failing to provide for me. I did not know what to do, so I just lived as well as I could, spending most of my time alone, reading holy scripture and praying that God would take pity on me.

'Then one day, quite unexpectedly, Lord Percy came to me. He had heard that Anne had become the mistress of the poet Thomas Wyatt. He was curiously calm: a strange sort of vindictiveness had overcome him. He would talk about nothing else: he felt Anne had betrayed him, and he was sick of his constant thoughts of her. Of course, I had no sympathy, and soon we were arguing again. He even went so far as to accuse me of arranging that Thomas Wyatt should seduce Anne in order to spite him.'

Lady Percy paused. She stiffly got up from her chair and, taking a pair of sticks from the side, walked to the window. Looking out across the park, she went on, 'At this distance in time, after nearly forty years, I can see things more clearly. He loved that woman so completely that he was emotionally incapable of loving anyone else. Even though she loved other men, and loved some of them more than she loved him, he never accepted the fact. It destroyed him.'

'Do you not feel angry?' asked Rebecca.

She turned round. 'Yes. Of course. But to tell you the truth, I feel greater anger towards the king. He pursued Anne Boleyn for years, as if she was his quarry. She flirted with him and seduced his imagination, and he was enraptured. He forced her to break off with Wyatt and, although she refused to be his mistress, she said she would marry him if he were not married to Queen Catherine. Shortly afterwards, in the summer of 1527, the king secretly began arrangements for a divorce. Realising that he was serious in his desire to make her queen, and worrying that her secret marriage to Lord Percy would become known, Anne panicked. She told the king that she had been betrothed to Lord Percy, but she did not tell him that they had consummated their marriage. The king, being in love, believed everything she said, and simply accommodated this new information within his plans. He secured a papal bull allowing him to marry whomsoever he wanted after he was free from Catherine, even a woman who had been betrothed to another man. The only limitation on such a marriage was the condition that the intended wife's first union had not been consummated. Of course, Anne's had, and so she was obliged to keep the truth secret.

'For Lord Percy, Anne's new relationship with the king was heart-breaking. His father died that same year, and, although Henry was now the earl of Northumberland, he had no love of life or his title. If someone had run him through with a sword, or poisoned him, I think it would have been a blessed relief to him. He behaved strangely, even going to court to give presents to the king simply so he could see Anne from afar. She refused to speak to him. The king, piqued that Lord Percy had once been betrothed to his queen, began to persecute him, forcing him to give up lands and estates. Lord Percy gave the king everything. He just wilted away into a despondent malaise.

'And then, quite quickly, Anne ceased to reign over the king's heart. She was in her mid-thirties, her beauty was fading fast, and her failure to produce a son marked her out as being not favoured by God. The king decided that her lack of divine grace showed that she was not to be trusted. Cruel, despicable man ...' The countess shook her head, remembering. 'Everybody hated everyone else. I hated Anne for ruining my life. I hated my so-called husband. Lord Percy hated me, *and* Anne, *and* the king. And the king hated us all too. Everyone was afraid of him. But as soon as he started to think of getting rid of Anne, Lord Percy suddenly came to life again. He thought he might finally win her ...'

'My lady, why did the king hate you?' asked Clarenceux. 'You said he hated you all?'

'He was so intoxicated with his own power that he despised anyone who questioned what he did, or created obstacles or difficulties. He hated anyone who stood in his way, whether that person was a pope or a mere woman. I created difficulties for him because I said publicly that Lord Percy had been married to Anne Boleyn, in my attempt to have my marriage annulled. When the king was ardent to win Anne's love, and marry her, I was an irritant. Ultimately, of course, he tried to divorce Anne on the grounds that she had previously been married to Lord Percy – just as I had said. But then it was pointed out to the king that if he divorced Anne and acknowledged the earlier marriage between her and Lord Percy, this would make his daughter Elizabeth illegitimate.'

'I'm sorry, my lady, but why?' Rebecca asked.

The dowager countess faced Rebecca. 'My girl, as your heraldic companion can, I'm sure, confirm, there were very specific rules laid down about the succession to the throne at the time of

Richard the Third. Correct me if I am wrong, Mr Clarenceux, but there are two conditions in the Act known as *Titulus Regis* that prevent a royal child from inheriting the throne. Is that not so?'

Clarenceux had been thinking of the hatred that passes down from kings to lords, and from lords to lesser men – especially if the king be a man like Henry the Eighth, and indulges himself to excess. He paused, collecting his thoughts. 'Yes, there are two conditions. If one of the parents – either the king or the queen – has previously been married, and if the royal marriage took place in secret, then their offspring are barred from inheriting the throne. As a result, Edward the Fifth and his brother Richard Plantagenet were both removed from the line of succession. Although *Titulus Regis* was specifically repealed by Henry the Seventh, to allow his wife to retain her royal dignity, it remains a potent threat to the queen. The circumstances described have already led to the deposition of a monarch once, and they could again. There is a precedent.'

The dowager countess lifted one of her sticks as if to accentuate what she had to say. 'Mr Clarenceux, I am impressed. You see, Widow Machyn, if Lord Percy and Anne Boleyn were married, and the marriage consummated as he claimed, then the same factors apply to our present monarch, Elizabeth. For the king and Anne Boleyn were married in secret. Even if the king was correctly divorced from his first wife – which he was not – then the prior marriage of his second wife still means that Elizabeth is illegitimate.'

'Hence "the fate of two queens" . . .' murmured Clarenceux.

'What was that?' asked Lady Percy.'

'I was just reminding Goodwife Machyn that her husband declared that the fate of two queens depends on the chronicle,' said Clarenceux.

'True. Mary of Scotland should indeed inherit the throne of England, and return this kingdom to the fold of Catholicism. But somewhere I was interrupted. It is important that I tell you about the king. For in response to the realisation that it would disinherit Elizabeth, he decided not to divorce Anne but to have her beheaded on a charge of adultery. And in order to twist the knife into Lord Percy even further, he made him sit on the commission that tried Anne. Now you see why I claim the king was cruel. He was like a boy playing with us, as if we were all tiny creatures. Any sign of trouble and he was ruthless – cutting off heads as that same boy might pull the legs off a cranefly. He had already forced Lord Percy to make him his heir and sign over all his estates to him. Now he made him judge his own wife – the love of his life – for adultery. And because Lord Percy saw Anne Boleyn as the cause of all his misery, he joined in with those on the commission who sentenced her to death. But unlike them, his reasons were personal, because she had been unfaithful to him. Of course, the king publicly announced that Lord Percy had denied marrying Anne; but the truth was otherwise. They had been married. The marriage had been consummated. Anne had been unfaithful. She had lied to the king. And ultimately the king had decided it was better to kill her than admit his daughter was illegitimate.'

Rebecca wanted to sit down. The story had weakened her. But still she stood, facing the old countess. 'My lady, what has this to do with my husband?'

'After Lord Percy declared he would never live with me, he spent much of his time in Wressle Castle. He was there when Robert Aske and the rest of the men involved in the Pilgrimage of Grace sought his leadership against the tyranny of the king. But Lord Percy had no stomach for the fight. After Anne's death, his reason for existence was gone – and not even fighting the king, who had so recently had her tried and beheaded, could rouse him. Lord Percy had, after all, exercised his own vindictiveness in sentencing her. That last summer he spent at his house on Newington Green in Middlesex, and there he died. I believe he poisoned himself. He was only thirty-five. And he left very specific instructions regarding his funeral arrangements.'

'Did my husband arrange his funeral?'

'He did indeed. Sir Arthur Darcy took your husband to see him just before he died, and he gave Goodman Machyn instructions for the conduct of the service and the construction of his tomb. He also gave him a document that he treasured above everything else he possessed.' The dowager countess paused, looking from Rebecca to Clarenceux. Then, very slowly, as if it pained her to say the words, she added, 'It was proof of his marriage to Anne Boleyn.'

Clarenceux's skin suddenly tingled from his neck and face down to his legs and feet. 'What? Proof that . . . that Queen Elizabeth is illegitimate?'

'Exactly, Mr Clarenceux. He gave Goodman Machyn the original marriage agreement, signed and sealed by an official notary, the bishops of Durham and Rochester, and the queen's chaplain. It is unquestionable proof that Anne Boleyn had previously been married, before she was secretly married to the king.'

Rebecca felt herself trembling. *Henry – my husband – knew this all these years and never spoke a word about it. How was he able to conceal it?*

She looked at Clarenceux. His brow was furrowed. 'But why did the chronicle not begin until 1550? If Henry Machyn had been guarding the document since 1537, why did he not start writing it then?'

'Goodman Machyn came to me when my father died – he saw to that funeral too. It was the year after Lord Percy's death. He told me he had received the document and asked me for advice. I asked him whether he believed it should be destroyed. He said no. I asked him whether it should be used; he said not at that time, no. But if it looked as though Elizabeth might ever come to the throne, then it should be produced. I agreed. In 1550, when Edward the Sixth was ill and likely to die, Goodman Machyn came to me again, with Sir Arthur Darcy and the man who eventually became known as Sir Percival. We agreed how the marriage agreement should be guarded: by a fraternity of nine men who, when gathered together, would be able to locate it no matter what happened to the keeper.'

'But, my lady, that is my whole point,' said Clarenceux. 'We cannot locate it. The names of the Knights simply spell "Lord Percy" and their dates point to the month of his death. Nothing reveals the whereabouts of the document at all.'

The countess was silent for a long time. 'Mr Clarenceux, I have told you as much as I can about this document. I do not know where it is; I entrusted its location to Goodman Machyn. If his instructions are insufficient to find it, then perhaps it is lost to us. In which case his death will have been in vain.'

'But I still do not understand. How am I to interpret the chronicle?'

'I do not know the answer, Mr Clarenceux. But one thing I can tell you is that the answer does not lie here in Sheffield. Lord Percy never liked coming to my father's house. It was the only place where the servants refused to obey his commands over mine.'

Clarenceux stared at the old woman, unable to believe that she did not have the answer he sought. He looked down at the book, still cradled under his arm. *Henry Machyn did not tell me what I need to know. He had too high an opinion of me. He thought I would see something that I simply cannot see.*

Then a possibility struck him. 'My lady,' he said slowly, 'does the book of Job mean anything special to you?'

'From the manner of your asking, I am sure you already know the answer to that question. It means nothing to me – but to Lord Percy, it meant everything. He read from it every day.'

'His epitaph!' Clarenceux said. He looked from Rebecca's startled face to Lady Percy's. 'Your ladyship, do you know what the epitaph on Lord Percy's tomb is? Is it from the book of Job?'

'I do not know for certain,' she said. 'I have never seen it. But on his second visit, Goodman Machyn did say that he was going to add some lines of scripture to the tomb.'

Clarenceux punched the palm of his left hand. 'Now I see. We

have come to the wrong place. The key lies not in the dates themselves but in another document, one written in stone. I was a
fool, a blind fool. "Lord Percy, June 1537" – it was a direction
to go to the tomb, not to come here. We need to return to London
as quickly as we can.'

The countess put forward her sticks and walked towards
Clarenceux. She looked at him. 'I trust nonetheless that this visit
has proved worthwhile. I strongly suggest you allow Goodwife
Machyn a night to rest before you take her back to the south.
She looks weary and I notice that she holds her wrist as if it
pains her. In fact, you might find a slight delay profitable. Since
I never did get my annulment, I took advantage of my status as
Lord Percy's widow to take his personal papers and account
books. You will find several boxes of them in the muniment
room.'

Clarenceux frowned. 'I do not follow you, my lady.'

'Yes, you do. There are certain myths and legends about Lord
Percy and Anne Boleyn that you might like to check for yourself. Some are true, some are not. You will know when you see
the papers.'

60

Richard Crackenthorpe nudged the corpse with his foot. He put down the candle on the cellar floor and kicked the body harder. The candle flame guttered with the swirl of the air. He kicked the corpse again; this time it just moved like a heavy lump of meat.

He cursed and took a deep breath. How was he going to explain this to Walsingham? Daniel Gyttens had known where the chronicle was. Somewhere called 'Summerhill'. It had to be near London. Gyttens had specifically said that Rebecca spoke about the need to go back there, to check the chronicle. But where was Summerhill?

Still unable to believe that the man was dead, Crackenthorpe knelt down and felt for a pulse. There was none. For a moment he rested his head on his arm. Then he stood up straight. He was bloody, tired and dispirited.

Suddenly he decided to take out his frustration on the body. He kicked it again, and again. He felt the ribs break beneath his foot as he stamped down on them, anger surging through his body. And then he thought of Clarenceux. The rush of hatred that the thought brought on made him reach for the knife at his belt and plunge it through the eyes of the corpse, one by one, before slicing through the throat and breaking the vertebrae of the neck, so he could hold the eyeless head aloft in the candle-light.

'Behold the head of a traitor,' he snarled. The jaw hung slack. A little slow blood crept from each eye socket. It looked like a skull. Then he hurled the head as hard as he could against the wall of the cellar.

61

It was late. Clarenceux sat hunched over a table reading documents by candlelight in the second-floor chamber he had been assigned by Richardson. Paper account books bound in vellum lay in boxes on his left; piles of folded deeds lay in a chest on the floor beside him. On the table was a round-edged deed box containing a number of copies of letters.

He picked up a letter in Spanish. It mentioned another letter, one dated 2 May 1536, and a report by the imperial ambassador, Eustace Chapuys, to his master, the Holy Roman Emperor. It stated that King Henry the Eighth had decided to rid himself of 'his mistress' who called herself Queen Anne, because she had been married to Lord Percy more than nine years earlier and had consummated the marriage, as many people then at court were ready to testify. The letter added that the king would divorce her if she were not convicted of adultery.

Clarenceux unfurled another small roll of paper, bound with a faded ribbon. He read the address and the date: Eustace Chapuys to the emperor, 2 May 1536. This was a copy of the original report, in French, to which the other letter had referred. Chapuys had written:

I have not written sooner to your majesty on the particular subject of the divorce of the king and Anne Boleyn, because I was naturally waiting for the issue of the affair one way or the other; but it has since come to a head much sooner and more satisfactorily than one could have thought, to the greater ignominy and shame of the lady herself, who has actually been brought from Greenwich to this city under the escort of the duke of Norfolk . . . The reason is that she has for a length of time lived in adultery with a spinet-player of her chamber, who has this very morning been confined to the Tower, as well as Mr Norris the king's most favoured groom-in-waiting, for not having revealed what he knew of the said adulterous connection. Lord Rochford, her brother, was likewise sent to the Tower six hours earlier. I hear moreover, from certain authentic quarters, that before the discovery of the lady's criminal adultery, the king had already resolved to abandon her, for there were many witnesses ready to testify and to prove that more than nine years ago a marriage had been contracted and consummated between the said Anne Boleyn and the earl of Northumberland, and that the king would have declared himself much sooner had not one of his privy councillors hinted that he could not divorce himself from Anne without tacitly acknowledging the validity of his first marriage and thus falling under the authority of the pope, whom he fears. This is certainly a most astounding piece of intelligence . . .

Clarenceux read through the passages again, his mouth open with astonishment. 'Nine years earlier' was the critical point: 1527, when the king had decided to marry Anne Boleyn despite her previous 'betrothal'. If the information that Chapuys had received from 'certain authentic quarters' was correct, Anne Boleyn had lied to the king about not having consummated her marriage with Lord Percy. And if he divorced her, the king would have had to acknowledge Elizabeth was illegitimate, just as the dowager countess had said. So he had executed Anne instead.

Clarenceux exhaled slowly. Somehow, somewhere, the proof of all this was in his possession. It was important that he see the epitaph written on Lord Percy's tomb in Hackney. If that gave him the key to the chronicle, and allowed him to find the original marriage agreement, he would have sufficient authority to go to Cecil and to bargain with him.

There was no time to waste. He would copy these letters and they would set out in the morning. But, late though it was, Clarenceux's curiosity urged him first to reach for Lord Percy's household account books. This would be his only chance. He lifted the pile and found the volume for the year beginning Michaelmas 1532, and looked for the entries relating to November and December.

62

Thursday, 23 December

The stay at Sheffield Manor had been extraordinary from almost the very moment of their arrival. The strangeness did not lessen at their departure. Lady Percy embraced them both in the hall and gave Clarenceux a purse containing more than twenty pounds to cover the expenses of their return journey – 'including horse hire, should you need it'. A new riding horse was provided for Rebecca. The dowager countess put her hand on Rebecca's arm just before she mounted and made a point of telling her that she could trust Mistress Barker – the purpose of which neither Rebecca nor Clarenceux could fathom. But when Clarenceux enquired as to her meaning, Lady Percy shook her head.

'Secrets are like daggers, Mr Clarenceux – best kept hidden until you need to use them.'

'Then tell me, why you are helping us? What do you have to gain from this? Why are you still concerned, so many years after Lord Percy and Anne Boleyn died?'

'That is a simple question to answer, Mr Clarenceux,' she said with a stiff expression. 'Anne Boleyn ruined both my life and my chances of having children. She had a daughter, I did not. Her daughter is now queen – and a Protestant, an enemy of my faith. She not only has no place in my physical world, she deserves no place in my spiritual one either. I am an old woman now, and doomed to purgatory, or worse; but if there is anything I can do to end the plague of vice and heresy that that godless woman Anne Boleyn spread across England, then I will do it. Dead or alive, my soul will not rest until England is once more within the fold of the true faith and its illegitimate queen and her ilk dead and buried. God does not approve of kingdoms ruled by heretics and bastards, Mr Clarenceux.'

Clarenceux nodded, saying nothing more on the subject. He bowed his final farewell, then turned and led Rebecca out of the hall and into the courtyard, where the ostler and stable boy were waiting with the horses.

Their journey back south was much faster than that going north. The disappearance of the snow and a few dry days meant that the roads – although still thick with mud – were much easier. There were very few other travellers with Christmas almost upon them. Most people were at home preparing for the end of the Advent fast and the twelve-day feast. In addition, the moon was now past its first quarter, allowing them to consider riding beyond dusk, confident that they would find their way to the next inn when darkness fell.

The mood of their journey was a mixture of urgency and anxiety. To Rebecca it seemed ironic that their destination was a place of great danger and yet they were struggling to get there as fast as possible. But she too was eager to push on: to discover the whereabouts of the document that her husband and others had died protecting. There would be no peace of mind until it was found. And when it was in their possession – what then?

'What are you thinking?' she asked Clarenceux as they rode through a ford overshadowed by trees in a thickly wooded part of Nottinghamshire.

'How bitter Lady Percy was. I was contrasting her motive – hatred of Elizabeth and everything the queen stands for – with that of your husband. I remember when he came to me that night, he said to me: "One can only remain faithful to the queen *and* God if the queen herself is faithful to God." And I clearly remember him saying: "At some point you will have to decide whom to obey: the Creator or His creation. Are you prepared to live your whole life in fear of that moment?" Your husband was not a bitter man. His motives were much more earnest, honest and honourable than those of Lady Percy.'

Rebecca rode on a little way. 'Henry wanted to obey what he thought was God's will. Lady Percy wants to impose it on others. You and me included.'

He looked at her. 'When we find this document, I am not sure I want to put it to the uses that Lady Percy hopes I will.'

'I can hear Henry saying that that makes you more of a coward than a Catholic. But he didn't see the bitter creature she has become. He would only have seen the countess in distress all those years ago, when he came to her to ask for advice. Myself, I am glad you feel as you do.'

'What about you, Rebecca? What do you hope for?'

'For life to return to normal. I don't want to start a revolution. I don't want to be stopped from praying in my own way. But nor do I want to see a Catholic woman on the throne if she is going to set about burning people on account of what they believe. God moves all our hearts, and if He moves them in different ways, who among us has the right to burn a fellow Christian for it? The sin lies in the lack of understanding, not in the divergence of faith.'

'You are a good woman, Rebecca. Your goodness deserves respect.' But as he said these words he was thinking, *Your goodness is a threat to those in power. It gives you the moral strength to refuse their orders. I pray that the Lord watches over us, and saves us. For I do not believe this is going to end well.*

63

Walsingham stood with a piece of paper in his hand, looking out of the window at the walls of the Tower. 'Give me one good reason why I should spare you.'

Crackenthorpe was sweating, even though the room was not warm. 'I have done my best. I have taken risks – but only because you wanted me to.'

Walsingham turned to face him. 'Risks? You have no idea what you are talking about.' He noticed Crackenthorpe looking at the piece of paper. 'You want to know what this says, don't you? You are wondering whether it is a warrant for your execution.'

Crackenthorpe said nothing.

'Did Gyttens say anything useful before he died?'

'Mr Walsingham, the man said everything – repeating what the other Knights said about the chronicle, about the Arthurian names, about his—'

'So why did you have to kill him?'

Crackenthorpe ran his fingers through his hair, and felt his hand shaking. 'He knew about the chronicle – where it was being kept. He said that the Machyn woman had mentioned that they had to go back to somewhere to look at it. The place was called Summerhill but he would not tell me where that was – which county, or which town. It could be a dozen places. Please, Mr Walsingham, I have not done anything but what I have done in pursuit of your instructions.'

'That's enough. Don't bleat at me. I know that you were following my orders. And personally I am glad you exceeded them. When a man is killed and someone has to take the blame, that person is you, not me. And when you have transgressed so far that I have to let you go to the gallows, I shall be glad that you are going to be hanged, because otherwise it would be me. The same will be true of your successor. It is a difficult balance – between a powerful instrument who is prepared to torture a man to death and one who is so fearful of the law that he is ineffective.'

Crackenthorpe simply stared at Walsingham.

Walsingham scratched his beard. 'It is just possible – *just* possible – that that word *Summerhill* has saved your life.' Walsingham folded the piece of paper in his hand twice and placed it carefully in the fire. He remembered the days of his youth at Scadbury Park, and the old crumbling house on the side of the hill and its eccentric old-fashioned inhabitant.

'Has anyone visited Lord Percy's house?'

'No, Mr Walsingham.'

'What about the tomb in Hackney Church?'

'No one has been there, Mr Walsingham. At least, not Clarenceux.'

'Keep your men watching. In both places. I am going to Chislehurst, to make some inquiries of my own.'

64

Sunday, 26 December

It was late. They were tired, in the chamber of an inn in Bedford. They had spent four days riding, even travelling on Christmas Day itself after attending a church service in the morning. They had avoided the processions, with their antler headdresses, costumes and mummings, and kept on, riding despite the cold in their hands and feet.

'Within two days we will be in London,' said Clarenceux quietly as he unfastened his doublet and hung it on a clothes rack before the fire.

It was a sombre moment, the recognition of just how soon they would be at the end of their journey.

'I feel like saying that I want to run away from it all, that I just want it to be over,' said Rebecca. 'But I suppose that's not true. The last thing I want you to think is that I am a coward.'

'I would not blame you if you ran away,' he said. 'But I cannot back out now. I don't know whether it is a matter of pride or honour but there is no doubt in my mind. Too many people have died. People I love depend on me. And I need to clear my name.'

Rebecca continued to undress. 'Pride, I think, is the way people see themselves. Honour is the way other people see them, no? I think you want to bring this dangerous time to a conclusion because you are an honourable man, not because you are a proud one.'

Clarenceux stood in his shirt, feeling the cold of the room.

'Maybe.' He watched her as she removed her gown and stood in her shift. 'There are plenty of things I do not feel proud of, and things I would like to do that would make me feel ashamed, but perhaps I can console myself that I have at least acted honourably.'

She picked up her gown and looked him in the eye. 'You could have acted otherwise, less honourably. Many other men would have done. That is something you can be proud of.'

With that she came over to the bed and lifted the bedclothes and got in. She lay there watching him. His legs still showed signs of scratches and cuts but he had regained his strength. His shoulders looked huge, his arms strong.

Clarenceux pulled back the bedclothes. She turned over on to her side, away from him.

He settled himself into the bed, aware of her motionless silence. 'What is the matter?'

After a long pause she said, 'I think things that I should not think, and feel things that I know are wrong. You are more honourable than me.'

He was uncertain what to say. 'I have often thought tenderly of you.'

Rebecca shifted on to her back and looked at him. 'And I of you. You know that.'

He looked at her face upon the pillow, at her hair, and imagined reaching forward to touch her. He had done so once before, when he had touched the mole on her face. But he had done that then without thinking; it had been natural. If he did the same thing now, he would be a changed man. Not changed like Lot's wife into a pillar of salt, but into a more loathsome thing: a guilty man, disgusted with himself. What he truly desired was wrong – and the fact that she knew it too both burnt in his heart and made him strong. *She trusts me not to touch her, and that trust is what gives me the strength to resist. And I know it is the same for her too: she knows I trust her.*

'Let us sleep now, Rebecca.'

65

Monday, 27 December

Cecil looked out of the window at the boats moored on the Thames and saw the sun bright on their masts and rigging. A barge was being rowed up the river, taking someone from the Tower to Westminster. He heard the clock in his chapel chime. Eleven o'clock. *Where is Walsingham? Two hours late – this is not like him.* He strode from the writing chamber through the next room and to the top of the stairs overlooking the courtyard of his house. 'Where's Walsingham?' he called to the groom waiting at the foot of the stairs. The young man looked terrified, and shook his head. 'Go and find him.'

Days of anxiety had come upon him and weighed him down. While there had been progress he had been calm, thoughtful, methodical. Now it was almost two weeks since they had last heard news of Clarenceux's whereabouts. And Cecil was torturing himself with one thought above all others. *Clarenceux has taken the chronicle out of the country. I have failed.*

He returned to the writing chamber, to go through his list of consequences. He had written two sides of paper, thinking through each eventuality; but as he knew only too well, the truth was probably stranger than anything he could imagine. He set down the papers again, and let his mind return to the problem of Hackney Church.

It *had* to be Hackney. The names of the Knights all pointed to Lord Percy, and now he could see that the dates suggested

June 1537, the date of the late earl's death. Alnwick, Wressle – these places might have once been Percy's favoured homes but this was very definitely a London plot. The search of Percy's old house at Newington had revealed absolutely nothing. Nor was there much advantage in going to Sheffield. The dowager countess had never loved Lord Percy, never even spent much time with him. The tomb had to be the key.

But it was now the twenty-seventh. Walsingham had had men located in Hackney, near the church, for a full week. And there had been nothing. Any news would have been better than this silence – even if Clarenceux had been marching on London at the head of an army, that would have been something to work on. But no. The plot had simply dissolved and Clarenceux had disappeared. Somehow the wily herald had eluded him.

Cecil sighed again, shut his eyes and tried to calm himself. He could feel his heart beating like that of a man facing the gallows.

He picked up another piece of paper, containing the epitaph on Lord Percy's tomb. It had been very carefully transcribed but there was nothing surprising or suspicious about it. On one side it said:

Here lieth interred *Henry* Lord *Percy*, Earle of Northumberland, Knight of the most honourable Order of the Garter, who died in this Towne the last of Iune, 1537, the 29th year of Henry ye 8th.

And on the other side of the monument there was a quotation from the book of Job, chapter seven, in which Job explains his desire to die. How apposite for the earl of Northumberland, who certainly wanted to die after the execution of Anne Boleyn. But it had nothing to do with a Catholic conspiracy or a chronicle.

'Mr Secretary, sir. He's here!'

The groom he had asked to find Walsingham came into the chamber followed by Walsingham himself. Walsingham was filthy from the mud of the roads but he strode in despite his dirt, holding his hat in one hand. He had not even bothered to remove his sword.

'Summerhill, in Chislehurst, Kent,' he said. 'Clarenceux has definitely been there – with the Widow Machyn. They left together on the sixteenth, according to the report of one of the cottagers on my cousin's estate.'

'The sixteenth? Eleven days ago? And no word yet from the ports?'

'None – unless it has arrived since I've been in Kent. I came straight here.'

'Who owns Summerhill?'

'A Catholic sympathiser – or so I suspect – by the name of Fawcett. My cousin says there have been priests in the area in the last twelve months, and although no one knows where they go, Summerhill is the most likely place. It is an old house, with many nooks and corners.'

'Have you arrested Fawcett?'

'No, he seems to have disappeared. Which is suspicious in itself.'

'Probably hiding in one of his own priest holes,' said Cecil, putting down the paper containing Lord Percy's epitaph.

'I will send Crackenthorpe to search the property with his men. They will find him, if he is to be found.'

'No doubt. But we want this man alive.' Cecil poured two glasses of white wine from a flagon on the table and handed one to Walsingham. 'I have to say I am worried, Francis. I am beginning to think I have been wrong. All the time you have believed that Clarenceux is the ringleader of this plot, but you did not convince me. I was waiting for some certain evidence, and none was forthcoming. But evidence is not truth: I should have remembered that. I suspect I have given Clarenceux the benefit of the doubt too often and for too long. Now we have eliminated almost all the others from any real culpability: only Clarenceux and the mysterious last Knight remain at large.'

'He has been to Scotland, France, Spain and the Low Countries in the course of his career.'

'Quite. He could be anywhere in Europe. I suspect you have been right all along: he *is* the protagonist. And to think my wife and sister-in-law stood as godmothers to his daughter . . . I have been too trusting.'

'Sir William, you should not be so hard on yourself. You have done all you could, I am sure.'

Cecil stiffened. 'I'll thank you, Francis, for not patronising me. You know as well as I do that if one works as hard as one possibly can, and still fails, then there is no merit in the work or in oneself. It is only success that matters. If you and I foil nineteen plots out of twenty to kill the queen, we will have failed.'

'Do not worry. We will not fail.'

'Good,' snapped Cecil. 'Looking at your filthy state, I trust there is something more substantial than wishful thinking and womanly compassion underlying that rhetoric. You can begin by renewing the guards watching the south coast ports, including the quays and hythes of London. If Clarenceux has tried to leave the country, I want to know. If he has already sailed I want to know when he left and where he was going. As for Summerhill – search it all the way down to its foundations.'

66

Clarenceux and Rebecca rode into St Albans at dusk. The dark clouds and the lack of moonlight discouraged them from pushing on too far. After supper at an inn, the Fighting Cocks, they removed themselves from the hall and went to their chamber in silence. Both were mindful that this was their last night on the road. Both were thoughtful. The candle of their time together was about to go out.

There was little to do but be together. Rebecca washed in a basin of warm water brought by one of the inn's servant boys and Clarenceux talked to her from where he sat on the bed, looking up from the transcripts of the letters he had made at Sheffield Manor. Afterwards they spoke of their childhoods and experiences in later life – from hardships to past Christmases, diplomatic missions and marriage. Both of them had to admit that, in comparison to Lady Percy, they had been lucky.

At that they fell silent. Rebecca was quiet as she climbed into bed. Clarenceux knew she was thinking about her husband. He wanted to comfort her, and the fact that he could not hurt him. He could offer her no real solace at all. He stayed sitting on the edge of the bed.

'We need to plan for tomorrow,' he said. 'From here to London is twenty-one miles. If we leave at eight of the clock we will be there just after noon. We could go straight to Hackney, skirting around the city. Or we could return the way we came, and place the chronicle in safekeeping with Julius. Or we could go to what is left of my house and hide the chronicle in the remnants. Having been ransacked once, it is probably safe.'

'You decide. You're going to decide anyway.'

'I'd like to hear your opinion.'

'We should go straight to Hackney. Find the key to the chronicle as quickly as possible.'

'Interesting.'

'That is your way of saying you disagree.'

Clarenceux turned and smiled at her. 'You are getting to know me too well. I thought the same thing – but has it not struck you as strange that no one has stopped us on the road?'

'What has that got to do with it?'

'Think of it this way. How long ago was it we were being chased around London? Nearly two weeks. How many Knights had Walsingham tracked down by the time we left? He got to James Emery before us. He got to Lancelot Heath too, remember, and searched his house – but Heath was wise enough to hide himself. Walsingham also knew about William Draper, of course, and your husband. If in the space of just a few days he managed to track down five men, and search their houses, then he had a means to find all the Knights quickly. So, as we both realised some days ago, he has worked out the sequence of names and dates, and probably he knows that "Lord Percy June 1537" relates to a tomb, not Sheffield Manor. We took a wrong turning there – and, because we were wrong, we did something unexpected. I imagine he is fuming about the fact that he can't work out where we are. But if we walk freely into Hackney Church, we won't walk freely out again.'

'Then let us go to Julius first, and stow the chronicle safely there. It is nearly full moon. If it is a clear night we can ride on from London and travel to Chislehurst. Then we can go to Hackney the following day.'

He lifted the bedclothes and lay beside her. 'That is what I was thinking.'

'Are you also thinking that the proof we are looking for is hidden somewhere in Hackney Church?'

'I suspect it is. And that we will need the chronicle to find it.'

'That will be very dangerous.'

'It will.'

'We could take it with us.'

'That would be even more dangerous.'

With that they both fell into their separate thoughts.

'What are you thinking?' asked Clarenceux after a while, as the candle began to splutter.

'I was thinking about the queen.'

'What about her?'

'Do you think Lord Percy was her real father?'

'No. He couldn't have been.'

'Really?' She raised herself on one elbow and looked at him. 'What makes you so sure?'

'While at Sheffield I checked Lord Percy's accounts for the time of her conception, November or December 1532. He was in Northumberland. The queen, Anne Boleyn, was with the king, on his way back from Calais.'

'And you? What were you thinking about?'

'Similar thoughts. It is not fair to visit the sins of the father – or the mother – on the daughter. Seeing Lady Percy has shifted my heart somewhat.'

'You and I would make very bad revolutionaries.'

'Maybe. But as far as Walsingham is concerned, we will make very good ones after he has hanged me in chains and burnt you alive for treason.'

There was a silence. The candle went out.

Rebecca lay back on the bed. 'Please don't mention the burning again. Or your being hanged. Things are sad enough as they are.' After a while she asked, 'Do you remember the first bed we shared together? The one at Mile End?'

'Trying to stay apart instead of rolling together in the middle. Yes, of course.'

'This is the last night of our journey. Tomorrow we will be back at Mr Fawcett's house, and then . . .'

Clarenceux understood. They were both fighting their instincts. He put his arm round her in the darkness and felt her put an arm round him, laying her head on his shoulder. For a time they listened to each other's breathing. Clarenceux remembered how awkwardly he had held her before, not knowing what she expected of him. Now things were different. He was happy to be able to hold her, happy that she wanted him to.

'Good night,' he whispered, listening to her breathing.

'Good night,' she replied.

He kissed her hair.

67

Tuesday, 28 December

The decision to go to Chislehurst first meant they had to travel quickly, so they pushed their horses hard over the first twenty miles, crossing the Thames at Fulham about an hour after noon. There were no guards on the ferry nor at the nearby tavern, the Swan; a possibility that had worried Clarenceux. After that they encouraged their exhausted mounts to canter down every slope, forcing them on for the last fifteen miles. Even so, it was dusk long before they approached the rise up to Summerhill.

As the skies began to darken, so did their mood. They began to note the looks of strangers on the way, the inquisitive glances that asked no questions but wanted to know their business. One gentleman on a horse saw them and kicked his mount into a gallop. Their thoughts began to twist into the shadows that loomed among the trees on either side of the road. Apprehension crept into the corners of their minds. For both of them this meant long periods of silence, or short, terse conversations that betrayed their nerves.

'At least we can be sure of a warm hearth and a bed for one night,' said Clarenceux.

Finally, after many hours in the saddle, and with the colour drained from the landscape, and cold biting into their hands despite their gloves, they rode up the long slope. They saw the black clumps of trees and noticed here and there the straight edge of a wall against the near-dark sky. And they noted too the silence, the absence of movement, the lack of light.

They rode up to the gatehouse. Clarenceux dismounted and twisted the handle of the oak gate; it was locked. He pushed it but it did not budge at all. He knocked and he called, but several minutes passed and no one came. There was nothing but the bitter cold and the breeze shifting the leaves of the trees nearby.

'Do you still have money for an inn?' asked Rebecca.

'There's money enough, certainly,' muttered Clarenceux. 'That's not the point. Julius has servants – a wife too.' He picked up a stone that he had just kicked with his foot and hammered repeatedly on the gate. 'Julius! Julius!'

'Who calls?' shouted a thin voice from the far side of the courtyard.

'William Harley, Clarenceux King of Arms, friend of Julius Fawcett.'

He waited, rubbing his gloved hands together. Rebecca dismounted. A shutter in the gatehouse above them opened, and someone looked out in the gloom. It closed again and they heard voices from within. There came the sound of a heavy drawbar being dragged across and the gate being unlocked. It opened a little.

'Mr Clarenceux?' The man's voice was frightened.

'Yes. And Goodwife Machyn. Let us in, please; I must speak to the master of the house.'

'Mr Fawcett is not here. He . . . he has not been seen for several days.'

Whatever feelings Clarenceux had had on the journey, this surprised him. At the very least he had expected to find Julius here – not the cold darkness of an unlit house.

'Will you please let us in even so?' Rebecca asked. 'We are returning two of his horses – and we need your hospitality for the night.'

But the reply was guarded, fearful. 'How do we know you are who you claim to be?'

'What is this? A trial?' snapped Clarenceux. 'If you would shine a light, you would recognise me. We were here two weeks ago, guests of Mr Julius Fawcett, whom I have known for upwards of twenty years.'

There was a muttering in the darkness. One of the men – with a rasping, old-sounding voice, who had not previously spoken – said, 'Very well, Mr Clarenceux, we trust you. But you must understand, terrible things have happened here today. A man has been killed. We are all shocked. To tell the truth, we are at our wits' end.'

The gate swung open. Clarenceux and Rebecca led their horses into the blackness and waited while the gate was shut and locked and the drawbar heaved back into place.

'We are sorry, Mr Clarenceux,' continued the old servant. 'Mr Fawcett told us never to use a light if we are uncertain who is at the gate. He used to say the advantage lies with the—'

'. . . The man with the sword,' Clarenceux interrupted. 'Yes, I know. What has happened?' He emerged into the dimness of the courtyard and, having handed the reins of his horse to one of the servants, walked in the direction of the hall.

'Not that way, Mr Clarenceux, please. The hall door is locked because of a terrible tragedy. James Hopton, Mr Fawcett's chamberlain, was killed by a royal sergeant-at-arms . . .' The old man's voice faltered.

'Crackenthorpe?' asked Clarenceux.

'Sir, I do not know the man's name.'

They entered the house by way of the kitchen, through a small door. The high room was mostly dark but the light of a fire on one of the great hearths and a single rushlight on the large round table in the centre cast a faint gold glow upon their faces. The man who was talking to them was indeed old, thin-haired and with missing teeth: they both recognised him from their earlier visit as one of Julius's clerks.

'Whatever his name, he was the most brutal man I've ever seen. Like a soldier on the field of battle. He forced his way into the house this morning with a large number of men and proceeded to search every room. Mr Hopton was one of the few of us still here. Mr Hopton tried to stop the sergeant in charge but he simply took out a sword and held it against his throat as if to threaten him. And then, suddenly – without any warning – he sliced with the sword, cutting Mr Hopton's throat. We were too shocked to do or say anything. The strange thing was that it was almost as if the sergeant had not meant to do it. But he killed Mr Hopton as he stood there. He *killed* Mr Hopton. After that he calmly went where he wanted and so did his men – while Mr Hopton's body was left in the hall in a pool of blood. He and his men turned over furniture, ransacked Mr Fawcett's library, and ripped open cushions. He even stepped over Mr Hopton's body on the way out ... Kicked it too, he did; he *kicked* Mr Hopton's body ...'

Clarenceux put his hand on the man's arm as the old voice choked with the pain of the memory. 'Calm yourself. Listen. Tell me your name.'

'Francis. Francis Shepherd.'

'Goodman Shepherd, take a deep breath and tell me the whole story. What happened before the killing? You said that Mr Fawcett has not been seen for several days. When did you last see him?'

Francis Shepherd wiped his face on his sleeve. He shook his head and went to the light stand. His hand trembled as he tried to light a second rushlight from the first, but eventually it caught. He inserted it at the correct angle and stood looking down, the new flame casting a huge shadow on the high wall of the kitchen behind him.

'On Christmas Day, in the early afternoon, the whole house-hold was in the hall. The master was here, his wife and about six or seven customary tenants, a few leaseholders and all the servants and the gardeners, thirty-five of us. Then a gentleman came demanding entrance. He was the young man who used to stay sometimes at Scadbury Park, Francis Walsingham. He was announced and Mr Hopton and I went to see him. In a very haughty tone he ordered us to take him to Mr Fawcett. I went back into the hall, to seek the master's word on the matter, knowing that Francis Walsingham was not welcome; but Mr Fawcett had gone. So had his wife. They had both vanished. As soon as they heard the name Walsingham they got up and left the hall together. And we have not seen them since.'

'That explains Julius. But where is everyone else? Where are all the rest of the servants?'

'Sir, ten men were arrested by Walsingham in the hall that same afternoon. After he left, many simply left of their own accord. I cannot blame them. Had I been younger I would have left too. We were all frightened. This morning there were only six of us here. That was when a large number of soldiers arrived: thirty men, maybe more. We were just shoved to the side as the sergeant in charge forced his way in. Mr Hopton stopped him in the hall and told him he had no right to enter. That was when the sergeant-at-arms killed him.'

'The man in charge – was he a tall, dark-haired man, with a distinctive mark?'

'He was. Very dark hair and a scar right across one side of his face.'

Clarenceux looked up at Rebecca. 'How did he know?'

She said nothing.

Clarenceux put his hand to his forehead and felt the cold perspiration. He turned back to Shepherd. 'I do not understand how ...'

And then he remembered. He looked at Rebecca. 'They must have caught Daniel Gyttens.'

For an instant Rebecca did not know what he meant. Then she too remembered. She inhaled suddenly and held her breath, putting her hands over her face, not wanting to see anything, or hear anything. 'It's my fault,' she whispered. 'I said the name Summerhill ... It's my fault. Oh, Lord almighty, in the name of Jesus's mother, I am sorry, I am so sorry ...'

Clarenceux was silent. He looked down at the table, trying to collect his thoughts. Eventually he said, 'What has happened has happened. We cannot dwell on one mistake. Mr Hopton's body – is it still in the hall?'

Shepherd wiped the tears from his eyes, and nodded.

Clarenceux looked at the other men who had come into the kitchen with them. There were both elderly servants too. They looked terrified. 'How many others are left here tonight?'

'Sir, just we three,' said the man who had taken the reins of Clarenceux's horse. 'Everyone else has gone. My name is Jack, groom of the stable. This is Thomas, groom of the hall.'

'You did well to stay. I commend you. I assume none of you will object if Goodwife Machyn and I spend this night in the rooms we stayed in two weeks ago?'

'Sir, we would welcome your company, and thank you for it. But those rooms are mostly ruined,' said Shepherd, recovering himself. 'The furniture is broken, and the linen scattered.'

'We will make do. Will you two stable our horses and bring in our belongings?'

'Sir, we will. Immediately.'

Clarenceux glanced at Rebecca. She was motionless, head downcast, her hands at her sides. He understood. *She does not want to meet my eye for fear of what I might say. But this is no time for recriminations. I need her now more than ever. I need her to remind me to stay strong.*

He looked around the kitchen. He walked to some shelves along the wall and saw what he wanted, took down a couple of wax candles and lit one from the rushlight and set it standing on the table. The other he set down beside it, on its side. Rich golden light spread around the kitchen. The servants would not have spent their master's wax candle so freely but they appreciated Mr Clarenceux's doing so.

'Is there anything to eat?' he asked. 'Some bread and meat perhaps?'

'There is plenty of cold meat, good white bread from this morning, cheeses, ale, wine and pears and apples.'

'Just bread and meat will do,' Clarenceux said. 'But first' – he paused, looking at Rebecca – 'first we will go into the hall and lay out the corpse of Mr Hopton.'

'Us? Why?'

'You must have laid out a corpse before. You know what to do.'

'I do, but it's not me, it's . . .'

'Sir, it is not a fitting task for a gentleman,' Shepherd objected. 'It is women's work. We will send for someone from the village in the morning.'

'It is not fitting to leave a good man in a pool of his own blood either. Goodwife Machyn will help me. I want to see his body. I want to touch it, and I want to remember him. I want to remember many other things too. Tomorrow I might also have to kill a man, and that man might be Sergeant Crackenthorpe. If it is, it will be revenge for many deaths – Will Terry, Goodman Machyn and Mr Hopton among them.'

'But why?' insisted Rebecca again. 'I will help you if I can. But why do you want to lay out this man's corpse now, in the dark? That won't be revenge.'

'Do you forget the old ways so quickly? Before the old religion was banned, we used to watch the night through with a man when he died.'

'What has got into you, Mr Clarenceux?'

'The fear of God, Goodwife Machyn. And I want to keep it that way. For if I fear almighty God, and keep Him close, then my fear of Sergeant Crackenthorpe will be as nothing.'

And with that Clarenceux picked up both the lit candle and the spare one, left the kitchen, and walked into the great hall.

Rebecca knew that she would never forget that night. She was tired and hungry, she was confused and grieving; but most of all she was frightened. She had been increasingly scared on the way to Summerhill but nothing had prepared her for this. For what was truly alarming was not that Walsingham had discovered that they had been at Summerhill, nor even that Crackenthorpe had searched the house. It was Clarenceux's reaction. Ever since their meeting with the dowager countess he had been more and more self-possessed. And now his composure had gone a stage beyond anything she could have predicted. He had re-entered the mental world of the soldier, in which action is instinctive, the mind attentive and the soul not afraid of anything.

He is preparing himself to confront death.

The shadows in the hall were high on the walls. Tapestries and armour looked down on them. They had been safe – too high for Crackenthorpe's men to reach. Clarenceux saw the corpse and set down the candles on either side of the head. Mr Hopton's face wore an open-eyed, shocked expression – a look of dismay, not pain. His neck had been cut cleanly but the lower part spilled out over the upper, with tubes and white membranes visible. The pool of dried blood lay black on the flagstones around him, smeared here and there by the passage of boots. A rivulet had started to run towards the wall before it had congealed on the cold stone.

Clarenceux directed Shepherd to set up a trestle table in the centre of the hall. When he had done so, the two men lifted the corpse and placed it on the table. Candlelight flickered on the pallid skin. The heavy, lifeless arms were already stiff; Clarenceux drew his knife to cut the clothes off. But at that moment Rebecca walked up behind him. 'There is no point. We have no shroud.' Seeing that he had not yet closed the dead man's eyes, she did so, setting the head straight and pushing back the broken skin of the neck.

Clarenceux stood looking at the dead face. He reached forward and touched it. 'I wanted you to see it. It is right that you and I should see the result of your slip of the tongue. Not so that I or anyone else can blame you – the good Lord knows we all make mistakes. But to see what Walsingham does. I need to feel angry, Rebecca. And I need you to be angry too – so that you want me to feel angry, to kill. All compassion is now a weakness. I am going to leave the chronicle here tomorrow. And you are going to come with me to Hackney, to keep watch when I go into the church there. I will enter as a soldier and as a Christian. If my enemies are waiting for me, then I will fight. And if God is not with me, then I will die.'

He leant forward and kissed the forehead of the dead man. He made the sign of the cross, and walked away into the darkness of the hall.

68

Wednesday, 29 December

aylight. Feathers. And the sound of trickling water in the next chamber.

Rebecca stirred in the bed, surfacing from a very deep sleep. She had left the shutters open and could see the ripped mattress and broken bolsters spilling their contents around her. She blinked, and remembered the previous night, when they had looked into the room and seen that the bed ropes and mattresses had been slashed and the bedding scattered. Hearing Clarenceux splashing water on his face in the next room, she sat up, aware that she too should be getting ready to leave. She pushed back the covers, climbed off the remains of the mattress and walked over to the basin in the corner. Seeing that there was no ewer she hurriedly pulled her dress on and went through to his room.

He was kneeling, half naked, at the foot of a makeshift bed, splashing his upper body with cold water. He glanced at her but said nothing when she entered. From his silent manner she sensed his resolve, the coldness of his mind.

She knelt down beside him to wash her face and hands. He stood up without saying a word, pulled on his doublet and walked over to where the chronicle lay. He picked it up and slowly returned to her. He placed his hand gently on her shoulder. She paused, still leaning over the basin.

'When you are ready, come to the chapel.'

*

The chapel at Summerhill was small and, like the rest of the house, very old. The paintings on the wall were dark from the soot of so many candles over the years, and the roof – a narrow barrel-vault – was similarly blackened. One stained-glass window gave a greenish light to the chancel and left most of the rest of the chapel in shadow. The crucifix above the screen had been defiantly in place – against the law – until Walsingham's visit. Now it stood propped up against the altar, having been smashed down by Crackenthorpe's men.

Clarenceux was kneeling on the tiled floor, his head bowed before the altar where three candles were burning. The chronicle was also on the altar, placed before a silver cross. A sword, an unsheathed dagger and a small boot knife lay on the ground to his right.

Rebecca knelt beside him, on his left, and they both began to pray.

O Lord, who art in Heaven, praise be to Thee and hallowed be Thy name; hear my prayer.

First, remember the soul of my dear departed husband, Henry Machyn. No man was ever kinder. May he dwell with You in Paradise.

Forgive me for the uncleanness of my mind and the sins I have committed in thought, word and deed. Forgive me for the betrayal of Mr Fawcett after his kindness to me. Protect Mr Fawcett and his wife wherever they now be.

Today Mr Clarenceux will go as one entering the lions' den.

Lord, in Thy mercy hear my prayer. Give me strength this day, and the resolve to do justice to those who have sinned against You. Let me not fail. Let my sword do Thy work if it be Thy will.

Protect my wife and daughters. Wherever they are, give them strength and keep them in virtue and in Thy tender care.

Protect my friend Julius who has shown me such kindness and favour, and whom I have led into great danger. Safeguard him and his wife. May they one day be rewarded in heaven for their faith in You.

He will pray to You to protect him, as he did that day when crossing London Bridge. Please hear his prayer, for it is my prayer too.

Give me the strength to be with him when he has need of me in doing Thy work.

Lord, in your mercy, guide him and protect him, for all our sakes. Give me the patience and time that I may earn his respect. Without him, my life is an ever-darkening horizon.

Protect him, please, for he gives me strength. Amen.

Lord, have mercy on the souls of the departed, especially those recently deceased, who have died in Thy name. William Terry, Henry Machyn, James Hopton and the two soldiers whom I killed. May they all come to Thy glorious and eternal kingdom.

Protect Rebecca Machyn. Forgive me for leading her into danger. Her presence now is everything to me. She gives me strength.

Lord, guide me as I go forward in Thy name. Amen.

He looked at her. 'Are you ready?'

She nodded.

They both got up. Clarenceux bowed to the altar and bent down to pick up his weapons. He slipped the small knife into his right boot, strapped on his sword, sheathed his dagger and bowed again. She also bowed, and left the chapel at his side.

In the hall James Hopton's body was still lying on the trestle table where they had left it the night before. Clarenceux went to the dais and picked up one of Julius's heavy black robes that was draped over the table there. He put it on, staring at Hopton's body, and made the sign of the cross.

When we look at the dead – especially those who have died for a cause we believe in – our self-belief and our belief merge into one.

He lingered a moment longer then crossed himself again and marched out of the hall.

69

They rode from Summerhill to Greenwich and took their horses on the ferry across to the Isle of Dogs. From there they rode to Mile End and asked John Crawley, the landlord of the Rising Sun, and his wife Iseult whether anyone had come asking questions about their previous visit. No one had. So Clarenceux talked to them about the roads, paths, buildings and bridges in Hackney. Was there any news of guards in the Hackney area? Crawley said that men had been seen loitering in the area but that was all. No one was sure if they were still there or not. Clarenceux questioned him further about the layout of the village: how many crossings over Hackney Brook were there? And where did those paths lead? After an hour they left.

They approached Hackney from the south at two o'clock – just as the tower bell of St Augustine's was chiming. The sun had broken out of the thick winter clouds and cast patches of light on the grass on either side of the road. People were carrying wooden crates of chickens into London and riding with their copes laced up against the cold. There were businessmen in fashionable dress, a carter with a load of slates for a new London house, and tinkers and vendors with packhorses laden with baskets of purses, brass pans and iron scissors for market stalls. Several cowherds were shifting their milk cows back to their home fields. Further along, a farmer was driving a flock of sheep along the highway.

The country around here was entirely grazing: there was no arable farming at all. Clarenceux knew it from trips north in the past, when conducting visitations or when travelling out of London in his youth. Indeed, he had stayed at the Mermaid Inn in Hackney on several occasions, and once at the Flying Horse. The old Percy house still stood in the north of the parish; he had attended a funeral mass there once. And there was a substantial brick house in the village of Homerton belonging to the Machell family, where he had attended a wedding – Brick Place, it was called. Alongside that house was a path through to the churchyard. Although he could hardly claim to be intimate with the locality, he was not on unfamiliar soil.

Clarenceux drew in the reins and pulled his horse to a halt at a crossroads. He could see the spire of St Augustine's Church in the distance, peeping out from between the tops of trees, golden in the afternoon sun. There was an inn a little way further ahead on the right, beside a ford through Hackney Brook.

A robin alighted on a branch overhanging the road. It sang a brief song and cocked its head on one side before flying off.

'Here is where I leave you,' Clarenceux said, looking along the road to his right. It was a grassy lane lined by leafless beech trees and an old wall. 'I want you to ride straight on, through the ford, and into the village. Go past the church and see if there are men in the churchyard. If you see anything suspicious, keep going – just ride straight out and find safety. If there is no one, ride into the yard of the Mermaid Inn and ask to leave the horses there while you see the landlord. But don't go into the inn. Come back and find somewhere discreet from where you can watch the front of the church. Remember, if the worst happens, just ride for safety.'

'And you? What about you?'

'I will go by this lane, on foot. If all is well, then I will come and find you. If not . . . well, you will know what to do.'

'Mr Clarenceux . . .'

He swallowed, and did not look at her, 'We have no time now for speeches. We must be strong, and trust in the Lord.'

Rebecca shut her eyes. 'Before you go ...'

But he dismounted, and placed his reins in her hand. 'Goodbye, Rebecca,' he whispered. 'Live well and give thanks to God often.' And without another word he slapped the horse's rump with his gloved hand, causing her to start moving forward.

Rebecca rode on for a little way with her eyes still closed. She whispered a prayer for him. Only when she came to the brook did she look back and see him there, a solitary black-robed figure, waiting.

When she looked back a second time, from the far side of the brook, he had gone.

Clarenceux hurried along the grassy lane on foot. John Crawley had said there were two small bridges to the east of the ford, one stone-built, the other wood. The nearer one, the one made of wood, led to a lane that went round the back of Church Fields. The stone-built one led into Homerton, coming out not far from Brick Place.

He walked briskly, feeling the hilt of his sword beneath the robe. He saw the first bridge, fifty yards off the lane, with trees leaning over it. He walked on. Two hundred yards ahead, with reeds growing in the marsh on the near side, was the second narrow bridge, with newly built stone piers and ruts where small carts had churned up the mud on the approach path. This was the one he wanted.

By now Rebecca will be at the Mermaid Inn. He crossed the bridge and walked towards the whitewashed houses at the top of the lane. This was the village of Homerton. He turned left into the wide curving street and continued walking past Brick Place to the pathway he knew, which led to the back of the church.

Here his pace slowed. On his left there were gardens, surrounded by a high stone wall. Ahead was Church Fields, and beyond that was the churchyard. If anyone was on patrol there he would see them long before they could recognise him.

He glanced to his right; a herd of cattle was standing in the field in deep mud around a cattle trough. There were no men in sight.

Now he was thirty yards from the churchyard ... twenty ... ten. Here was the gate.

A gust of wind from the north chilled his right cheek. There was a woman carrying a basket in the churchyard. Otherwise nothing. No one. He paused and watched her leave, unconcerned by his presence.

He walked into the churchyard, towards the porch on the south side of the church. He could see a tall brick house on the far side of the churchyard which had many small windows. *Anyone could be looking out. But maybe no one is. Keep going – keep going until someone or something forces you to stop.* He came to the porch and went inside. His pulse was racing. He placed his hand on the door handle and twisted it. It was unlocked ... *Keep going. This is God's work; He will protect you.*

He pushed the door open: it swung with a creak on its iron hinges.

The church was full of daylight, with wide broad-arched windows. Some paintings on the walls had been whitewashed over, and the stone altars denuded of their vestments. No cross stood above the rood screen. But all these things were of less interest to Clarenceux than the one unassailable fact: there was no one inside. No troops, no spies. *No one.* A tremor of joy ran through him and he closed the door, bursting with anticipation. He walked quickly into the nave and looked along the length of the building, his eyes noting the tombs and monuments. In the south aisle there was a very impressive-looking effigy, but in his excitement his eyes struggled to find the epitaph. When he found it, the name was Haskins. So he moved to the next, and the next, checking wall plates, chest tombs, brasses. His eyes skimmed inscriptions, looking only for names, reading: *Liddiard ... Leech ... Jones ... Halloran ...*

And then he saw it, in the north aisle. It was very plain, for a monument commemorating an earl. There was no figure. Clarenceux's mental image of the tomb, with an effigy of the earl reclining in stone, reflecting on his too-short life, had been completely wrong. The actual grave was marked only by a plain marble-topped chest tomb set into the wall. An elegant box. The marble had no words, no inscription. Along the front there was a clearly carved inscription in English – easy to read as the winter sun was casting the carved letters into shadow.

> Here lieth interred *Henry* Lord *Percy*, Earle of
> Northumberland, Knight of the most honourable
> Order of the Garter, who died in this Towne the
> last of Iune, 1537, the 29th year of Henry ye 8th.

The inscription was so unprepossessing that for a moment Clarenceux believed his interpretation was wrong. He took his glove off and ran a finger along the lines of the lettering. *This was nothing to do with the chronicle. My fears of being discovered here by Walsingham were all unwarranted.* Nevertheless, he took another look and read the words carefully, just in case he had missed some code or other hint. He reached for the writing materials he had brought in the pocket of the robe and copied the inscription, kneeling down and leaning on the marble surface.

Then he stood up, disillusioned. *There has got to be more to this than meets the eye.* He wondered if some object nearby might cast a shadow, thereby picking out a certain series of letters. He stood back and moved slightly to one side but there seemed to be no change to the inscription, nor any shadow or marker. He looked at the stained-glass window above the tomb, searching it for any script or scene that might give a clue to the interpretation of the chronicle. Nothing seemed significant: the window was much older than the tomb. However, in drawing away from the tomb he noticed that there was another inscription in the stone on the end. It was the single word, in capital letters:

ESPERANCE

He felt a shiver of anticipation and alarm at the same time. This was not just Lord Percy's motto – it was the word with which Machyn had ended his chronicle.

He crouched down and inspected the lettering. Then he shifted himself to the opposite end, to see if there was a word there. And then he gazed, astonished, at the tomb. Clearly this *was* the place intended by Machyn. Carved in small Roman capitals was a torrent of Latin:

MILITIA EST VITA HOMINIS SUPER TERRAM ET SICUT DIES MERCENARII DIES EIUS • SICUT SERVUS DESIDERA TUMBRAM ET SICUT MERCENARIUS PRAESTOLATUR FINEM OPERIS SUI • SIC ET EGO HABUI MENSES VACUOS ET NOCTES LABORIOSAS ENUMERAVI MIHI • SI DORMIERO DICO QUANDO CONSURGAM ET RURSUM EXPECTABO VESPERAM ET REPLEBOR DOLORIBUS USQUE AD TENEBRAS • INDUTA EST CARO MEA PUTRUDINE ET SORDIBUS PULVERIS CUTIS MEA IRRUPUIT ET PECCATUM APERITUM EST • DIES MEI VELOCIUS TRANSIERUNT QUAM A TEXENTE TELA SUCCITITUR ET CONSUMPTI SUNT ABSQUE ULLA SPE • MEMENTO QUIA VENTUS EST VITA MEA ET NON REVERTETUR OCULUS MEUS UT VIDEAT BONA • NEC ASPICIET ME VISUS HOMINIS OCULI TUI IN ME ET NON SUBSISTAM • SICUT CONSUMITUR NUBES ET PERTRANSIT SIC QUI DESCENDERIT AD INFEROS NON ASCENDET • NEC REVERTETUR ULTRA IN DOMUM SUAM NEQUE COGNOSCET EUM AMPLIUS LOCUS EIUS • QUAMPROPTER ET EGO NON PARCAM ORI MEO LOQUAR IN TRIBULATIONE SPIRITUS MEI CONFABULABOR CUM AMARITUDINE ANIMAE MEAE • NUMQUID MARE SUM EGO AUT CETUS QUIA CIRCUMDEDISTI ME CARCERE

For one throb of his heart, Clarenceux felt the satisfaction of knowing what the Latin meant and where it had come from. It was from the book of Job, chapter seven, where Job justifies his will to die. Those last words – *am I a sea or a whale that you surround me in prison* – were a strange adjunct to what had gone before. Indeed, they made a conundrum in themselves; but that was why Clarenceux remembered this passage so well. He had never understood that line – what did it have to do with Job's lamentation? *The embossed cover of Machyn's chronicle is marked with waves and fish. Both inscriptions on the ends of the tomb link to the book. Is the proof of the marriage inside this tomb, placed there during the funeral by Henry Machyn?*

Suddenly he heard the iron hinges of the door and marching footsteps on the flagstones. A shaft of sunlight through the window caused him to shield his eyes as he rose to his feet but there was no doubt what was happening. Six men were lining up, three on each side of the door. They were all wearing different liveries – one a wine-red doublet, another a black tunic, another an old fur-trimmed jerkin – but all were armed with side-swords. And they were all under orders: none of them spoke. They just stood to attention in their motley garb, like a group of parish militia men on muster day.

He heard a woman's voice screaming outside, in the distance. He recognised it as Rebecca's. 'For the sake of Christ's mercy,' she was yelling, 'Mr Clarenceux! Get out ... save yourself.'

There was nowhere to go. There was only one door. He looked everywhere for an alternative exit, but there was none. He could do nothing but watch helplessly as two more men entered. Each of them was holding a rope tied to one of Rebecca's wrists. She was struggling, twisting backwards and forwards, trying to loosen the knots and break away. But they had tied her well and were brutal in the way they handled her. 'In the name of God!' she screamed as they hauled her inside, one reaching down and grabbing her hair. But when she saw Clarenceux standing there, not escaping or even trying to avoid the guards, she realised the futility of her struggle. She became still, staring at him as if he had betrayed her.

'They were waiting in the Mermaid Inn,' she said coldly. 'The bastards were waiting for us ... They've sent a messenger to Walsingham.'

A ninth man, who appeared to be the captain, entered as she spoke. He stepped straight across to her and struck her hard in the face. 'Shut up, woman!' he shouted. 'You two – search that man. If he has any weapons, take them. Bind him. And you, lock the door. We will wait here until Sergeant Crackenthorpe arrives.'

Clarenceux considered his chances. There was time yet to draw his sword. Two men were holding Rebecca: it would be seven against one. Better than that: there were only two men approaching him and he would have the moment of advantage. But then the captain called out, 'Don't even think of drawing a weapon.'

Clarenceux shifted his gaze away from the approaching men to the captain. He saw the long barrel of the gun that the man was pointing at him. He glanced to the other side of the church. He could run across the nave: it was difficult to shoot a running man. There was a chest tomb in the south aisle; maybe if he could get on to that, he could smash his way through the window. But breaking the glass would take time, and he would be an easy target. They would shoot him. And they would still have Rebecca.

The first of the guards pushed him roughly back against the wall and grabbed for the hilt of his sword beneath his robe. Clarenceux let him take it, and the dagger too. He let himself be turned and shoved face first into the wall beside the tomb as the guard roped his wrists together behind his back, drawing the thin rope very tightly against the skin.

'Tie him to the screen,' commanded the captain. 'The woman too, on the other side. Keep them apart.'

As Clarenceux was forced towards the chancel screen he tried to come to terms with his inaction. He had been prepared for this; he had been ready to fight. And now, somehow, in a matter of seconds, he had been overwhelmed. He felt a rope being passed around his waist and his body firmly tied to the oak upright of the screen, and then another looped around his neck.

They had led Rebecca to the screen in the south aisle. Clarenceux felt ashamed; he did not want to look at her. He did not want to see a sign of recrimination in her face for leading her into what had, in retrospect, been an obvious trap. Walsingham had *known* – and was able to place a large number of men here, quietly, dressed as travelling gentlemen, and keep them here for days, weeks.

The plot is dead now. The candle has spluttered and gone out. And our lives are following the same course.

The captain stationed two men to guard the door. Three others were ordered to watch Rebecca and three to watch Clarenceux. The sun was almost gone from the south windows; the light in the church would soon start to fade. Clarenceux looked at the earl's tomb, silent, still, with the dust settling on it as it had for the last twenty-six years. *Is the proof of the queen's illegitimacy hidden inside that chest? If it is, then that was a bad place to hide it. We might have come here incognito and seen the inscriptions; but we could not have opened the tomb without arousing attention. Perhaps that is why Henry Machyn arranged for there to be nine Knights – to work together to open the tomb. But then why the chronicle? And why the reference to the book of Job? The sea, the whale. And there was something odd too about an earlier part of the inscription. It should have read* cutis mea aruit et contracta est. *Or something like that – something about Job's skin becoming wrinkled and furrowed . . .*

His skin . . .

At that moment, as Clarenceux looked up and saw the very last ray of sunlight disappearing from the furthest corner of the furthest window, he realised. It was sweet food for the soul. At last, he understood the secret of Lord Percy's tomb – Henry Machyn's secret.

70

ergeant Crackenthorpe strode into the church, with all the appearance of a powerful and proud man in his hour of glory. But in truth his heart was burning. There was a rush of fire in his body – it raged in his chest and in his limbs – and it was a desire, not a pride or any sort of reflection on what had happened. He had not been able to ride at Walsingham's gentle pace, merely smiling to himself at the thought of questioning Clarenceux. He wanted to rip the man limb from limb. He wanted to flay him alive – to cut the strips of skin off his back and pour salt on to the bloody flesh. He wanted to drive his heel into the man's hand, feeling the satisfaction of breaking each bone.

Three soldiers accompanied him into the church. They waited at the back while he advanced towards Clarenceux. Clarenceux expected a punch to the face or body. He braced his stomach muscles, but no blow came.

'How fitting that God should have delivered you to me in this place. I worship the almighty that puts you at my mercy. But I have no mercy. I swore a long time ago that I was going to do to you what they used to do to traitors in the past: cut your guts out and then burn them in front of you. In France they tie a man's arms and legs to four horses and pull the body apart.'

Clarenceux drew himself up to his full height and looked Crackenthorpe in the eye. 'Where is Walsingham?'

'Still on the road. He is probably savouring the thought of

341

what you are going to tell him as much as I am the thought of making you talk.'

'Have a thought for your soul, even if your name is that of a murderer.'

Still Crackenthorpe did not punch him. Instead he said, 'Do you know why I rode on ahead?'

Clarenceux said nothing.

'It is because Mr Walsingham does not approve of some of my methods. He thinks I am a killer with no self-control. But as you can see, I know what I am doing. I could inflict a lot of pain on you – and I will. But when I do so, it will be for my benefit, not for his, nor for the sake of obtaining information. You will talk not because of anything I do to you but because of what I do to the woman.' He glanced at her, tied to the wooden screen, looking down. 'Pretty thing she must have been. Your mistress now?'

Clarenceux said nothing.

'It will hurt you even more, what she suffers. You see, I know what it is to torture a man. I don't just hurt his body – I hurt his soul. I draw it out by hurting the people he loves. I know from experience. Only it happened to me when I was young, and adversity makes the young grow stronger. It just weakens and kills men and women past their prime. When I torture you, I will feel good because your pain will remind me how strong I have become. But you ... First you will weep, then you will talk, and then you will die.'

'Walsingham is not alone in despising your methods. God does too.'

'Spare me the sermon, Mr Clarenceux. In these matters you are an innocent. You will only make things worse. For her.' He smiled. 'When I think of what I am going to do my body feels hard and strong, like my mouth watering at the thought of drink. I like that feeling. I relish the humiliation of a woman, of rendering her powerless. Her powerlessness makes me feel powerful, and increases my pleasure. Or I can give that pleasure to others, and that also is power.' He turned to the two soldiers standing guard over Rebecca. 'You two, take the woman back to the inn. Despoil her, both of you – do whatever you want with her.'

Clarenceux shut his eyes as the men untied the rope binding Rebecca to the screen.

'Mr Clarenceux,' she called, 'we will fight them with love. Be strong. Trust in the Lord . . .'

'For Christ's sake shut her up!' yelled Crackenthorpe.

'Trust in the Lord, Mr Clarenceux,' Rebecca repeated. Then one of the men yanked her jaw open and thrust a rope through her mouth, tying it behind her head. The two of them dragged her out of the church. The hinge of the door creaked open and the guards slammed it shut behind them.

'Are you wondering why I do not want to have her myself? It is because seeing you in pain will give me greater pleasure.'

'I would spit in your face if this were not a holy place.'

'Your religion weakens you, Mr Clarenceux.'

Clarenceux stared at Crackenthorpe and searched for something to say. All he could think of was the scar on the man's face. 'That scar,' he said, 'I like it. It reminds me that a man tried to kill you.'

Crackenthorpe fought to retain his composure. Then he let fly with a punch, and connected with Clarenceux's jaw. Clarenceux's head was knocked back against the carved wooden column to which he was tied. He tasted blood in his mouth, and his tongue felt a loose tooth. The double blow affected his sense of balance. He felt sick.

As he retched and spat out the tooth, he heard the creak of the door. The diminutive figure of Francis Walsingham walked into the nave, followed by four men in his black livery. Crackenthorpe wheeled round.

Walsingham approached, looking at Clarenceux's bloody face, his groggy half-closed left eye. He gestured to the tomb of Lord Percy. 'You have a lot of explaining to do.'

'I have nothing to explain.'

'Come, Mr Clarenceux. Your playing at rebellion is over. I might have believed you before, when you claimed ignorance; I even let you go. But you betrayed my trust then and you have proved yourself my enemy since. We know who the Knights of the Round Table are. We have interrogated your comrades, and although they tried to protect you, we know the truth. We know the encoding of Lord Percy and the date of his death: who but a herald would have thought of centring a plot on the tomb of a dead lord?'

Walsingham looked up and around the church, as if surveying it for the first time. He turned back to Clarenceux. 'But what is the significance of this place? Is this a mustering point for your rebellion? Am I to expect that troops are descending on this spot, as we speak, from Essex, from Suffolk, from the Midlands? From the north? Is this another Pilgrimage of Grace? To the tomb of the earl of Northumberland, the man who refused to lead the first Pilgrimage? I want an explanation, Clarenceux. And I want it now.'

Clarenceux shook his head. 'The men who organised this plot are all dead. Henry Machyn. Sir Arthur Darcy. John Heath. I came here to learn what ... what it might have entailed, to explain it to Sir William Cecil.'

'You can explain it to me.'

'I would have done,' whispered Clarenceux, 'if Sergeant Crackenthorpe had not ordered the rape of Goodwife Machyn before you arrived.'

Walsingham looked coldly at Crackenthorpe. 'It is this man we need to torture, from whom we need to extract information, not her. Why did you issue such an order?'

Crackenthorpe pointed to Clarenceux. 'This man's weakness is not in his body but in his conscience. Hand her back to me, and allow me to slice off her breasts in front of him. Before I've made the first cut, Mr Clarenceux will agree to do whatever you want. I guarantee it.'

Walsingham stared at Clarenceux. 'A poor revolutionary you would make, if the pain of one miserable widow defeats you.'

'I have . . . been thinking . . . much the same thing myself. That is why I am a herald, not a revolutionary.'

'Where is the woman?'

'I sent her to the Mermaid Inn,' Crackenthorpe told him.

Walsingham turned to the men behind him. 'You two, fetch her. Bring her back here.'

Then he turned his attention to Clarenceux. 'Let us talk about this as gentlemen. Your cause is over. Whatever rebellion you wished to foment is not going to happen. You are going to be executed, both you and the widow. The only question is how we do it. Now, let us suppose you give me the chronicle of Henry Machyn and tell me the significance of Lord Percy's tomb over there. In return I will ensure that both of you are hanged, and you are not quartered and Widow Machyn is not burnt at the stake or treated to any further humiliations.'

'How am I to give you the chronicle?'

'You will tell me where it is. I will send Sergeant Crackenthorpe to fetch it. When he delivers it to me, I will countermand the order for your quartering and her burning.'

Clarenceux shook his head and murmured, 'You misjudge me, Walsingham. You misjudge us both. The weapons I hold are . . . sharp.'

'You will die a traitor's death.'

'And when the plot is enacted, so will you.'

Walsingham angrily turned away.

Through his blood-covered eyes Clarenceux saw that his bravado had opened up a chink in Walsingham's armour. The man had no idea what the plot entailed.

'Mr Walsingham. I reserve my claim to innocence in all these matters. But I suggest a deal of another kind. You will release all the Knights of the Round Table and every one of those people whom you suppose to be my associates, including Mr Julius Fawcett, if you have him, and I will deliver the chronicle to you – on two conditions. The first is that Sir William Cecil is present and the second is that we exchange the chronicle and prisoners at my own house.'

Walsingham frowned. 'Why? Why should I listen to you? Or even think of having any part of a deal with you? In a short time you will be dead, Clarenceux.'

'If I must be a martyr, Mr Walsingham, then so be it. But I do not think you want that to happen. Because you will have failed. My death and that of Goodwife Machyn will not be the end of things. I have had no part in any plot against her majesty; but now, having seen that tomb, I know what will happen. And there is nothing you can do to stop it.'

Walsingham's face darkened. Clarenceux was bringing his most feared nightmare to the forefront of his mind – the unforeseen, unstoppable plot. He walked to the tomb in the north aisle.

'Open this,' he shouted angrily to the men waiting in the church. 'Now!'

All the men in the church jumped to his service, including those stationed at the door. Only those near Clarenceux stayed at their posts. Even Crackenthorpe wandered nearer. Clarenceux watched.

'You, go and find a crowbar. The rest of you break the cement with your swords.'

'My offer is still on the table, Mr Walsingham,' Clarenceux called. 'You will have some explaining to do when you have desecrated a holy grave and found nothing.'

'Shut up, or I will have Crackenthorpe hit you again.'

'This is a church, Mr Walsingham. A house of God. And you are digging up a man who has had a holy burial.'

When the man returned with a crowbar, they set to work, hammering its edge under the marble slab. The church was filled with the ringing noise, which echoed between the arches and in the arcade above.

'Tonight will be almost full moon,' Clarenceux said. 'If you agree to my terms, I will go and fetch the chronicle myself, this very evening. And then, on my return, you can pass your prisoners over to my care.'

'Damn you, Clarenceux! Hold your tongue or I will have it cut off!'

'You do not know what this plot is about, Walsingham. You need my help.'

The clanging noise of the crowbar against the masonry continued to ring out and echo. Then it stopped. Instead there was a grinding noise as the top of the tomb was shifted.

There was silence.

'What do you see?' Clarenceux sneered. 'Let me guess. A lead coffin. Any dried flowers in there from the earl's widow? I thought not.' Walsingham turned away from the grave and walked slowly back to Clarenceux. 'So, will you agree?'

'Sergeant Crackenthorpe wants to kill you with his bare hands. I am inclined to let him do so. You have one chance to explain this.'

At that moment the door creaked open and two men led Rebecca Machyn back into the church. Her dress was torn away at one shoulder and she was limping. She looked straight at Clarenceux and saw his bloody face. 'God is with us, Mr Clarenceux,' she said bravely. 'God is with us.'

'Tie her to the screen,' said Walsingham.

Clarenceux felt a chill at the sight of her. His argument gave way to a cold, blank stare. 'I will explain myself, Mr Walsingham, tomorrow at noon, in the presence of Sir William Cecil and the rest of the prisoners, whom you will hand over to me.'

Walsingham held Clarenceux's gaze for a long time. He said nothing. His grey eyes flickered over Clarenceux's face, not caring for the blood. He turned and walked down the nave. 'Crackenthorpe!' he called. The sergeant-at-arms hurried to his side and followed him from the church.

Light was fading now. The soldiers and guards waited where Walsingham had left them, not daring to leave their posts but no longer strictly standing on ceremony. Clarenceux looked at Rebecca: she was staring down at the flagstones on the ground, her shoulders slack, despondent.

Walsingham and Crackenthorpe returned after nearly ten minutes, Walsingham's short, quick steps contrasting with the slow, lengthy strides of Crackenthorpe, who followed just behind.

'Clarenceux. You will ride from here this evening to where the chronicle is kept. Sergeant Crackenthorpe will accompany you, along with three of his men. Of course, you will be tied. You will hand over the chronicle to me tomorrow at noon, at your house, as you have asked. If you do not, Widow Machyn will be burnt alive and the other surviving prisoners will go to the gallows as traitors, and be hanged, eviscerated and quartered.'

'Who are the surviving prisoners?'

'Robert Lowe, Nicholas Hill, William Draper, Michael Hill and James Emery.'

'You can keep William Draper,' mumbled Clarenceux. He found it hard to speak. Too many names had not been mentioned.

71

It was going to be a cold night. The sky was deep blue already, the last light of day fading fast. There were few clouds. The road was clearly visible in the moonlight, like a steel blade across the hills ahead of them; and the puddles they approached reflected the silver-touched wisps of clouds.

The guards roped Clarenceux's hands together in front of him but took away his gloves. They tied a cord to the reins of Clarenceux's horse and fastened the other end to Crackenthorpe's saddle. A noose was placed round Clarenceux's neck. Crackenthorpe held it loosely in his hand.

Clarenceux wanted to lead them away from the route he had actually taken with Rebecca, so he directed them along the road to Kingsland and from there up to Newington Green. The tall shape of the house in which Lord Percy had died stood there, severe in the moonlight, overlooking the green. They rode through Islington and then past the inns gathered around the Angel.

Crackenthorpe was silent. He only spoke when he saw they were approaching the city. 'You did not bring us by the most direct route. We should have gone down the highway to Bishopsgate.'

'No one told me I had to come by the most direct route, Sergeant Crackenthorpe. That did not form part of the deal.'

'If this is a trap, you can guarantee I will tighten this rope round your neck. With great pleasure.'

Clarenceux searched for a strategy. Riding through the moonlit city – seeing the lines of roofs and the stationary carts outside the shops, the barrels of water, the puddles in the centre of the muddy street – he knew that he had only a short time to detach himself from these guards. Even in the moonlight everything seemed more *real*; the darkness was death itself, closing in on everything he could see. With his hands tied together he could not bend down and reach his boot knife. Every time they passed into the shadow of a house or a wall he worked furiously at the knots binding his hands, and little by little they grew looser. But still they were too tight for him to slip them and rid himself of the noose round his neck.

Keep calm. Opportunities will arise. There are still twelve miles to ride before we come to Summerhill.

At Bridge Gate there was a moment's chance. Crackenthorpe had to dismount and explain his business to the captain of the guard. But the men accompanying Clarenceux moved him into the moonlight and watched him closely. One, Christopher Fraser, forced him to hold out his hands, so they were not concealed by the folds of his robe. Unable to see the marks where the twisting rope had bitten into Clarenceux's skin, he nevertheless held on to the ropes around his reins and neck. Eventually Crackenthorpe reappeared, and the five men rode across the eerily empty darkness of London Bridge. With the moon almost directly ahead, shining down the street, there was no shadow from the high houses on either side. Clarenceux's knots remained tight.

Moonlight reflected off the high roof of Southwark Abbey and the whitewashed frontages of houses on the road south. It touched the leafless branches and twigs of the trees on either side of the road; no tree cover concealed Clarenceux for long enough to work on loosening his hands or reaching his knife. He tried to think ahead: was there a curve in a road around a hill? Or a valley? But he could not think of any place where he could lead Crackenthorpe to escape the glare of the moon. Some other distraction was required.

'How did Henry Machyn die?' he asked, as they approached Peckham.

Crackenthorpe said nothing.

'How did Daniel Gyttens die?'

Still no answer.

Clarenceux could sense the seething hatred. The very fact that he had asked such direct questions seemed to create waves of anger within the man. He felt the rope about his neck and knew that Crackenthorpe could simply pull on it, hard, and strangle him; and until he could get his hand on his boot knife there was nothing he could do to stop him.

He persevered. 'You must have served in someone's company – if only in the militia. How come you and I are so implacably opposed? We have much in common. Were you at Boulogne?'

Still Crackenthorpe said nothing.

'What have I done that has so offended you? Even between thieves there is respect. Yet you plainly have no respect for me. Or for Goodwife Machyn.'

Silence. Just the steady sound of their horses' hooves as they passed between the houses on the highway through the village. But Clarenceux was twisting his hands to and fro every time he passed into the shadow of a house, pausing when the moon shone again on him.

'Earlier, when we were in the church, you said you knew from experience what it is to have the soul tortured, and that you derive satisfaction from inflicting pain on your enemies. What was it that made you so? What hurt you in the first place?'

'If you had grown up on the Marches of Scotland, in Westmorland, as my brothers and I did, you too would have seen many atrocities. You too would have preferred to commit acts of brutality than to suffer them.'

Clarenceux passed another house and wrenched his hands a fraction of an inch further apart, stretching the rope and giving his fingers that bit more freedom, but tightening the knots a little more. Then the moon was on him again.

'Most people would have learnt to sympathise from such an experience.'

'It is weakness – and weakness is common.'

'So, do I understand? You are afraid that you would be of no value to Walsingham if you did not derive satisfaction from inflicting acts of cruelty?'

'Walsingham himself told me how he relies on me to push my prisoners for information further than he dare go.'

'And if you kill a man, and get caught for it? Does that not concern you – that you take the blame for his commands?'

'I am proud that I serve.'

'You are a bloody fool for it.'

Crackenthorpe did not answer. He just yanked hard on the rope round Clarenceux's neck – so hard that Clarenceux choked and started to fall, unable to help himself. He landed heavily on his shoulder on the frozen ground. Suddenly he felt the rope pulling his neck: Crackenthorpe was dragging him along the ground, throttling him, as if he were on the gallows. Frantically Clarenceux clawed at his neck with his tied hands, trying to grasp the rope, feeling the ground slipping away beneath his robed shoulders, and trying to stop the deadly knot biting into his throat. So tight was the noose that his cold fingers could not find a grip. Eventually he forced them through, as the terror of asphyxiation gave way to waves of nausea.

Crackenthorpe reined in his horse. Clarenceux lay panting behind him. He pulled the rope from around his neck and gasped. And in his gasping he rolled on to his knees and reached down to his boot, drawing out the small knife tucked inside. He slipped it into his right hand, slowly got to his feet and walked towards his horse.

'The rope, sergeant,' observed one of the men.

'Pick it up and put it back round his neck.'

Clarenceux took a deep breath and leant forward for the rope to be replaced. Crackenthorpe immediately pulled it tight, almost pulling Clarenceux over. He stumbled forward. 'For pity's sake, let me breathe,' he shouted, reaching up to loosen the knot, and turning round to prevent the moon from revealing the tip of the blade in his hand.

'I have no pity for you. Nor for that whore, Machyn's widow.'

Clarenceux mounted his horse. 'She is no whore,' he muttered.

'Not any more she isn't.' They started walking forward.

'What do you mean?'

'She is dead.'

Clarenceux felt the fear rise up, overwhelming him like an excrutiating noise. He had to struggle to make his voice heard. 'Walsingham's part of the deal was to release all the surviving prisoners. He said that I had until midday to return with the chronicle.'

'I am not going to let you return by midday. They are all going to hang. As for the whore – Walsingham was never going to release her. He waited until I had removed you and then hanged her at the Kingsland crossroads. That was why he accepted your deal.'

Clarenceux passed into the shadow of a house. He did not try to loosen his bonds or even manoeuvre the knife to cut the rope. All the life had gone out of him. He remembered the last night of their journey, when she had fallen asleep on his breast.

'There have been too many deaths,' he said, staring at the moonlight on the leafless branches alongside the road. 'Too many people have died. You kill and kill; you are cruel, vindictive – a despicable dreg of humanity.'

Suddenly Crackenthorpe's voice was furious in the silence of the night. 'And was it me that did all the killing? What about you, a heretic and a murderer? How can you preach to me like this when you killed my brother?'

Clarenceux swallowed, remembering the two men he had killed. 'Your brother?'

Suddenly he realised just how cold the night air was, how cold his hands were, how cold the stars, how cold the world.

'Now do you understand why I want to hurt you?'

Clarenceux said nothing. The desolate landscape within him was changing fast. The barren rock was melting in the flow of hatred and the instinct for survival. So, Rebecca was dead, united with her husband. But he would show her departing spirit that he would avenge her death. He would avenge all the deaths – including that of Crackenthorpe's brother, for he too had been a victim.

Moving into the shadow of a dense copse, he shifted the knife in his hand and cut part of the rope binding his wrists. Gradually, inch by inch, he loosened the tied knot, keeping the rope in sight.

Only a mile to go now. But his heart ached. He thought of her – the last time he had ridden this road had been with her. What was the last thing she had said to him? *God is with us.* And before that she had said, *We will fight them with love. Be strong, Trust in the Lord.* She had knelt beside him just that morning in the chapel at Summerhill, and prayed beside him Her absence burnt within him. The tears came to his eyes – he could do nothing to stop them.

Up the road towards Summerhill they rode, with the moon silvering the trees, the road and the old battlements of the great tower. Reflecting in the glass of a high window. Highlighting the wood of the gate.

Clarenceux's pulse was fast. Still he waited, each step the horses took being one step nearer the time of his revenge. He thought of touching the cold corpse of James Hopton the previous night, the man whose neck had been sliced. The killer was riding beside him – so close that he had to be vulnerable.

Another hundred yards to go, another fifty.

'We have searched this house already,' said one of the men. 'Just yesterday.'

'The heretic murderer has been back here since,' answered Crackenthorpe.

Then all of them began to dismount. Clarenceux draped the reins of his horse round the post to one side of the gate.

'You, knock on the door. Rouse the gatekeeper,' ordered Crackenthorpe.

'No,' said Clarenceux. 'No. That will not be necessary. The chronicle is not in the house. Follow me.'

Crackenthorpe's huge figure remained by the side of his horse, silhouetted by the moonlight. He considered the risks. 'Very well. Stephens, you will guard the horses, keep them ready. You other two will come with us. But first I want to fasten this rope tighter around the prisoner's neck.'

Clarenceux stopped and allowed Crackenthorpe to tighten the noose. He held his hands close against his body, so as not to let the rope around his wrists fall away.

'This way,' he said, leading the three men to the left of the gate and alongside the stone wall. He listened to the sound of their footsteps behind him in the frost-covered grass.

He was trembling. Here the path alongside the house was in shadow, and he could hardly see it. Nor did he know exactly where he was heading. All he knew was that the overgrown access to the tunnels beneath Summerhill was somewhere near, forty feet beyond the corner of the outer courtyard, as Julius had said. He trampled through the undergrowth searching for the darker shades, moving first this way, then that, following every possible pattern that might indicate the exposed rock and the tunnel entrance.

'Where are you leading us?' asked one of the men, stumbling through the bracken.

'To the chronicle.'

And then he saw it. Beneath the silhouette of a pair of trees there was a patch of complete blackness and overgrowth. The vague trail of a flattened path led in that direction.

'This way.'

Clarenceux walked on to the old path and approached the opening. *Sir John Fawcett ... sixty-seven paces ...* He reached for the side of the tunnel and brushed away some loose brambles and bracken. 'It's in here.'

'We need a light,' said Crackenthorpe. 'Do you two have a lantern?'

Neither of them did.

Crackenthorpe turned in the moonlit wood, sensing something was not right. 'Why did you not say that the chronicle is underground? We could have brought lanterns.'

Clarenceux's heart was beating fast. 'You did not ask. I do not need a light. I know where I am going.'

Crackenthorpe stepped closer to him. 'If you try anything, I am going to break your neck. I'll find the chronicle when I come back – and then I will have a light.'

Clarenceux felt the rope bite into his throat and turned into the tunnel.

Sixty-seven paces . . .

The three men were following him. The tunnel's width – it was about six feet wide – prevented them all walking together: two were immediately behind him and another at the rear. He guessed that Crackenthorpe was the one at the rear as there seemed to be very little slack in the rope around his neck. He tried to control his breathing, which was rapid and heavy; it seemed to echo against the chalk walls. He moved over to the right-hand side of the tunnel and in the darkness allowed the ropes to fall from his hands, trying to leave them where the guards would not step on them.

Thirty-one, thirty-two, thirty-three . . . Carefully he reached up and took hold of the rope around his neck and drew it a little forward. *Thirty-nine, forty, forty-one . . .* One man was now very close behind him. Clarenceux began to cut through the rope, sawing with the blade. *Fifty, fifty-one, fifty-two . . .*

Crackenthorpe stopped suddenly. 'What's that noise?'

In the suddenness of his stopping the last strand of the rope broke and fell from Clarenceux's hand.

He had to run. Into the darkness. Now.

'He's cut the rope – after him!' roared Crackenthorpe.

Raising his right arm Clarenceux pushed himself forward, feeling for the stone protruding from the chalk at head height. He heard the unsheathing of swords and the sound of feet pounding on the tunnel floor. They were so close, and they were running unafraid, not knowing what lay just a few steps beyond. *Where is the stone?* He had lost count of his paces – but knew that he had covered more than sixty-seven since entering the tunnel. *How many more? Is the stone still there?* A foot from behind knocked Clarenceux and he stumbled, and stooped, and ran on. *Have I missed the stone?* There was no time; he lunged for the wall itself, risking the fall.

And then he felt the stone and his other hand felt the opening. He flung himself to the right, and into the narrow passage. Immediately two screams of terror filled the tunnel, echoing in the shaft as the men plunged straight over the edge and fell into the nothingness of the drop, their eyes suddenly opened to death, their bodies sounding like slabs of meat as they smashed down on to the rocks at the base of the shaft.

Two screams echoed in that tunnel. Only two.

Clarenceux could hear heavy breathing in the darkness nearby. He sensed a man getting to his feet and heard the *ting* of a sword as he picked it up off the stone floor.

'Fraser!' shouted Crackenthorpe. 'Ridley!'

No answer.

Clarenceux's hands trembled as he felt the chalk. He inched further round, feeling for the continuation of the main passage, listening for the sounds of his pursuer but able to hear only his own heavy gasps for air. Down he crept, hands feeling the clammy walls, until he sensed that he had found the spot where he had stood with Rebecca on the day that Julius had shown them the tunnel for the first time.

Rebecca. Eyes with the love of a starlit night. Beloved. Hanged.

A scrape of cloth against stone alerted him. He crouched down, leaning against the corner of the passage floor, listening. He heard Crackenthorpe's sword scratch the rock; he heard his footsteps. The man paused.

Clarenceux tried to calm his breathing. He could run down into the deeper passages and risk being lost, or he could tuck himself against the wall of the passage further down and hope that Crackenthorpe missed him. But the passage was not wide enough; there was a good chance that he would be noticed. And Crackenthorpe would stab down with his sword. He felt for his boot knife: he had dropped it somewhere. He had no blade at all.

He heard footsteps again, this time more purposeful. He listened. But it seemed that Crackenthorpe was going back up the tunnel.

Still he did not move. As the footsteps faded, Clarenceux lay on the cold chalk thinking about Rebecca. He could not control his thoughts – he lay there for ten minutes or more, dwelling on the memory of her face, his own face wet with tears. Not until he remembered that he had betrayed Julius's family secret was he able to break his cycle of thoughts about her. And that new thought made him no happier. He had revealed the knowledge of the tunnel to a stranger and an enemy. Moreover, he had to take the chronicle to Walsingham, to force him to give up the other men. By noon. And Crackenthorpe knew that. He would probably ambush him on the way.

Clarenceux wiped his face, gasping for breath in the musty air. He could hear nothing now except a distant moaning somewhere far off. One of the men who had fallen into the shaft had not died instantly. Then the moaning stopped.

Clarenceux stood up in the tunnel and listened. He started to move back up the slope, towards where he guessed the staircase must be which led up into the house. He moved forward carefully, slowly running his hand along the left wall, mindful that from this side there was nothing to stop him falling into the shaft if he lost count of his steps.

Suddenly a burning torch appeared in front of him, having come down the stairs from the house. Clarenceux froze. *Can this be one of Julius's men?* He crouched, praying wordlessly with all the will in his heart that it was someone from the house come to find him. The figure was advancing. Still all Clarenceux could see was the flaming point of light. On it came, bobbing up and down with each footfall.

If that is a friend, his gait shows he is keen to find me.
But that is not the way a man walks normally.
That is not a normal man.

And with that thought Clarenceux realised he was looking at
the dark hair of Richard Crackenthorpe in the torchlight, just
fifty feet away. The man had gone through the house and terrorised
the old servants within into giving him a light and revealing the
staircase. Now he was striding down the tunnel, sweeping the
torch from one side to the other with his left hand, a drawn
sword in his right. His gait was bold and spoke of fury. But he
was not reckless. Clarenceux could see him slowing and inspecting
the ground carefully.

Crackenthorpe moved the torch up and down the walls on
either side. Then the torch swept around the passageway – and
he saw Clarenceux crouched ahead of him.

Clarenceux rose, turned and ran. He rushed straight down to
the foot of the passage, reaching out for the rock, hearing the
heavy footfall of Crackenthorpe running behind him. The light
of the torch behind was too weak to see the cavern wall at the
foot of the tunnel, and he crashed into it hard, twisting his fingers
and hands, scraping his shin and bashing his head against the
rock. But he pulled himself to his feet and pushed himself towards
the right, remembering that there were several passageways leading
off.

He ran down another tunnel in total darkness, hands
outstretched, feeling the curve of the chalk wall and hoping to
find a turning. On he went, tripping here and there on the uneven
floor, realising that there was no hope of remembering his way
back. The tunnels curved – he did not know whether he had
turned a corner or simply followed the passage. Soon he was
hopelessly lost, running and turning without reason or logic until
he slowed and stopped, and struggled to calm his panting, listening
out for footsteps.

He heard them. Crackenthorpe had been able to run much
faster, by the light of his torch. He was not far away.

Clarenceux stretched out his arms again and started running – running endlessly, it seemed, in a dream-like darkness. Patterns appeared of shapes and colours, as if he had pressed his fingers into his eyes. And still he heard the chasing steps. On he went, knowing he could run faster if he did not play the blind man with his hands out, bashing into walls as he went, twisting in the tunnels as if escaping from a devil in a labyrinthine hell.

He turned a corner. Suddenly Crackenthorpe was there in front of him, and Clarenceux was blinded by the torchlight. 'Halt!' yelled Crackenthorpe, as he lunged towards him, sword at the ready. Clarenceux turned and started running back the way he had come, hearing Crackenthorpe's heavy footsteps close behind. With the torchlight so near he could see the mouths of tunnels curling away into the unknown; but then he would take a turning and be plunged into the dark, until Crackenthorpe caught up.

Turning after turning he took – splashing through the cold water of a shallow underwater stream at one point – only to hear Crackenthorpe keep up the chase.

When the man with light meets the man with the sword, the man with the sword always has the advantage – but here the man with the light is the man with the sword. If only I could find my way out of these tunnels. O Lord, save me. Christ have mercy! He is almost on me again. I cannot carry on much longer.

Water. Julius never mentioned that there was a stream down here. That was a landmark. I should remember, so I can use it to navigate.

He hastened down a tunnel and decided he would return to the stream. He had run on ahead in darkness now for a minute or more, with the torchlight appearing only at intervals behind him. Now he dived into another tunnel, and felt a sharp corner with his hand. He hid immediately around the turn, in the shadow. He waited, breathing heavily. Too heavily. Crackenthorpe would hear him and stab round the corner with the sword.

But Crackenthorpe did not come.

Clarenceux listened, fearfully. There was no sound of footsteps. Just the slow drip, drip, drip of water.

He looked back round the corner.

Darkness.

I cannot even hear him. Could he have fallen and let the light go out?

Clarenceux went round the corner and crept back along the way he had come, sniffing the air for signs of the burning pitch of the torch. He tensed himself, fearful that Crackenthorpe had put out his light on purpose, and was waiting for him, sword drawn.

He felt another corner with his fingers and turned, heading back through the tunnel he had run along only a moment before. Again he paused, listening. More dripping water, this time falling not on to rock but into an underground pool or lake. And then he heard something else, like a faint shuffling of feet. The sound of two pieces of metal knocked together.

Clarenceux took a deep breath and moved in the direction of the sound. He stepped carefully, not wanting to trip and fall. There ahead, perhaps forty yards away down a tunnel, was just the faintest hint of light. Quietly he inched forward towards it, listening, prepared to run at the slightest sign of Crackenthorpe's being aware of his presence.

The light was growing stronger. *It is coming from round that corner. What would I do in Crackenthorpe's position? I would place the light somewhere to attract my enemy, like a moth, and then I would hide where he cannot see me. In the darkness of one of the adjacent tunnels.*

But at that moment Clarenceux heard the clang of something metal hitting another metal item It was followed almost immediately by the sound of another metal item striking the floor, hard.

He crept closer, coming to the opening, his back pressed against the wall of the passageway. The flickering light was just round the corner, and illuminating the far side of the passage. He crouched down, listening, fearing the darkness at his back but fearing the light even more.

He inched forward, until one eye could just see around the corner.

Crackenthorpe had found the long, chapel-like chamber. Clarenceux recognised the columns of chalk and the aisles on either side: the shadowy niches around the long nave. Crackenthorpe was examining a gold or gilt-silver flagon on the altar at the far end of the room. He had lit several candles and propped his torch against a carved crucifix in the middle of the hall. He looked at the jewelled crosses on the walls and the chests of treasure saved from the monasteries, lost in a golden glow of his own. Then he set down the flagon, returned to the torch, picked it up and saw Clarenceux.

Clarenceux did not run. Instead he slowly entered the nave. He stood there openly, bold and unarmed.

Crackenthorpe's eyes were fierce in the torchlight. 'You have no sword.'

Clarenceux took another step forward, along the stone nave, and then another, and another. And as he walked forward, creeping from the shadows in the aisles around them came men on silent feet. Several of them were bearing swords, others holding knives. There were servants in old doublets, grooms in old tunics, and two men wearing breastplates.

Then Julius stepped forward, in his black robe. 'He cannot be allowed to leave. He must be killed.'

'Julius,' said Clarenceux grimly, not turning away from Crackenthorpe, 'I will do the killing, if you will give me a sword. Would you ask your men to light the rest of the candles.'

'I will not have you risk your life.' Looking at Clarenceux, he added, 'Besides, you have already been blooded, it seems.'

'Julius, this is Richard Crackenthorpe, the man who killed your servant James Hopton, my friend Henry Machyn, and my servant William Terry. He has sworn to kill me too. As it is his fate to die in these passages, I urge you to let me do the killing.'

'It is safer for us to do it together.'

'Julius, I need to kill this man – for revenge, for my own sake.'

Julius considered for a moment. Then he unbuckled his own sword, stepped forward and handed it to Clarenceux.

Still Clarenceux did not take his eyes off Crackenthorpe. He took the weapon, unsheathed it and threw aside the scabbard. He stepped forward.

Crackenthorpe did not back away. He and Clarenceux circled in the light of the candles and torches. The only sounds were their footsteps as they moved in the almost still air of the underground nave. Candlelight glinted off the treasures around them but they saw none of it. Neither man allowed his gaze to shift from the other.

Crackenthorpe made the first sudden lunge, aiming high, hoping to catch Clarenceux off guard and dart in with a slash to the ribs; but Clarenceux was not off guard. He was concentrating on the man shifting before him. When the high lunge came he was able to swipe it away.

Frustration will be his downfall. Take your time. Beat off his attacks until he makes a mistake.

Crackenthorpe raised his sword, willing Clarenceux to second-guess his target; but Clarenceux was quick enough to escape the threatened cut. They circled again. Crackenthorpe darted forward a second time, going first for Clarenceux's sword-arm shoulder, then slashing at his throat. Clarenceux was slower to avoid the second cut. The blade just nicked his skin: its closeness was a warning. Crackenthorpe was younger, stronger and faster than he was, and he had no less reach.

Again they circled. Crackenthorpe grimaced with intent as he thrust forward to Clarenceux's chest. Steel edge met steel edge, sparks flying in the candlelit nave. Clarenceux hurled his weight into the blows, seeking to knock the blade out of Crackenthorpe's hand by striking it with force at an angle. But although their blades struck seven, eight, nine times, Crackenthorpe retained a firm grip. He almost strolled around the cave, so consumed by the fight that he seemed to have forgotten it would be his last.

The candles on the altar guttered as the two men swirled around and attacked again. Crackenthorpe – now moving with his left arm outstretched, hoping to catch Clarenceux's sleeve or collar – rushed forward suddenly and thrust his blade towards Clarenceux's chest. Clarenceux parried the blow, stepping to one side, drawing his own blade back across Crackenthorpe's cheek, slicing through the soft skin and exposing the teeth and gums for the instant before the blood welled and started to flow. Encouraged, he brought his sword down with a clang on Crackenthorpe's as the man lunged for revenge. With another blow Clarenceux tried to strike the blade out of the man's hand. But Crackenthorpe was not beaten yet and, seeing an instant of opportunity, darted forward with his blade and stabbed Clarenceux in the left-hand side of the abdomen.

The pain shot through Clarenceux and he crumpled up, losing his balance, staggering towards a column of rock. The servants watching there drew back, horrified and tearful. Clarenceux lifted his head and saw Crackenthorpe's face looking down on him: a vengeful spirit. Clarenceux's own body surged with pain and submerged into the easy weakness of inaction; but the will to inflict a fatal wound on his enemy was still strong. No matter that he had failed to play the game of patience, he would never stop fighting this man. He would fight him in this world and the next.

Crackenthorpe saw the doubled ferocity of his opponent and slashed down with his sword as Clarenceux tried to get up, seeking skin but finding a raised sword and guard. He slashed again and thrust, catching Clarenceux's arm as he knelt on the ground, drawing blood. Another slash, cutting Clarenceux across the ribs. Clarenceux could not bring his sword up quickly enough to defend his body, and threw himself to one side, partially taking cover behind a column of rock as he scrambled to his feet, parrying blows as he did so. Then he too charged, striking Crackenthorpe's sword away and getting in close, forcing Crackenthorpe against another column of rock with his shoulder. He punched upwards with the palm of his fist and tried to lift his sword to Crackenthorpe's throat but it caught on Crackenthorpe's leg and he was forced to twist out of the way as Crackenthorpe brought his own sword up and slashed. But Clarenceux was not retreating now. He swept down with a great cry of hatred, slashing and cutting Crackenthorpe in a torrent of fierce blows, slicing the man's face, his arm and his chest. Crackenthorpe backed away for an instant and then charged back into the scything strokes that meant his death, thrusting and slashing with his sword, hardly hitting Clarenceux's blade but finding his arm once, twice, then his shoulder and his thigh, sending Clarenceux falling again. Suddenly he saw his chance for the kill – one last moment of glory to revel in his strength, his ability to dominate his fellow men, which had been the greatest pleasure of his life. He raised his sword for the final killing blow on Clarenceux's head – only to be shocked by the thrust upwards into his throat of Clarenceux's own blade.

Crackenthorpe teetered, hearing the splash of his own blood on the floor, trying to understand what had happened, and at the same time trying to bring his blade down on his victim. But all his understanding, focus and strength had gone. It had burst out of him. Suddenly Clarenceux withdrew his blade and Crackenthorpe no longer knew why he was standing with his arms in the air, or holding a sword; he no longer knew anything at all.

The sword fell first, and clattered. Then the body collapsed heavily.

Julius's men rushed forward when they saw Crackenthorpe fall but Clarenceux put up a hand. 'Leave him,' he shouted, still kneeling. He rose shakily to his feet, breathing heavily. He lifted his sword and paused, looking down at the huge dying man. Then with hatred and fury burning within him, he brought it down with all his force and cut through Crackenthorpe's neck, the metal blade ringing on the stone floor as the head rolled away.

He sank back to his knees. 'God is with us, Rebecca.' He pressed his face to the floor.

72

⁂

larenceux felt the most intense pain as he was carried back up the spiral staircase into the house. They had to twist his body. 'Put me down!' he roared. 'Put me on my feet.' Both the men trying to carry him instantly complied. Clarenceux's was a voice to be obeyed, especially when he was in pain.

He panted for a moment, recovering his strength. Then, with his hands on the stone steps, he began to push himself up. A man followed with a lantern. Clarenceux passed the chamber on the ground floor and carried on crawling until he reached Julius's study on the upper floor. The small door was open, and he pulled himself to his feet.

'Go ahead,' he said to the man with the lantern. 'Just go straight through to Mr Fawcett's library. I will follow.'

'Sir, wait, you need help. You are still bleeding.'

'No, not now,' gasped Clarenceux, feeling the pain in his belly increasing suddenly.

He leant against the door jamb until he had gathered his strength to walk to the next doorway. Several men were now clustering around him. Halfway across he fell. Two men were quickly at his sides, lifting him. 'Help me through to the library,' he said, seeing the light ahead.

Once they had hauled him into the library, Clarenceux once more sought the refuge of the doorway, keeping himself on his feet.

Julius appeared, having run up the stairs. 'William, what are you doing? Sit down. I'll have someone carry you to bed.'

'No, Julius. Four or five men will die at noon if I do not hand the chronicle over to Mr Walsingham.'

'After all this, you are going to give it up?'

'He is going to hang them – at best. He may even have them burnt for heresy. I have no choice. Enough men have died. Enough women too.'

'You cannot be in your right mind, William. Look at you. You have been stabbed in the gut – I can see the blood still coming – and you have two, three deep cuts to your arms and several other wounds, including a cut to the chest. Never mind going to London – how are you even standing up?'

'God is with me, Julius. I am to save these men. He has given me a plan. I need your help. I need you to take me to the city. Take me in a cart if you have to – but, damn it, get me there quickly, before noon.'

Clarenceux's declamatory voice, given force through his pain, echoed in the room and in the minds of everyone present.

At length Julius spoke. 'I will accompany you – with as many men as I have spare horses. But first you will let Lychorus dress your wounds.'

Clarenceux gestured to a book press on the far side of the room. A pile of books were stacked at its foot. 'Over there, at the bottom of that pile, you'll find the chronicle.'

Julius went over to the pile, took the topmost books off, and lifted the chronicle. He set it down on the table. Once more the golden gleam of a candle touched it. So much of Julius's study had been damaged by Crackenthorpe's soldiers, so many books torn apart, that its intactness gave it a certain aura.

'Thank you,' said Clarenceux, pointing to another heavy vellum-bound volume that was lying on a shelf nearby. It had been mutilated and the cover was loose. 'May I also borrow this? I trust you won't be needing it for a day or two.'

73

Thursday, 30 December

No one troubled them on the return to London. If any of Walsingham's men were watching the road, they did not confront Julius and his company of fifteen men.

Clarenceux was carried in a cart, covered in blankets, and was silent most of the way, sometimes biting his lip against the pain. They made a fast pace in the bright morning air. Clarenceux felt confident he would not die: the wound in his abdomen had continued to bleed for a long time but now had stopped. He knew that he should see a surgeon, but he did not even mention the word – and would allow no one else to do so either. There was no time. Besides, the spectre of death by surgery still haunted him, as it did every man who had seen what military surgeons could do. As he knew well, untrained women in rural parishes sometimes performed surgical operations on injured people who then lived. Military surgeons undertook the more complex operations, requiring considerably greater knowledge and dexterity – and half their patients died after a few days. The only explanation was that it was God's will. *We will keep clear of surgeons.*

At London Bridge, Julius talked to the guards. They were uncertain but could not prevent him and his men from passing. At Bridge Gate the company was simply waved through. But thereafter they were followed. At Ludgate the cart passed under the arch that Clarenceux knew so well, and rumbled over Fleet Bridge.

For a moment it seemed that the nightmare was receding. But Clarenceux reminded himself that it only seemed that way. There was no guarantee that the cold-blooded killing was not about to resume.

They stopped outside the house in Fleet Street. Clarenceux threw off the blankets and signalled to Julius to knock as he manoeuvred himself to the edge of the cart and let himself down on to the ground. He glanced at the following guards, who had remained at a safe distance. Two of Julius's men supported him as he tentatively walked towards his front door.

It did not open.

Even if all my servants have left, Walsingham should be here. And he should have the prisoners with him. And why are those guards watching?

'Knock again.'

A minute went by. This time the door did open. A gaunt, white-haired old man with a deeply lined face looked out nervously.

'Thomas, I *am* glad to see you.' Clarenceux could not help but smile.

Thomas's eyes alighted on Clarenceux and his face lit up. His expression was beyond mere happiness. 'Sir, I had given up hope! I thought ... Oh, Mr Clarenceux, sir,' and in his emotion he rushed forward and knelt in front of Clarenceux, and kissed his hand.

Clarenceux pulled his servant to his feet and embraced him gently. 'Thomas, a fine welcome, for which I thank you heartily. But tell me: is anyone else at home? My wife? Nurse Brown?'

'No, sir, I am here alone. Nurse Brown has left the city. The other servants have not returned. But Mistress Harley and your daughters are well, sir, and still with your sister-in-law in Devon. Your house is not yet fit for their return. I came back to do what I could to mend things, but much has been damaged.'

'Thomas, my heartfelt thanks. Has Mr Walsingham called in the last day or so? Or anyone else of his following?'

'No, sir, no one. I have been here all the time.'

'I see.' Clarenceux looked along the street to the west and saw the carts and packhorses approaching the city, and the street vendors, water carriers and milk carriers. He turned and looked the other way, towards the city wall and Ludgate, the bridge and the broken shape of the tower of St Paul's. Walsingham's guards were still watching him from just this side of the bridge.

'Julius, what time is it?'

'About noon, I would say, William. We are on time. The bells will ring soon.'

'It would appear that I have been deceived. Francis Walsingham has defaulted on his part of our bargain. But he is acting under the protection of Sir William Cecil, her majesty's Secretary. What would you advise me to do? Go to Walsingham's house by the Tower? Or pay a visit to Mr Secretary Cecil?'

Clarenceux did not wait for an answer. Instead he turned and, pointing west, limped back to the cart, aided by Julius's men. 'Go with God, Thomas,' he called as the cart jolted and began to move westwards. 'I will be back later. And thank you.'

It was only a short journey from Fleet Street to Cecil House, in the Strand. Julius rode ahead through the gates and into the courtyard. When the gatekeeper sought the meaning of the intrusion Julius calmly asked that the man announce the arrival of Mr William Harley, Clarenceux King of Arms. Without waiting for a refusal, he led all his men up to the door of the grand house.

'For heaven's sake, can't you see this man is in great pain?' he snapped at a servant who stood in their way and dared to suggest they should not enter without being invited.

'Then he needs a surgeon. Sir William cannot satisfy you on that score,' the man replied indignantly.

'No, but Sir William has many other scores to settle with me,' replied Clarenceux, his arms on the shoulders of two of Julius's servants. 'And he will need more than mere surgery if he fails.'

After this exchange, twelve of Julius's men accompanied their master and Clarenceux into the great hall of Cecil House while the other three remained outside, looking after the horses in the front courtyard.

A minute later Cecil came into the hall. His eyes went straight to Clarenceux. He saw that another gentleman was present, dressed in a similar black robe.

'My greetings on seeing you, Clarenceux, would be glad and hearty; but today you come unexpectedly and accompanied by men I neither know nor trust.'

'That, Sir William,' replied Clarenceux firmly, 'is because you trust the wrong men. Or let me be particular. You trust Francis Walsingham – a man who has tried to kill me, who has allowed a royal sergeant-at-arms to murder a boy in my service, William Terry, as well as an old man, Henry Machyn, and this gentleman's chamberlain, Mr James Hopton – this gentleman being Mr Julius Fawcett of Summerhill, Chislehurst. Forgive me if I appear rude by not waiting to be invited into your hall, but you and I have too much talking to do to waste time on courtesies.'

'Then tell me, Clarenceux, what is your explanation for the charges of high treason against you?' Cecil's eyes settled on Julius for a moment, then returned to him. 'Correct me if I am wrong, but you have failed to produce a seditious document in your keeping, you have harboured others guilty of the same crime, you have resisted arrest, murdered two servants of the Crown and – worst of all – you have sought to encompass the overthrow of her majesty the queen herself. That is treason as laid out in the Great Treason Act of Edward the Third – you cannot deny it.'

More of Cecil's men were coming into the hall, six servants in his household livery and eight guards wearing breastplates. Julius's men were now outnumbered, and, standing around Clarenceux, they began to feel uneasy. But Clarenceux himself did not flinch.

'Sir William, you do not know this but I will tell you freely. You can add to that list of crimes that I have killed not two but five so-called "servants of the Crown". Last night I killed the sergeant-at-arms, Richard Crackenthorpe, in a duel; and I led two of his men to their deaths. I believe their names were Fraser and Ridley. If you want proof, Crackenthorpe's head is in the back of the cart in your front courtyard.'

Clarenceux looked at Cecil, daring him to speak. But Cecil was taking his time. Suddenly Clarenceux's declamatory voice filled the room, rising with the emotion of the remembered killings. 'And do you know why I killed Crackenthorpe? Because he had sworn to slay me for accidentally killing his brother. It was a personal matter. These men might have been paid by the Crown but they were not acting in its interests. They were serving themselves, using their royal authority to further their own ends – to bully, intimidate, steal, rape, injure and murder the queen's subjects. That is what you do not understand, Sir William. And nor does Francis Walsingham. You are too far removed from real events to see it. There is no plot. I repeat: *there is no plot*. It is all a figment of your terrified imaginations. You, in your great house, with the ear of the queen – what do you know about the way other people live their lives? You are so sheltered from danger you fear every gathering of men is a conspiracy. Walsingham and Crackenthorpe – acting supposedly under instructions from you – have killed a number of people who never sought to overthrow the queen. They may have had their secrets but they were not revolutionaries. Now I want revenge for . . .' But Clarenceux could not go on. The thought of Rebecca caused him to flounder in a sea of despair.

Cecil was shaken but he remained in control of himself. 'Then explain to me the meaning of the chronicle of Henry Machyn. You cannot deny you have seen it and have possession of it.'

'I agreed to hand it over this noon to Francis Walsingham at my house. It would appear he does not want it, for he defaulted on our agreement. He did not attend. That is how seriously he takes your plot, Mr Secretary. But more – let me tell you that he guaranteed the lives of the men he has mercilessly imprisoned in return for this book. Where are those men? As it happens, the book does indeed refer to a secret document that would enable the overthrow of the queen. I am sure I only need mention the marriage of Lord Percy and Anne Boleyn and you will know exactly what I am talking about. You are one of the few who will understand how serious such a plot *could* have been. But this was a secret to be kept, not a plot to be enacted. However, if I do not have Walsingham at my house in Fleet Street within the hour – with all those whose freedoms he has promised – and with you in attendance, then I will give myself over to bringing it about. And I will give my dying strength to undermining the authority you have built up, and which Walsingham exercises in your name, and which Crackenthorpe exercised also, because I am sick to my very soul with the deaths of innocent people.'

More men were coming into the hall, alerted by Cecil's servants. But Julius's men stood their ground.

Cecil walked forward, towards Clarenceux. 'There is no plot, you say?'

'Not if you do not want there to be one.'

'You mean, *you* are the plot.'

'No, Sir William. Upon the life of my daughter – your wife's god-daughter – there is no plot. I have possession of a chronicle, that is all. And that chronicle gives me certain knowledge that you understand, and I understand, but which Francis Walsingham does not understand and very few would.'

Cecil held his gaze for a long time. When he eventually spoke, his voice was low. 'Very well. Today is your day. As long as you can guarantee that the future is mine. Do we have a bargain? Do I have that guarantee?'

'We will see – if Walsingham complies. You have my word.'

Cecil turned to a man standing nearby. 'Find Walsingham as quickly as possible. Tell him this, *exactly*: if he has made an agreement with William Harley, Clarenceux King of Arms, he is to observe it in its minutest detail, or face a charge of high treason. Tell him to hand over the prisoners he has promised by two of the clock, on pain of death and forfeiture of his estates. Tell him that exactly as I have said it to you.' Cecil turned to Clarenceux, 'And rest assured, William – I hope I can call you William still – if Walsingham fails, then you may have his head, to add to your collection.'

Clarenceux tried to bow but the pain in his abdomen prevented him. 'I am grateful for your trust, Sir William.'

'Good. My men will escort your company to your house and I will see you there at two of the clock.'

74

There was little furniture left in Clarenceux's hall. Thomas had done a good job of tidying up but the spaces on the wall where his round mirror and paintings had hung told a quiet story of loss. The smashed plasterwork above the fireplace still testified to the destructiveness of Richard Crackenthorpe and his men. Nevertheless, Clarenceux was happy to see the place again. He was especially pleased to see the elm table in its usual place.

'I have not attended to your study,' said Thomas as Julius's men helped Clarenceux to a chair that had been prepared for him. 'With all the papers and documents on the floor – I thought it best to leave that to you personally.'

'Thank you, Thomas. You have done well. I am pleased.'

Clarenceux asked for the elm table to be brought across the room and positioned in front of his seat, and he had Machyn's chronicle placed on it. Julius instructed half his servants and retainers to wait outside as there would be insufficient room within. A mug of ale was brought for Clarenceux, and the first sweet taste was like an instant of homeliness.

Sir William Cecil arrived shortly afterwards with a good company of men. He walked briskly up the stairs, with guards preceding and following him. A plush seat was carried up from a neighbour's property and he took his place beside Clarenceux. He looked at the table and the chronicle, and the array of men before them.

'Francis is going to think he is on trial.'

'Good,' Clarenceux replied.

Cecil shook his head gently. 'If he comes, and if he does as he has agreed, he is still under my protection, Mr Clarenceux. I hope you don't make unwarranted statements that would prejudice your case, or any threats that will throw the burden of shame back on yourself.'

Clarenceux said nothing. He understood.

Walsingham's footsteps sounded on the stairs. He was alone.

He was wearing his usual attire of black doublet, small ruff, black skullcap and black hose; but Clarenceux noted a certain distinction in the lace at his throat and on his cuffs, and that he was wearing a sword. The latter was not technically permitted. Francis Walsingham was not a knight, and therefore not allowed to walk around the city's liberties displaying a blade. But Clarenceux knew that the sword served a more subtle purpose: to remind Cecil that he acted under his authority and with his protection.

'Good day, Francis,' Cecil began. 'I am glad you have come. It would appear that we owe Mr Clarenceux an apology. He tells me there is no plot, and that there never was any plot, against her majesty.'

Walsingham looked coldly at Clarenceux, as if examining him. Then he turned back to Cecil. 'Do you believe him? Would you believe him if he told you he has persuaded her majesty to return the Church of England to the Roman fold? The man is a liar, a traitor and a heretic.'

'Well, Francis, that may be your opinion. But we do not prosecute or punish people simply on the strength of your opinion.' Cecil paused for a moment. 'And if we have acted against people in the past on that account – prosecuted them, punished them, searched their premises, damaged their possessions, threatened them – then that was wrong. Do you not agree? And if it has been done under my protection, that constitutes an abuse of privilege, no?'

'Sir William, you and I have a difficult balance to maintain. As you yourself have said, the stability of the ship of State is all-important. If I remember your exact words, you said: "If a mariner falls overboard, we do not turn the whole ship round. I would rather that innocent men drown than the ship be unsteadied."'

There was a shifting among the men in the room. Cecil remained calm. 'How many innocent men have drowned, exactly?'

'That depends on what you mean by innocent.'

'How many?'

'Two have died. Both royal servants – one outside the Machyn house, killed by Mr Clarenceux; and the other in the alley north of the churchyard of St Peter's, also killed by Mr Clarenceux.'

'Let me repeat the question. How many?'

Walsingham hesitated. 'I will allow that Clarenceux's servant boy and Daniel Gyttens should not have died.'

'And Henry Machyn?'

'Henry Machyn was a traitor and a heretic. He was not innocent.'

Clarenceux could contain himself no longer. 'Henry Machyn was merely the guardian of a private document. He never plotted against the Church or the State. He was guilty of nothing more than writing a chronicle – one that is not remotely seditious.'

Walsingham's eyes narrowed. 'But if you look in that chronicle, what does it say under the date of the fifteenth of June 1552? And the sixteenth of June 1553? It *is* seditious, I'll have you admit.'

Cecil held up a hand to silence Clarenceux. 'I believe, Mr Walsingham, that now is your opportunity to put that theory to the test.' He gestured to the book. 'Here is the chronicle of Henry Machyn.'

Walsingham looked at the vellum-bound book. Everyone else looked at him. He stepped forward and picked it up. The cover was loose, and almost came away in his hand. But he paid no attention to that. His eyes went straight to the uneven script. He squinted as he tried to read. He set the book back down on the table and turned the pages. He started reading silently again, looking for the incriminating entries. He found nothing under the first date he examined, so he turned more pages, looking for another date. Again he found nothing. Increasingly frantic, he turned back to the start. A sneer of satisfaction came across his face as he found an entry for the thirteenth of June 1550 and glanced up at Clarenceux. Then he read the entry, and realised that it was not incriminating. After checking six or seven more entries, he set the book down.

'Read the last entry,' Clarenceux commanded.

Walsingham turned the pages brusquely, looking occasionally at Clarenceux, until the last page was revealed. He read it silently.

'Read it aloud,' ordered Cecil.

Walsingham looked Cecil in the eye and held his gaze before turning to the book. 'It says: "The eleventh of December. Harry Machyn writer of this chronicle died, being killed by the order of Richard Crackenthorpe, queen's sergeant-at-arms. Esperance."' And that,' said Cecil, 'is the basis on which you have killed innocent people, in the name of her majesty, Mr Walsingham?'

Walsingham tossed the heavy book on to the table. 'The word "Esperance" appears on Lord Percy's tomb – it points to Machyn's complicity . . .'

'In what, exactly? His complicity in what?'

Unnerved by Cecil's smooth opposition, Walsingham looked round the room for support. Every face told the single story of deserved revenge. He turned back to Cecil. 'Sir William, you know about the messenger sent from Scotland. You know about the assassin sent to kill William Draper. There *was* a conspiracy. You and I discussed it many times.'

'No. You told me about it. Did I ever tell you to kill anyone? Did I ever instruct you to do anything except take the precaution of searching this very house? And when you did search it, did you find anything? No. Yet you clearly intimidated this man, wrecked his property, murdered his servant, and drove his wife and daughters out of their home.'

'I was looking for the chronicle . . .'

'And now you have found it. Does it justify your behaviour? I think not. So, what are you going to do? What is going to be your final conclusion on this matter?'

Walsingham said nothing.

'I have a grave suspicion that, without my intervention, you would have hanged Mr Clarenceux and told me that all was well because you had foiled the plot. But the only crimes that have been committed have been committed by you and your hirelings. That is how it appears to me.'

Walsingham swallowed. 'I will ensure that Sergeant Crackenthorpe faces the full penalty of the law.'

Cecil looked away. 'It is too late for that.'

'He is dead,' said Clarenceux.

Walsingham's mouth opened. He searched for words but none were forthcoming. 'God have mercy on his soul,' he eventually said in a hoarse voice.

'God will do nothing of the sort,' retorted Clarenceux. 'Do you think it was an accident that I ended up like this, with wounds to my body, arms and legs? You gave him instructions to kill me once he had the chronicle, so I would not return today by the appointed hour. You were not here at noon. You never had any intention of honouring your side of the deal we struck yesterday in Hackney Church.'

Walsingham looked towards the door.

'Don't turn away from us, Francis,' said Cecil. 'Explain to me first your understanding of the bargain. Mr Clarenceux and you were to meet today, at noon, in this house, when he would give you the chronicle and you would release the prisoners, is that correct?'

'Those that were still alive.'

'And how many is that?'

Walsingham looked at the ground. 'Five men,' he said at last.

'Where are they now?' snapped Cecil.

Walsingham looked Cecil in the eye. 'If I have been harsh, it was because you wanted me to be . . .'

'Answer me, Mr Walsingham. Where are they now?'

'In the Tower, in my house and in the safe house in Bishopsgate.'

'You admit they are not here, then. So, Mr Clarenceux is telling the truth. You had no intention of fulfilling your side of the bargain. You clearly did not expect Mr Clarenceux to return safely and fulfil his.'

'Where is Rebecca Machyn?' demanded Clarenceux, his voice trembling. 'You said five *men* are still alive. What about her?'

Walsingham looked terrified. 'Sir William, I implore you, what I have done I did with a good conscience, in all faith and fidelity to—'

'Just answer the question.'

'No!' shouted Walsingham. 'I will have no more of this! I will not be interrogated as if I were a criminal or a traitor. I have laboured day and night to do what was asked of me, with knowledge only of a conspiracy in progress. And as you yourself have said, Sir William, if we succeed nineteen times out of twenty to keep her majesty safe and fail on the twentieth, what then? We have failed completely.'

'What about Rebecca Machyn?' insisted Clarenceux.

'She is still alive – I am innocent on that score at least,' shouted Walsingham. 'But she is guilty – she is as guilty as Clarenceux himself!'

No one spoke. The words echoed in the minds of all the men present. Walsingham realised that everyone in that room had taken his words as proof of his prejudice. But for Clarenceux, it was as if a heavenly choir had started singing and releasing doves of peace. The grief he had known was gone. Tears welled in his eyes.

'Where is she?' he asked.

'Bishopsgate.'

Cecil turned to Clarenceux. 'It would appear that you, Mr Clarenceux, are indeed the injured party. But we still have to bring all this to a resolution. What should we do now?'

Clarenceux wiped his eyes and looked at Cecil. 'The way forward is clear. I made a deal with this man: the lives and safety of all those he is keeping prisoner in return for the chronicle. The two conditions were that we make the transfer in this house and that you be present, Sir William. Here is the chronicle, on the table before us. We are in my house. You are present. We lack only the prisoners. As an officer of her majesty the queen, I am prepared to stand by my side of the bargain if Mr Walsingham stands by his.'

'Good,' said Cecil with a sigh. 'I was hoping you would say that. Mr Walsingham, you have two hours to assemble everyone here, in this room, including the Machyn woman. Mr Fawcett, outside in your cart I believe there is a head. Could you dispose of it, please? The gate on London Bridge is the traditional place. Now, I would like to have a private word with Mr Clarenceux, so if you will all vacate this hall, I would be much obliged.'

Everyone waited as Walsingham marched out of the room. Then they filtered out, murmuring and talking among themselves. Thomas was the last to leave. He bowed to Cecil and Clarenceux, then closed the door to the stairs behind him.

Cecil looked at Clarenceux. 'At my house earlier you said that there is no plot. But you also mentioned the marriage between Lord Percy and Anne Boleyn. I also was privy to the message from Scotland that sparked off this hunt for conspirators. So I do know that you are either lying to me on your own behalf or lying to me on behalf of others.'

'But I was—'

'No buts. You have heard me accept your side of the story publicly and without reservation. And I appreciate that you were not the architect of whatever plot was, or is, afoot. I often thought that Walsingham was too quick to regard you in that capacity. I know that you are not a rebellious man by nature. You like structure. You like order. You like family pedigrees and coats of arms described in arcane language. You have a family, and although you are a follower of the old religion, I know that that is because you are of a conservative nature. Walsingham could never understand these things because you too neatly fitted his conception of what a Catholic conspirator must be. Do you follow me?'

'Yes, entirely, Sir William.'

'Walsingham will learn from this experience. What I have in mind for him requires him to learn many hard lessons – and more innocents will drown, it is true. But we have a woman on the throne, a headstrong woman, and she is very vulnerable. She is also the most powerful of all the monarchs of a Protestant leaning, so she is doubly vulnerable – to the foreign assassin's bullet as well as the English Catholic's knife. And she refuses to name a successor. I am a good deal older than she is; but if between us Walsingham and I ensure she lives long enough to marry and pass on the Crown safely to another generation, then we will have done our duty.'

'I understand.'

'So . . . Am I right in thinking that you have discovered proof of the Percy–Boleyn marriage?'

'Yes.'

'Where is it? Is it in the chronicle?'

'No.'

'Tell me where.'

Clarenceux considered his reply. Honesty, he decided, was the only possible course of action. 'Sir William, it seems safest to me that I do not tell you. Your business is to protect her majesty above all else. I know the whereabouts of the most dangerous document you can imagine. Whom could I trust to keep it more than I trust myself?'

Cecil said nothing.

'And you have just declared in the hearing of a number of witnesses that there was indeed no plot. It would be better for me to destroy the document myself than allow it to be kept by someone else.'

Cecil sat forward and spoke in a low voice, looking deep into Clarenceux's eyes. 'No, do not destroy it. We may need it.'

'I am sorry, what did you say? We may *need* it?'

'Yes. Let me put it this way. Some of us are privy to the events of 1536. I have known for a long time of the existence of the marriage agreement. I presume you know the name Chapuys?'

'The ambassador to the Holy Roman Emperor. I've seen copies of his letters on the subject of the marriage and on the execution.'

'And you will be sensitive to the fact that we have not always had a Protestant monarch. And we may yet have another Catholic. I am sure that it does not matter greatly to God one way or the other – that is where you and I differ, perhaps – but I will use whatever means are necessary to ensure there is no revolution in the name of a Catholic God *or* a Protestant God. Do you understand me?'

Clarenceux looked carefully at Cecil's face.

'It is no more than what I have just done for you, is it not?' Cecil got up from his chair. 'I hope and pray that we have an understanding, Mr Clarenceux. You will keep that document safely and very secretly. And if ever I need it, you will produce it for me.' Clarenceux made an attempt to get to his feet. 'No, stay seated, Mr Clarenceux. You word of honour is as good sitting down as it is standing up.' He offered his hand.

Clarenceux hesitated for just a second. Then he shook it.

'Good. I will see you in two hours.'

When Cecil had gone, Clarenceux sat for a long time in his chair by himself. He thought back to the moment when he had stood in this hall with Henry Machyn, and accepted the chronicle. He remembered telling the boy William Terry not to reveal the whereabouts of the book. He remembered the interrogation at Walsingham's house, and the hellish night in the cellar, awaiting death, and then the heavenly sunshine on being released. With a flinch he recalled the two guards he had killed, one of whom had been Crackenthorpe's brother. And killing Crackenthorpe himself in the cavern. He owed a great deal to some people. To the warden of the Skinners. To Tom Griffiths, the pelterer. He owed an immense amount to Julius. But most of all he was indebted to Rebecca. He owed her his life, for she had moved the chronicle at the critical moment, risking death to save it from falling into Crackenthorpe's hands. She had been the one who had understood the meaning of the Knights' names. But most of all she had been with him throughout. He would not have been able to keep going if it had not been for her support.

For three weeks I have lived in fear. But I have learnt much. In Walsingham's cellar I realised that I would prefer to die than live a hated, unworthy existence. And in that dark churchyard, waiting for Rebecca after escaping from William Draper's house, I learnt that God alone is not enough. Those words haunted me that evening and they still do. But there really is no mystery. Men and women need one other – otherwise our struggles would simply be unbearable.

75

Sir William Cecil was the last to return to Clarenceux's hall. His guards appeared and took up their posts on either side of the door. He apologised for being late and walked past Julius's and Walsingham's men to his seat.

Cecil glanced at Walsingham and noted that the sword he had worn so ostentatiously earlier had gone. He cleared his throat. 'Mr Walsingham, Mr Clarenceux, Mr Fawcett. I do not wish to prolong this business any longer than is necessary. As far as I can see, all that needs to happen now should be a simple handing over. Given the emotions and reputations involved, I suggest we exchange as few words as possible. Mr Clarenceux, I believe you should be the one to take matters forward?'

'Thank you, Sir William. Mr Walsingham, you and I had an agreement, to exchange the chronicle of Henry Machyn for all the prisoners surviving, together with the restoration of all our property, including mine. I understand that Daniel Gyttens and Henry Machyn are now dead. Even so, I believe that there were seven other Knights of the Round Table. You said five survive, apart from Henry Machyn's widow. Where are the other two?'

'The identity of one man eluded us. I cannot answer for Lancelot Heath either. My men never found him. We searched his house and his brother's inn by London Stone but there was no sign of him.'

'And you arrested no one else in connection with him – his brother or sister, for example?'

'No.'

'Then that leaves five men and Rebecca Machyn. Present them.'

Walsingham turned to two of his own guards. 'Bring them.'

Clarenceux waited patiently as the footsteps sounded on his staircase. The prisoners filed into the room and stood in a group in the middle. They looked like beggars, such was the filthy state of their clothing and bodies. Three faces were new to Clarenceux: Nicholas Hill, James Emery and Robert Lowe. Michael Hill, in an old black tunic, looked thin and very frail. Although only a few days had passed since Clarenceux had considered him still handsome for a man of sixty years, his face was now drawn and full of bewilderment. A younger man had had his arm round him as they had entered; Clarenceux guessed this was his son, Nicholas Hill. In a fawn doublet with leather lacing on his cuffs and brown hose, he was powerfully built and had a look of efficient service about him. James Emery wore a long black coat that was now in tatters. Rebecca's brother – the blacksmith, Robert Lowe – was recognisable from his huge chest and his burnt and callused hands. William Draper stood slightly apart from the others, his face still badly disfigured where Clarenceux had broken his nose.

Rebecca looked worst of all. The joy had gone out of her face. Her long hair was dirty and lank; her dress more torn than when he had last seen it. There was dried blood on her filthy hands. For an instant Clarenceux's heart tightened in a fist of rage; then he relaxed. *It is over now.*

Clarenceux reached forward and lifted the book from the table. He held it up for Walsingham, and sensed a sneer in the small man's face. Walsingham had been humiliated, and his protector had failed him. He, Clarenceux, had played tricks on them. Walsingham must have been wondering how Cecil had been manipulated. But he knew he had to accept the chronicle.

Walsingham stood in front of Clarenceux. He reached forward and took the book from his hands. 'This is still evidence.'

Cecil answered. 'It is also still the property of Mr Harley, Clarenceux King of Arms, to which you have already done enough damage. I trust you will return it to its rightful owner when you have had sufficient time to examine it, in line with your agreement with Mr Clarenceux to restore all the prisoners' property.'

Walsingham said nothing. He turned and marched out of the room with the chronicle under his arm, followed by his guards.

'That, I believe, concludes our business,' said Cecil. He rose to his feet. 'Gentlemen, Goodmen, Goodwoman – I will leave you now. I hope that this affair is soon forgotten, and that those of you who have recently been intimidated by the late Sergeant Crackenthorpe, acting beyond his authority, live the rest of your lives free from the taint of treason and heresy.' Then, turning to Clarenceux, he bowed. 'Sir, your circumspection has saved the day. You have my deep respect. My salutations to your wife and daughters, when you next see them.' He paused, then he too walked to the door, his men following behind. 'Good day to you all.'

And then he was gone.

Julius came forward. 'William, I too must be going. It will be dusk in half an hour. And although we will be riding by moonlight, we have been up all night. So . . .'

Clarenceux struggled to his feet. Julius tried to stop him and then realised he would not be stopped. The two men embraced.

'Thank you for helping me,' whispered Clarenceux, clutching his friend tightly.

'Thank you for trusting me,' Julius replied. They broke away, each man looking at the other. 'When you are well, you must come down to Summerhill.'

'I will, gladly. I look forward to it.'

Julius turned and approached Rebecca Machyn, still standing with the men in a silent, uneasy group. He took her hand, even though it was covered in dried blood, and kissed it as if she were a lady. 'My blessings and my gratitude, Goodwife Machyn. Thank you for all you have done for my friend. My house will always be open to you – I will not forget that you are a keeper of my secrets.'

When Julius's men had left, there remained only the Knights of the Round Table, Rebecca and Thomas. Michael Hill, James Emery and Nicholas Hill embraced one another. William Draper walked away from them, and stood by the wall. Rebecca did not move at all. The fact she did not come close to Clarenceux worried him.

'Goodwife Machyn, now that Sir William has gone, please, take his seat.'

She came forward without a smile and sat down.

'I know you will all want to go home. But first I would like to say a couple of things. The Knights of the Round Table is no more. Forget your Arthurian names and dates. They mean nothing now. Such organisations are dangerous. What began as a means of keeping some information alive turned into a wave of fear that nearly destroyed us all. Mr Draper, I can see that you only tried to save your own neck. I cannot blame you for that. But you did betray your fellow men – including me – without warning us. You let Henry Machyn go to his death. You were prepared to let men die, you informed on your fellow Knights, and you spoke unwisely at Holyrood and in London. You are free to go now. But I hope our paths never cross again.'

Draper did not move. 'My face, my rib – you did these things to me.'

'No, you brought them upon yourself. And if you wish to compare wounds, then let me show you the stabbing in my gut, the gash in my thigh, the deep cuts on my arms and shoulders. These wounds were inflicted by Sergeant Crackenthorpe because of information *you* provided. Do not even think of blame or revenge; God will surely crush your soul. If anyone in this room has a right to vengeance, it is this good woman, for the loss of her husband. Now, you have one chance to leave without the enmity of us all. I suggest you go now.'

Draper hesitated. Then he went.

'My friends, you are free,' said Clarenceux. 'And you have your property back. I am glad for you.'

None of the four men said anything until Nicholas Hill stepped forward. 'It is fine for you to say it is all over, Mr Clarenceux; but speaking for us – it is not. We undertook once, many years ago, to guard a document with our lives. If we lose that document, and have no control over its whereabouts, we will have failed.'

Clarenceux had not expected this. He took a moment to collect his thoughts. 'You are living in a daydream, Mr Hill. The majority of this country has turned against the old religion. They will not accept a Catholic queen now. Their experience of the last one – with all the burnings and killings in her name – has shown them that whatever the faith of their queen, it is peace that matters most of all.'

'But it is God's will! It is a matter of legitimacy, the right line,' insisted Nicholas Hill.

'I would strongly counsel you not to make an enemy of Sir William Cecil. Today he saved all our lives, mine included. He could just as easily reverse that.'

But Nicholas Hill was angry. 'You talk about Mr Draper betraying us – but *you* have betrayed us, Mr Clarenceux. You gave the chronicle to Francis Walsingham. We could have hidden it, we could have fought . . .'

Clarenceux slammed his fist down on the table. 'Don't be a fool! Do you think that that book is worth all our lives?'

'But you gave it up,' said the blacksmith, Robert Lowe. 'Walsingham has it now. What is to stop him simply picking us off one by one?'

'It looks as though you are the fool, Mr Clarenceux,' said Nicholas Hill.

Clarenceux glared at each of the men before him. He started to undo his doublet, wincing with the pain in his shoulder and ribs. 'I doubt that any of you would ever have discovered Henry Machyn's secret. It was never in your grasp. *If* all of you had gathered together: Sir Lancelot, Sir Owain, Sir Reynold, Sir Dagonet, Sir *Percival*, Sir Ector, Sir Reynold, King Clariance and Sir Yvain; and *if* you had realised that your names all spelled LORD PERCY; and *if* you had put all your dates together and realised that they pointed to the death of Lord Percy in June 1537, and *if* you had all agreed that the key to the secret lay in the wording on Percy's tomb in Hackney Church, then you would still be none the wiser. You would not have found the document.'

'How do you know?' asked Michael Hill.

'How many of you can quote the book of Job to me in Latin? Chapter seven, to be precise, beginning at the first verse.'

There was silence.

'Any of you? No? Well then. There is a long passage of Latin on the side of Lord Percy's tomb that ends with the strange phrase *Numquid mare sum egö auı ıeluı quia circumdedisti me carcere*. That means roughly "Am I a sea or a whale that you surround me in prison". Only if you had seen the chronicle would you realise that it had a sea and a whale embossed on it. But even that would not have been enough. Only if you were intimately familiar with the whole of that passage from the seventh chapter of the book of Job, would you have realised that there was a mistake in one of the verses. It should have read *cutis mea aruit et contracta est* – "my skin is wrinkled and contracted". The inscription on Lord Percy's tomb does not. It reads *cutis mea irrupuit et peccatum aperitum est* – "my skin is broken and a crime is revealed". Henry told me when he gave me the chronicle that only I would understand the secret – and now I see why.'

'So,' snapped Nicholas Hill, 'where is the document? You still gave Walsingham the chronicle. He will now find it . . .'

Clarenceux pulled a large piece of vellum from his doublet. It was heavily folded and smeared with blood. 'This is your document – the original marriage agreement between Lord Percy and Anne Boleyn. Witnessed by a notary public and two bishops.' He tossed it on to the elm table.

There was silence. Each of the men peered forward, none of them daring to say anything or even to touch it.

'Where was it?' asked Michael Hill.

'Until this morning it formed the vellum binding of Henry's chronicle. Henry had it bound around a blank book to hide it, in the year 1550. That same year, he started writing a day-to-day account of his life inside the book, to ensure it and its precious cover would be kept in perpetuity. His chronicle did contain a secret – only it lay in the binding, not the text.'

All four men approached the table. James Emery picked up the document, and held it reverently. 'This amounts to proof that Queen Elizabeth is illegitimate?'

'Practically. It is proof of a pre-contract of marriage on the part of one of her parents – and that was good enough to remove Edward the Fifth from the throne eighty years ago.'

'In that case, we should publish it immediately.'

'Then you would be a fool. All of you would be publicly executed and so would I. And our deaths would amount to nothing – for Sir William Cecil would immediately deny that the document is genuine. He would simply label it a forgery.'

'But it is *proof*, you said so yourself. It is true,' said Nicholas Hill.

Clarenceux shook his head. 'What is proof? You think it has anything to do with the truth? Believe me, no one has as little respect for the truth as those in power. Men like Sir William Cecil suppress unpalatable truths every day, and they only admit something is *proof* when it suits their purposes.'

'Then what do you intend to do with it?' Emery asked, still holding the document.

'Exactly what Lord Percy wanted.'

'What was that? How can you know?' asked Michael Hill.

'A fair question. The answer lies in the fact that the story behind this document is a tragedy. Lord Percy met and fell in love with Anne Boleyn. And she loved him. But the king stole her and she proved fickle. She grew to love the king because he wooed her with power. Lord Percy, who had known high status and power all his life, could see that she was being manipulated, and knew that the king would tire of her one day; but she turned against him. It drove him mad, and the king started to manipulate him too in his madness. At the end, after he had been forced to sentence his own true love to death, he simply had one wish: that this story not be forgotten. He gave the document to Henry Machyn to look after, not so there would be a revolution against the king but simply so that someone would know that the woman he had loved all his life was his wife, that she had been stolen from him, and that once she did love him.'

No one spoke.

'We will keep it from now on,' said Nicholas Hill coldly, taking the document from James Emery. 'We were entrusted to guard it and we will continue to do so.'

Clarenceux did not move. 'No. You will leave it with me. I gave Sir William Cecil a promise that I would look after it in return for your lives and property. If it leaves my possession, none of us will be safe or trusted ever again.'

Emery broke away from the group and walked across to the window. It was beginning to grow dark. Clarenceux glanced at Rebecca. She had not moved but sat staring ahead. Nicholas Hill looked closely at the document, but he could not read it in the dying light. He passed it to his father, who glanced at it and set it carefully back on the table in front of Clarenceux.

'I think Mr Clarenceux's counsel is wise,' said Michael Hill. 'We are not men of action. Nor are we revolutionaries. None of us can use this document.'

Robert Lowe looked at Rebecca. 'I wish you and your husband had never met. You and he have made me feel like a gullible, easily led man. I don't expect to get an apology from you in this gentleman's house, but next time we meet ...' He looked at Clarenceux, bowed briefly, said 'Good day to you,' in a polite but cold voice, then turned and walked to the door.

In silence they listened to his rapid footsteps on the stairs.

'I think we should leave too,' said Michael Hill, looking at his son. 'Mr Clarenceux, please forgive us for what must appear to you ingratitude. It's just that for years we have prepared ourselves to face imprisonment and death for the sake of this secret. That gave us strength throughout our recent ordeals. Even in the Tower I knew that my suffering had a greater purpose – that it would bring about a change. It is difficult for me to accept that there will be no change. But I know that I should be grateful, and I *am* grateful – doubly so on behalf of my wife and son. On all our accounts, I thank you.'

Nicholas Hill said nothing. He simply went to his father, put his arm round him to support him and led him to the door. Emery followed them, without a word or a backward glance.

Clarenceux and Rebecca listened to the men going down, and the front door closing. The light in the hall was growing dim. Neither of them spoke.

'Are you going to talk to me?' he asked after a while.

'What is there to say?'

'What happened in Hackney?'

'I don't want to tell you. What happened is between me and those men's consciences. It is over. Forgotten.'

Clarenceux leant forward. With the light fading rapidly he could only indistinctly see her face. She was not looking at him. 'Shall I ask Thomas for a light?'

'No. The darkness is good.'

'Why do you say that?'

'Because it hides my tears.'

Clarenceux felt reprimanded, chastened. There could be many reasons for her tears but the most obvious left him feeling guilty. 'Is there anything I can do?'

'No.'

He sat back again. 'Rebecca, what is on your mind?'

She sighed. 'After it was all over they put me in a brick cellar. It was cold and damp. I wanted to die. And in those dark hours I saw myself as I truly am: a poor widow. I have no money, nor any trade. I cannot continue Henry's business. No one would want to marry me with nothing to my name. My best hope is to become a servant in Mistress Barker's household and there end my days.'

She paused, wiping her eyes.

'I realised there in that cellar how much I was fooling myself, being with you. You are married; you cannot protect me. I am no one's woman: no one's daughter, no one's wife, no one's mother. Any man with a knife and the inclination can violate me and walk away. Who will defend me? What is my word against a man's, when no one will speak up for me? I was fooling myself by pretending that you and I have something in common, that I could share something with you as my husband did. It wasn't true, and it isn't true.'

Clarenceux closed his eyes. 'You are not just a widow, Rebecca. You are a much-loved woman. And you have much love to give, too. In the church, at Hackney, you said we would fight them with love.'

'I am sorry for that.'

'No. I am glad that you said it. I am glad of your closeness to me. Lying next to me, all those nights, I wanted your respect so much that I never touched you, even though I longed to. And in the church, your words urged me to be strong – for you as well as me. I kept thinking of you on the way back to Summerhill. On that journey Crackenthorpe told me you were dead, and the very thought caused me so much pain, so much ...'

'What has happened to Crackenthorpe?'

'He is dead.'

'You killed him?'

'Yes.'

'Thank you.'

'You do not need to thank me.'

'Nevertheless, you have avenged Henry's death as well as my ordeal.' She paused, nervous, trying to find the right words – words that she could bear to hear herself saying. 'They kept me in the cellar where he died. Walsingham's guards told me. They also told me about what they did to him before they killed him – cutting strips of skin off his back, burning him, and other terrible things.'

They fell silent. One church bell began to ring in the distance. Very soon other bells were ringing too, including the bell of St Bride's nearby.

'Will you go down to Devon to find your wife tomorrow?'

Clarenceux felt the pain in his abdomen and shoulder, and remembered what difficulty he had had just walking up the stairs and across the room. 'Not tomorrow, no. It is a long way. But soon.'

They fell silent again.

'What will you do with Lord Percy's document?'

'I have not had much time to think about it. I have to keep it safe. Sir William Cecil wants me to guard it for him.'

'He will use you. He is a cunning man.'

'Maybe. But it is still in my possession. And we are still alive.'

'Under the rule of a Protestant queen.'

Clarenceux lifted his hand. 'Don't say that. Don't be like the others. You told me that you did not want a revolution, but only to be safe. That is what you have got.'

Rebecca smiled weakly. Then she realised Clarenceux could not see her face in the darkness of the hall, so she leant forward and took his hand in hers, and gave it a little squeeze.

'Yes, and I am grateful. I just wish there was something I could do for you to make you as grateful to me.'

He felt for her hand and held it in his. 'You have already done enough. You saved my life. You worked out the sequence of letters in the book. You gave me strength in Hackney Church. Most of all you are still alive. I saw what a world without you looks like, just for one night, and it was so cold. I do not want to see such a world again.'

'Sweet words, Mr Clarenceux. But you understand my meaning, I am sure. Your wife will soon return and, when she does, you will be glad. She will not want me around, and nor will you. I understand now.'

'What do you understand?'

'You. And her. After Crackenthorpe arrested you, in this room, she and I talked upstairs in your study And I did not understand then what it is about her that you love. The two of you seem so different. At times on our travels I thought perhaps you do not love her. But now I see that you do. For you, love is a matter of honour – just as it was for Lord Percy. He could not change and nor can you. Honour, duty, love, respect – all these things are the same to you. You are intrinsically loyal – you protect those you love as a matter of duty and those you love depend on you. You have built your own world around yourself, and you will defend it with your life.'

'And now you too are now part of that world.'

'No. No, I am not. And I never can be. I was – but only while you were alone and in need of me. Now I must stay away from you. For both our sakes.'

The prospect of being apart from her all the time was an emptiness. 'This afternoon, Rebecca, sitting in this seat, I was alone for a short while. And I found myself reflecting on all the events of the last week. And I thought of all the people to whom I am grateful. And the more I thought about it, the more I realised that I owe more to you than to anyone else. It's not just that I owe you my life, it is everything you—'

'But that is what I am saying, Mr Clarenceux. You cling to the past. For you the past is one long series of triumphs, adventures and splendour, and wondrous proud moments, and honourable gentlemanly things. You genuinely love the past. For me the past is not something to love. It is hunger, through not having enough bread. It is pain, the loss of three babies. The loss of my husband. Can't you see that?'

Clarenceux said nothing.

Her voice was urgent, convinced of her rightness but struggling with emotion. 'The big difference between you and Francis

Walsingham is that the past means little or nothing to him. For him only the future counts; and he does not love it, he fears it. I am like that too. I fear the future, I really do.'

Clarenceux shook his head. 'I don't know. But the bells will ring soon. Will you stay here tonight? I do not know if I have a bed left intact. But you are welcome to it if I do.'

'Mr Clarenceux, thank you, but I will take my chances. I cannot stay here any longer. Not with you.'

Clarenceux wiped his face with his hand. 'I know that it is selfish and unfair of me to say so but I cannot agree with you. I need you—'

'No, Mr Clarenceux, you need your wife. You love her. Imagine she were threatened – nothing would stop you defending her. Whatever you may feel at this moment, you know you would never forgive yourself if you let her be hurt. I can see now that you never touched me because you were protecting her, your marriage, and everything else that you believe is right, and good, and proper; everything else which is part of the life you have built around you.'

Clarenceux suddenly knew that she was right. It struck him straight to the bone. He looked for some way to persuade them both that she was wrong, but knew that he would be lying if he tried, and doing her a disservice as well as himself.

'Where will you go?'

'I will find somewhere. Home maybe. Or someone's stable loft.'

'Stay here, Rebecca.'

'Is Thomas here still?'

'Yes, downstairs. I told him I would call if I needed anything. But—'

'Then he will look after you. You don't need me.'

'Rebecca, please.'

She rose from the chair in the darkness and bent over him, and kissed his forehead. 'Goodbye, Mr Clarenceux.'

He looked up and saw the outline of her face. 'Rebecca, I . . .' But he could not find the words. 'I am sorry if I have hurt you.

I never meant to upset you ... I still want to make you happy.'

She put her hands either side of his face. 'I know. That is the one thing I cannot forgive you for.'

And then, second by second, she was further from him, further away and leaving. She was walking across the room, feeling her way. He heard her steps on the stairs, and then the front door opening and closing.

Clarenceux sat alone in his hall, in the darkness, his face wet with tears.

76

Lady Percy was sitting in her dark chamber at Sheffield Manor. She had been in the same chair all afternoon, looking across the park, hoping to see a messenger. None had come. A little rain had fallen, and the clouds were heavy in the sky as the evening drew on. Still she sat, waiting.

After a while Benedict Richardson came with a lamp. She was unresponsive, and declined his suggestion that she should eat. After a few more questions, to which she made no reply, he reached out to close the shutters to the window.

'Leave them,' she commanded.

'But my lady—'

'You may go.'

He looked at her, and at the empty fireplace, then bowed and withdrew.

Lady Percy's thoughts had sunk into darkness with the passing of the day. No message had come. The Knights of the Round Table had been betrayed – she felt it. And with them she too had been betrayed. It seemed to her that the flame that had scorched her all her life, burning her through the years, had suddenly gone out.

She looked for her sticks by the light of the candle that Richardson had left. She set them before her, stood up and walked to the window. Slowly she leant forward and rested her head on the frozen leaded glass.

Out there, in the cold darkness, the queen of England's rule held strong. Lady Percy knew it as a dark reign: a reign without true light. But it seemed to her at that moment that what lay beyond the window was less significant than what lay on this side.

'I am a Talbot and I am a Catholic,' she whispered to the glass, 'and I will never give up hope. I swear by almighty God and this great darkness in which He has wrapped us, I will have my revenge. It is my destiny. That will be my changing from maiden to woman, not my marriage.'

She remained at the window for some minutes before turning and slowly shuffling along an unlit stone corridor towards her bedchamber.

77

larenceux remained in his chair for a long time after Rebecca left. Minutes turned into quarters of an hour, and the first hour came to its silent end in the darkness. Eventually Thomas came up to the hall bearing a candle.

'Thank you, Thomas.'

'Mr Clarenceux, sir?'

'Yes, Thomas?'

'Will things return to normal now? Are you going to stay?'

'Yes, I am staying.' He sighed heavily. 'When I have regained my strength, you and I will go down to Devon and bring back Awdrey and the family. Then things will be more or less as they were before.'

'That is good, sir. It would be good if things got back to normal. There is one mattress that was not too badly damaged, in the guest room. I picked up all the feathers and stuffed them back in as well as I could, before I sewed it up. It should suffice for a few nights.'

Clarenceux looked up at the old man in the candlelight. 'Thank you, Thomas. Thank you for all you've done for me.'

The servant bowed his head. 'Sir?'

'Yes, Thomas?'

'I was wondering, in my time going to Devon and coming back, what was the meaning of Henry Machyn's chronicle? It has been much on my mind.'

'The meaning of the chronicle?' Clarenceux thought back to when he had received it; to Henry Machyn's worried face. He thought too about the moment when he had seen his study wrecked, with parchment and paper all across the floor and his father's portrait smashed. Then he had seen the wood of the door in a new real light, as if he had no possessions but was fighting his way through the world, and the whole world was a strange place. He thought too of Walsingham's cellar, and of searching for Rebecca in the cold churchyard. Finally his mind rested on the image of Rebecca herself, declaring to him that she was unimportant and had nothing, but still determined to go her own way.

'The meaning, Thomas, was *esperance*.'

'Sir?'

Clarenceux smiled. 'It was the last word in the chronicle. It means hope. In all our struggles, the last word is hope.'

Author's note

This is a work of fiction but it was inspired by some extant historical documents created by and referring to real historical characters. The real Clarenceux King of Arms in 1563 was one William Harvey (not Harley), who was appointed in 1556 and died in 1567. The real Henry Machyn was one of William Harvey's London friends: he was a merchant taylor, funeral arranger and parish clerk, who died in November 1563. Machyn's name would have faded into obscurity if it had not been for his chronicle or 'cronacle' (as he himself called it). He began writing in 1550, shortly before the death of his brother Christopher. According to the official copy of his will, he left his chronicle to 'Master Clarenceux' (i.e. William Harvey).

Sometime after the death of William Harvey, the chronicle was acquired by the great collector Robert Cotton (d. 1631). It thus became part of what was without doubt the greatest library of English historical manuscripts ever assembled by an individual. This massive collection was later moved to Ashburnham House in Westminster where, on 23 October 1731, a terrible fire destroyed the building. Many manuscripts were lost altogether. Many others were rescued as flames consumed their outer edges – Machyn's manuscript was one of these. Its binding, margins and spine were all burnt away; only the central portion of each page survived. For the next hundred years these charred pages lay loose and unsorted in a box in the British Museum. Eventually they were put in order by Sir Frederick Madden in 1829 and edited by John Gough Nichols, being published as *The Diary of Henry Machyn, Citizen and Merchant-Taylor of London* in 1848. A growing interest in sixteenth-century history brought it to wider notice, and so Henry Machyn was included in the first edition of the *Dictionary of National Biography*, published in 1893.

In 1999, when working at the Royal Commission on Historical Manuscripts, I was commissioned to rewrite the entry on Henry Machyn for what was to become *The Oxford Dictionary of National Biography*. Over the course of the twentieth century his self-taught style of writing had led to his text being studied as one of the few examples of phonetic spelling to survive from the Tudor period. In addition, his unusual choice of words – which verged perhaps on dialect – meant that his chronicle was not just valuable to social historians, but a key work for linguistic scholars too, especially for those who wanted to know how English sounded before Shakespeare and how different regional accents could be mapped for the early period. But where was Henry Machyn originally from? Was he a Yorkshireman or a Londoner? Being a historian rather than a linguistic expert, I set about answering this question in a purely historical way, through archival research. I found the official copy of his will, which was previously unknown, in the Corporation of London Records Office, together with another family will. Using these documents and other archival sources, the family origins could be shown to lie in northern Leicestershire. I then pursued my interest in Machyn further, drawing upon references to him in the Merchant Taylors' records and other parish sources. The result was an article, 'Tudor Chronicler or Sixteenth-century Diarist? Henry Machyn and the Nature of His Manuscript', published in *The Sixteenth Century Journal* (volume xxxiii, 2002, pp. 981–998). This remains the fullest account of his life and work.

In the course of my research I followed up a reference in Machyn's chronicle to the painter-stainer John Heath (d. 1553), father of Lancelot Heath, who was a witness of Machyn's will.

One line in Heath's own will (which is now in the National Archives, PROB 11/25/Bucke), inspired this book:

Item I give and bequeath to the Knights of the Round Table if I do it not by life time twenty shillings to be spent at Mile End.

Machyn mentioned this bequest in his chronicle, stating under an entry for 22 March 1563 (the day of John Heath's funeral) that the Painters and the Clerks 'had twenty shillings to make merry with all at the tavern'. But it was the reference to the 'Knights of the Round Table' that attracted my attention. Having also written an article for the *ODNB* on Thomas Talbot, one of the founder members of the Elizabethan Society of Antiquaries, I knew there were various societies that had huge political importance. Indeed, the original Society of Antiquaries was suppressed due to its growing political influence. I thought about that reference to 'the Knights of the Round Table' for the next ten years.

Machyn's chronicle is not a seditious document but it is an extraordinary one, describing the drama of day-to-day life in early Elizabethan England, and detailing a very large number of executions for treason and heresy.

Recently a new edition, entitled *A London Provisioner's Chronicle, 1550–1563*, by Henry Machyn has been created under the auspices of Professor Richard Bailey, and made freely available online as a joint publication of the University of Michigan Press and the Scholarly Publishing Office of the University of Michigan Library (http://quod.lib.umich.edu/m/machyn/). Incidentally, this allows clarity as to the meaning of 'drawing' in the phrase 'hanging, drawing and quartering'. It does not normally refer at this period to disembowelling but the process of dragging the condemned person to the gallows. A good example is that of Mr William Thomas: Machyn states that he was arraigned at the Guildhall in May 1554 and sentenced to 'suffer death, to be drawn and quarted'. Machyn goes on to say that some days later, on 18 May 1554, Mr Thomas:

'was drawn upon a sled . . . from the Tower unto Tyburn . . . And he was hanged and after his head struck off and then quartered. And the morrow after his head was set on London Bridge and three quarters set over Cripplegate'.

Clearly the sentence of 'drawing' resulted in the man being 'drawn' in a sled, publicly, to the place of execution – not to having his entrails pulled out of him while he was still alive.

As mentioned above, the original binding and the beginning and end pages were lost in the fire in 1731, and so, in developing the plot in this book, I had some freedom to invent two entries that Machyn never wrote – specifically the first and last lines. However, the other quotations from Machyn's chronicle are present in the original (although I have modernised some spellings). The quotation from Machyn's will is similarly a genuine one. The epitaph on Lord Percy's tomb in Hackney church is likewise accurate, and *Esperance* was an actual Percy family motto – although the additional lines from Job were not on the original tomb. Many other elements of the story are based on historical reality – the collapse of the spire of St Paul's, the parishes of residence of the protagonists, the timing of the full moon in December 1563, Sir William Cecil's patronage of the young Walsingham, Cecil's house on the Strand, the location of the Bull's Head tavern, the appearance of Sheffield Manor, Lady Percy's Catholic sympathies, the existence of chalk caverns in Chislehurst, the layout of Hackney in Elizabethan times, and Eustace Chapuys's letter to the Holy Roman Emperor, to point to just a few. Creating the story has been an interesting experience for me as a historian, juggling with past reality, allowing some facts to fall and inventing others to suit the fiction. Sir William Cecil and Francis Walsingham were genuine characters, of course, as were Lord and Lady Percy and the royal individuals. Richard Crackenthorpe and Julius Fawcett are fictitious characters. Three historical individuals have had their names changed. One is William Harvey himself. Another is Henry Machyn's wife, who was actually called Dorothy Lawe or Lowe (not Rebecca). Daniel Gyttens – one of the actual signatories of Henry Machyn's will – was correctly Davy Gyttens.

The possible illegitimacy of Queen Elizabeth is a tantalising mystery. As stated in the book, the Act of Parliament *Titulus Regis* (1484) did establish two circumstances for the illegitimacy of Edward V – his father's pre-contract of marriage with another woman (Eleanor Butler), and the subsequent marriage *in secret* to Edward V's mother (Elizabeth Woodville). Henry VII repealed this Act shortly after gaining the throne in 1485, and had the original cut out of the records and burnt; but copies did survive and were known in the sixteenth century. On top of this, it is worth noting that it was the *circumstances*, not the Act itself, that removed the boy from the throne: the Act was passed a year after Richard III had taken the crown from his nephew on the grounds of illegitimacy. So it is fair to argue, historically, that Queen Elizabeth was similarly vulnerable at the start of her reign, for her circumstances were similar to those of Edward V. To be precise, her father had been previously married (to Catherine of Aragon) and his second marriage (to Anne Boleyn, Elizabeth's mother) took place in secret. Although it could be said that Henry VIII's first marriage was annulled, there remained a question mark over Anne Boleyn. If she too had previously been contracted to Lord Percy, before marrying Henry VIII in secret, then Elizabeth was illegitimate on her mother's side as well as (arguably) on her father's.

Did Lord Percy and Anne Boleyn actually marry? There seems little doubt that marriage was discussed. The evidence principally comes from three sources. First, there is Chapuys's letter of 2 May 1536 to the Holy Roman Emperor (published in Pascual de Gayangos (ed.), *Calendar of Letters, Despatches and State Papers Relating to the Negotiations between England and Spain, volume v part ii: Henry VIII, 1536–1538* (London, 1888), pp. 107–108 and quoted in part in this novel). This clearly states that Henry VIII originally sought to be divorced from Anne Boleyn by claiming that she had married Lord Percy before 1527, and it goes so far as to state that they had consummated the marriage. Second, there is Henry's papal permission in 1527 to marry a woman 'who has already contracted marriage with some other person, provided she has not consummated it' – quoted in E. W. Ives, *Anne Boleyn* (Blackwell, 1986, p. 79). Thirdly there is the evidence of Mary Talbot, the countess of Northumberland, who attempted to annul her marriage to her husband Lord Percy, earl of Northumberland, in 1532 on the basis that he had admitted to her he had previously been contracted in marriage with Anne Boleyn (Ives, *Anne Boleyn*, pp. 79, 207). These three independent pieces of evidence suggest that Anne Boleyn had indeed been contracted to marry Lord Percy prior to 1527. In addition, it may be significant that Chapuys stated in his letter that there were many witnesses willing to testify that Anne Boleyn had been married to Percy. However, Henry VIII was not above concocting stories to suit his political ends, and that included forcing people to act as false witnesses. So, while it is probable that some sort of contract between Lord Percy and Anne Boleyn was made, whether or not they exchanged vows and had sexual intercourse prior to 1527 is a matter for speculation. As in all ages, even if 'the truth' is known, its meaning and importance are relative – and heavily dependent on the political vicissitudes of changing times.

(Ian) James Forrester (Mortimer)